Albert Pillet,

The African Fabiola; or, The church of Carthage in the days of

Tertullian

Albert Pillet,

The African Fabiola; or, The church of Carthage in the days of Tertullian

ISBN/EAN: 9783741176012

Manufactured in Europe, USA, Canada, Australia, Japa

Cover: Foto ©Andreas Hilbeck / pixelio.de

Manufactured and distributed by brebook publishing software
(www.brebook.com)

Albert Pillet,

The African Fabiola; or, The church of Carthage in the days of

Tertullian

THE

AFRICAN FABIOLA;

OR,

THE CHURCH OF CARTHAGE

IN THE

DAYS OF TERTULLIAN.

TRANSLATED FROM THE FRENCH

BY

JOSEPH P. O'CONNELL, D.D.

PREFACE.

THE mass of cheap trash that constantly floods the country proves how vast is the number of those who read as they walk or play—for amusement. On the other hand, the dearth of serious, instructive, and really valuable books shows that but few seek solid information or apply themselves to real study. It is said of Victor Hugo that he once replied to a person who complimented him on the success of one of his tragedies: "*If the people desire nonsense I'll give it to them.*" The depraved tastes of the multitude never lack a Hugo; but, on the contrary, always find many and very ready caterers, and hence morality and religion almost invariably are made to suffer. The insatiable appetite for light and amusing reading craves and will have food, good or bad. Unfortunately, that generally offered is unwholesome, if not absolutely poisonous. That *our* repertory of light reading is very meagre and insufficient needs no better proof than that few Catholics make any scruple to sell, buy, or read productions like those of Lever, Lover, Marryat, and Scott.

Fully convinced, therefore, that a good, interesting, and instructive book is a boon and a treasure, I have devoted my leisure moments to the translation of this. That it deserves a place by the side of "Fabiola" and "Callista" has been decided by the unanimous verdict of Catholic France, and is substantially proved by the many editions through which it has run.

The reverend author—once a vicar-general of the diocese of Rouen—has most ingeniously inserted in the course of the story the pith of three masterpieces of the great Tertullian—"On Female Dress," the "Apologeticus," and his address "To the Martyrs."

St. Perpetua, the heroine of the story, and St. Felicitas, the one a noblewoman and the other a slave, cannot fail to be doubly interesting to Catholics from the fact that they are both inserted and daily mentioned in the Canon of the Mass. What a beautiful idea and how indicative of the Catholic spirit of that Church which knows no distinction of *bond or free, Jew or Gentile*, to enroll and enshrine the patrician and the slave side by side in the very Canon of the Mass!

In our day and time, when so many weakly yield to the ordinary temptations and trials of everyday life and seem incapable of appreciating the glorious heritage of the faith, it may be well to show them even a single example of what our ancestors did and suffered to maintain and transmit that faith to us.

The following extract from a letter to the publisher will serve to show the opinion had of this book in France:

"... I read the book when it was first published, and it left a lasting and very favorable impression on my mind. Now that a third edition is about to be issued, I have, at your request, reread it carefully. The reperusal has confirmed my previous opinion. It is a good book; the plan is happily conceived and well carried out. In imagery and language the style is appropriate, chaste, nervous, and dignified; the tale is interesting, the plot skilfully managed, and the characters well defined. To its credit it may be said that it frequently reminds one of Cardinal Wiseman's 'Fabiola.'

"But its chief merit is that it is so eminently religious and moral. Every Christian family can accept it without hesitation; the young can read it without danger to faith or morals; it is a book which cannot be opened without experiencing a feeling of admiration and respect for that holy religion which can elevate souls and hearts to such an eminent degree of sanctity and heroism.

"May you give us many such books as this; by so doing you will merit the esteem and gratitude of all good men and of all the friends of wholesome and instructive reading.

"Permit me to congratulate you, and to sub-
scribe myself,

    Your very humble and faithful servant,

            LEJEUNE,

        Hon. Canon and Professor of Theology in the
             Faculty of Rouen."

———

The translator desires to call attention to the
fact that he has not followed the French in the
magnificent extracts taken from the works and
put into the mouth of Tertullian. He has gone
back to the originals, and has given a far more
nervous and literal translation than was given in
the somewhat diluted French imitation.

BROOKLYN, EASTER, 1881.

———

" If a modern Christian wishes really to know what his forefathers
underwent for the faith during three centuries of persecution, . . .
we would advise him to peruse those imperishable records, the
Acts of the Martyrs, which will show how they were made to die.
We know of no writing so moving, so tender, so consoling to faith
and to hope, after God's inspired words, as these venerable monuments. And if our readers, so advised, have not leisure sufficient
to read much upon this subject, we would limit him willingly to one
specimen, the genuine acts of SS. Perpetua and Felicitas. . . . If
the reader would compare the morbid sensibility and the over-
strained excitement endeavored to be produced by a modern French
writer, in the imaginary journal of a culprit condemned to death,
down to the immediate approach of execution, with the unaffected
pathos and charming truthfulness which pervade the corresponding
narrative of Vivia Perpetua, a delicate lady of twenty-one years of
age, he would not hesitate in concluding how much more natural,
graceful, and interesting are the simple recitals of Christianity than
the boldest fictions of poetry."—*Cardinal Wiseman's* " *Fabiola.*"

CONTENTS.

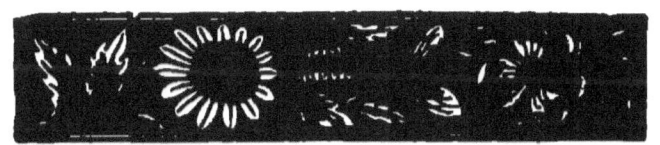

THE AFRICAN FABIOLA.

CHAPTER I.

THE MESSAGE.

THE sun was verging towards its setting; the evening breeze gently fanned the blue waters of the sea that laved the *proud and happy Carthage, after Rome the glory and pride of the world,* as the ancients used to call it. After a day passed amid the occupations and fatigues of painful toil, the merchants and artisans strolled in groups along the wharves or among the rows of date, fig, and olive trees, which in that sandy soil bore such excellent fruit. Among the promenaders some—and they were the majority—talked of trade, of the arrival of many and richly-laden vessels; others discussed the news of the day— namely, that new religion, so mysterious in its tenets and austere in its practices, and which, after having *seduced* so many poor persons and slaves, after having defied for two hundred years all the efforts of science and all the power of

9

the Cæsars, was beginning to invade the wealthiest families and the very senate itself.   Some,
oblivious of business and of the gods, recalled, in
the ardor of their patriotism, the ancient grandeur of Carthage, so long the formidable rival of
Rome; they gloried in memories awakened by
the names of Hannibal and Cannes, and cursed
the luxuries of Capua, which had enervated their
invincible legions, and the blush of shame suffused their brows at the recollection of Scipio
and Zama.

At some distance above these animated groups
there appeared a solitary pedestrian; he wended
his way slowly along the aqueduct, that stupendous marvel, which, from mountains forty miles
distant, conveyed water to the city and the fort-
ress of Byrza.   This man was scarcely middle-
aged, and was wrapped in an ample cloak, similar
to those then usually worn by the *philosophers.*
He appeared to be buried in deep thought.   On
seeing him one would naturally be led to think
that, being a stranger to that nature which dis-
played its glories above his head and under his
feet, he saw only through the soul, that all tem-
poral things were too petty and contemptible in
his mind to bestow a single thought upon them.
He was tall and well shaped; his masculine and
regular features wore that air of dignity which is
the attribute of lofty virtue, of habitual self-com-
mand, and profound thought; yet one would have
sought there in vain for that sweet calmness which

tempers dignity and makes it attractive. His broad forehead, already furrowed by deep wrinkles, bore all the marks of premature old age, and the locks which flowed on his shoulders had become white long before their time. His penetrating, flashing eye shot forth lightning glances full of the beauty and power of his genius; occasionally these became gloomy and dark—ominous precursors of the dreadful tempests which raged in that fiery soul. Everything in this man seemed superior to human nature, for he seemed an exceptional being, who had nothing in common with the ordinary weakness and frailty of men. And yet, on looking closer, one was impressed with a vague, unaccountable feeling of extremism, which, by instinct and temperament, narrowed the boundaries of virtue, sought the purity of the angels among the children of Adam, the holiness of heaven in this world of misery and sin; so that if this man should ever descend into the arena of controversy, he would be terrible, implacable, and would play with his opponents as the lion with the weak lamb. Another language would be necessary for his thoughts, another logic for his attacks, an eloquence altogether new for his genius, thunder-strokes for his wrath, irony hitherto unknown for his contempt, and for his ambition greatness and glory such as are not to be found in this world. This man was called *Septimius Florens Tertullian*, and, as he now appears before us, he was in about the fortieth year of his age.

Having reached the angle whence juts the prom-
ontory of Carthage, he entered the city by the
broad way which led to the citadel. On the right
and on the left arose magnificent dwellings and
sumptuous palaces, with swarms of slaves awaiting
the arrival of their lordly masters. Theatres and
public baths built of costly and precious marbles,
adorned with elegant sculpture and beautiful sta-
tuary, bespoke this the quarter of the leading
citizens ; here all the aristocracy of Carthage
sought to dwell. Above the citadel appeared the
imposing front and elegant brazen doors of the
temple of Juno, the precincts of which had been
more than once reddened with the blood of innocent victims. Within, this temple was said to
have been a marvel of richness ; gold, precious
stones, and other gifts of wealthy, designing, or
ambitious pagans met the astonished gaze on
every side. As if to insult the people who had
conquered it, the city had spared nothing to make
it a second Capitol.

Tertullian, for so shall we call him in future,
cast only a look of contempt on all this worldly
magnificence. At the sight of the theatre his
glance paused for a moment. As he thought of
the shameful scenes which were there enacted,
and which daily drew thither crowds of the dissipated and voluptuous, his face flushed with indignation and shame. Just as he was passing
before the temple it so happened that the high-
priest, still robed in his sacrificial trappings, was

slowly descending the steps, followed by some of his priestly attendants. Tertullian saw him; he paused suddenly; his whole frame shook and trembled convulsively, his face grew pale, distorted, and livid. He cast a withering, contemptuous look upon the high-priest of the false gods, and, halting in front of the temple: "Unclean divinities!" exclaimed he with clenched teeth, "sacrilegious idols! how long will ye insult the Christ, my God? When shall my eyes behold his cross lifted up radiant and triumphant over all these mutilated ruins?" Fortunately, he was not heard or understood by the high-priest, for a wave of the pontiff's hand would have been enough to have set his followers on the *blasphemer*, to tear him to pieces, mayhap would have been the signal for a bloody persecution capable of devastating the metropolis and all the churches of Africa! A few moments later Tertullian knocked at the door of a splendid mansion, which, at a later period, was destined to be converted into a magnificent basilica by the piety of the faithful. A Nubian slave admitted him.

Recent in design, construction, arrangement, and ornamentation, this mansion was a model of elegance, splendor, and convenience. It had the *porticus*, or porch, laid in beautiful marbles, the *atrium*, an open space, around which ran a row of alabaster columns, covered with foliage, birds, and beasts, that seemed to live and move under the magic chisel of the artist. The latest freaks of luxury and fashion, the richest gifts of the East, soft and beautiful carpets, lofty bronze candelabra, busts, vases, tripods, paintings in all the glow of freshness of color, statues poised in their niches, tables of odoriferous woods brought from afar and transformed by Carthagenian skill into marvels of art, brilliant stuffs, Chinese silks, gold and silver embroideries, furniture fashioned by the hands of masters, couches of the most graceful designs and tastefully incrusted with ivory— everything had been collected together in this mansion to please the eye and to flatter vanity.

In sultry climates like that of Carthage, where under a burning sun the heat of the day becomes oppressive, the effeminate children of wealth spare no expense to cool the atmosphere artificially, so that besides awnings, tapestries, and ample curtains which served to keep out the sun and heat from the rooms, immense marble basins were constructed in the centre of the halls and courts to receive the constant streams of fresh water which fell into them, day and night, in limpid jets and cooling showers. These fountains refreshed the air, pleased the ear by their sweet murmurs, and conveyed to the fatigued and enervated senses a feeling of vague tranquillity, which lulled into repose the indolent man, the delicate and dainty female. Such was the home now opened to Tertullian, who was immediately ushered into the presence of its mistress by a youthful female slave.

Softly reclining on a couch, a young woman

held in her arms and silently contemplated with
an ineffable smile of happiness a new-born infant
asleep upon her bosom. So deeply was she buried
in her sweet reveries that she took no heed of
the stranger who stood before her. In the full
flower of youth, in all the bloom of beauty, rendered more touching and heightened by the pallor
of her face, consequent upon her recent sickness,
one could easily see by her modest air that she belonged to that new religion which not only purified but at the same time ennobled the heart of
woman. But being merely initiated, and as yet
only imperfectly enlightened regarding the spirit
of that religion, although pure and chaste, she was
far from that perfection which despises pomp and
display; about her were scattered rich garments,
mantles, costly veils, diamonds, jewels, gold and
coral bracelets; and necklaces blazing with brilliants
lay in profusion on tables of porphyry or sandal-
wood. Near the couch lay an infant's cradle,
which, judging by the ornaments and workman-
ship, must have cost the mother sums which could
have supported many a poor family.

"Vivia Perpetua—for I cannot call you sister,
still less daughter—Vivia, do you know me?"
Tertullian's voice trembled with emotion as he
spoke.

"O father! why this severity?" replied the
young woman, springing from her couch. "How
have I incurred your anger to be thus treated
with a harshness of which I have as yet seen no

example among the Christians, my new brethren!
Oh! dispel not the happiness which God has given
me, but increase it rather by blessing the happy
mother and new-born infant." She threw herself
at his feet as she held up her child to him.

"*May He from whom all paternity derives its
name, in heaven and on earth—may the Father
of our Lord Jesus Christ* bless you and this your
little infant. Vivia, you ask why my speech is
severe, why I call you not to-day by the name by
which the priest loves to address the children of
the true God. In your house my eyes discover
only the luxury, the display, and the ornaments
of a pagan mansion! Look around you! And
it is *here*, forsooth, that you meditate on the holy
law which you have vowed to embrace! *here* it is
that you study the life of the God who came into
this world to save you! *here* that you worship
and pray! *here*, Vivia! . . ."

"Father, of a truth it is here I have lived all
alone for nearly six months, since the departure
of my noble husband, until my lonely seclusion
was recently beautified and gladdened by the
presence of this innocent and beloved infant;
here it is that I find happiness in rehearsing the
pious and holy instructions received from you
and the venerated ministers of God. Believe the
sincerity of your humble child. Here have I
wept sweet tears of gratitude at the recollection
of God's goodness in having condescended to open
my eyes to the light of the Gospel. The thought

of all that his beloved Son suffered for all men and for myself, in particular, is always present to my heart and that blessed spirit which I think you call by the name of angel, and which ever stands by my side, is my witness that I often bow my face into the dust to implore the grace of purification in the saving waters of baptism, even had I to pay my blood to purchase the happiness of that mysterious regeneration!"

"Vivia, beware; presumption, the daughter of pride, has seized your heart, and presumption leads to apostasy; we have but too many proofs of this. Before having engaged in the struggle you proudly defy suffering and death! Only see how you love riches, how you cling to ease, how you pride yourself and exult in your noble alliance with your husband, and then say if it requires a great deal to weaken and overcome the courage of a weak woman, of a young neophyte! And this child, in whom centre all your affections, whose first smile, whose first lisp you already await with such impatience—this child, whom you seem to idolize—this child, if . . ."

"Father, father, spare me! crush not the frail creature who implores your compassion! Oh! this child is indeed dearer to me than all the world. At the bare thought of being separated from him my heart feels a pang of grief such as no language could express; and yet, sooner than betray Christ, my Saviour, I would consent to leave this cherished infant an orphan on the world. If God demands the sacrifice, he will give me, I hope, the strength and the will."

Her utterance gave way, and she fell back, pale and in tears, on the couch, convulsively clasping her infant to her bosom.

The great soul of Tertullian could not help the betrayal of some emotion. Speedily mastering his feelings, as if condemning a weakness unworthy of his character :

"Vivia," said he, "God forbid that I should doubt the truth of your protestations ; but, blind mortals as we are, we know not even that which takes place within ourselves, and the heart of man is an abyss full of terrible mysteries even to himself. I am glad to be able to persuade myself that you have not forgotten your promises, that you continue to desire the grace of baptism, and that, in accordance to the instructions given you, you are preparing yourself for it by humble and fervent prayer. But if you have clearly understood the spirit of that holy religion which you seek to enter, why all this elaborate and scandalous superfluity of raiment and ornaments, which Christian humility condemns and Christian modesty rejects ?* From the moment a woman has had the happiness of knowing the true God and the true history and condition of her sex, display and ostentation in dress should be carefully shunned.

---

* Here and elsewhere throughout this work we make Tertullian quote his own words as often as he is introduced to the reader. The words here given are from his "Treatise on Female Dress."

She should rather go about in humble garb and affect simplicity of attire, thus accompanying Eve, mourning and repentant, and even by her very garments expiating that which she inherits from Eve—the ignominy of the first sin and the odium that attached to her as the cause of human perdition. Woman was the first infringer of the divine law, and woman caused the fall of him whom Satan dared not to tempt. Vivia, the sentence of God on your sex lives in this age; the guilt, of necessity, must live also. And because she brought about the ruin of God's image, man, and the consequent introduction of death into the world, the Son of God himself had to suffer and die. In her exile from the fair bowers of Eden, where she had spent so many happy days, the sorrowing Eve contented herself with the coarse garment fashioned for her by God's hand; while you, her daughter, must needs have the soft fleeces of the Milesians, the silks of the Chinese, the purple of Tyre, the costly cloths of Babylon, gleaming pearls, flashing onyx-stones, gold wrung from the mines, and lying mirrors to flatter your vanity. Can it be possible that you have never reflected or did not know that all this vain display is simply the funereal pomp of woman in her condemned and dead state, and that their discovery and use is to be attributed to Satan, the chief of fallen angels?

"Since the light of grace has fallen on my soul —*for I have not been born, but have become, a*

Christian—I have read in our sacred books that the fallen angels allowed themselves to be ensnared by the seductive charms of the daughters of men. Hence those monstrous alliances which provoked God's anger, and his regret at having broken his eternal repose by creation.* Less to repay the criminal enjoyment which they desired than to multiply the temptations which caused the weak to fall, these evil spirits revealed to woman the secrets which their cunning had discovered. They taught her the use she could make of the precious metals, the virtues of certain herbs, the advantages to be derived from the sheen of jewelry and gold in necklaces and bracelets, the art of dying wool in purple and other brilliant colors. They knew that all desires and wishes to please by corporal means and forms were an outrage to God, an occasion of ruin and sin to their unwary victims. Vivia, such is the shameful origin of all this pomp and splendor to which you still cling. . . . And yet, if you are a Christian, you and God will one day judge these fallen angels. How will you feel on your way up to the tribunal to pronounce eternal sentence on them ? How will you dare to condemn those whose gifts you prized and coveted !

"Leave gold to its natural uses, and set not such value on what barbarians, wiser than we, despised so far as to forge into chains for their cap-

* This fallacy of Tertullian and other ancient writers regarding the "loves of the angels" for the daughters of the race of Cain has long been abandoned as absurd.

tives. Because these stones which you call precious are rare, do they cease to be what nature made them—insignificant pebbles fashioned by the caprice and art of man, polished by dint of labor, cut by patient toil, to be hung on the ears of women foolish enough to plume themselves on this borrowed splendor? Why, by an unnatural blending, seek to unite and mix colors separated by Almighty God? Is it not folly to adorn one's self with pearls that have lain buried and unknown for ages at the bottom of the sea, which, after all, are but the slow product of a disease peculiar to shell-fish?

"I am aware, Vivia, of all that prejudice can oppose to these holy maxims; in vain will you excuse yourself on the plea of rank, great wealth, early education. Reflect well that, before God, you and I and all men are but vile mites, miserable sinners. We have forfeited the right of lifting up our heads; our place is in the dust. The humblest of your slaves, if she has more virtue, is more exalted than you in the eyes of Him whose judgments are not formed from external appearance and glitter. You would fain plead birth and nobility of lineage! But the Christ, whom you desire to serve, waited to be born until his Mother's nobility had disappeared and was hidden under the squalor of poverty. Her ancestors had been exalted and wore the kingly crown, but God caused the throne to crumble under their feet and the sceptre in their

hands; the descendants of the renowned and
opulent Solomon had to earn their bread by the
sweat of their brow. Christ spurned worldly
greatness, and by so doing he branded it by his
contempt and stigmatized it by his anathema;
and it is because he lived without glory, without
pomp, without honors, that I hail and adore him
as my Saviour and my God.

"Will you tell me, Vivia, that the broad do-
mains and the wealth in which you find so much
self-satisfaction were bestowed on you to satisfy,
at any cost, all the whims of your indolence, all
the wild dreams of your vanity? When God
bestowed them so lavishly on you he had in view
an object far more exalted than you have hitherto
imagined; he wished you to be the representative of his providence. All around you are the
poor, the first-born of his Church and kingdom,
the living members of his Incarnate Son. Vivia,
leave to pagan women all these vain ornaments,
these costly trifles; use your wealth nobly by
giving bread to your hungry neighbor, raiment to
suffering mothers and indigent children; redeem
captives; send assistance to our brethren who, for
having openly confessed the faith, have been violently stripped of their possessions. Your name
will be blessed, and that of God still more, as
by your hand he will heal many wounds and dry
many secret tears."

In humble silence Vivia had listened to the
grave and severe words of the Christian priest.

For the first time she felt ashamed of the luxurious life which she had hitherto led, and saw all the emptiness of the vanities which she had loved. But vanity, her life-long idol, soon rose to check this first impulse.

"Father," said she, raising her head, " I admire your virtues; they are great like your faith, exalted and sublime like your genius; but do you not exact too much from a weak woman who has but just been born to the new and austere life of the Christians? Doubtless, my heart is not yet sufficiently detached from the cherished heirlooms of my ancestors; but from the moment I renounced the worship of idols I can truthfully say, unless I deceive myself, that my heart has admitted no reprehensible affection, and that I am induced to wear these ornaments by scarcely another motive than that of pleasing my noble husband and some few friends still left me in the world. Permit me to say, father, that at my age and in my position it would be unbecoming in me to clothe myself like one of my slaves. And, after all, is it not enough to preserve the heart pure and unsullied?"

"What think you of me, blind woman?" exclaimed Tertullian; "do you hope to deceive me as well as yourself? Look into your heart, examine it before God, for whom there are no mysteries. Dupe not yourself: when you bedeck yourself with so much care you are influenced by a secret wish to please, to attract attention, and that

wish is not blameless. It springs from a bad
principle, from the sin within us; it contains a
mighty peril, although you know it not—the re-
suscitation of that terrible passion which is never
entirely dead either in the heart or the senses.
Why expose yourself to danger, Vivia! Why
brave the storm that may crush us! The man
who has grown old amid warfare and mortification
still trembles under hoary locks, and woe to him
if he does not fear! the precipice is near and the
fall almost certain! And you, in all the fervor
of youth, in the very infancy of your faith, you
who perhaps never yet mortified by the austeri-
ties of penance your delicate and pampered body,
you imagine that you, forsooth, are safe, and may
walk unscathed on burning coals! Insane and
haughty presumption, that may one day cost you
bitter tears! The foundation of salvation, the
impenetrable buckler of salvation, is a wholesome
diffidence in one's self.

"Let us suppose for a moment that you have
what you certainly have not—all the holiness and
strength of an angel. Even in this case would it
be lawful for you to glory in yourself! Christ has
condemned vainglory; he has forbidden it, and
has made humility equally obligatory on virtue
as on talent; and yet you deem yourself irrepre-
hensible at the very moment that you take pride
in that body which, as you will soon be told by
the Church, is moulded of clay and shall soon
crumble into dust! Ah! Vivia, do not deceive

yourself thus; as for myself, I know but one legitimate reason to be proud of the body: it is that it may be torn and tortured by the hand of the executioner, mutilated by the teeth of the wild beast in the amphitheatre, or be slowly consumed by fire for the name of Jesus Christ."

"O father!" cried Vivia, "into what new world do you usher the young catechumen! Never before even in the assemblies of the Christians have I listened to such sublime lessons. My weakness stands appalled in their contemplation, and in spite of myself my heart taxes them with excessive severity. I again ask how can there be criminality or guilt when there is none in the heart?"

"Did they teach you also," rejoined Tertullian, "in these Christian assemblies to judge of the words of the priest according to your own wisdom? However, I will not allow myself to take umbrage at your obstinacy; I pity your blindness. Your heart, as you allege, contains no guile; is this also the case with those who gaze at and admire you tricked out in such elaborate finery? One of our apostles has said that there are persons *whose eyes are full of adultery and have no peace in sin.* Vivia, such persons are many; in spite of the spread of our holy religion, we live in the midst of pagans, and they are all the slaves of voluptuousness. Even among our own brethren some are still weak; do you wish to scandalize and make our neophytes totter to their ruin?

Are you not afraid that this worldly frippery may not fire the worst passions in the hearts of the pagans? It is not sufficient for us to fly evil; total immunity from guilt requires that we avoid being the occasion of sin in others. When we shall stand before God's tribunal we must render an account of the souls lost through our fault.

"In defiance of the laws, but of laws which are impotent, I see plainly that but slight shades of difference separate the so-called good and virtuous women from the hapless victims of public immorality. Both classes affect the same fashions, the same postures, the same proud and bold carriage. Both are insanely vain of their persons, employ the same means, or rather the same artifices, to attract the eyes of the public, same ornaments on their brazen foreheads, on their necks the same chains, on their shamelessly naked arms the same bracelets. I understand this similarity and uniformity of dress. Where is the pagan woman truly chaste? Where is the young widow who does not occasionally call to mind that she lives in the city built by the ill-famed Dido? Where is the young woman who does not know that among the divinities who claim her incense there is one whose very name we Christians cannot pronounce without loathing and horror? But, Vivia, you aspire to belong to Christ, the son of a spotless Virgin, and you cannot avoid guilt and live as do these women whose very religion favors, encourages, and deifies the

basest passions; it is more than enough to be
obliged to breathe the same air and speak the
same language that they do.

"The future is a book equally sealed .to both
of us; God has not given me the power to read
from its pages as he did to the favored prophets
of old. Hitherto he has mercifully spared the
great Church of Africa, and, while the blood of
martyrs deluges less peaceful lands, we have had
only days of quiet and contentment. But this
long peace, I fear me, has enervated our hearts;
their restoration imperatively demands a conflict.
The storm that has spared us until now may fall
upon our heads at any moment if it should please
God to blow it to our shores, and in such an
eventuality it would be almost certain that you
as well as I would be summoned to descend into
the arena. Let the great day of martyrdom
come. I ask you, Vivia, are those delicate arms
ready to exchange bracelets for iron chains?
Will those feet, so daintily encased in embroidered slippers, permit themselves to be rudely
thrust into gyves? Will the broadsword find
a place to smite that head so bejewelled or that
neck so laden with strings of emeralds and
pearls?

"Open, then, your eyes to the light while it
is yet time; do penance for the past, cast aside
whatever clashes with the spirit of the faith you
profess, renounce all this worldly display that you
must certainly and solemnly do before you can

ever be permitted to receive the grace of baptism. Believe me, Vivia, the religion of Christ has abundance of ornaments incomparably more valuable than those you have heretofore esteemed. Let your countenance draw its whiteness from simplicity, its rosy tints from modesty; paint your eyes with bashfulness and wreathe your lips with the sweet fragrance of silence. Let no barbarous trinkets disfigure your ears, but implant in them the word of God, infinitely purer and more precious than jewels and gold; bow your head to the glorious and royal yoke of Jesus Christ. Clothe yourself with the silk of uprightness, the fine linen of holiness, the purple of modesty. Thus arrayed you will attract the eye and win the love of your God, and on the great day of resurrection an angel's hand will single you out and lead you in triumph to the presence of Christ."

After her momentary flash of pride had passed away the young woman bent her eyes on the ground; she felt as if crushed by the weight of such piercing and powerful words. She resembled the reed which at the first breath of the blast lifts its feeble stem, as if essaying to cope with the storm, but, being weak and feeble, it soon bends to the earth, and there lays until the storm has passed. With the skill and tact of an experienced combatant, Tertullian had watched the reflection of Vivia's thoughts on her fair and open countenance, awaiting the proper moment

to strike the final blow and lay the victim prostrate at the foot of the cross without giving her
time to recover.

"Vivia," cried he, in a tone still more grave
and dignified than before—"Vivia, he who ad-
dresses you is not Tertullian, the unworthy
priest, the *miserable sinner*, but the representative of the Church of Carthage, the messenger of
our holy bishop, your father and mine. Do you
remember the day when, on your knees and in
the presence of a numerous congregation of the
faithful, you begged him with tears to be initiated in the religion of Christ, and to be prepared
according to the usual course of instruction and
probation prescribed for catechumens? A low
murmur of joy and satisfaction ran through the
assembly, and every eye was turned to heaven to
thank God for his goodness and mercy. The
saintly pontiff told you, with deep feeling, how
he rejoiced at opening the fold and adding one
sheep more to the flock. · His voice trembled as
he stood before the altar and entoned the canticle
of thanksgiving, which we all took up with such
fervent gladness. Do you remember how, when
you arose from your knees, so many venerable
matrons, holy virgins, and spotless maidens
crowded around you, calling you by the sweet
name of sister, and embracing you with the kiss
of peace? Do you remember the joy and the
tears of your mother as she clasped you to her
bosom, kissed you, and told God that she had

lived long enough since her beloved child had now become a Christian? And still, Vivia, you have saddened the heart of the holy bishop, your father. The Church of Carthage has been scandalized, your pious mother is inconsolable, for it has been reported in the congregation of the faithful that you waver in your promises, that flesh and blood have regained their sway over you, and that, still a slave to ease and vanity, you designedly postpone the day of your baptism. The pagans openly boast that you never have deserted their ranks, and that you will soon appear again in their temples in the company of their wives and children.

"Vivia, reflect on the scandal you give; engrave on your heart the words which I am charged to bring to you from our venerated pontiff: 'Let this woman do penance; let her wipe out the bad example which she has given; let her, by trampling under foot all her pagan display and pomp, begin from this day to lead a live of humility and mortification.' Vivia, I have delivered my message." And Tertullian sped away, without even saluting the young woman, whom he left terrified and heart-broken.

CHAPTER II.

VIVIA belonged to one of the oldest and noblest families of Carthage. On her mother's side she reckoned among her ancestors the celebrated Hamilcar or Barca, who for five years struck Italy with terror and desolation, and saved his country from the invasion of the fierce and warlike Numidians. Spain saw him landing boldly on her shores with a few small vessels, nor did he depart until he had conquered many tribes and laid the foundations of Barcelona, to which he had given his name. His fame, however, was destined to pale by reason of the renown achieved by one of his sons, the celebrated Hannibal, who when yet a child had sworn so implacable a hatred of the Romans that lapse of time only intensified it. He was a warrior as indefatigable as he was great and skilful; he marched across the Pyrenees and the Alps, and fell like an avalanche on the fertile plains of Italy. Having been victorious on the banks of the Ticino and the Trebia, and later at Thrasymenus, at Cannæ he crushed the Roman legions, commanded by Paulus Emilius and Varro,

and for a while the *people-king* trembled behind
their walls. The enervating repose of the Car-
thagian troops at Capua saved Rome; Hannibal
was recalled to Africa, was defeated at Zama,
exiled to Carthage, and ended his days by poison
to escape being surrendered to the Romans.

Vivia's father was a lineal descendant of the
haughty and vindictive Hanno, the implacable
enemy of Hannibal, of whose power he was jealous. After long years of rivalry, which not unfrequently caused the shedding of blood, and
menaced the peace of the entire city and the weal
of the republic, the two families became united
by marriage; the grandson of Hanno took to wife
the granddaughter of Hannibal, and thus these
two powerful and hitherto unfriendly houses became allied and united.

Hanno Vivius, at the time our story begins,
was a hale old man, from sixty to sixty-five years
of age. In his youth he had studied law and elo-
cution. Gifted with talent and an extraordinary
memory, he soon rose to prominence among his
fellow-students; but the ardent mind of the youth
was not content with the honors of being a good
speaker; it seemed to him that the blood which
coursed in his veins called him to higher aims;
it was not in a hall or the narrow limits of a debate that he could maintain the prestige of his
line or fittingly serve his country. Besides, the
lawless hordes of Numidia menaced Carthage as
they did in the days of Hamilcar; swarms of pi-

rates from barbarian coasts preyed on their commerce, made descents on their shores, massacred
the old, enslaved the youth of both sexes, and
vanished in their fleet barks laden with rich
booty.   He decided, therefore, to choose the
profession of arms, and subsequently commanded
many military and naval expeditions.   He led
this busy life for fifteen years, was always successful, was twice honored by a public triumph,
and solemnly crowned in the principal temple of
the capital.   When the fatigues of war and his
many wounds compelled him to retire into private life, the gratitude of his fellow-citizens followed and conferred upon him the highest offices
of the magistracy.

Hanno had not inherited the rancorous diposi-
tions of his race ; he was frank, open, generous,
and was every inch the soldier.   At the head of
armies his humanity and justice won for him the
affection of his subalterns ; in the senate, where
his birth entitled him to a seat, in the discharge of
the weighty matters assigned to his management,
he had shown fidelity to duty, impartiality, a soul
superior to bribery, and love for the people.   He
was of a mild and easy disposition, was a tender
husband and a loving father, and, although not
entirely free from the prejudices of birth and position, still his army of slaves had sufficient reason
to be satisfied with him.   These had only to do
their duty faithfully, to be submissive, punctual
in preparing his meals, punctilious in caring for

his favorite steeds, careful to keep his hunting implements ready and well furbished; this done, he was satisfied, and required nothing more of them. They were, therefore, well off for those times, when slaves were treated with such merciless inhumanity; when, for a slight fault, a trivial oversight, or because such was the will of a capricious owner, it was nothing unusual to have them whipped unmercifully until they were covered with wounds and blood.

From his tenderest years in the camp, but especially since his participation in the government of the city, Hanno had often heard mention made of the new religion. He knew but very little about its tenets, he only picked up from public report that the Christians affected great austerity and retirement; that they secretly met on certain days to celebrate their mysteries; that they mutually gave assistance to each other in sickness and want; and that, having been once initiated by certain immersions, they were no longer permitted to appear in the temples, or to assist at the public sacrifices; that they held themselves bound to suffer patiently confiscation, exile, and even death, rather than acknowledge the gods of the nation. He had been informed, and was inclined to believe, that, under cloak of great moral purity, they perpetrated, in their secret assemblies and under cover of night, the most abominable crimes, such as fornication, adultery, and incest—nay, that they even butcher-

ed their children and feasted on their mangled
limbs. Accordingly, Hanno despised and instinctively hated the Christians; nevertheless, as
they punctually paid their taxes, served faithfully
in the army, and were useful citizens in their
trades or professions, he leaned to the opinion
that they ought not to be dealt with very rigorously, certainly that they should by no means be
put to death.

A man of this stamp could not well be a profligate in the full force of the term. He would
never consent, like so many of his friends, to vio-
late his marriage vows, to insult the tears or humiliation of a dishonored wife by thrusting her
aside to make way for a new and criminal alliance. He took care that all his surroundings
should bear the stamp of decency—a fact highly
honorable to him in an age so deeply plunged in
corruption. This morality, however, never went
further than what was required by the exigencies
of *decorum.* He loved society, visited his friends,
and was a constant frequenter of the public baths,
like all the aristocracy of the city. In his morals
he was no rigorist; his conversation was jovial,
and for very good reasons he was exceedingly
lenient to what he called the levities of youth.
Nor could it be ascribed to calumny that he bore
the reputation of being a lover of gaming and
good cheer. All this put together will give a
pretty faithful outline of what Vivia's father

Although brought up in paganism, her mother soon manifested a sincere hatred for vice. From her tenderest years Julia—for such was her name—was cited as a model of mildness, modesty, and virtue. The licentiousness which sat enthroned in the temples, which was unblushingly paraded on the stage, and pervaded every conversation, inspired her with an indescribable disgust that protected her youth against the allurements of the world. She felt, as if by instinct, that reserve and modesty should be the distinguishing attributes of womanhood; that in youth she should live hidden under the protecting wing of a pious and prudent mother; that as soon as she became free she should watch over her heart, see to the proper government of her home and children, and, by kind affection, render herself the pleasing companion of her husband. Accordingly, she always shunned the society of those of her own age in whom she discovered levity of character or a taste for boisterous amusements. Being rich, talented, and beautiful, she could have had a whole host of admirers; this was then the custom; but she appeared in the family circle only at meal times, answered curtly and always with gravity the questions addressed to her, and lost no time in returning to her apartments, to continue, with her slave, her needle-work or to amuse herself with her music and harp. Such a course soon discouraged and drove away, one after another, all the young triflers and idlers who sought to

please but only annoyed her by their artful protestations and flattery.

Julia saw but very little of her father. All
her affections had been centred in her mother and
an orphan cousin ten years her junior. She had
watched over her cradle and had kindly lent herself to be her companion in all her childish games.
She used to dry her tears, console her in her brief
troubles, and thus her affection for the child grew
until she could not bear the least separation from
her. They shared the same room by day, the
same chamber by night. Whenever Julia strolled into the country or along the seashore Potamiena—for so the orphan was called—was her inseparable companion; hand in hand they thread-
ed the streets of Carthage, followed by the old
female slave who had charge of them. Their
mothers smiled upon and admired this mutual
attachment. One day, however, Julia returned,
or rather was brought, home alone! Potamiena,
the beloved orphan, the dear *little sister*, had
disappeared, and no one ever again heard anything about her. Julia's grief was so great that
for many months her health gave cause for anxiety. She wished to live for her mother's sake, for
she was her only consolation. Nevertheless, she
never ceased to weep for her lost friend. More
than twenty years had elapsed since this terrible
misfortune had happened, and yet whenever she
heard Potamiena's name tears filled her eyes.

In obedience to her mother's wish, in her sev-

enteenth year she became the wife of Hanno
Vivius, who bestowed upon her an immense
fortune, an honored name, brilliant qualities, a
loyal and devoted heart. Her own wealth being
even greater than that of her husband, she felt
in duty bound to put her house on a footing
equal to that of the most opulent in Carthage,
and, thanks to the judicious taste of Hanno, her
mansion soon became the centre of attraction for
the aristocracy of the entire city. She did the
honors with the tact and affability which she had
acquired by her training and the rule of life
which she had marked out for herself. Ere long
these frequent and merry reunions became a
source of pain to the virtuous Julia. They
shocked her sense of delicacy, for it was the
ambition of each one to prove himself in advance
of his fellows in the knowledge of fashionable
worldliness, vice, and scandals; in them but little was to be heard regarding subjects of national
interest or morality; much about pleasure and
intrigue, while occasionally objects the most
sacred were made the subject of pleasantry and
ridicule. Julia could never accustom herself to
join in conversations which always smacked of
levity, and from the time she became a mother
she ceased to appear at these reunions, alleging
as an excuse her duty to her children, which she
could not, she said, permit to devolve on merce-
nary hands. Hanno was not deceived as to the
real motive of this conduct; he did not wish to

pain the wife he loved ; even among friends he gayly and playfully undertook to excuse and defend her conduct.

Being now free and all absorbed in the management of her domestic affairs, in superintending her numerous slaves, and in attending to the due administration of her monetary interests, neglected by the carelessness of Hanno, Julia still found time to satisfy her own generous impulses. Very different from others in her station, who think only of enjoyment, and forget the wants of the poor, she was never happier than when she found an opportunity of assisting the needy. Before she came to the knowledge of Christianity, she practised one of its greatest virtues, and there can be little doubt that she was indebted to her munificent liberality to the poor for the happiness of finding and embracing at a later period that heaven-born religion which placed charity at the head of her precepts— charity which was unknown to the pagan world, and reckoned as a weakness by her philosophers. She bestowed especial care on widows and orphans, and from every quarter of the city the indigent flocked to her for relief. She had the gift of enhancing the value of her gifts by the kind and cheerful manner observed in bestowing them ; she had always a kind word to soothe the heart at the same time that she bountifully supplied the means of appeasing hunger.

Julia gave birth to several children, all of

whom she herself nursed. Two of them had
died in the cradle, a third had been taken away
at the age of seven, his face having been fright-
fully eaten away by a horrible cancer. She bitterly wept over this child, who had caused her
such care and long watching, and she often
bathed with her tears the splendid monument
which she raised to his memory. Poor mother!
she yet ignored the sweet consolation of prayer,
which calms the most poignant grief and whispers to the heart the mysterious words of hope!
She knew not then that she would one day find
in God's bosom and in all the glory of immorta-
lity the idolized child torn from her affections by
a cruel disease. As yet she could only commune
with his *shade*, which she was taught to believe
wandered around his tomb, she felt desolate
and broken-hearted as she turned away after
having repeated the *eternal farewell* of the pagans.

And yet in all the bitterness of her grief
Julia never once forgot that three children still
remained to her who also had sacred claims upon
her affections—two sons in their boyhood, both
of whom had made their mark in the most celebrated schools of Carthage, and a daughter, a little the senior of both, and who, in more ways
than one, was the living image of her mother.
She was affectionate and obedient, very much
attached to her brothers, and was especially
remarkable for great kindness to the slaves ap-

pointed to wait on her. She was ever ready to
assist them in their tasks, visited and even tend-
ed them during their fits of sickness. If she ever
happened, in a moment of impatience, to treat
them harshly, her good nature soon returned,
and she hastened to make amends for her conduct by giving them presents and caresses.

The reader has already guessed, no doubt, that
this was Vivia of whom we have been speaking.
And yet, notwithstanding all we have said,
Vivia had more faults than one. Being extreme-
ly sensitive, the slightest contradiction irritated
her; but her resentment was short-lived and devoid of rancor. Her great and versatile talents
had developed in her at a very early age the
germ of self-love. She liked to display her ac-
complishments in conversation, where she could
give loose rein to her teeming imagination; she
was a pleasing conversationalist, and when she
broached a historical question or an important
subject her hearers continued to listen even after
she had ceased speaking. These, indeed, were
the topics which won her preference; she knew
she would here command admiration, and praise
was by no means a matter of indifference to her.
Her character was somewhat wavering and irreso-
lute; her will lacked energy. Occasionally she
did show resolution, almost enthusiasm; then
she appeared capable of making great sacrifices;
but the fire soon died away, and then, as if a reaction had taken place, after a violent effort or too

great a strain, she relapsed into her usual indeci-
sion.   Her mother did everything in her power
to remedy these defects; her anxiety became
alarmed at the thought of the consequences that
might possibly arise therefrom in after-life; but
all her wisdom and advice had proved abortive.
Vivia listened, candidly avowed her failings, and
promised amendment.   But this demanded something more than her own reflections and the desire to please her mother: she lacked a supernatural motive, and this her religion could not
give her.

Unhappily for her, nature, too, had lavished all
her gifts upon her.   To nobility of birth, remarkable talents, wit, and a flow of language
she joined uncommon beauty, rendered still more
captivating by a dreamy air full of languor and
expression.   All Carthage talked of her; even
her very father never lost an opportunity of
praising her, even to her face.   Much less would
have been sufficient to inspire her with vanity;
and so, from her fourteenth year, she made it a
study—I should rather say a labor—to improve
her personal appearance and attractiveness by all
the adjuncts of adornment and dress.   Covered
with diamonds and precious stones, she shone radiant in the blaze of costly necklaces and bracelets ; her dresses were of the costliest materials,
and dazzled the eye by a display of the richest
and most beautiful embroidery in gold and silver.
Let it be said, however, to her praise, and in the

interest of truth, that her moral conduct was ir-
reproachably pure.

Such was the family of Vivia, when an event
that could not have been foreseen occurred and
radically changed the internal status of this family, with whose habits and character we have
ust been made acquainted.

CHAPTER III.

AMONG the slaves given by her mother to Julia at the time of her marriage to Hanno was one named Rufina, who was about the same age as her young mistress. The fairness of her complexion showed plainly enough that she belonged to no African race, but was sprung from some one of the tribes that dwell in the mild climate of Europe. Always grave and pensive, she was ever respectful to her superiors and affable to her equals, yet she never shared in their merrymakings and wanton dances. Whenever her occupations allowed her a few moments of liberty, she either retired to her humble chamber or strolled alone in some solitary walk in the garden. Occasionally she would be heard singing in some unknown tongue, and though the listeners understood not the refrain, the air affected them singularly; there was something so sweet in the voice, so touching and melancholy in the tone! They who heard paused to listen until tears came, as they invariably did, and put an end to those weird melodies. On certain days she as-

44

sumed a more animated and lively strain; but such days were few, and she speedily relapsed into her habitual melancholy. As may be easily imagined, the curiosity of her companions was aroused in no small degree, and each of them had formed her own commentary. "She is a hypocrite," cried one. "Just think, at her age people naturally love enjoyment and dancing; in every climate youth laughs and skips, and still, no matter how we try, we have never yet been able to induce her to join us in our amusements. By this affected gravity she flatters herself, of course, that she will ingratiate herself into the good graces of our sedate mistress, and it must be acknowledged that in this she has succeeded but too well already."

"Perhaps," said another, "she is some great princess, the daughter of some barbarian king, reduced to slavery by some unlucky accident. Her pride is wounded, and she feels humiliated in our society and in the performance of the tasks which she has to share with us. I have seen her refuse more than once the presents offered to her."

"I have heard it said," rejoined a third, who loved to play the blue-stocking, "that somewhere away beyond the sea there exists a custom of initiating young women in a mysterious life of contemplation and reverie. They do not wed or live in cities, but wander in forests or retire to some solitary island. They are a kind of prophetesses or sibyls, are summoned to the council of the king, are the sovereign arbitresses of peace and war, and when the battle is raging a prophetic frenzy seizes them and they intone magic songs to infuse their own maddened spirit into the souls of the combatants. I have strong suspicions that Rufina was formerly one of these women, so highly esteemed among barbarous tribes, and that she disappointed the hopes of some prince or chief, and was in consequence deprived of liberty and sold as a slave."

"In my opinion," broke in a swarthy old crone, whose features wore all the evil traces usually furrowed by envy and hate, "I have found out the secret of her moping ways. Rufina may be a hypocrite, as you say, and I do not doubt it, but I have my reasons for believing that it is at our cost that she gradually wriggles herself into the confidence of our young mistress. I do not trust her sweet ways more than I would the fawning of a young tiger. I have secretly and carefully watched all her movements, and I can assure you her sadness is no longer a mystery to me. The *chaste* Rufina has simply opened her heart to the amorous pleadings of love. I am sure of what I say, and I even know the person. He is a slave like herself, and his name is Revocatus. You may have seen him yourselves, for his master often sends him to ours on errands. Only hear me out, and you will become as convinced as I am.

"First of all, judging by his color, Revocatus and she must be from the same or a neighboring country. I saw them both when they came to Carthage, and they arrived at the same time. Afterwards I found out that when they were put up for sale they earnestly entreated to be disposed of to the same purchaser or master, and when this was refused she became so enraged that she could not restrain her lamentations and tears. Although he commanded his feelings better, still he betrayed great mortification at the separation. Very often, while our *pensive* Rufina is singing at the end of the garden in that gibberish that nobody can understand, I see Revocatus creeping along the wall outside until he gets to a place where he can stop and listen to her. In all probability those airs, that seem so melodious and weirdly sad to us, are the love-songs of her country, and convey to him her sorrow at not being able to be his bride. Having set myself on their track, I redoubled my watchfulness, until I finally detected them in their interviews and heard them conversing in their unintelligible language. Their interviews are always pretty long; they seem to be constantly discussing some very interesting subject—no doubt some plan or other to regain their liberty, to escape from their owners, perhaps in order to be able to love and live together."

Such were the judgments passed on the young foreigner, who had not the slightest suspicion of what was being said of her. Entirely absorbed in the performance of her duties, she did not seem to notice even the cutting remarks, the sly hints, and open rebukes of her companions. Invariably full of kindness and consideration for them, she never lost an opportunity of pleading in their behalf, and her winning ways often spared them from the reprimands and punishment which they frequently deserved. This generosity, instead of mollifying, only embittered them the more, so they resolved to compass her ruin in the estimation of their mistress. The old negress's revelations were, therefore, very well timed. Accordingly, they all went in a body and accused Rufina of holding secret and frequent interviews with Revocatus. This they did, as they averred, because, "for the honor of the house, it was high time to put a stop to such an intrigue."

Ever since her mother had made her a present of Rufina, Julia had never ceased to remark, and had always admired, the gentleness and devotedness of her slave. Her retiring ways, her modesty, that constant melancholy which gave an indescribable charm to her person and voice, all united in interesting her mistress in her favor. In the course of time Julia had placed implicit confidence in her; she usually kept her in her apartments to enjoy her company and conversation, and treated her more like a daughter than a slave. The accusation was a grave one, adroitly planned and strongly corroborated by all the slaves, who unanimously asserted that they had *seen*, certainly and surely *seen*, all that the old crone had previously related. The accusation, therefore, fell on Julia like a thunder-clap, and her first impulse was to hand her slave over to Hanno, to be punished as severely as the cruel laws of the times would permit. Luckily she did not act upon the impulse. It would be more just, she reflected, to question her and hear what she had to say. In spite of appearances, might she not, after all, be innocent? She summoned her to her presence. When they were alone:

"Rufina," said she, "why have you deceived me? Have I not been always kind to you? I grieved for your unhappy lot, and strived to render it less painful. I had confidence in you, and you know it; I permitted you alone to have charge over my very children as often as I was called away by other occupations. I imagined that you were devoted and virtuous, and you have deceived and betrayed me!"

"Kind mistress, truly you have been good, too good to me, and my gratitude to you will last as long as life; but, alas! what can a poor slave do? All her blood poured out to the last drop for you would be but insufficient payment for such a debt! But I to deceive you! I to betray you! oh! never, never!" And her eyes, overflowing with tears, were lifted to the face of the noble lady.

"Tell me, then, Rufina, what mean those mysterious songs in which you occasionally give utterance to your thoughts and feelings? They pleased me even though I understood not their import; hence I have frequently asked you to sing them to me, or to hum them over the cradle of my children. Whenever I heard them I invariably experienced a strange feeling, which even now I cannot account for. What, then, is this poetry? Is not magic its soul, or rather, as I am more inclined to think, is it only the ardent, impassioned expression of these tender sentiments to which I had imagined you a total stranger; for, I once more repeat, I had faith in your virtue?"

"Noble mistress, believe the word of your humble slave; what I sing are no weird songs. How could I, a poor unlettered female, have been able to study that mysterious science of which I had never even heard until I came hither? Still less are they calculated to convey the sentiments to which you alluded just now. Possessing nothing, and destined to remain, in all probability, in slavery as long as I live, on what object could I possibly bestow the affections of my heart? I am but too well aware that I could not dispose of it without guilt. I am your slave, I belong to you whole and entire; my life itself is in your hands. My whole ambition is not to displease you, and I am but too happy when I succeed. In obedience to you and to while away the leisure moments allowed me by your kindness, I have been accustomed to sing those airs;

they are those of fatherland; my mother sang them by my cradle as I did by that of your fair children. They are the only goods, the sole treasure, brought by me when I landed in your country. Save the happiness of serving you, they are my only consolation. But, if such be your pleasure, my lips shall utter them no more, and in future I shall commune in silence with my own thoughts and memories."

There was so much candor and meekness in these words that Julia felt herself deeply moved and sorry for having reproached her so cruelly. Could such qualities co-exist in the heart with deceit, hypocrisy, and the guilt of which she stood accused? She determined, however, to find out the whole truth, were it only to confound the jealousy of her slaves. With this design she assumed a milder tone, and said:

" Rufina, you are acquainted with a slave named Revocatus, who comes hither occasionally to do his master's errands. Is it true that he stops to speak with you in private, and prolongs his interviews beyond the bounds of propriety? I do not wish to be rash in giving credence to evil reports, but such conduct is calculated to ruin you. What motive or reason can you have for thus making yourself an object of derision to your fellow-servants and of my husband's resentment in case of discovery? Rufina, take my advice, shun this Revocatus, about whose moral character I know absolutely nothing."

"Kind mistress mine, I am ready to make the sacrifice you demand, and should deem myself culpable were I to disobey or displease you; but if you would condescend to allow your lowly slave to defend herself in your eyes, I would say that this Revocatus has been my friend from childhood and the companion of my earliest years. The same day and country witnessed our birth, one roof sheltered our cradle, one breast suckled us both; we lived and grew up together in the fond hope that death alone could, but haply that even that would not, separate us. Sweet dream, doomed to be dispelled, alas! even in our early youth! O noble mistress!" continued she as she cast herself in tears at Julia's feet, "Revocatus, whom I must see no more in obedience to your commands, is the child of my poor mother; she bore us together in her bosom, and together ushered us into the world. Had you but condescended to notice him you could not have failed to remark how we resemble each other; this is so evident that people always note it, and assert they never before saw anything like it between brothers and sisters, or even twins such as we are."

"Arise, Rufina," exclaimed the noble lady, giving her hand to Rufina, who covered it with kisses—"arise, you are a noble girl. I believe you are innocent; forgive me for my momentary suspicions and the pain I have given you. From this day I shall look upon you no longer as a slave. Be my companion; aid me to bring up my children; you love them, and they return your affection. My Vivia especially cares only for her mother and you. You have been so kind to her always—in sickness you never leave her for a moment; you can rely on her and my gratitude. Go meet your brother often; speak with him when and where you please; my pleasure is that you do so without hindrance or molestation. As for your wicked traducers, they have deserved punishment, and it shall be meted out to them this very day."

"Blessings on your head, noble mistress; I am now happy indeed, since you believe in my innocence and permit me to see my fond brother. My late sad misfortune is no longer a cause for grief; my condition, heretofore so irksome, is now become so pleasant that I shall love it for the future. You have assured me of your confidence, and you have had the condescension to approve of Vivia's affection for me. Be pleased to permit me to add, however, that there is one thing wanting to all your favors of this happy day, this is forgiveness for my companions; I beg it on my knees. They never dreamed of doing any harm, no doubt; appearances deceived them, and they were actuated only by zeal for the honor of your house. Pardon them, then, I beseech you, and never let them know that my entreaties obtained their forgiveness."

"Generous girl, how can I refuse? Who taught

you so well the way to my heart ? At what school
have you learned lessons so exalted and marvellous that, though I admire, I can never hope to
put them in practice ? What ! your companions,
in their jealousy at my preference for you, lay an
infamous plot to accomplish the ruin of one who
never did them an injury ; they plan and profer
against you a charge of such a nature as to have
brought terrible punishment upon you, and yet
you beg on your knees that they be pardoned'!
Wonderful maiden, what a strange philosophy is
this of your country ! Say, say, what is the name
of your people. Give me your history ; unravel
the deep mystery in which you have hitherto
shrouded yourself."

"My history, noble lady, contains nothing
worthy of interest for a mind so exalted as yours ;
it is the history of a hapless and obscure person
who passes unnoticed and unknown in the world,
and is forgotten as soon as she has disappeared.
Judging by my long voyage to Carthage, where
the unforeseen happiness of serving you awaited
me, my native land must be far, very far away ;
but what matters the distance to me, since I may
never again behold it ?   I was born in the most
remote part of Gaul, hard by the straits that separate it from the British Islands, whither Cæsar, it
is said, carried his victorious arms after he had
conquered my country. All that I have ever
heard of my ancestors is that the Romans called
them *barbarians ;* why, I know not, unless it be

that the Gauls won many battles against them, and planted their standards on their proud capitol. Being an old soldier, my father used often to tell Revocatus and myself of the courage and warlike deeds of the Gauls; but I was too young to understand all he said, and since I have forgotten them. My mother used to interest us with subjects that pleased me far more; of these I have retained a more vivid recollection.

" I was only ten years old when my father died, nor had I the consolation of being near him at his last moments. Having faithfully clung to a cause which he deemed noble and holy, he was loaded with chains, dragged from our home, and a few days after was put to death by the sword of the executioner.

" Being poor, and encumbered by her two helpless children, my widowed mother worked hard to support us by her labor and the produce of a small plot of ground tilled for her by her compassionate neighbors. Five years after she went to rejoin in a better world him whom s'.e had never ceased to mourn; labor and sorrow had worn her away prematurely. Our grief was bitter and deep; at the age of fifteen we became orphans without other support than the little plot of land and a poor cottage, our tenure of which was soon threatened by merciless creditors. As we had no one to help us, no influential friend to protect us, we were cruelly stripped of everything and driven from our little patrimony, which would

have satisfied my desires and all my brother's
ambition. In this manner were we forced to bid
a tearful adieu to the tomb of our mother and to
the cottage that had sheltered our childhood. But
our misfortunes were not to end even then ; as
the land and cottage did not realize a sufficiency,
we were compelled to forfeit our liberty in order
to liquidate the debt; this was in accordance to
the laws of my country.

"We were put on board a ship bound for the
coast of Africa. The voyage was long and unpleasant ; frequent storms kept us in constant danger
of shipwreck and death. But this fate had no
terrors for Revocatus and me, for we would
have died together and would have tenanted the
same grave. While the sailors trembled with
fear and importuned all their gods for delivery
and assistance, my brother and I used to sit quietly and watch the lightning as it flashed from the
heavens, or listen to the rumbling of the thunder
and the still more terrible roar of the waves dash-
ing against the sides of our laboring ship. But
it was not the will of heaven that we should die
together. We arrived at Carthage ; in spite of
our prayers and tears we were obliged to separate for the first time in our lives. I became the
slave of your noble mother ; Revocatus fell to
another master. This is our history, and you
now see that it contains nothing to claim your
attention."

"You are mistaken, Rufina ; the cruel and undeserved misfortunes of your family and of yourself interest me and fill me with compassion. The gods have not given me a heart of brass or stone. Misfortune always wears a sacred aspect in my eyes, no matter the head on which it may fall. But continue, Rufina; the day is waning and you have not yet satisfied my curiosity. Answer my questions frankly. What sort of songs are those you sing? What poet composed them? In what school have you learned that sublime philosophy of which you have given me a specimen by asking pardon for those who sought to do you such cruel injury?"

"Sweet lady, it was an easy task to inform you of what I had been up to the happy hour that made me your slave. At present I am at a loss to make myself intelligible, and to find the proper terms to translate my meaning and my thoughts. I shall endeavor to do so, however, since you wish it; fortunately, you are blessed with mental qualities that will supply whatever may be wanting in my poor speech and explanations.

"I have never assisted at your religious ceremonies or entered your temples. The religion of Gaul, or at least of that portion of it to which I belong is not that of Carthage; indeed, it is essentially different. I presume, however, that in your worship, besides sacrifices and the rites peculiar to each country, you have chants or hymns, in which priests and people join. From our childhood we are taught to sing these, and as we

advance in age and their acquisition they become
our most pleasing occupation.   They are so beautiful and pure that they fill the heart with rapture.   The husbandman guiding his plow repeats
them to the echoes of the mountains; young
women and maidens fill the house with their
beauty and melody while they ply their domestic
tasks; in the gloaming and by the twinkling star-
light the shepherd enlivens his solitary watches by
repeating them.

   " These canticles are of the greatest antiquity,
and were composed by inspired writers; the spirit
of sublimity and religion pervades them; they
lift up the soul beyond the things of earth and
give birth in the heart to the noblest aspirations
of virtue.   Here they extol the wonders of creation, there they convey the loftiest conception of
the Omnipotence from which it sprung.   ' God,
Jehovah, is great; he is wonderful in his works.
The heavens proclaim his glory, and night de-
clares it unto night.   He said: *Be light made,
and the light was made.*   The stars answered:
Lord, behold, here we are.   He poised the earth in
the immensity of space.   He imprisoned the vast
and stormy ocean in its bed, and appointed a little sand to be a barrier to its fury.   He stretched
out the clouds like a garment; he wrapped them
in mists as an infant is wrapped in its clothing.
At his voice the heavens spread themselves as a
tent, the sun rejoices as it comes forth like a
giant to run its course.   The mountains lifted

themselves up, the valleys lowered themselves; the fountains were opened and the rivers burst forth. At his command the lightning flashes from the clouds, darting from the east to the west, and the thunder gives forth its voice. He looks upon the earth and it trembles with fear. He touches the mountains, they quake and melt like wax before the fire.'

"Occasionally, too, our chants breathe the milder tone of thanksgiving and love. Thus, when we praise God's mercy and providence: 'How good is *Jehovah!* His paternal love reaches from age to age, embraces all generations and peoples. He gives his sun to embellish and fructify the earth; he sends the dew and rain to the fields to bring forth their fruits. He hearkens to the cry of the fledgling and sends him food. He provides grass for the toiling ox as he patiently draws the plough along the furrow, and clothes with beauty the flowers that bedeck the fields. His eyes follow the footsteps of the innocent and virtuous. If the injustice of men drives him into exile, he is with him in the desert; if they bind and cast him into prison, Jehovah bears him company to console his captivity. He is a guide, a protector, a friend, and a father, who cannot abandon or forget his children.' These are some of the subjects treated in our canticles; they are musical and pleasant to the ear, but a thousand times more so to the heart that can understand and relish them.

"In this world the number of the rich and happy is small indeed! Suffering, misery, and tears are the lot of the majority. Some, like myself, are torn from home and country and have to weep for their eternal loss. And hence our canticles teem with sentiments appropriate to every phase of grief. They call to Jehovah's mind that, 'The poor is entrusted to thy care; thou art the helpless orphan's undying father. Thy hands wipe away the tears of the afflicted, and make easy the hard pallet of the sufferer. One day the powerful man shall fall from the pinnacle of his greatness, and the indigent shall rise triumphantly from the dust. The proud one who exalted himself like the cedar of Libanus in a moment is no more; the passing traveller saw him fall, sought him, but he was not to be found. Lord, thou seest our tears shed in exile for our lost country. Being slaves in a strange land, our canticles of joy have ceased, but our country, our true country, together with our lost liberty, shall be soon restored, and then we will intone the eternal canticle of joy and gladness.'

"Would, good mistress, that I could rehearse to you all the beautiful things contained in the canticles of my religion! If they have often stirred your heart when sung by a poor slave and in a tongue unintelligible to you, imagine how they speak to the heart that loves and understands them! I have not much courage or strength, nor do I pretend to have; I wept long and bitterly when death took away those whom I loved; I wept when I was left a poor, helpless orphan, when I was sold, wh·n I was forced away from my home and country, when I was torn from my brother, the only and last one left me in this world. But I remembered the lessons taught by my mother, her mildness and patience when afflictions fell upon her. I remembered how she sang those canticles and what consoling balm they brought to her soul. I merely followed my mother's example when, like her, I sought to solace my grief by repeating the canticles she used to sing and had taught me; and thus my sorrow became less poignant and my tears less bitter. These canticles of my religion and fatherland are so beautiful and so sweet! Such poetry, as you would call it, is more than human, and could not have been the work of man."

Julia's soul was moved to its depths. Admiration, fear, respect, and love thrilled every fibre of her heart and produced mysterious and pleasing sensations never felt before.

The name of God, now heard for the first time, his omnipotence in creating the heavens and the earth, his care in guiding and controlling them, his goodness, that extends to the orphan, the prisoner, the unhappy, and yet forgets not the patient ox, the bird, the flower, or the blade of grass—all this was strangely mysterious and incomprehensible, and introduced her into a new world.

" Dear Rufina, continue, I beseech you. How
beautiful the philosophy taught in your country
must be since it has inspired such noble ideas and
poetry so sublime ! Oh ! why was I not born in
that Gaul which my ignorance despised as the
miserable home of savage and bloodthirsty
tribes ? "

" Good and kind mistress, I do not very well
understand what you mean by the term philosophy. In my younger days I was told to mistrust
it as a vain and empty pursuit. In our old Neus-
-tria there are no such schools as you have for
your sons in Carthage. All that I know I learned
from my parents, but principally from a kind old
man who came into our neighborhood from
Rome. Even now I can almost imagine I see
him sitting among those whom he called his
brethren, but more frequently his dear children.
How sweet the face! how calm the brow!
how mild the glance! how musical and persuasive the language! One felt that it gushed
from the very depths of the heart, laden with all
its strength and treasures. His words never
failed to touch my heart, and on my return home
I used to repeat and impress on my memory
the beautiful things we had heard.

" The good old man bade us farewell one day,
to go visit others of his children who longed for
his presence ; we were never more to see him,
alas ! Wicked men whom he sought to reclaim
conceived a hatred of him, and mercilessly mur-

dered him, despite his silvery hair and great virtues, and his last breath was a prayer for his
enemies.

" God forbid that I should dare to argue with
a person who claims all respect and deference!
You are of noble birth, while I am only a poor
slave. You are distinguished for intelligence
and knowledge ; I am of lowly station and without education, as I have already informed you.
Do not imagine, then, that I would wittingly say
aught to wound or condemn even the youngest
of my equals ; how much less would I you, who
are my noble mistress ? Oh! could you have
heard that venerable man ! that it had been
given to you to have known him and his virtues,
to have witnessed, as I have, all his wonderful
and good works ! Had this been your good fortune, I am confident your faith and mine would
be identical.

" He recognized not the numerous divinities
adored in Carthage, many of whom I hear mentioned by my fellow-slaves. He taught us that
there is but one God, eternal, before all ages, omnipotent Creator, only Lord and sovereign Master of the universe; that he is infinitely wise,
just, and good, filling by his immensity all space,
the heavens, the earth, and the sea ; that
he is the invisible witness of all our thoughts,
words, and actions ; that, in his infinite mercy, this God gave us his only, beloved, and
eternal Son, who, by an incomprehensible mys-

tery of love, condescended to assume our nature, to suffer and die to save our fallen and
guilty race; that he will one day judge all mankind, will give infinite happiness and glory to
those who shall have led good lives, but will in-
flict eternal chastisement on the wicked.

"I have heard it said that the morality inculcated by some religions is very lax—nay, that
they foster and flatter the most grovelling propensities and unnatural crimes. I know not how
much truth there may be in this accusation, and
can scarcely bring myself to believe that it may be
true. Vice should be branded always, and virtue
honored. But he who instructed me in my infancy inculcated on his hearers the necessity of
cultivating the most delicate modesty and purity.
An evil thought is enough, he used to say, to
separate us for ever from our all-holy God; hence
we guard ourselves not only against evil but
against its desire or even thought, for our hearts
must be as pure as our bodies. *God searches the
heart and reins.* With us marriage is held in
honor, but perfect continency, which we look
upon as a gift from heaven, is honored still more.
Hence those who observe it, in order to attain to
greater perfection, compose a class of their own,
and enjoy especial privileges.

"We pray often, and are taught that prayer
should be the utterance of a pure and innocent
heart. We look upon obedience as a virtue;
consequently we practise it with readiness and

alacrity, no matter who be the master to whom we
may belong. It is thus I have always served you,
dear mistress, since I became your slave. We
are commanded to love and assist one another
with all patience and mildness. Quarrelling,
hatred, and revenge are strictly prohibited. If
we are despised, persecuted, plundered, or beat-
en, we are instructed to suffer in silence, to love
those who hate us, to pray for those who persecute and calumniate us; the more we are injured the more we ought to endeavor to pay good
for evil; this is our sole way of taking revenge.

"Such, then, noble lady, is, so far as I have
been able to explain it, what you call our philosophy, but what we designate as our doctrine. I
have conveyed it to you but very imperfectly, not
that I wished to dissemble my faith and what I
have been taught. Woe to me if I be ashamed
of my faith! I do not forget that the blood of
a martyr courses in my veins; you understand
now what I meant when I told you that my father's head fell by the sword of the executioner
because of *his fidelity to a noble and holy
cause.* In like manner it was from the lips of a
glorious martyr that I learned the little that I
know of the doctrine in which I had the happiness to have been brought up."

"For some time past, Rufina, I suspected that
you belonged to the new sect. Guard and
cherish the religion of your childhood and country; it is beautiful, although severe; its maxims

are pure, but, in my opinion, very difficult in their observance. Hitherto I only knew it from what I had heard said of it by flippant or prejudiced men, who, as I now clearly see, misrepresented and slandered it. Your frank explanations have set it before me in its true light. I admire it, and feel that my heart commences to lean towards it. Some time, perhaps . . ."

Rufina fell on her knees and was about to speak, when a messenger came to say that the evening meal was ready.

CHAPTER IV.

For some days after this conversation Julia appeared more pensive than usual. Hanno and the children questioned her in vain; she evaded all their enquiries. Completely absorbed in her own thoughts, she constantly dwelt on the simple but touching words of her slave, so that her mind could not shake off the contemplation of that wonderful system of belief, and the still more marvellous teaching of the Christians regarding virtue and charity. Although of a noble family, well educated, and confessedly intelligent, she had hitherto had but the most limited and crude notions regarding the Deity, while a poor girl who could not even read, who was born in a cabin in a barbarous country, had spoken to her in the most sublime strain regarding God, his nature, his perfections, his providence, as well as the creation and the government of the universe! "How wonderful is her God!" said she to herself; " how admirable in his unity and marvellous in his power! Oh! how consoling must it be to love a being so good!" She felt tempted to fall on her knees at his feet and exclaim : " *O God of Rufina ! thou art my God.*"

As we have already stated, Julia had a natural love for virtue ; she had a horror of vice, while everywhere she saw nothing but depravity in morals, indecent amusements, and shameful excesses. Nor could she disguise the fact that these excesses were authorized by her very religion and sanctioned by the example, nay, by the very worship, of some of her gods. Hatred begotten of pride, dissensions, implacable rivalries, lawless ambition, deadly revenge, insatiable greed of wealth, were the life and soul of the ever restless pagan world. The rich were proud and cruel to their slaves, but recklessly squandered their money and the income of their vast estates in the most vulgar enjoyment and debasing pleasures. The poor were despised, and when old age came they had only to die of want ; the widow and the orphan were left to shed their bitter tears in neglect and squalid misery. Among the Christians, on the contrary, morality was pure and virtue honored ; their repasts were temperate, no excesses or levity of speech ; the rich were neither proud nor ostentatious, but humane and charitable, and treated their slaves not only kindly but fraternally. They bestowed alms liberally as well as judiciously, so that bread and clothing were never wanting to their poor. Peace and harmony dwelt among them ; they seemed to have but one soul and one heart.

Julia's soul was too noble and honest not to remark this striking contrast. She felt herself drawn towards a religion that harmonized so thoroughly with her own intelligent mind and virtuous instincts. The more she reflected the more clearly she saw it. Nothing now remained but to brave public opinion and the fear of her husband's displeasure. But grace soon came to aid the accomplishment of the work begun by a slave.

Her daughter Vivia, then in her twentieth year, fell seriously ill. The devoted mother had now but one thought, that of watching over her beloved child and snatching her from the grasp of death. Her post was always by the sick-bed; but an angel in the shape of a young woman was her constant companion, watching and praying. This was Rufina, for she wished to share with the mother the cares and fatigues of Vivia's sick-room, as well as of the affections of her heart.

"How kind you are, Rufina dear!" was Julia's constant exclamation. "You were the only one that pitied my little Dinacle when a horrible cancer was slowly eating away his fair face and made it so loathsome that his own father could not bear to look on it. But you alone did not shun him; you vied with his mother in courage and care, and in washing his horrible sores, although you could not have the incentives which naturally support a mother's love; and here again your inexhaustible devotedness keeps you day and night by my child's bedside! Your generosity overcomes my heart. How can I ever repay you?"

"Good mistress, why recall my poor services to your lost child? I did but my duty, and have you not every right to my labor and assiduity? Had Heaven heard my prayers he had not died; but my poor prayers were not worthy to be heard. Your noble boy was taken from you, but he is waiting for his mother in a better world."

"That time has not drowned my sorrow you know full well, Rufina, for not a day passes that I do not weep for his loss. He was so young, so affectionate, and so beautifully fair before that mortal disease had disfigured him! What a brilliant future did I weave for him in my imagination, until death came and rudely dispelled my dreams! Cherished Dinacle! Of him nothing remains to me save the cold ashes that I so often water with my tears. I lost two others, but they died in infancy—like flowers in the bud; these I had scarcely seen; they knew not their mother, and they died, too, without suffering or pain. But not so my Dinacle; he both knew and loved me, and oh! he suffered so much before he died. Seek not to soothe my sorrow; let me weep without consolation and without hope."

"O dearest mistress! would that you had the Christians' faith! For them death is but the separation of a few days. Among us, when a mother loses her infant, she weeps, indeed, because she is a mother; but she is soon lifted up, and, with a heart full of hope and eyes fixed on heaven, exclaims: 'Dear babe, He who gave you to my love has recalled you to his own paternal bosom. Blessed be his name! I shall soon go to rejoin you, never more to be separated."

"But what assurance have you that such hope is not fallacious?"

"God's; for he is the sweet consoler of afflicted mothers."

"But Dinacle belonged not to your religion; he believed not in the God of the Christians."

"God has ways unknown to us; his mercy is infinite."

"Might this be true, Rufina? . . . Dinacle would not be wholly dead—would still live somewhere! But who would take care of him? Who would bind his sores and soothe his racking pains?"

"Your child suffers no longer; he has shuffled off the body, and with it all the sores that distressed you so much; he is now living a new life."

"Where is he, then?"

"In heaven—which belongs in an especial manner to little children, and whither both his little brothers have gone before him."

Rufina's eyes beamed with heavenly radiance and joy.

"In heaven! my beloved child in heaven!" cried the mother, as she instinctively sprang to her feet and clasped her hands.

"My dear brother Dinacle is in heaven!" murmured Vivia, whom they had thought asleep, but who had heard the whole conversation.

She stretched out her hand to the lowly slave, who grasped and covered it with affectionate and ardent kisses; for she, too, was overjoyed at having confessed the faith, at having conversed about God and heaven, and at having brought consolation to the heart of a disconsolate mother; she had noted, too, the tears of happiness glistening in the eyes of her young mistress. "O God of love!" said she in her heart, "perfect the work thou hast commenced; these are worthy of knowing and loving thee."

Meantime Vivia's malady grew daily more and more alarming, and science had exhausted all its efforts in vain. All hope was lost. Julia, a prey to the most agonizing grief, endeavored by every means in her power to stay the life slowly ebbing away. Rufina prayed: "Good and merciful Saviour, thou who hadst pity on, and gave back to, a weeping mother the son who was being carried to the grave, take compassion on my mistress; spare and preserve to her her dying child. Take my life instead; I offer it to thee with all my soul. Break not the heart of her who has been so kind to me; protect the life of her dear child, in order that they may unite with me in honoring and serving thee."

The angel of prayer bore to Christ's feet the humble and generous petition of the slave.

Death had not struck the final blow, but remained hovering, so to speak, over the young invalid, who continued to linger for days, speechless and unconscious. An occasional stir or a feeble sigh was the only indication that life was not entirely extinct.

On the evening of the fifteenth day, after having taken a potion administered by her mother, she fell back quietly on her bed and closed her eyes as if in quiet repose. Julia gazed long and silently upon her ; but, whether from excess of fatigue, or by the will of Providence, her head drooped, and then deep sleep fell upon her. " God be praised ! " said the attentive slave ; " this rest will be a precious boon to my poor mistress, and I can pray more at my leisure." Saying this, she sank on her knees at the foot of Julia's bed in such a position as to enable her to watch over both.

A subject so interesting and sad would afford material for a grand picture. On an ebony couch inlaid with ivory lay a maiden wan and pale ; her long tresses fell waving over a neck whose blue veins moved tremulously at every pulsation of the sleeper's heart. Her sharp but clear-cut features told, however, of long and severe suffering. Did not the movement of her breathing cause the rich coverlet to rise and fall gently, one would have thought that she had just died. By her side a woman, still in all the bloom of beauty, with a face stamped with an expression of grief

peculiar to, and experienced only by, mothers ; at
a little distance below a young woman clad in
the humble dress of a slave, her arms clasped in
fervent prayer, her eyes raised to heaven, her
countenance beaming with faith and love, while a
sweet and heavenly smile flitted on her lips.

But what neither the skill nor genius of the
artist could have reproduced was the mysterious
drama then taking place in the soul of the mother.   Julia meantime was profoundly buried in
sleep.   Suddenly, to the amazement of Rufina,
her head was lifted up as if looking at some object, and she seemed to be listening attentively to
a voice speaking to her.   Her animated countenance faithfully reflected the many and strong
emotions passing in her soul ; there was fear,
terror, and a sadness bordering on despair ; then
joy, admiration, hope, and gratitude.   At one
time she drew back her head and covered her face
with her hands as if in terror ; her respiration
grew labored and her countenance became fright-
fully distorted and pale ; then, as if freed from an
oppressive weight, she breathed more freely ; her
face grew cálm ; a smile played on her lips ; her
brow became radiant ; sweet tears coursed down
her cheeks ; while her hands, being alternately
lifted up and clasped on her bosom, left no room
for doubt that the impressions then received were
those of joy and gladness.

Without losing sight of her mistress for even
an instant, Rufina redoubled her fervor, under the

intuitive feeling that she was receiving a revelation from heaven. Drawing from her bosom a little wooden cross received from her dying mother and treasured with religious care, she pressed it to her lips, bathed it with her tears, begging of God the recovery of the dying girl and the conversion of her mother. Never had her heart uttered a more fervent, earnest prayer.

"Rufina, dear Rufina," suddenly cried Julia, bursting into tears and throwing herself into her arms, "*your God is mine*—I, too, am a Christian!"

"I have lived long enough, O my God! since my beloved mistress has come to the knowledge of thee."

" Rufina, dearly beloved sister, call me no longer by the name of mistress. It would be more fitting that I should call you so, because through you have I come to the knowledge of the true God, through you have I obtained the recovery of my child—for Vivia will live in order to become a Christian, like her mother and yourself."

" God alone gives light ; so, too, he alone brings back from the gates of death. To him, and to him alone, be all glory, benediction, and thanks!"

" What you say is right, Rufina: the light that enlightens the soul, as well as the impulse that moves the heart, comes from God ; who but he can wrest the victim from the jaws of death ! But it is to your exalted virtues and fervent prayers that I owe the twofold gift received from him."

"I have been told by the venerable apostle of my country that God does not regard the merit, but shows mercy to whom he pleases. Say not, therefore, that God has shown you mercy for my sake, who am a miserable sinner and the last of the Lord's servants. You have kept yourself pure in the very bosom of corruption; you have been kind and merciful to your slaves, charitable to the poor, the friends of God. He has witnessed and blessed your good works, and to-day he crowns your virtues and your charity."

"Seek not, dear Rufina, to impose on me by an excess of modesty. In my dream—but no, it was no dream, but something real and true, a voice from heaven—in that vision I saw you as clearly as I do now; and it was you that saved my beloved child from death; it was you, too, that asked and obtained for her mother the grace of becoming a Christian. But before I relate to you this vision, which I shall not forget as long as I live, permit me, Rufina, my sister, to kiss the little cross which I saw you draw from your bosom, and which you have put back, no doubt, as I see it no longer in your hands."

The slave could not refuse. The humble cross was presented to the noble patrician, who lovingly and respectfully pressed it to her lips.

"Now, then, my good Rufina, sit by me, give me your hand, and listen."

Not to disturb the peaceful slumber into which

the young invalid seemed to have fallen, she thus began in a low voice:

"After a long struggle sleep overcame me. Immediately a most appalling spectacle presented itself to me. I saw Vivia struggling in the throes of a mortal agony; she writhed her arms, her eyes, haggard and bloodshot, seemed to burst from their sockets, while she continually cried: 'Oh! to die so young. Oh! I cannot, I will not die.' As I bent over her bed, wet with perspiration, I tried to quiet her, but in vain. I clasped her to my bosom, and, in answer to her piercing cries, said: 'No, my dear child, you shall not die; the gods are not so unjust, so cruel as to take you away in the spring-time of life; and, merciless as the Fates are said to be, they will not cut the thread of your young days. Your mother's tears and your youth will move them to pity.'

"My eyes now fell on a hideous phantom that I had taken no notice of, but which, no doubt, had been the cause of my child's alarm. His giant form towered above the bed; his eyes flashed with fiendish satisfaction, like those of a tiger tearing his prey; sometimes he laughed aloud, as if in mockery of the tears and lamentations of his victim. Nigher and nigher came he, as his bony fingers prepared to clutch my child's heart. I rushed at him to keep him off. 'Who are you?' cried he in a terrible and hissing voice—'who are you to dare to cope with me? Read! my name is written on my forehead: *Death! Perdition!* Cease your feeble and useless efforts. Your daughter, the pride of your life, the idol of your heart, belongs to me. Only look and you will see the futility of your struggles; they cannot stay for a single instant her fall and my triumph.'

"I turned and saw an open grave; hard by a deep, black pit, whence rolled clouds of dense smoke mixed with lurid flames, that exhaled all around the most sickening stench and the stifling fumes of brimstone and pitch. Shapes the most hideous to the eye were busily at work casting into the pit thousands of victims, whose shrieks of despair and terror filled the air. I saw them falling, falling, dragged lower and lower. Their awful cries of despair rang in my ears more clearly and heartrending than ever went up from a crowd of slaves cast to the famished lions and leopards of the arena.

"I noted with astonishment that all these victims had also a name written on their foreheads in letters of fire: *Adulterer, murderer, miser, proud, glutton, infidel,* etc. Every one had at least one, but many had several. I strove to turn away my eyes from this frightful spectacle, but a power superior to mine prevented me. In my terror I endeavored to hide my face in my hands, but I could not move them; they hung as if palsied or chained to my side.

"Now a piercing shriek fell on my ear. I recognized Vivia's voice; the monster grasped my daughter's heart with his left hand, and with his right pointed to the grave and the yawning gulf. Other phantoms no less hideous crowded around bearing red-hot chains, which they began to wind all around her. At this juncture, Rufina, you appeared; the monster shuddered and trembled as if he acknowledged in you a power superior to his own; my daughter's heart being freed, she breathed more freely; the grave and the pit closed half way. You were quite calm, Rufina; with eyes raised to heaven you poured forth a flood of prayer irresistibly powerful, yet quite unintelligible to me. You had taken out the identical little cross which you just now gave me to kiss, and you held it over my daughter's head so that it seemed to touch it. All the monster's fury seemed as if it had been curbed by some powerful chain; some one seemed to strike down his arm every time he tried to reach my daughter's heart. He reminded me of a panther struggling at the bars of his cage to fly at his prey.

"Meanwhile the monster still remained and continued to hiss and struggle unceasingly. I am totally at a loss to explain what you did next, dear Rufina. Your face became dazzlingly brilliant, a ray of light shot from your fiery lips, and it appeared to me that drops of fresh blood oozed from your little cross and fell slowly on my forehead and on Vivia's. It was like a cooling balm, but infinitely more refreshing than anything I had ever felt before. Then a bright light shone in

the room and on the bed ; so soft and pure was it
that the light of day was only shadow and darkness in comparison. In this I saw a woman so
marvellously beautiful, so unearthly fair, that the
world never saw the like. She was clad in garments whiter than the untrodden snow. Instead
of a crown of jewels, such as queens wear, hers
was composed of stars more effulgent than the
brightest stars in the firmament. Her appearance was full of lofty dignity, while sweetness
beamed from her eyes and sat upon her lips.
Oh! how differently do men represent the false
divinities that I have heretofore worshipped in
my blindness. But this woman, Rufina, was all
heavenly ; her beauty was wholly divine, and so
dazzling that the brightness of the sun would
pale before it.

"She was surrounded by a troop of fair-haired
children, of whom I could only see the heads and
expanded wings, the rest being enveloped in
clouds. Innocence, happiness, and love beamed
in their faces ; their voices sounded like sweet
music and thrilled through every fibre of my
heart as they sung to this woman, if indeed she
may be called a woman : 'Hail, full of grace, the
Lord is with thee, the purest and most perfect of
creatures! Blessed art thou among women ;
and because thou wert worthy to bear in thy
womb the Word made flesh, all nations shall vie
in glorifying and proclaiming thee blessed.'

"She gazed on you, Rufina, with ineffable sweet

ness, as a fond mother does on a beloved child. You were speaking to her, doubtlessly, for your lips were constantly moving. 'Daughter,' said she to you, and the angels hushed their song, 'your humble prayer reached my throne in the highest heavens; I have presented it to the Lord, and he has granted your petition. The girl shall live because you have prayed for her; she shall live in order that she may become a Christian'. She will one day give glorious testimony to Christ, my Son; her name shall be great in heaven and on earth, and it shall be praised and honored to the end of the world.'

"Then, turning to me: 'My child,' said she, 'although very imperfect, your virtues and your abundant alms have not been forgotten by Him who knows and sees all things; he has had compassion on your lamentable blindness. For a long time this humble slave (pointing to you), who is far your superior in the eyes of heaven, has presented the most fervent supplications to the throne of grace that your eyes might be finally opened to the light. God in his goodness gives you back your child from the brink of the grave and of the gulf that you saw yawning at her feet. Believe; adore him who alone is worthy of adoration and love.' I then felt as if a hand was placed gently on my head. The vision had disappeared.

"How can I describe what I felt? A strange joy filled my soul; it seemed as if a new life and

a new heart had been given to me. Faith, like a
beam of sunlight, had shot into my soul. I believed; prostrate on the ground I adored the true
God, ignored by me so long; sister, I was at last
a Christian like yourself. It was at this point
that I returned to consciousness. But who can
this woman be whose incomparable beauty is sur-
passed by her still more wonderful sweetness?
Who are those children that sang with such ravishing melody? Can you tell me, Rufina?"

"Kind mistress, she whom you saw once dwelt
in an eastern country; she lived a lowly and sor-
row-laden life. She was the daughter of the ancient royal line of Juda, and her name was Mary.
When God decreed to save man by becoming man
himself, he chose her on account of her humility
and immaculate purity. Without any detriment
whatever to her spotless virginity she became
the Mother of Christ. She stood at the foot of
the cross, and his blood and tears flowed upon her
when he was dying for us. This disconsolate
Mother survived her Son's death for many years;
but now she is with him in heaven, crowned by
him with glory and power. But how shall I
make you understand all her goodness, tenderness, and love for men, whom she looks upon as
her children? No one could; still less, then, can
I, who am but a poor ignorant woman.

"Those whom you saw in your vision and
whom you imagined to be children are not such;
they are God's angels, the noblest and purest

of all his creatures. Created by his omnipotent voice, these blessed spirits see God face to face; they praise, adore, and bless him without ceasing, and never depart from before his throne save to bear his commands or to do his bidding. It is our belief that one of these angels is appointed to each of us in order to guide and protect us. Being a faithful friend, a devoted brother, a sure guide, we follow him cheerfully; being a powerful protector, we constantly call upon him in all our trials and difficulties."

The result of this wonderful series of events was that Julia, in spite of the prejudices of birth and education, courageously declared herself a Christian. In the Church of Carthage she was justly looked upon as one of its leading members, both by reason of her zeal for the faith and her great piety. Vivia, having been restored to health miraculously, soon followed her mother's example, and had her name enrolled on the list of catechumens. The poor slave from Gaul was set free. She made use of her liberty to consecrate herself by a solemn vow to the Spouse of virgins, without, however, quitting the noble lady who had become for her a friend, a companion, and a sister.

But it is high time to return to the young woman whom we left writhing under the grave and severe reprimands of Tertullian.

CHAPTER V.

THE STRUGGLE AND THE SACRIFICE.

AFTER the priest's abrupt departure Vivia remained for some time as unconscious as if she had been stricken by lightning. Her infant struggled in her arms apparently unheard and unheeded. With her glazed look, parted lips, and pallid countenance she bore a strong resemblance to one of the marble statues in her own *atrium*. The struggles and wailing of the child finally succeeded in arousing her. Having quieted the infant, she placed it in its cradle, where it soon fell into the quiet slumber of innocence. The mother threw herself wearily on a couch. Just then a slave entered the apartment to wait upon her mistress as usual.

"Thanks, Verecunda, for your attentiveness, but I wish to be alone," said the young patrician. "However, in case my mother or Rufina should come, you will admit them. With this exception I wish to see no one."

"Noble mistress, may I be permitted to ask if you have heard bad tidings from your valiant

the hands of the cruel Numidians and been carried in chains into their sandy deserts?"

"I have received no tidings from Jarbas for
nearly a month. Although I cannot but tremble
for the safety of a man of his courage and bra-
very, I hope, however, the Lord watches over him
and has saved him from the misfortunes which
you seem to dread."

"Why, then, do you refuse my customary services and shut yourself up in the solitude of your
apartments? If you feel unwell permit me to
watch by your side. Is not this the duty of a
faithful slave?"

"I fully appreciate your attachment, good
Verecunda. There is no cause for anxiety. I
simply desire to be alone, and nothing more."

"Oh! then, the stranger who has just gone
away was wanting in respect to the noble daughter of Hanno, and I am not surprised at it, for
the young companion who has been introduced to
you by him told me just now that she was afraid
of him, that he had a severe and scowling look,
and that his voice, although she heard it at a
great way off, had filled her with terror. It is
evident that this man has annoyed you, for you
are still very pale, and it is easy to see that you
have been weeping. However, you need only to
say one word, and if this bad man comes again
one of your brawniest slaves shall hurl him from
the door."

"You know not what you are talking about,

my poor Verecunda. Why do you listen to the foolish prattle of a silly girl who perhaps finds amusement in making fun of you? The man whom you accuse of insolence and wickedness, this *stranger* whom your imprudent zeal would spurn from the door, is as well known to you as he is to me; you have seen him frequently both here and in the assembly of the faithful. That was Tertullian, the glory of Carthage, the intrepid defender of our faith, the terror of pagans, whom he crushes by the thunders of his eloquence. But you have tarried too long already. I repeat, I wish to be alone; go then, Verecunda; in case I need your services I can easily call you hither."

The slave withdrew.

The feelings and heart of the young patrician had been so strained and wrung that the moment she found herself alone she burst into a violent fit of weeping; tears brought her relief and the power of calm reflection. She repeated mentally all the admonitions of Tertullian, whose every word was for her an oracle, so deep was her respect for that extraordinary man. His celebrated "Apology, or Defence for the Christians," had just been published; it had won and was then receiving the attention and admiration, nay enthusiasm, of the entire Church. Vivia had read this masterpiece of reasoning and eloquence, and looked upon *the priest of Carthage* as a man raised up by God and imbued with the spirit and power of Christ to vindicate his religion, to confound the so-called wisdom of the world and the detestable pride of the Roman emperors. She ran her eye over and examined one by one all the worldly vanities that surrounded her and on account of which he had so severely reprimanded her, and then it seemed to her as if the costly necklaces and golden bracelets burned her flesh, like red-hot iron. The evening breeze, too, seemed to rebuke her worldliness as it gently waved the rich drapery of her couch, while the blaze of numberless lamps was reflected everywhere from gold, ivory, jewels, and precious stones. Everything round about her, even the very cradle and her infant, seemed to recall and re-echo the stern reprimands of the priest. She felt like a criminal revisiting the scene of his crime, when in his trembling fear he imagines every one he meets to be an accuser or a witness, every sound to be a denunciation and a demand for justice.

Taken all in all, Vivia was really an excellent person; she had been formed in the school of her pious mother and the devout Rufina. From the time of her renunciation of paganism her faith had never wavered, although she had not given proof of much eagerness in preparing for and hastening the time of baptism. It must be said, however, that at the time of which we write many persons remained for years in the order of catechumens; also that the bishop was not very

urgent in the matter, as he feared they might
relapse into idolatry through temptation, family
influence, or evil habits not yet entirely overcome; nay, he profited by this delay in testing
their sincerity and giving them more ample instruction. In justice to Vivia it must be said
that there was some excuse for her neglect if we
consider the preparations necessary for her marriage, the festivities of the occasion, and the duties of her new position.

But now all her faith was aroused, and new
thoughts crowded tumultuously into her soul.
She had abjured paganism before God's altar;
had asked to be admitted among the followers of
Christ; the waters of regeneration were about to
cleanse her; and, in spite of all this, she had continued to lead a most worldly and unmortified
life. Her home and table were as lavishly furnished as any of the pagan aristocracy, and, as she
had been justly asked, what was there in her dress
and surroundings to distinguish her as a Christian? Did she not wear her hair as long and as
fashionably as if she were a pagan? Did she not
use the same essences and wear the same stuffs?
Did she not bedeck herself with the same brilliants,
display, and splendor? Was her retinue of slaves
less numerous, her chariot less burnished, and her
fiery steeds less richly caparisoned? She blushed
for shame at seeing herself so effeminate and
worldly while her heart and engagements bound
her to a religion which preaches simplicity, mo-

desty, and mortification! "What!" thought
she, "I believe in and adore a God born in a
lowly stable, in poverty and obscurity, a God
whose hands knew the fatigue of constant and
rugged toil, and who had not where to lay his
wearied head, while I do not scruple to live in
ease, to deny nothing to my tastes and caprices,
and occupy myself only in what amuses or, at
best, only prevents indolence from being irksome.

"Christ fasted in a desert; his life was one of
penance and retirement. He shed tears often,
and although his ineffable sweetness may have
sometimes wreathed his lips into a kindly smile,
it must have been seldom, so great was the bitterness of his soul! He willingly delivered his
body to suffer for me! His limbs were torn
by the scourge, his head crowned with thorns,
and a hard cross his bed of death! And I—my
life is spent in ease and enjoyment! No expense
is spared in providing my table with the most exquisite food! A diadem crowns my brow, I live
amid perfumes and bathe in aromatic waters, and
when night falls I repose on soft down encano-
pied in silken curtains! Oh!" said she, striking
her breast, "how long shall my heart be heavy?
How long shall I have the name of a Christian
and the habits of a pagan? How long shall I
love vanity and lies? Because gold and silver
shine in my dress, because I sparkle with diamonds, because people look at, admire, and praise

me, is my soul on that account less poor, less
miserable, less naked in the eyes of him who cannot be deceived by vain appearances?   What
shall I answer him one day when thousands
whom I might have relieved will accuse me before his tribunal of having left them to die of
hunger and want?"

Thus did faith and grace goad this heart so
laboriously won to God by the prayers and self-
sacrifice of a poor slave.   But the rival of the Almighty was not wanting even here with his lies
and deceitful arguments; before Vivia had time
to form a final and firm resolution he gently
prompted the thought:

"But what reason can there be to make this
change so suddenly? Such a course could not fail
to excite public remark.   What would people
say of the noble Lady Vivia were she to follow a
manner of life so little in keeping with her birth
and rank?   Hanno loved to see his daughter admired, and would he be indifferent, or rather
would he not be filled with indignation and
anger? What would the proud Jarbas say when
he should return crowned with laurel and find
his wife living on scanty fare, clad like a woman
of humble rank, and would look in vain for the
richly-robed and bejewelled form that he loved?
True, hitherto he seemed to be inclined towards
the new religion; still, he had neither said nor did
anything definite.   Might it not be possible for
him to grow zealous for the old religion, and, in

this supposition, might he not force her to an apostasy which would disgrace her for ever among the Christians; or, in case of resistance, might he not ignominiously repudiate, cast her forth from his house, and deprive her of her darling infant? The laws gave him the right of doing all this, and, even if they did not, had he not sufficient influence in the city to be able to act as he pleased with impunity?

"At any rate, she had not yet been baptized, and she could wait until she had been before making up her mind and coming to a final resolution. It would be the height of imprudence to advance only to recede again; such a course would only give scandal to the Christians and a triumph to their enemies. After all, had not the priest been actuated by and spoken under the impulse of mistaken zeal? No doubt he was a man of learning and merit, but he was quick, choleric, and as unsparing to others as to himself. Perhaps, with too much confidence in overweening knowledge and virtue, he delights to bend others to his own ideas and to lord it over their minds and hearts. Without pushing the sacrifice too far, might she not do just as well by retrenching gradually in the matter of dress, yielding a little less to vanity and ease, and assisting a few poor families? God could not require more from a young woman of her rank and position."

Alas! such is the sad condition of our fallen nature. We know what is good, pure, holy;

we admire and love it ; our hearts have still aspirations for virtue. Like the wounded bird that
would fain soar to the clouds as of yore, but soon
falls exhausted to the ground, we too experience
moments of fervor and lofty aims, our strength
fails, and we stop short at the beginning of the
race that a moment before we were so anxious
to run. After having been held in check for a
little while our nature reasserts itself very quickly, and the recoil only gives it more nerve and
stubbornness ; the struggle is fierce, and one in
which the inner man is frequently worsted and
overcome.

Vivia was undecided, her heart was fluctuating
between two conflicting resolutions. She had
not followed the dictates of grace ; on the contrary, she had imprudently listened to all the
suggestions mentioned above, so that the good
impulses first received had vanished, and left her
reduced to such a state of apathy that she offered
but very feeble resistance to the suggestions of
her heart and enemy. God took compassion on
her, for when she was, perhaps, on the point of
yielding, Rufina's hand gently lifted the curtain
that hung across the entrance to the apartment.
She had been informed by the young slave that
Vivia had given orders that there should be no
intrusion on her privacy, and had felt some alarm
in consequence.

"Pardon me, dear Vivia," said she as she
kissed her forehead—"pardon me if I intrude on

your retirement; but, in spite of Verecunda's assurance to the contrary, I felt apprehensive on the score of your health, and am come to offer you my feeble services and best endeavors."

"God be thanked, my dear Rufina, your fears are entirely groundless. Had I been indisposed I would have sent for you without delay. Can I ever forget all your kindness and care when it had pleased God to afflict me with suffering? Somehow this evening I felt a desire for silence and privacy. You are aware . . ."

"May God preserve me from imprudence, dear Vivia! I respect the secrets of your heart, and have no desire to pry into them; but you look paler than usual, and your eyes still bear the traces of recent tears. Dear lady, something distresses you. I shall go and and pray that God may console you in your sorrows."

She turned to leave the room.

"Stay by me, good Rufina," exclaimed Vivia; "do not leave me when I stand in especial need of your kindness. It was God that sent you to me. Can I hide anything from you? Have I not given you my heart to read for years and years past? Ah! why pain me by questioning my confidence in you?"

"Dear Vivia, I have never wilfully given you the slightest pain, you have been always so good to me! But there are sorrows that compel secrecy and which may be told to God alone. In this world of exile, alas! where is the heart that

has not been sometimes broken by some weighty
sorrow, too deep for human utterance or consolation ?"

"Dear and kind friend, I am in great distress
indeed, but my distress is not what you imagine,
nor like anything in my past experience ; hitherto
God in his mercy has always tempered and pro
portioned my trouble to my weakness. A terrible struggle has been going on within me, and I
known not how it will end. I would like to be able
to make the sacrifice generously ; I feel that God
demands it, and that my mind would then be
easier and more at rest ; but my nature rebels and
resists, and you know but too well how weak I am
in such a struggle. Do help me, then, Rufina,
and pity the young neophyte whom your prayers
saved from death and perdition."

"God alone, dear friend, can give you the
victory in this struggle, whatever it may be ;
man's voice is but a hollow and impotent echo.
Can the reed resist the storm by leaning on another reed, or is the blind man's foot more steady
because another blind man leads him ? Place
your trust in God, from whom is all our strength.
He requires not what is impossible, and his
fatherly kindness always tempers the wind to
the shorn lamb. By his assistance you conquered
Satan and burst the chains of a long slavery.
Victory is assured to you in virtue of the name
and omnipotence of Jesus Christ."

"How happy you are, Rufina, to have known

and loved from childhood this holy religion that
demands so much courage and virtue! How
often since my conversion have I envied you
this happiness! Why was I called so late?
Why was I born to a lofty station and to a name
made illustrious by generations?"

"I am at a loss to understand you, dear Vivia.
If your call was a little later than mine, is that a
proof that God was less good and merciful to you?
Is the sheep that he has gone in search of
into the wilderness and has brought back on his
own shoulders less an object of his love and care
than the one that was born in the fold and never
left it? If he has bestowed on you an illustrious
name and birth, remember that it is in your power to increase their lustre, and that your example
and courage must necessarily have great influence
on the multitude. Who knows what incalcula-
ble good you may be destined to do the Church
of Jesus Christ, now so humble and despised?"

"What my future may be, I know not. But
I have many reasons to fear it will be neither so
holy nor so useful as your charity for me would
fain make you believe; but to come to the point,
let me explain to you the gist of my difficulty
and trouble. Well then, dear Rufina, you must
know that Tertullian has been here and has most
severely reprimanded me for the way I live,
which, he says, is wholly unbecoming in a Christian woman. Oh! had you but heard him! How
severe his words! How miserable I felt in his

presence! How he wounded me to the soul, especially when he turned to go and said that I was breaking my dear mother's heart and scandalizing all the Christians in Carthage! Is it possible that I have been so wicked?"

"It is not for me to judge you, dear Vivia. Being only an insignificant member of the flock, I have learned from my childhood to listen, to obey, not to argue. For me the priest's voice is sacred, his word that of God himself."

"But to renounce and sacrifice the dress and ornaments that become me so well, and which, after all, are nothing but what suits my age and rank!"

"Are not modesty and simplicity a thousand times more precious ornaments to the Christian woman than those that fade with time and can be bought with gold? One of our apostles forbids the use of these vain ornaments to the servants of Christ; would this man, inspired by God himself, have laid down this prohibition had the subject of dress been a matter of indifference?"

"But, my dear Rufina, when I examine my own heart I can find nothing to accuse myself of on this score. It seems to me that I love with my whole heart the God whom you taught me to know, and that I regard it as the greatest misfortune to displease or offend him. Oh! say, I beseech you, that I am not a castaway."

"Entertain not such a horrible thought; it would be an outrage on God's love. No, he has not cast you off, and the sacrifice which he now demands at your hands is but a new proof of his goodness to you; he wishes you to be all his. Oh! how difficult it is to reconcile the perfect love required by him with attachment to the things and vanities of the world! Let us not deceive ourselves, dear Vivia, nor lightly imagine that we are all innocence. Our heart is a deep and dark abyss into which we cannot peer very far; but God's eye fathoms it to its lowest depths, and there detects, perhaps, many blemishes which escape our feeble glance. Before that thrice holy God *no man knows whether he be worthy of love or hatred.*"

" How say you, dear Rufina? You who have been so invariably kind, you who have loved me always like a mother, you now clothe yourself with severity, and your words are almost as harsh as Tertullian's. You decide against me without mercy; you require of me your own exalted standard of virtue and perfection, and that is too great for my strength. O Rufina! you love me no longer."

And the young patrician burst into tears and cast herself into the arms of the pious freedwoman.

" God is my witness that I love you more than myself, and that, had I the power, I would gladly die a thousand deaths for your sake; do me not, therefore, the injustice of questioning my affection for you. You have condescended to permit

me to regard and love you as a child; it was in
virtue of this sacred title that I always gave you
advice whenever you required it. Vivia, your
faith is strong, your virtue beyond the possibility
of a doubt; but you are young, accustomed to
ease, to flattery, and utterly inexperienced in the
painful trials of life, and hence you have never
yet learned to what sublime abnegation and heroic
sacrifices must the soul aspire that has been once
enlightened by God and called to practise the
lofty maxims of the Gospel. Vivia, hearken no
longer to the voice of nature and conquer your
own heart; this is a triumph worthy the daughter of the model Christian mother, Julia!"

"But what will the world say, Rufina? I shall
be accused of folly. . . ."

"*The wisdom of the world is but foolishness.*
The Christian is not the slave of the world, nor
does he accept it as his judge; he bows only to
the judgment of God alone. Remember, Vivia,
that *you are one day to give glorious testimony
to Jesus Christ, and that your name is to be for
ever great in his Church.* Your destiny is exalted indeed, and one that I should be tempted to
envy were I not the lowest of the Lord's servants."

"O Rufina! it shall never be said that Vivia
was so fickle and ungrateful as to thwart the glorious destiny marked out for her by Providence.
How or in what way I am to bear testimony to
Christ my Saviour I know not, but, at all events,

I am ready and willing to do so, even if it be required of me to write it in my blood. O Rufina! my generous friend, my second mother, to whom I owe more than life, to-day you give birth anew to your loved Vivia; through you God will triumph in my heart. Will he forgive my long resistance to his graces?"

" Fear not, Vivia; God's love is infinitely merciful. Obedience and sacrifice will ensure pardon. Let us unite in thanking God for his goodness; let us praise him with all the angels and saints."

Vivia fell on her knees, and with tears and prayers asked God's pardon for the past, promising at the same time that in future her life should be one of mortification and retirement. The pious Rufina knelt and prayed by her side; she seemed like an angel uniting her pure and unsullied accents to the ever imperfect prayers of a child of Adam.

Both remained long on their knees communing with God, for they both felt very happy—the one for having found courage and strength to make the sacrifice, the other for having at last found her beloved child in God entirely submissive to the yoke of Jesus Christ. As it was now high time to retire for the night, the two separated after having tenderly embraced each other. Vivia had formed a grand and heroic resolution such as faith alone can inspire. The angels could now weave her crown of martyrdom.

CHAPTER VI.

THE PLOT.

A FEW days after the events above narrated two men met at the distance of only a few paces from Vivia's mansion. They were busily engaged in planning a wicked scheme that would one day culminate in the most disastrous results.

It has been already stated that Tertullian, upon leaving Vivia, had met the high-priest of Carthage issuing from the temple. The sight had fired the ardent soul of the great Apologist, and had made him cast a look of indignation and contempt on the miserable pontiff of paganism. Olympianus (for such was the high-priest's name) hated the Christians, as a matter of course, and Tertullian's contemptuous look wounded him to the quick; but in dealing with a man of Tertullian's fame the pontiff readily understood that prudence and caution were necessary. His ulcerated heart cried for deep revenge, but for a revenge that, while it would be sure, would entail no evil on himself. Being as cowardly as he was rancorous, he had resolved to bide his time and watch his opportunity. Meanwhile he consoled himself with the thought that, sooner or later, said opportunity would certainly present itself.

Already Christianity had made rapid progress in spite of all the opposition of human wisdom, and, what was worse still, of the profound and universal corruption of morals. Even where it had suffered most it had succeeded in tiring out the violence of its enemies. The blood of the martyrs was the seed that invariably brought forth a new crop of Christians. Like a young oak on a mountain-top, which, while it bends to the storm and seems doomed to destruction, only strikes its roots broader and deeper into the rocky soil ; its trunk grows higher and higher, until at last its lofty head woos a calmer air above the clouds, and seems to look down upon and laugh at the storm; thus, too, had Christianity grown and spread in spite of all obstacles ; it had invaded the village, the city, the camp, the tribunal, the senate, and the very palace of the Cæsars. The old paganism, as a system of worship, had grown effete and was living out its slow agony in temples now almost empty, and at the feet of abandoned and despised idols. To give it a semblance of activity and life it became necessary to employ all the excitement of the savage games of the amphitheatre, the combats of wild beasts, the feast of martyrs' blood flooding

Carthage, like Rome and Athens, had her apostles at a very early day. A few slaves and poor people formed its first Christian congregation. But soon some noble and wealthy families embraced the new doctrines, and every day served to swell the number of Christ's flock. Not only in the city but in all the neighboring provinces churches were founded and committed to the care of saintly bishops. The Church of Carthage grew apace and soon became a metropolitan see. After the lapse of one century its primate presided at a provincial council which was composed of no less than three hundred of his suffragan bishops.

Being so far from Rome, and separated from the West by the sea, Carthage had never engrafted on her civilization their ideas, manners, and customs, and hence she had not hitherto followed their example by persecuting the Christians. If we except an occasional cry raised against them in the temples at the instigation of the priests, or a passing slur flung at them, as a mere matter of form, in the senate, nothing was done against the Christians or their assemblies. Their places of meeting were well known, and the worshippers took little or no precautions to avoid notice.. But a slighted passion and wounded pride were destined to disturb this long peace very soon.

At this time there lived in Carthage a wealthy and influential young man named Jubal. He was tall, handsome, and well educated, but hot-

headed, impatient, and irascible. At an early
date he had flung himself headlong into the vor-
tex of pleasure; at twenty-five he seemed to have
drained to its dregs the cup of criminal indulgence; ho feared neither the gods nor men; he
ridiculed the first and haughtily scorned the second. Hence he spurned all restraint, and opposition to his lawless desires only aroused his angry
passions—nay, he sometimes made use of the dagger of a slave to make away with those who incurred his resentment or thwarted his designs.

An acquaintance, based rather on courtesy than
friendship, had long existed between his father
and Vivia's. They both loved good cheer, and
indulged in it as the enjoyment most suitable and
befitting to their station and years. As they
spent much time at the table and occasionally in-
vited thereto some younger men, Jubal had sometimes sat at Hanno's board, and in this way had
chanced to see Vivia before she was married.

He had not been insensible to the charms of
the patrician maiden; her beauty, set off as it
was by costly garments, her ready wit and conver-
sational powers, had made a deep impression on
his heart. One day, as he chanced to sit by her at
table, he felt emboldened in his conceitedness to
whisper to her some words borrowed from the repertory of phrases which young libertines have
always ready on their lips. Vivia, aglow with
indignation and modesty, courageously resented
the insult, and, casting a withering glance of cou-

tempt at him, " *The dove's place,*" said she, rising
"*is not near the hawk!*" She then took a seat
by her mother.

Shame and rage choked the voice of the imper-
tinent Jubal. In spite of all his pride and ef-
frontery he could not articulate a single word.
He grew pale with anger for an instant and bent
a satanic look upon Vivia. Those who noticed
him expected one of his usual outbursts of passion when angered, but, to their surprise, he
simply slunk away, muttering to himself as he
went. Vivia trembled, and, for the first time in
her life, she felt afraid of the young libertine, on
whom hitherto she had never bestowed a thought
save one of contempt.

Jubal retired with vengeance in his heart ; the
words of the young patrician were ringing continually in his ears ; the noble pride of her glance,
the mortal affront received, the mocking smiles
with which his humiliation had been welcomed,
were like so many fiery arrows in his vitals. In
vain did he seek to divert his thoughts by a long
walk along the beach, and forgetfulness in the fa-
cile pleasures of his rank—nothing could lay the
demon in his breast, and the image of the haughty
Vivia haunted him everywhere. The darkness
and quiet of the night were powerless to calm
his feverish agitation; even during his short
snatches of heavy and troubled slumber he invariably imagined he heard the hated words,
" *The dove's place is not near the hawk !*"

A hundred times had he thought of summoning nis faithful *Bravo* to revenge him ; but Vivia belonged to an influential family that would not allow such an outrage to go unpunished. He alone would be suspected of guiding the assassin's hand, and would inevitably be brought before the criminal judge; this judge was a near kinsman to Hanno, and consequently would be interested in his condemnation and punishment. The slave was certainly devoted to him, but, in case of arrest for the assassination, he might lose courage when put to the torture and divulge the name of him who had given the poignard and designated the heart in which he was to bury it. The proud young man was afraid of death, and so had to devise other means of revenge.

There are men who will stoop to anything to attain their object. Devoid of principle and honor, and loving nothing in the world save themselves, they refuse to employ nothing that may procure them success in satisfying the cravings of their passions. Jubal was one of these. His wounded pride required either Vivia's dishonor or her blood in revenge for the insult done him. To compass this, the villain disguised his hatred, played the role of convert to morality, and became the constant eulogist of Vivia's virtue and purity. Feigning great attachment to and respect for her, as well as sincere regret for having unwittingly offended her, he had sent a friend of both families to demand her hand in marriage. In case of compliance he had resolved to rid himself of her by poison, and thus his vengeance would be satisfied while her fortune would serve to procure him every luxury and pleasure. But Vivia not only rejected his suit with disgust, but had succeeded in having him refused access to the house.

Such was the man whom the high-priest of Carthage had now sought. He was well aware of Jubal's hatred to Vivia, and so persuaded himself that he had but to encourage the young man's evil propensities to make him a ready and willing tool. Olympianus was too cunning and guarded to betray aught of his private resentment to Tertullian; Jubal would only have laughed at him. His plan was to fan Jubal's hatred against his haughty enemy to induce him to denounce and arraign her before the governor as amenable to the law by professing a proscribed religion, and in this way to give the signal for a persecution. Were this once set on foot he had every hope that, as the victims would be many, Tertullian's blood would avenge his own slighted and wounded feelings.

"Jubal," said the high-priest, "you are aware that the ancient religion of our forefathers is falling into disrepute; the tutelary gods of Carthage, that bestowed on us so much glory, influence, and wealth, are being shamefully neglected; solitude and silence begin to reign in their temples, while little more than the sacrifice of a few victims on great days is now seen there."

"Is it only to listen to your ridiculous lamentations," replied the choleric Jubal, "that you have brought me hither? What do I care about your religion? If your gods grow decrepit, is it my business to make them young again? If they cannot help themselves you ought to acknowledge rather that they are very contemptible gods and deserve richly the disgrace and contempt into which you say they are fallen. Let me tell you that I regard your Jupiter, your Apollo, and the rest of them, as mere men who died long ago, and I care no more about them than I would for the carcass of the vilest slave. The only god I want is pleasure; why should we set up others through ignorance, superstition and fear?"

"Jubal, I know that your notions regarding the gods are shared in by many; philosophers and sages have thought as you do, and, to be candid, I must confess that many of our own priests privately scoff at our creed, and that it is only their personal interests that induce them to retain their lucrative offices. I myself would be willing enough to let our *immortal* gods die; but what I cannot bear and what must shock even yourself, is that a new religion, coined by an obscure Jew who was ignominiously put to death for his crimes, aims at lording it over the entire world, and marches so arrogantly and de-

fiantly to enjoy the triumph that it so confidently
promises to itself.   Jubal, this religion is spreading from day to day; it has already wriggled
itself into some of the first families in the city,
and your mother, it is said . . .

"Yes, my mother, like a great many other
ladies, belongs to the new sect and makes no
secret about it.   I will tell you, furthermore,
that she would like very much to make me join
it, under the pretext of reforming my morals,
which she is pleased to think a little too lax.
Poor woman! it is only what may be expected,
for she has long since forgotten that she was
once young herself; at her time of life pleasure
is out of season, and so she has become smitten
by an insane love for this new religion; she has
exchanged one superstition for another, that is
all.   Let us hear your business; I have no time
to lose and am on my way to a jovial party.
What are you driving at, and why do you bother
me with such nonsense?"

"That is the way with all you young men;
ye are so full of fire, impatience, and restless-
ness, that ye want old men to be in just as much
of a hurry as yourselves.   Go, then, Jubal, rush
away to your boon companions, they are waiting for you very impatiently no doubt; you are
the leader, the master of all their feasts. . . . My
object was to talk to you about Vivia, that
haughty patrician that scorned your proposal and
thus deliberately added another insult to the old

one. . . . But I must not detain you, as you are in such a hurry to attend to far pleasanter business."

At the name of Vivia Jubal sprang from his seat like a tiger when he sees his prey; his breast heaved with a flood of hatred and revenge.

" Vivia!" he hoarsely cried, " Vivia! that hated name fills me with rage and opens a wound so deep that two years have not been able to heal it. Why do you speak of Vivia? What have you to say to me about her?"

" That, like your mother, she is a Christian."

" Her contempt and coyness made me suspect it. I recognize in this that hypocritical sect that pretends to despise all pleasure and to practise such absurd self-denial. Well, I ask once more what do you want?"

" Jubal, can you not understand? Meantime you burn for revenge, and the bare mention of her made you tremble with rage only a moment ago. If you hate her so deeply, if you wish to be revenged on her, what stops you? She is a Christian, I repeat; denounce her to the governor and demand the enforcement of the law."

" Do you imagine the governor is not aware that there are Christians in Carthage? He knows it just as well as you and I. But as they pay their taxes and appear to respect his authority he lets them alone, and, after all, he is right. In my opinion the Christians have as much right to adore their crucified God as you and your fel-

lows have to adore the gods of your Olympus.
Simple old man, you talk to me about revenge
and you have nothing better to suggest than a
ridiculous and clumsy plan ! Never mind, Jubal
has struck on something better; he does not
wish to share with any man the satisfaction of
punishing Vivia's insolence and contempt."

"Then why have you waited so long ? Confiding
in the influence of her family and the protection
of a husband for whom she jilted you, she quietly
laughs at your impotent and wordy anger as if
you were nothing more than the meanest slave in
the city."

The crafty old man here paused to see what
effect his words would produce on the young
nobleman. Jubal's face flushed scarlet; the
blow had told home.

"She defies me !" cried he after a pause; "she
dares me ! she trusts for protection to her name,
to the reputation of the soldier-husband of whom
she is proud to be the wife ! Well, then, I swear
that, before many days, there will be blood spilled
in that *powerful* family, even if I have to pay for
that blood with my head."

"Be avenged, Jubal, it is your duty and your
right; but you need not pay such a price for even
so sweet a revenge. Let me give you a friendly
and prudent advice. It has been currently reported that Vivia's husband permitted himself to
be cajoled by the honeyed talk of a certain Tertullian, who is a priest and the oracle of his ac-

cursed sect. I know to a certainty that previous to his departure for the army he had many private interviews with him, and had a decided leaning toward the new religion. Since then I have been assured that he made no secret of it in camp, and that our soldiers are equally outspoken in their dissatisfaction. This has caused much discontent and bickering, and hence it would be very easy to direct the minds of the soldiers to a solution of all these difficulties; and when Vivia would be a widow . . ."

" It would be easier to stab her !"

" Jubal, passion is blind in a young and fiery bosom like yours. I repeat, be revenged, but do not needlessly expose yourself to danger. When Vivia shall be a widow, go to her boldly and ask once more for her hand. If she repeats her haughty refusal, then lose no time; denounce her as a Christian in the presence of the governor and the senate. If necessary I can hound on some of the mob to shout as they do in Rome—*The Christians to the lions!* Then you have only to sit in the amphitheatre and glut your eyes and your vengeance in the streaming blood of your proud enemy."

Had the young nobleman been able to see the heart and the motives that actuated the pagan priest in fomenting his anger and thirst for revenge, that his object was Tertullian's, not Vivia's, destruction, he would have spurned both him and his suggestions. But he was duped into

the belief that the hoary old reprobate was simply
aiding him to be revenged on the woman he detested; the thought of gloating over her agonies
and blood in a public amphitheatre so over-
powered him with anticipated pleasure that it
made him deaf and blind to every other consideration.

"Well, then, all I ask is that I shall be able to
say that it was I that compassed her death and destruction. This is my claim and my revenge; I
shall be satisfied when I shall behold the lions tearing her limb from limb. Yes, Vivia dared to insult and defy Jubal; let her then prepare her
tears, and when the dagger shall have pierced the
heart of my successful rival, then will the *hawk*
attack the *dove*, and her mournful complaints
shall not save her from his sharp talons."

The two wretches had arrived at a mutual understanding; they could now go their ways. The
old priest sought repose. In his imagination he
already saw Tertullian in chains on the rack;
he heard the death sentence, and his ulcerated
heart swelled at the thought. Jubal sought his
usual company, where he was received with boisterous chidings and welcomes. He drank deeply
as usual, but, to their great surprise and contrary
to his habit, he withdrew before midnight and
long before the debauch was over. Their surprise and commentaries were not ended before
Jubal had found and accosted his slave.

"Afer, your master seeks to be revenged."

"When did your faithful slave ever refuse you?"

"I can rely on you, I know, when I pay you well; men like you regulate their actions according to their interests; your services when wanted must be bought with gold."

"A poor slave like me is not personally interested in the quarrels of his master. If, then, he exposes himself to danger in his cause is it not right that he should be paid? Do you reckon as nothing the violence he must needs do to himself in order to shed the blood of a man or woman that never did him any harm? A few days ago, for instance, when you ordered me to stab that young Christian slave who was foolish enough to refuse the honor proffered her by you, when I found her only a weak, poor thing the dagger shook in my hand; and when I heard her dying words: *Unhappy man, what have I done to you?* a strange shudder ran through me, and as I fled I said to myself: *Afer, you are following a bad trade!*"

"A truce to your hypocrisy, you old rascal!" said Jubal with a sneer; "your soul is as black as your hide, and your heart, if you have one, is as cold and as unfeeling as the steel of your dagger. For a handful of gold or your freedom you would murder your own master. Gold then you shall have more than ever before, and if your hand does its work well this time I will set you free in due and legal form."

"Gold! gold! O master, how beautiful is gold, how it gladdens the heart! But liberty! that is worth all the gold on earth. Then could I see once more my native woods and flowing streams; the air and broad plains of my youth would restore vigor to my limbs and elasticity to my sinews. I would again pursue the fleet gazelle and would once more encounter the desert lion! Haste, master, to make known your wishes; name your victim that I may run to strike the blow and rush back to gain gold and liberty."

"You shall have both, Afer, provided your dagger does not miss the heart you are to strike. But you must remember that this time your business is not with a coy maiden or an old slave guarding her mistress; it is with a sturdy soldier, the general of our troops in Numidia, the husband of Vivia. His guards love and are devoted to him. Yet there are fault-finders and grumblers in his camp; he is strongly suspected of a leaning towards the new sect, called Christians, and our old veterans are indignant at it. Chime in with the malcontents; you are full of cunning, as I am well aware, and you will require it all to ensure the success of our project. Be deliberate in your haste, mature well your plans; for if you make the slightest mistake, a single word or sign from Jarbas would be enough to send you to your fathers, if indeed your fathers have a place in the land of ghosts. Have a care not to divulge the fact that you belong to me; you might

be suspected and the torture might wrench from
you your secret. Assume whatever name you
think best and explain your motive for visiting
the army in such a way as to preclude inquisitive
curiosity. It will take you three or four days to
get there; so you will have plenty time to think
over and arrange your plans on your journey.
Let me charge you once more to be cautious; do
not strike until you find your man alone and
asleep, then strike so quickly and aim so straight
that he will not be able to have time to utter
even a cry. You understand me, Afer? Go,
and do not wait for daylight, so that you may leave
the city unnoticed. Here is gold for you, and remember that when you will be able to say to me
on your return : *My dagger found your enemy's
heart,* I will give you twenty times as much as
this contains.

He handed his purse to the slave, who grasped
it greedily and soon transferred it to his belt.

"Generous master," said he, "the noble Vivia
may prepare her mourning weeds and choose another husband if she will. Before the moon shall
have finished her monthly course Afer will have
avenged the powerful Jubal, and will be back to
demand the reward of his fidelity and services."

The city was still buried in darkness and her
inhabitants in slumber when the slave set forth
and sped along the road on his way to the camp.

CHAPTER VII.

BISHOP NARCISSUS.

WHILE these plots were being hatched in silence the Church of Carthage, suspecting no danger, had abandoned itself to great rejoicing. From all parts of the city the Christians flocked to a grand gathering of the faithful. This was to be held in a spacious villa near the mouth of the harbor, the property of a wealthy widow, a near kinswoman of the bishop. It was beautifully situated; on the land side it was sheltered by dense woods, while seaward it commanded a magnificent view of the water, which rolled and rippled up to kiss the sward and the feet of the beholder. As the crowd was too large to find room in any one room of the house, it was thought expedient to erect an altar at the end of a long alley overshadowed by trees just then bursting into leaf. To the right and left of the altar, and slightly raised above the place set apart for the clergy, there were two covered seats; from this it was evident that some foreign bishop was on a visit to the primate of the metropolis.

The prayers preparatory to the Holy Sacrifice were recited in the deepest recollection. Thanks were given to God for the prolonged peace vouchsafed to the Church of Africa, for the steady and rapid increase of the faith; a memento was made for all the churches, but more especially for those suffering persecution, where the martyrs needed strength and confessors patience to bear the weight of their chains, the pains of exile, and the toil of the mines. Petitions were offered for the pagans, that their eyes might be opened to the light, and they be brought to the fold of Christ; that the emperors, while they triumphed over the enemies of the empire, might themselves be conquered to the cross and cease from their futile efforts of two centuries to overthrow it. Upon the recommendation of their respective pastors many were formally admitted to the class of catechumens, to be prepared by instruction and retreat for the grace of baptism. It was now the hour for the celebration of the sacred mysteries.

First came the aged Optatus, Bishop of Carthage; he was followed by a venerable prelate, who, in spite of his hundred years, walked steadily and erect, bearing a pastoral staff, symbol of his authority and office. Despite his advanced age he ascended the steps to the altar with a firm tread and began the Holy Sacrifice. Faith and piety were written in every feature of his mild and noble countenance, while his deep humility and ardent charity made the tears swell up from his great heart and trickle on his silvery beard. Was it an illusion ! or did God wish to make a public manifestation of his servant's holiness ? Be this as it may, certain it is that many of the assistants affirmed that at the moment when, with hands trembling with reverential fear, he raised the consecrated host, a snow-white dove hovered around his head and girded it with a shining glory. The catechumens having retired as usual before the canon of the Mass, all the faithful received the Eucharistic Sacrament according to the rule then followed ; after this a hymn of thanksgiving recited in common terminated the service.

But who was this venerable bishop, whom no one could recollect to have ever before seen in Carthage ? Whence came he ? What could be the object of his visit ? The *pallium* worn by him at the Holy Sacrifice showed that he held a high position in the hierarchy of the Church, and yet when he had put off his vestments he appeared in the plain and humble garb of a hermit. Respect for the sacred mysteries had hitherto restrained curiosity, still every one waited impatiently for the moment when he would address them some words of greeting and blessing. But as the old man's modesty probably allowed him to say but little of himself, and as we are not equally as anxious as he was to hide his great virtues, we will endeavor to make him known to the reader.

He was called Narcissus, and was born in the first century of the Church. He might have,

and perhaps had, heard the voice of the Prophet
of Patmos; he had conversed with the immediate successors of the apostles, such as St. Clement,
St. Polycarp, and St. Ignatius of Antioch; he
had frequently consoled St. Pothinus of Lyons in
his prison, and had been an eye-witness of his
martyrdom.   Narcissus was now in his one hundred and twelfth year.   Having been born of
Christian parents and trained to the love of virtue, he became an orphan at an early age.   He
made use of his liberty in visiting the most
celebrated churches of his day and in studying
the doctrines of Christianity in the schools of the
apostolic men who, happily, still lived and shone
like beacon-lights in the Church of Jesus Christ.
In this way he amassed an immense fund of
ecclesiastical lore.   Unfortunately for posterity,
he left no writings, at least none have come
down to our times.

Nature had not been sparing of her gifts to
him.   He was tall, his features regular and manly; his broad and high forehead would have given
him an air of haughtiness had it not been toned
by the mildness of his glance and smiling lips;
his countenance was frank and open, like that of
a man who has nothing to hide or disguise; his
voice was clear and ringing, and his affability and
quiet cheerfulness gave a charm to his conversation which neither age nor misfortune could dim.
And yet this man had suffered cruel injustice.
At the time of our introduction to him age had

given him a slight stoop, indeed, but it had not diminished his vigor. His locks were thin and floated on his shoulders, while a beard white as snow swept his breast and gave him an air of venerable dignity which involuntarily compelled respect. His moral purity, the reputation gained by his vast erudition, his zeal in defending the faith against the attacks of nascent heresy, had caused him to be raised to the priesthood in spite of his own reluctance and opposition. Polycarp of Smyrna had imposed hands upon him, in the hope of attaching him to his own church; but Narcissus fled to Jerusalem, in order to hide himself in obscurity and poverty. God, however, had other designs on him. The place of his concealment was made known, and, a few years after, the clergy and people of Jerusalem unanimously demanded that he should be made their bishop. His entreaties and tears were unavailing, he was forced to occupy the patriarchal see first held by the apostle St. James.

In spite of all his efforts the fame of his virtues, his liberality, and wonderful miracles had spread far and near. With the sign of the cross or the touch of his hand he cured the sick, gave sight to the blind, hearing to the deaf, and speech to the dumb. Full of that faith that can move mountains, the elements and nature implicitly obeyed Narcissus.

Once, on the vigil of Easter, as the people were assembling for the celebration of the Divine Of-

fice, the deacons found there was no oil to feed
the lamps. As none could be procured, the
clergy and people felt very much annoyed; not so
the holy patriarch. "Bring some water," said
he quietly, "from the nearest fountain." When
it was brought he lifted up his eyes, uttered a
short prayer, and then, turning to the ministers,
" Now pour this into the lamps with a firm and
sincere faith, and remember that Christ our Lord
changed water into wine at the marriage feast of
Cana." To the astonishment of the entire congregation the water was changed into pure oil,
and all the lamps were filled. According to the
testimony of Eusebius of Cæsarea, some of this
miraculous oil was preserved for more than a
hundred years in Jerusalem.

However, neither his eminent virtues nor great
age were sufficient to shield him from the hatred
of some wicked and profligate men who vowed
vengeance on the holy bishop. Their animosity
was aroused against him because he had the courage to do his duty and reprimand them for their
crimes. Their first thought was to assassinate the
venerable old man; nothing was easier, since his
humble dwelling was open to all day and night.
When fatigue obliged him to interrupt his prayers
and studies he simply laid down on a mat, without undressing, and there rested for two or three
hours. But the fiendish enemies of Narcissus
desired revenge, and his death would not satisfy
them, for they knew his dearest wish was to die

and go to heaven, so that he used to complain lovingly to God of having been forgotten here below and having been left at his post beyond the usual time.

The evil spirit, that from the beginning has always taken delight in calumny as well as in blood—thus justifying his title to the name of *liar* and *murderer* given to him in the Scriptures —suggested to them a revenge far more painful to the tender heart of the saint. From his tenderest years Narcissus had given evidence of his great love of purity. He had been exposed to many dangers and temptations, had travelled far and constantly, had seen all the gay world and its seductions, and had passed through all unscathed. The demon of pleasure had tried all his wiles and arts in vain ; mortification and prayer had preserved the innocence of his young heart in all its virginal freshness and purity. Hence there was no hope of deluding such a man, now a centenarian ; he could be slandered, however ; his beautiful life and fair name might be blackened and the diadem of purity torn from his brow, at least in the estimation of the world.

At this time there lived in Jerusalem a woman who had long been a scandal in the city by reason of her dissolute life. She lived in the greatest dissipation and extravagance, and thus squandered immense sums of ill-gotten money, together with her own health and beauty. Dissipation brought on sickness and premature old age ; her dupes and flatterers abandoned her to destitution and misery. Urged by want rather than by a sincere repentence for her sins, she astonished everybody by making application to Narcissus' predecessor for public penance and baptism. At the expiration of the probation required in such cases she was received into the Church and placed on the list of the needy who were supported by the charity of the faithful.

Her accent and manners showed that this woman was a stranger; but no one could tell whence she came or what was her history. All that was known of her was that she had arrived in Jerusalem when she was young and beautiful; that she was constantly attended by a whole retinue of trembling slaves who obeyed her as if she were a very queen; that she had established herself in the most fashionable quarter of the city, in a mansion provided with every luxury that money could procure, and which soon became the very temple of scandalous dissipation and revelry. In the days of her splendor the haughty courtesan was one of the foremost in deriding and reviling that Church from which in the time of need she had to beg for daily bread. Many suspected the sincerity of her conversion, and time did not dispel their doubts. They made no secret of their opinion, which was that she had asked to be baptized and frequented the church only to obtain aid from the funds of the poor of Christ; so true is it that, no matter how impenetrable be the mask worn by hypocrisy, the real face concealed behind it can never be entirely hidden.

Such a woman was invaluable to the men who hated and had sworn to make the patriarch pay dearly for having wounded and humbled their pride. They had wealth and influence, and knew the power of both these engines to attain their object. Having arranged their plans, they repaired at night to the beggar's cottage. At first she was startled at the presence of three strangers at such an unusual hour; but soon her eyes sparkled with fiendish satisfaction; she saw gold in these men's hands; her covetous and greedy looks had not escaped their notice, and they argued favorably from it for the success of their scheme.

"Old woman," said one of them boldly, "we know who you are; we knew you very well when you passed under the assumed name of *handsome Juno*, when your youth and beauty drew around you a crowd of Jews and pagans, whom you fleeced and ruined without enriching yourself. We witnessed your mad extravagances; you revelled in jewels and gold; no king's table was more royally spread than yours, and your dwelling was more richly furnished than a palace. What have you of all this in your old age? Nothing but this miserable and dilapidated hut and that poor pallet. The crust you eat must be hard and bitter indeed; it is the bread of charity, the wages of lying and hypocrisy. Do not try to deceive us by false protestations; in the secret of

your heart you never abjured the religion of your
ancestors; you are a Christian only in name, as
every man and woman in the city is perfectly
aware; the very bishop is so persuaded of this
that he will refuse you in future the humiliating
pittance heretofore thrown to you. What will
become of you? However, if you feel so disposed you can gain money enough, this very day,
to return to your country, to purchase a slave to
wait on you, and to practise without molestation
the religion in which you were bred. Agree to
serve us and these purses shall be yours, and will
make you independently rich for the rest of your
life."

The wicked creature gladly accepted their terms
and promised implicit obedience to their wishes.
She must blast with her poisonous breath the
name of the venerable Narcissus; then would he
become the object of the people's scorn and contempt, instead of being, as he was now, their idol
and saint. She bound herself to accomplish this
by swearing an oath so fearful that it was considered by the very pagans to be inviolably sacred.

On the following day strange rumors were circulated among the class of the needy belonging
to the Church. Such persons are always ready to
pay attention to the most absurd accusations
against their benefactors. It was reported that
the patriarch had, surreptitiously and by pretending to a character which he had not, caused
himself to be nominated to the see of Jerusalem;

that his conduct in youth had been very reprehensible, and that it was to satisfy his passions, not to acquire learning as he pretended, that he had wandered from place to place. As usual these reports acquired volume by repetition; the people became excited, and indignation became louder and more violent until a riot became imminent.

The next day matters grew worse. A crowd of beggars gathered before the patriarch's house and loudly demanded his deposition as unworthy of the prelacy. "Put him out!" they cried; "expel him from the Church and the city! He is a villain! He is a ravening wolf that has usurped the shepherd's crook only to destroy the flock." Narcissus came forth and endeavored to quell the tumult, but his voice was drowned by the clamor, all he could do was to raise his eyes to heaven, thus mutely appealing to God in asseveration of his innocence.

At this juncture a woman wrinkled and bent with age made her way through the crowd, together with three men. Jerking herself into an erect position and facing Narcissus : "Wretch," she cried, "do you recognize me? Do you recognize in the woman so changed by years and misfortune the modest and virtuous maiden whom you seduced and then basely forsook after you had dishonored her? Do you recognize in her who went so long by the name of *handsome Juno* the bashful, innocent, and pure maiden known to her parents as Lucilia? I was their joy and their pride;

you and your wickedness made me their disgrace;
they were ashamed of me and drove me from their
door. Speak, do you recognize the gentle and
modest Lucilia ?"

Then, turning to the people: "This man,"
screamed she, "this monster, came to Corinth,
where I was born. That is now nearly sixty
years ago. I was then in my fifteenth year. He
came, as he said, to collect the traditions left by
the apostle Paul. Being Christians and holding
a respectable position in society, my parents received him with open arms. Their hospitality
was soon repaid by the blackest perfidy. He saw
me and I pleased him. Too confiding, alas, my
mother placed me under his care to be instructed
in the Christian doctrine, as I was then preparing
for baptism. He took advantage of my youth
and inexperience. . . . Some months afterwards he departed, to perpetrate new villanies no
doubt. As for me, I was dishonored, ruined,
spurned from my mother's bosom. I wandered
aimlessly and in despair through all the provinces
of Greece, parading from city to city the depravity taught me by this man, until I became tired
of my wandering life, and so, leaving Athens, I
came to this place; you all know the rest. On
this man then, on the base Narcissus, be all the
misfortunes of my youth! On him be this life of
guilt and scandal which he has caused! On him
be the shame that has hitherto been the lot of his
unhappy victim!"

The holy bishop, upheld by the testimony of his conscience and the grace of God, did not flinch under the dreadful accusations of Lucilia. "Woman," he said calmly, "in the name of our Lord Jesus Christ, I forgive you. He knows my innocence, and no doubt he will assert it in his own good time." As often happens, the fickle crowd now sided with the holy patriarch, and had it not been for his generous interference the imprudent and reckless Lucilia would have paid with her life for her rash and wicked conduct. Her miserable instigators, perceiving that the innocent victim whom they had resolved to destroy was on the point of eluding their toils, now cried out: "What the woman says is true, and we assert that Bishop Narcissus is certainly guilty of the crime laid to his charge. We have visited Greece frequently; this crime is still spoken of in Corinth, and we can produce proofs that leave no doubt in the matter. He did compass the ruin of this unfortunate woman whom you now threaten to stone to death. We are prepared to prove this on oath." Seeing the hesitation of the crowd, the first of the three men exclaimed: "May I be burned alive if what I say is not true." "And I," said the second, "may I be consumed by a slow and painful disease if my testimony is false." The third cried: "May I be struck blind for life if I calumniate this old man."

The irreproachable life and the well-known

virtues of the patriarch would have made it an
easy task for him to refute the charge and confound his accusers; but he chose rather to retire
into that solitude for which he had yearned so
long.   He was but too glad to cast off the burden
which he had unwillingly assumed; he departed
from Palestine, traversed Egypt, and passed into
Africa,* where he spent some years leading the
hidden life of a solitary.   The fear of recognition
kept him moving from place to place, until at
last a command from heaven sent him back to
Jerusalem and to the government of his see.

Nor did God fail to vindicate the honor of his
servant.   The hag Lucilia, torn by remorse on
her death-bed, was forced, as if in spite of herself, to give public testimony to his innocence.
Tortured with pain, and writhing in agony, she
constantly cried: *I slandered him!   I slandered
him!*   The men who swore to the slander were
visited by the vengeance they invoked.   The first
was burned to ashes, together with his whole
family and his house.   The second fell a victim
to a frightful disease which carried him off in
paroxysms of pain.   The third, terrified by the
fate of his accomplices, and fearing God's wrath,
made a public confession of his guilt.   Remorse
and tears brought on blindness.

This was the saintly and venerable bishop who

* The term *Africa* was first used by the Romans to designate the territory of Carthage after it had become a Roman
province.   It was only long after that it was applied to the
whole continent.   See Schmitz's " Manual."—[Note of Tr.]

had just celebrated the sacred mysteries. Prefatory to the benediction he spoke a few words of exhortation, urging the congregation to place their trust in God, who is always faithful to his people and to his promises, and sends afflictions only to render them more perfect. Then the Christians dispersed and wended their way back to the city in scattered groups.

CHAPTER VIII.

TOWARDS the evening of the above-mentioned day, in compliance with the request of Bishop Optatus, Narcissus related some of the incidents of his long exile in that charming simplicity of style which made his conversation so wonderfully interesting. Quite a number had collected; there were priests from the city, deacons in charge of the poor, some of the pious laity, and a few of even senatorial rank. There were present, also, some widows, venerable for their age, but still more so for their virtues. These were *deaconesses;* they spent their lives in visiting the poor, making garments for them, like Tabitha, instructing the catechumens of their own sex for baptism, and in preparing the friendless dead for burial. In the apostolic ages these devoted women were the type, the line, sketch, so to speak, of those grand institutions founded at a later period by the Church for the relief of every form of misery and suffering which the human family is heir to. Near the deaconesses sat a woman whom physiognomy rather than dress

131

proclaimed to be of noble rank ; this was Vivia's
mother, who, since her baptism, spent her whole
life in prayer and good works.   She was accompanied by her usual, nay, inseparable, companion,
the good and pious Rufina.

The venerable patriarch had narrated how he
had fled alone and at night from Jerusalem, disguised as a peasant, in order to elude the search
and pursuit of his flock; how he used to rest during the day near some sheltered spring and pursued his journey by the light of the stars; his
food was dates and his drink the waters of the
way-side rivulet. Trembling lest he should be discovered and forced to return to his flock, he finally
reached Egypt, where he hoped to find some
lonely spot where he might live unknown and
consecrate his whole time to meditation and
prayer.

But even on the banks of the Nile, in the vast
deserts formerly traversed by the children of
Israel before their entrance to the promised land,
in the deepest and darkest caves or tops of the
loftiest mountains, he sought in vain for a spot
untrodden by human footsteps. He had resolved
to penetrate into the trackless deserts of Africa ;
but sickness and fatigue prevented him.

"Sometimes," he continued, "I bent my steps
to the east and sometimes to the west, wandering aimlessly like Adam's first-born son after his
crime. Occasionally Providence conducted me
to some hospitable roof, where I met with gene-

rosity and kindness. At the sight of my bruised
and bleeding feet they used to have compassion
on the poor traveller, and used to press him to remain and rest. The invitation was generally but
too welcome to be refused. My more usual way,
however, was, when night came, to cast my staff
upon the ground and to abandon myself to undis-
turbed repose. God in his goodness watched
over his aged servant, and the roaring lions of
the desert retired to a distance, as if to respect my
slumbers.

"About twelve years ago, being persuaded that
I had no further duties to perform in this world,
that those who once knew me thought my bones
were mouldering in some unknown grave, I resolved to make use of the opportunity given me
by a merciful Providence. In this way I have
been able to visit in detail all the churches of Africa; I have passed through your city more than
once, always edified at finding so many evidences
of ever-increasing numbers and graces. Without
being recognized I have frequently assisted at
your assemblies; with you I have humbly sat at
our Lord's table, and my trembling lips have
drank out of the same cup the adorable Blood of
Jesus Christ, our common Saviour.

"But God has spoken; my tears and prayers
were not worthy of obtaining the happiness for
which I so ardently longed—to die without a
name in the silence of solitude. He wills that I
return to my people, and wield once more the

pastoral crook which my hands have forgotten
how to grasp. His holy will be done! but before
I turn my steps to Jerusalem, so long the beloved
city of God, I am obliged to execute a commission, or rather to convey a sacred trust and de-
posit, to a noble lady who is a member of the
Carthagenian Church. Had it rested with myself I should gladly have carried it with me and
worn it on my heart until my dying day.

"A short time before the rainy season, and
only a few months ago, I happened to be in Alexandria. My object was to find some convenient
place for retirement and meditation. A severe
fit of sickness detained me in the city. A charitable widow who lived in the remote suburbs had
afforded me a shelter and care. Her charity and
kindness had so won upon me as to induce me to
make known to her that I was a priest; but I
revealed neither my name nor rank in the Church.
I had determined to carry both secrets with me to
the grave.

"The patriarchal see was then vacant; the
clergy and people had not been able to meet to
provide a successor to the late bishop, who before
his death had not failed to mark the ominous
sounds of the coming storm upon his church.
Woe to the provinces governed by weak or designing men! They are incapable of stemming
the tide of popular fury, while, to retain a title
that flatters their pride or avarice, they basely
smother the voice of humanity and conscience.

Like Pilate, in order to retain the favor of their master, Cæsar, they condemn even the innocent and spill the blood of the just.

"Aquila, the prefect of Alexandria, has no personal hatred to the Christians; he esteems their virtues; he readily bears witness to their patriotism and obedience to the law, nay, in the beginning he was openly favorable to them. But the moment he found that his conduct was carped at and that public opinion censured his tolerance, a speedy change was made in his words and actions; the Christians were sought out and cast into prison; the priests were horribly mutilated, either by having their eyes plucked out, or by having their right hands struck off, as if in punishment for having celebrated the sacred mysteries. Some were tortured until their bones were dislocated, others were made lame, and in this crippled condition were condemned for life to work in mines and quarries. Worn out by inhuman treatment, by overwork and insufficient food, they died a slow and lingering death.

"Meantime the people clamored and cried for blood, more blood; the governor was constantly reminded that at Rome, Nicomedia, and elsewhere the Christians were made to serve for the amusement of the public in the amphitheatres, and that this was the only way to intimidate and arrest the progress of this wicked sect. The timid Aquila yielded in this also.

"How can I describe to you the frightful

scenes I have so often, alas! contemplated!
Words can give no idea of the violence and cruelty employed against our holy martyrs. They
were held naked and suspended in the air and
beaten until the bones protruded from the flesh;
vinegar and salt were poured into their living
wounds; their sides were torn with iron claws
until they were one mass of ragged and bloody
flesh, after which they were roasted over a slow
fire. Others were beheaded or cast into the
sea; this was the mildest punishment, and was seldom employed except when the executioners were
too fatigued and wearied to continue their labors.

"Each day brought new Christians to replace
those who had gloriously consummated their confession of the faith. No rank, age, or sex was
spared. Young men and children torn from
their mothers' arms were put to the torture, and
quailed not before the scowls and yells of the mob
drunk with fury. After the wheel and the rack
had done their work, some were tied to two different trees, bent for the purpose, and thus torn
limb from limb by the recoil. I have seen old
men covered with blood and dragged through the
streets; the populace pelted them with stones,
beat them with sticks, and lashed them with
whips and thongs. Their souls had gone to God's
footstool long before the fury of the mob had
ceased to outrage and mangle the misshapen mass
of their dead bodies.

"Meantime a spectacle no less appalling was

attracting vast crowds to the different circuses in
the city; many generous confessors whose courage no tortures could overcome had been led
thither and had been exposed to the fury of wild
beasts previously goaded to madness by pain and
hunger. But, O wonderful power of our Lord
and Saviour! it often happened that, although
goaded on by red-hot irons, the leopards, lions,
tigers, and bulls respected the holy martyrs and
turned all their fury against the executioners. A
youth, not yet twenty years of age, stood erect in
the middle of the amphitheatre; a heavenly joy
beamed in his countenance as, with arms outstretched in the shape of a cross, he poured forth
his prayer. Thrice did the tigers and lions rush
upon him to tear him; thrice did they stop
short and cronch at his feet, as if held back by
some invisible power. A furious bull was set
upon the youthful athlete, but, having come up
to him, turned suddenly on the pagans and gored
many of them. The undaunted hero continued
to pray as if he neither saw nor heard aught of
what was taking place around him; his lips were
yet moving in prayer when a soldier struck off
his head with a sword.*

"One day there was brought to Aquila's tribunal a delicate young woman, who, though clad
in the humble garb of a slave, appeared nevertheless to be of noble birth. To the first interro-

* See "Acts of the Egyptian Martyrs under the Governor-
ship of Aquila."

gatories put to her she boldly made answer that she was a Christian, and would be happy to die for Christ, her Saviour, and *her beloved Spouse.* The word *spouse* gave occasion to horrid blasphemies and brutal jests among the crowd; but she, without betraying the slightest fear or confusion, raised her voice and repeated: 'I am a Christian, spouse of Christ my God, and I consider it the greatest happiness to shed my blood to the last drop for him.'

"The governor spoke to her kindly at first, promising if she would renounce the faith to set her free and give her in marriage where she could enjoy position and wealth. 'If you consent to sacrifice to the gods,' he said, ' the wealthy master to whom you belong, and who holds the highest rank in the city, is ready and willing to share his name and fortune with you.' . . . ' Do not lose time, she answered, but attend to what you call your duty. I will never have any other God nor any other spouse than Christ my Saviour.'

" Furious and beside himself with rage, Aquila commanded the executioners to seize the innocent slave. In spite of her entreaties her veil was torn away, and a face full of beauty and maidenly confusion was exposed to the astonished gaze of the spectators; the cruel ministers of the governor remained as spell-bound with astonishment as if they stood in the presence of one of their goddesses from Olympus. Seeing this, the courageous martyr, fearing to lose her crown, cried aloud : ' I despise your false gods and infamous goddesses ; I am a Christian and the betrothed of Christ. Why do you tarry ? '

" Her words, and especially her lofty bearing and tone, irritated the executioners. They rushed upon her like wild beasts. They vied with each other in discovering and inflicting new methods of torture. Vain efforts ! For two long hours their rage vented itself upon her. Her whole body is one continuous wound, and blood flows from every limb ; her beautiful countenance is bruised and disfigured. The intrepid virgin never ceases to praise and bless the Lord. '*Blessed are they*,' exclaimed she, ' '*who are called to the feast of the nuptials of the Lamb !* How pleasing and sweet it is to suffer for the beloved One ! Chaste and divine Spouse of my soul, who hast signed with thy blood our redemption and our peace, behold the hour in which thy betrothed is about to ratify in her blood the august alliance to which thou hast vouchsafed to invite her.'

" At last the governor gave orders to have her remanded to prison, in the hope, no doubt, that her sufferings would induce her to sacrifice to the gods. They knew not the strength that God gives to his own ! The generous martyr had but one regret, that of seeing the solemn hour of her sacrifice delayed, and, after having stanched her wounds with her veil, she turned her whole attention to prepare herself by prayer

for a new confession of the faith.   She had not
long to wait.   On the morrow she was again
presented before the governor and tortured even
more cruelly than before.   As she remained
steadfast, she was sentenced to be cast naked into
a cauldron of boiling pitch.

"Tears filled the eyes of the chaste.virgin;
her modesty then would be insulted at the very
instant that she was to go, full of love and gladness, to be united to her Spouse.   I saw her clasp
her hands and fall on her knees. 'Noble Aquila,'
she said, 'in your mother's name, in the name of
your own wife, I conjure you to modify your sentence. I fear not death; it is the object of my
most ardent desires; I see its approach with transports of joy which you cannot understand; but
oh! do not permit this outrage, order rather that I
be put as I am into the cauldron.   You see what
courage and strength Jesus Christ, my God, gives
to those who put their hope in him.'   God
touched Aquila's heart; he granted her request,
and the execution of the sentence was entrusted
to one of the guards named Basilides.

"This officer treated her with the most delicate
consideration and shielded her on the way from
the insults of the rabble and their obscene and
blasphemous ribaldry.   Moved by this unhoped-
for humanity, the holy martyr told Basilides to
be of good cheer, for she would obtain for him
the grace of conversion. She prayed for some
time, and then calmly placed herself in the hands

of the guard. They immersed her slowly into the seething pitch, and the glorious sacrifice was consummated.*

"A few hours before her second appearance at the tribunal of the governor, I succeeded in gaining access to her prison, and she received from my hands the adorable Body of Jesus Christ to strengthen her for the combat. 'Priest of God,' she said to me, 'I shall soon leave this world of sadness and sorrow. I was not born in poverty and slavery, as you may have imagined; my early life was spent in luxury and ease with a noble lady, my kinswoman, and a friend, a fond sister whose memory brings tears to my eyes even at this last moment, when I should think only of God. As I was playing one day on the sea-shore I was seized by pirates on their way from their hiding-places in the mountains, and was carried by them to their ship. At their arrival in Alexandria they sold me into slavery. God had pity on me; a fellow-slave took me into her confidence and made known to me the God of the Christians. I received Baptism, and blessed the kind Providence that had wrought my salvation by means of the misfortune I so bitterly deplored. After the lapse of some years I came into possession of a new master; I had grown to womanhood, and was considered rather comely and attractive. Alas! these vain gifts were destined to cause me many tears. My master conceived a passion for me, but I rejected his overtures with horror, for I had already promised in my heart to have no spouse other than Jesus Christ. I urgently begged the venerable Bishop of Alexandria to grant me the dearest wish of my heart; he solemnly consecrated me to the Lord and gave me the veil that I wore this day at the governor's tribunal.

"'For ten years I have been suffering from the constant attacks of the unhappy man whose notice I had attracted, but God in his infinite mercy protected me always, and frequently in a miraculous manner. I have faithfully kept the promise made to my heavenly Spouse at the altar. My master sought to be revenged for my resistance, to punish me for what he called my pride and fanaticism; he denounced me to the governor as a Christian, promising him a large sum of money if he could induce me to yield. But God was with me; I have confessed his holy name, I have gladly suffered for love of him, and I hope shortly to receive from his hands the crown and palm of victory. In this solemn hour pray for me, father, that my faith fail not; whatever be the kind of death that awaits me, my eyes will seek you out before closing for ever, and do you then bless me for the last time and point me the way to heaven.

"'In this world I have found only perils and sorrows, and have nothing to regret. Having been left an orphan in childhood, my grave, wherever it may be dug, will not be watered by the tears of a sorrowing family. There is but one person who would weep at the news of my death—a noble Carthagenian lady, that friend, that fond sister of my infant days, the sole witness of my abduction by the pirates. Kind and tender *Julia,* for that is her name, it seems to me as if I still hear her piercing cries and see her fainting in her nurse's arms! Father, pardon these memories, which savor perhaps of worldly ties and affections; but I loved her so much, and she was so gentle and affectionate to me! If it should ever be in your power, tell her that her loved Potamiena died thinking of her, and give her this veil, dyed in my blood, with my last request that she keep it as the dying pledge of my affection. When misfortune parted us she adored the false gods of her country; may her virtues have obtained for her the grace of knowing the true God.' "

The venerable Narcissus here ended his narrative; more than once did his trembling voice betray the deep feelings of his soul, and tears forced themselves into his eyes as he repeated the dying words of the martyr virgin. Leaning on the arm of the pious Ruffina, the noble Julia came forward and knelt to receive the precious keepsake, the blood-stained veil of her beloved Potamiena. Her tears fell fast and long upon it before she placed it in her bosom. She would fain have

thanked the holy bishop and expressed her gratitude and joy, but her lips moved inarticulately
and refused to form the words. Meantime, night
had fallen ; the priests and faithful gave thanks
to God and separated. Next day the aged patriarch, staff in hand, was once more on the road
to Jerusalem, to be received by the people with
the old cry of welcome : *Blessed is he who com-
eth in the name of the Lord !*

CHAPTER IX.

AFTER the interview spoken of in a previous chapter between old Jubal, the hired assassin, and his haughty master, no time was thrown away. Taking advantage of the remaining hours of night and stealthily gliding along the darkest and most unfrequented streets, the slave was a long way from Carthage when the first rays of the sun gilded the horizon.

Being accustomed to scale the steepest mountains, and being an expert swimmer, he advanced rapidly and indulged in the most pleasing dreams. It was certain, then, that in a short time he would have money enough to enable him to spend the rest of his days in ease. He would be free again, and would roam through his native wilds and woods. Once more would he lead the life of his youth, follow the same pastimes and expeditions to hunt the lion and the tiger. At these thoughts his heart beat high and gave new life and elasticity to his whole frame; he rather ran than walked, and night was far advanced before he could bring himself to take a few hour's rest.

On the second day, however, his face wore an
anxious look; he slackened his pace occasionally or halted altogether, as if to give himself time
for thought.   Sometimes he closed his eyes in .
deep meditation ; a moment after and he would
arouse himself, and his face would settle into an
expression of resoluteness and alarm.   What
could be the thoughts that were passing through
the mind of this man, so long inured to crime?

Afer had grown callous by dint of assassina-
tions; his blow was unaccompanied by remorse,
the dagger never shook in his grasp.   He used to
cast a calm look on the victim at his feet, but it
was to make sure that he had not missed his
blow ; having satisfied himself on that point,
he proceeded leisurely to wipe the blade of his
poniard and demand payment for what he termed
his fidelity.   But, villain as he was, he was prudent and cunning, and certainly not a man to
commit himself by overhaste or presumption.
When occasion required he knew how to wait;
when the impetuous Jubal would sometimes
complain of his slowness in avenging him the
slave would drawl out: "Master, the time has not
come yet; you can rely on your faithful servant."

When the negro began to reflect he began to
fear also; at one time he had almost made up his
mind to return to Carthage and brave his master's anger.   His was indeed no easy undertaking ; it was to murder not only a brave soldier

in the strength of manhood, but, moreover, the
leader, the general of an army, constantly surrounded by faithful guards. How get to him,
how find access to his tent, and even if he did,
would he find him alone or asleep? would it be
possible to stab him to the heart? The slightest
movement or cry would arouse the guards, and
then woe to the assassin! a thousand swords
would be upon him!

For hours did these thoughts fill the bosom
and conjure the most frightful pictures before
the mind's eye of the trembling slave. At one
time he imagined himself watched, manacled,
examined, put to the torture, overcome by excess
of pain; he seemed to hear the fatal sentence
pronouncing his doom. At another time he had
succeeded in gaining the tent of his sleeping victim, but, for the first time in his life, his dagger
had missed the heart; the bungling slave was
hemmed in by the enraged troops; he felt on his
creeping and bloody flesh the cold edge of their
swords; an involuntary groan burst from his
breast, a cold sweat covered his body, and the
few teeth left him by age chattered with terror.
The dastardly old villain clung to life more eager-
ly than the most pampered favorites of fortune.

Exhausted by this warfare of terror and imagination, he sat himself down at the foot of a
date-tree, whose shade protected him from the
burning rays of a midday sun. "I will go no
further," said he to himself. "What a mad fool I

was to have allowed myself to be duped by such
fallacious hopes! My master has promised to
give me wealth and liberty; he is rich, and can
easily give me gold; he has plenty of younger
and stronger slaves than I, and he can well afford
to give me my freedom. But if I am found out
will he come and put on my manacles? Would
he jeopardize his life for mine? My purse is
pretty well stocked, the road is open, and my feet
are still able to put a long distance between Carthage and myself. After all, I have no reason to
hate Lady Vivia's husband; he never injured me;
let him live then, and let me live too. Jubal has
a dagger as well as I; let him take his own revenge, it is his own business." After this he
felt eased, like a man who has cast off a heavy
load, and quietly stretched himself down to sleep.

The children of the desert very readily confide
their soliloquies to the discretion of the sands;
because, argue they, if the sands hear, and it has
never been proved they do, it is very certain, at
any rate, that they never talk. Hence Afer had
thought aloud, he was so confident of being quite
alone. No sound had fallen even on his ear,
which was so quick that it could catch the rustling of the distant grass waving gently to the
breeze; yet no sooner had he closed his eyes as
he disposed himself to sleep than he sprang up
like a wounded lion.

An old man stood before him. His dress told
his occupation very plainly; he was one of that

class of camel-drivers so numerous in the countries of Africa, who constantly roam from place to place in search of pasture for their cattle. A snow-white beard fell on his ample breast; his sharp twinkling eye, riveted in a sidelong glance on the slave, seemed to be busied in recalling some half-obliterated and distant recollections of the past.

"Am I mistaken?" he cried, after a short pause; "is not this you, Afer?"

"Importunate old man," answered the black slave, placing his hand on his dagger, "what business of yours is my name, and by what right do you ask it? Begone to your camels on the mountain, and do not annoy a tired traveller seeking to rest a little on his weary journey."

"Afer, now I know you to a certainty; I do not wish to annoy or bother you as you imagine; I am an old acquaintance whom you seem to have forgotten, one of your old companions in misfortune, but one so changed by grief that it is no wonder you cannot recognize me. Do you not remember poor Sylvanus, once the slave of the noble Hanno, and now the herder of a few lean camels?"

"Do I remember old Sylvanus! *By the great Juno,* I do not forget my old friends so soon; I remember full well the merry quips and pleasant parties that we so often enjoyed, and whiled away the time in while waiting for our gaming and carousing masters."

"Have a care, Afer, how you recall these old memories; they bring blood from a wound that time can never heal. I would just as soon be run through the heart with that dagger with which your hand toyed just now.' For old Sylvanus there are no longer any happy recollections, no pleasures in this world unless . . . But come to my tent; I overheard you, you talked about Jubal and Vivia's husband, whom your master commissioned you, no doubt, to despatch to Pluto. If I can assist you in any way you may count on me; I have no use for gold; what could I do with it? But I want revenge!" And the old man's eye lit up with so malignant a gleam that it made the black slave tremble.

A few minutes later they arrived at and seated themselves in the camel-herder's tent. A female slave, bent with age, served them with refreshments and then withdrew to go and milk the camels on the hillside.

"We can now talk at our ease," said Sylvanus. "Fatuma will not return until evening. Hide nothing from me, Afer; you would only lose time by trying to deceive me. Not one word of your soliloquy escaped me; my attentive ear drunk them all in greedily as they fell from your lips. You are on your way to the camp, and you are going thither to avenge some insult offered to your master; do not be afraid that I shall betray your secret. I said, and I repeat, that my thirst for vengeance allows me no rest day or night. Like yourself, I bear no grudge to Vivia's husband, and he is said to be a brave soldier, a lenient and kind master to his slaves; but she! Oh! if my dagger could but pierce her heart I'd die content. To stab the man she loves and in whose name she glories is to stab her! That is to taste and enjoy the sweetness of revenge! My heart swells to bursting at the glorious thought. O Afer! will you let me share with you this undertaking? You may rest assured you will never regret it if you do."

"Sylvanus, I am at a loss to understand one word of what you say. Why, I always thought you were so happy that I have often envied you. You are free, you breathe at will the wild breeze of the mountains, and your camels suffice for all your wants."

"Liberty, mountain air, and a few camels were once my dream of perfect happiness; but these have now lost all their value for me. At night, in my tent, and during the day in the shade of the palms, I can only sigh and weep. O Vivia, Vivia! shall I ever enjoy the sight of your heart's blood and hear the death-rattle of your agony?"

"Every one is loud in her praises, what can she have done to you? Perhaps she took the whim of amusing herself by having you whipped long ago? Or did she suspect you of some imaginary crime and have you put into the stocks or prison? Why do you hate her? Nay, if my memory does not fail me, I remember that it was her mother that obtained you your freedom, gave you money to buy your camels, so that you might support yourself and old Fatuma, whom she confided to your care."

"That is all well enough; I got liberty and a handful of gold, but I got not the dearest, the only object of my affections. And it was Vivia, the wicked Vivia, that robbed me of my jewel, my treasure, and ever since I have been the most unhappy of men!"

"What do you mean, Sylvanus! of what treasure did Vivia rob you? Ye gods! perhaps he is doating."

"Have you forgotten that I was once a father? The mate who had united her sad lot to mine died young and left me an infant daughter, sole pledge of our mutual affection. Fatima— for so we called her—was not destined to know her mother; I alone watched over her solitary cradle. To return to it more quickly, I worked hard to finish my daily task; gray dawn found me always at my toil; the thought of my child redoubled my strength and made me forget fatigue.

"How happy it made me feel when I returned to see her smile and stretch out her little arms to me! How I used to embrace and kiss and weep over her! Then my tears were sweet .and soothing; since they have turned to the bitterness of gall.

"If Fatima fell sick I used to sit all night by her cradle watching, administering to her wants, and soothing her pains. I used to warm her little hands and feet with my hands and breath, and when daylight called me to my task I used to tremble with anxiety as I confided her to the care of old Fatuma. My good mistress frequently permitted me to remain all day with my child. It would be very ungrateful to forget that even the kind lady herself often spent whole hours by the sick-bed and nursed my darling like a mother.

"Why did she not die then? Why did she not go to her mother in the grave? Fool that I was! I implored the immortal gods to spare me my child. Alas! the future was veiled from my eyes; I was then very far from imagining that I should one day accuse them of cruelty for having heard my prayers! Afer, forgive a father's grief! As for you, unless you have changed since I knew you, you no more care for our great Jupiter than for the Crucified, whom the godless sect of the Christians adore.

"Fatima thrived and grew; she was the image of her mother, the same mild and winning ways; by dint of caresses and affection she seemed to strive to take her mother's place in my heart. On my return from the fields she always ran to meet me, to wipe my sweat-covered face, and her caresses were always accompanied by words that were music to my ear and joy to my heart. She had water ready for my feet and food for my mouth ; her hands had spread my conch to make easy my slumbers, and in the morning I was sure to be gladdened by her presence before returning to my daily toil.

"A slave's lot is a hard one, Afer, as you well know ; the bread he eats is often steeped in his tears, as well as bought at the price of his sweat. After having toiled all day under a burning sun, in the cold and rain, to till the field of another, he must often labor also to please and amuse his master ; his heart has seldom the consolation of hearing even a kind word ; he must bend in silence to the supercilious caprices and tyrannical exactions of those who paid for him in the same way as they do for their horses. But the tender affection of my Fatima gave me courage to bear patiently my unhappy lot. When I sat near her I forgot all my sufferings ; a smile or a word from my darling child made me the happiest of fathers.

"Laws are cruel ; the pride and avarice of men have made them so. Being the daughter of a poor slave, Fatima belonged not to her father, but to her father's master. He had the right to tear her from my arms, in spite of my prayers and tears, to sell her to a stranger to be taken whithersoever he might please. Hanno did not do this, and I thanked him on my knees. At any rate, my darling would not be taken from me ! I could see and embrace her every day of

my life, and, when the time would come, I could
choose for her a husband that would be worthy
of her. Sweet hopes, whither are ye fled! It
was now, Afer, that the real misfortunes of your
old friend began.

" Years had developed Fatima's limbs, and had
brought into relief all her sterling qualities; she
was fifteen years of age. She was praised for
her beauty and admired for her modesty and
gentleness. People never grew tired of praising
her and her wonderful affection for her father.
She was the only person who seemed not to know
and esteem and appreciate all her good qualities.
She could not understand why people praised her
so much. ' Was not virtue a duty ? To love
one's father, to be devoted to him, was not that
a natural impulse to be found in every child's
heart ? '

" The noble Hanno's wife had been always
very kind to her; she proposed to attach her to
the immediate service of her daughter, and no
obstacle was found in the way. In waiting on
her young mistress, Fatima was not obliged to
make any change in the customary routine of her
past life. So I continued to enjoy her presence
every day, and her company during the long
hours of the evening. This was so pleasant to
both that we often forgot the hour for repose, we
were so happy in being together. Two years
glided away in this manner.

" I noticed, however, that Fatima began to lose

some of her natural sprightliness ; she became
graver and more serious, and her conversation
was no longer as gay as it used to be. Still she
was as good, as affectionate, and as officious towards me as ever. There was so much sweetness in her smile and affection in her manner,
that I always recognized the heart of my own
darling child, and hence I was afraid to question
her.

"Was Fatima concealing something from me ?
Could she, who was invariably so frank with me,
have some secret that she dared not reveal to her
father ? What extraordinary change was coming
over her ? Did she begin to feel the misfortunes
of her condition ? Was she worried by the petu-
lance or pride of her young mistress ? Was her
honor or virtue threatened ? Could her young
and innocent soul have been unwarily ensnared
by some tender affection or attachment ? Did
she think it was time to lay aside the garb of
maidenhood to assume that of wedlock ? I determined to put an end to my anxiety and distress by sounding her cautiously. She spared me
the trouble herself.

"One day I returned from the field at the usual
hour. My eyes looked for Fatima in vain ; she
came not to meet me. Alarmed and trembling
with fear, I asked myself what could be the
cause of her absence. The twinkling stars came
out one by one until they filled the heavens, and
still no footsteps of my child fell on my listening

ear. At last I heard a slight rustle. Here she was! I ran to clasp her in my arms. I stood as if smitten by a bolt from heaven.

"Fatima wore no longer the mean and dark-hued garment of a slave. A snow-white robe enveloped her whole person, a veil of the same color floated round her head and half concealed her beautiful tresses, while a golden cross sparkled on her bosom. There remained, then, no room for further doubt. She had been deceived, cajoled, entrapped; they had taken advantage of her youth, of her confiding innocence—she had been made a Christian! This, then, was the secret she had held locked up in her heart, and, O dotard that I was! I never even as much as thought of such a horror.

"I was struck motionless and dumb. She approached me trembling and with downcast eyes to embrace me. Her lips slightly touched my forehead; I heard her whisper the name of father. I returned to consciousness and spurned her from me with the wildest vituperation and rage. I saw her fall at my feet. She begged me with prayers and tears not to withdraw from her my love and affection. They were unavailing. I called down the most awful imprecations on her head; I cursed her, I raved like a madman, and left her with a solemn injunction never more to come into my sight. Mark me well, Afer, I did this because I had sworn such a hatred to the Christian religion that, had I a dagger at that moment, I would have plunged it remorselessly in my own child's heart!

"But it is time for you to retire to rest; the shades of night have fallen upon the hills, and my heart is so torn with harrowing emotions that I cannot continue for the present. I will do so to-morrow, and you shall hear my plans for the future. That the immortal gods have inspired me this time I am fully persuaded. Only rely on me and the success of your enterprise is certain, and I shall be permitted to gloat over my first instalment of sweet revenge."

Thereupon the two friends separated for the night.

CHAPTER X.

PAGAN FANATICISM.

SCARCELY had the first streaks of dawn appeared when Sylvanus and Afer were already astir

"Fatima," said the freedman, taking up the thread of his last night's narrative, " Fatima was my whole happiness and pride. I lived but for her ; her future preoccupied all my attention and care. The hardest toil, poverty, the darkness and the chains of a dungeon would have been as nothing had I my child by my side ; without her, wealth, possessions, happiness, and ease had no charms for me, and she had now put an impassable gulf betwixt us. I had cursed her and had flung her from me without mercy ! I had sworn never to see her more !

"Instead of appeasing, time only whetted my resentment. Whenever I espied her on her way to visit me, as she always hitherto had been accustomed to do, I invariably avoided and eluded her by taking some circuitous path. If she came upon me unawares, I turned away my eyes and hastened to hide myself in my cabin. In vain did she follow me; she used to remain for hours kneeling and sobbing at the door, imploring me to remove from her heart the heavy weight of my malediction and resentment; I let her weep and pray on without pity or compassion. I felt a strange satisfaction in torturing her in this manner; a sort of savage delight filled my soul when 1 reflected on the tortures she had to undergo on account of my sternness and obstinacy.

" Julia, the noble wife of HANNO, came to me repeatedly and gently upbraided me for my relentlessness : ' Your daughter,' she used to say, ' is inconsolable ; her grief would move the heart of a savage ; she had no thought of displeasing you when she became a Christian ; since then she has only grown better, milder, more modest, and obedient, so that she has become a model for her young companions.' I listened because I had no alternative, I never uttered a word, but always departed with a new instalment of hate in my heart.

" I had been informed by an old slave employed about the house that Fatima had been taken into the friendship as well as into the service of her mistress at one and the same time ; that she often kept her by her under pretext of wanting company or assistance, but in reality only to have an opportunity of vaunting the merits of the new religion ; she urged her to embrace it, promising her her friendship as a re-

ward, and by saying that after they would be
united in one faith and worship they would live
together like two sisters. She was a good judge
of a heart so tender and loving as Fatima's; her
persistent solicitations and wheedling ways were
sure, in the end, to overcome the feeble resistance of her slave. A fiery, fanatical priest, well
known to all Carthage, Tertullian, the oracle of
the modern atheists, gave the finishing stroke to
the work of my child's cajolement.

"Afer, no words could make you understand
my rage and hatred to Vivia; compelled as I
was to suppress and hide the passions raging in
my breast, I fell into rayless despair. My nights
knew no sleep, but as often as I became unconscious by dint of fatigue and grief Fatima seemed to stand before me. I imagined her always
shrouded in white, wearing that cross, the symbol of her base apostasy; at the sight I used to
spring from my pallet like a tiger wounded in
his sleep. My lips frothed maledictions upon
her and the hated patrician who had duped her
innocence and unsuspecting youth.

"When the hour for toil called me to work, I
doggedly plodded to the place assigned me. I
held aloof from my fellow slaves as much as possible; little by little they became accustomed to
my gloomy sullenness. Indifferent to everything, always absorbed in my own sad thoughts,
I took no note of the flight of time. I felt
neither the sweltering sun that bathed me in per-

spiration, nor the refreshing shower, that is as
welcome to the slave toiling in the field as it is
to the drooping bird and flower. In the evening
I slunk back in silence to the city, and while
everything in my master's mansion resounded
with music, feasting, and song, I sat solitary and
alone nursing my grief. If sorrow made me
weep, hate soon came to dry my tears. There
are strange mysteries in the heart of a father,
especially when all his affections are centred in
an only child.   Afer, you cannot understand
what he suffers when the ties that bind him to
that child are violently snapped asunder, when the
long hopes that lured him on and the dreams
that fed his imagination vanish for ever. The
gods sometimes send golden dreams to the pil-
low of the sick and the miserable, but with consciousness intensified suffering returns.   Nor do
you understand what it is to have deep hate
gnawing the heart day and night, to feel the
thirst of revenge burning and eating it away
without a moment's respite.   Frightful torture,
than which black Tartarus itself has nothing
more terrible ! For five long years this has been
burning up the blood in my veins and consuming
my very vitals !

"When I cursed Fatima, as I told you already,
I swore never to see her.   She was no longer my
child, from the moment she joined that accursed
sect, which is allowed to go on growing and
spreading when it ought to be smothered in the

blood of the last of its adepts. I am thankful to
the gods for having given me courage and
strength. I have been faithful to my oath, and
when it pleased Hanno to set me free, to rid himself, no doubt, of a bore, I coldly turned my
back on the roof that had sheltered my youth,
that had witnessed my joys and happiness as a
husband and a father, and subsequently my grief
and despair. I repaired with old Fatuma to this
lonely desert, whither the noise of the world
never comes. With me I brought the arrow still
rankling in the wound. I never cease to feel its
stinging barb. Afer, I shall die if I have not revenge.

"I have not revisited Carthage, that city of
sorrowful memories, since I was set free. I
knew not what had become of Fatima, not even
if she were still alive. Only a few days ago,
however, a young soldier returning from the
army passed through our mountains and rested a
night in my tent. He thought to interest me
with camp news, but soon perceiving that I paid
but little attention, he shifted the subject of conversation and spoke of city matters and of persons of note with whom he was acquainted. I
knew not why, but I had the curiosity to ask him
if Vivia still lived in Carthage, and what had become of one of her slaves called Fatima. 'Vivia,'
said he, 'never left the city, and still lives in the
same old mansion. No doubt she has become a
mother ere this. Like her mother, she too is a

Christian, as all the city knows. She even hopes that Jarbas, her husband, will speedily follow her example, thanks to the influence of one Tertullian, with whom he held sundry conferences previous to his departure for the army. He makes no secret of his sympathy for the new sect. In the camp his bodyguard is composed exclusively of Christian soldiers. Many are lond in their dissatisfaction, and the discontent is becoming more serious and threatening every day. As for the young slave whom you call Fatima, she became a Christian, like her mistress, a long time ago, and is a great favorite of hers. She picked her out a husband from the same sect; and, as if something unpleasant or ominous attached to the name of her childhood, she dropped it for that of Felicitas. This is the name she goes by at present.'

"So, Afer, after having renounced the ancient and venerable religion of her fathers, she wished to forget even the name that her mother and I gave her, and it was that detested woman, the woman to whom I owe all my woes, that selected and gave her a husband; and the man of her choice, the man to whom she made over my daughter, he, too, is a base deserter from the sacred cause of our gods. O revenge, revenge! Even if she whom I loved but too well were to perish, Vivia must die. Let her not reckon on the influence and protection of her husband, for before many days she shall weep in widow's

weeds; and then shall come the day when my
eyes shall feast on the spectacle of her dying
agony and blood. After that I shall return to
these hills to die happy."

The old freedman ceased. He was frightful
to behold. His lips continued to quiver and
move spasmodically, so that he looked as if he
were still speaking. He had risen and had
drawn himself up to his full height by a jerking
movement like that of a mechanical automaton.
His hand clutched a naked poniard, and seemed
only to be waiting for the order to strike. His
staring eyeballs shot fire, and revealed the fury
of the tempest raging in his soul. The black
slave, in his terror, did not dare to speak to or
even to look at him. He trembled as if he stood
in the presence of one of those imaginary giants
that used to terrify him in infancy, and who was
represented as being able to uproot a mountain
or hurl a man as a shepherd would a stone from
his hand.

"Afer," continued Sylvanus after a short
pause, "listen to the plan that I have been medi-
tating on since yesterday, and thinking about all
night: Vivia's husband is every day losing more
and more the confidence of his troops; the enthusiasm produced by his first victories over the
fierce Numidians has given place to dissatisfaction, as I have been told by outsiders, because he
does not follow them into their own fastnesses.
They call his prudence cowardice, and the sus-

picion of treason even has been whispered
about. It is rumored that he has come to a
secret understanding with the enemy, that the
outposts around the camp are neglected, and that,
while our brave legions are kept in disgraceful inactivity in their miserable intrenchments, the
wily barbarians are making ready to fall, one of
these days, on Carthage, to take it by surprise,
to burn her harbor and shipping, and to possess
themselves of her spoils and wealth.

" Time is precious, Afer ; let us not throw it
away in useless talk ; let us set out for the camp,
we can reach it before night by using our own
diligence and the fleetness of our camels. I will
pass myself for a man inspired by the gods, an
interpreter of their supreme will. I will excite
our soldiers, I will rouse them into revolt in the
name of our outraged gods, in the name of the
immortal Juno, the guardian of proud Carthage.
I will march at their head to Jarbas, and will demand that, as general of the army, he personally
offer sacrifice to Mars, the god of war. I will
tell him that ' this terrible god appeared to me
in sleep ; he commanded me to seek you ; his
altar must run red with the blood of your oxen ;
on this condition only can you accomplish the
overthrow of the indomitable Numidians and return in triumph to the walls of Carthage.'

" The altar, the victims, the sacrificator will be
ready. Jarbas will refuse, if it be true that he is a
Christian ; he is not the man to dissemble through

fear or to hide behind a cowardly falsehood. His refusal will be the signal for a revolt; the gods and our daggers will do the rest. Mine, for one, will not certainly fail; I want to send it all bloody to the wicked Vivia. My name is engraven on the blade, and she shall know that Fatima's father has begun the work of vengeance!

"I desire the glory and the honor of perfecting that work of vengeance. With you, Afer, I shall return to Carthage; I want to be the first to bear the news of Jarbas's death. In the commotion which it will produce, it will be easy to hound the mob on the Christians; the ears of the Senate will ring with that shout inspired by the gods: *The Christians to the lions!* At the thunder-tones of frenzied populace our magistrates will arouse themselves, perforce, from their criminal apathy. Then, at last, will these *atheists* be sought out and punished. Vivia, the wicked Vivia, shall not be able to escape the fate she so richly deserves; she shall die and I will see her! She shall die crushed by the fangs of wild beasts. Perhaps Fatima's blood would flow and mingle with that of her mistress! Well, let her, too, die! I was once her father, but I am her father no longer!"

As it may be easily imagined, Afer could not but approve of the revengeful designs of his old friend as well as of the plan proposed by him. The carrying out of Jubal's scheme had lost the ter-

rible difficulties and dangers of the evening before. Provided he could say at his return : *Master, you have been avenged; Vivia's husband is
dead*, the rest did not much signify to Afer. He
had neither love nor hatred for the Christians;
all he wanted was gold and freedom. If he were
once rich and free, he would let Sylvanus rage as
much as he pleased against those whom he called
infidels and *atheists*. He took good care, however, not to let his accomplice see this; he was
too cunning to betray himself and his thoughts,
so he simply signified his assent by shaking hands
with Sylvanus; then they both left the tent.

Let us turn from them as they hasten on their
camels towards the camp, in order to regale our
eyes on a smiling, pleasant scene such as Christ's
religion alone can present—let us back to the
great city. The saintly Bishop of Carthage stands
clad in the insignia of his high office and dignity,
and is surrounded by his clergy and flock. A maiden robed in white is at his feet; her brow wears
the purity of the angels whose name she bears,
while her looks, beaming with heavenly joy,
seem riveted on a flowing veil and a crown of
flowers lying on the altar.

CHAPTER XL

BEFORE Christ, born of a Virgin, had pronounced the words, *Blessed are the pure and clean of heart*, continency in its highest, most superhuman and angelical perfection was a virtue unknown in the world. One woman alone, she who had been chosen and fitted to bear in her womb the Word made flesh, had understood and practised it. Her soul, enlightened from on high, had fathomed its excellence; her immaculate heart felt all its heavenly and peerless value. Idolatry, born of united pride and voluptuousness, and destined unavoidably to result in the worship of the flesh and the deification of the passions, could not soar to the height of a virtue that does violence to and sacrifices the heart itself in its dearest attachments in order to make it worthy of God, the equal and the brother of the angels. The vestals of paganism, the priestesses of Gaul and the North, though they did not wed, still they never dreamt of the cheerful and voluntary immolation and unsullied purity of heart required in a *virgin*. Their faithlessness

and frailties were not unfrequently seen of men
and the law had penalties wherewith to punish
them.   God's eye *alone* could scan the heart and
detect the secrets of the soul, and where these
were evil *legal* continency was valueless.

Even among God's own people virginity was
not honored, and barrenness was a disgrace.
Having been vowed to the Lord by a rash father,
Jephte's daughter has but one regret: the promise being sacred and inviolable, and being a
virgin, she is doomed to live and die in that state;
she requests, therefore, of her father that she may
be permitted to retire to the mountains for two
months to *bewail her virginity* with her young
companions.   Unlike the daughters of her nation,
she can never enjoy the happiness of loving and
being loved by a spouse and prattling children.
Hence her grief and tears; hence, too, all the
merit of her gentle obedience and generous sacrifice.

The Gospel having been rejected by the house
of Juda and Israel, is announced to the nations.
A new, a heaven-born, spirit permeates and leav-
ens the whole mass.   Faith *renews the face of the
earth* and achieves wonders, charity recognizes
no longer any limits to its benevolent efforts, poverty has its enthusiastic admirers, humility seeks
and courts abjection and contempt, suffering and
death are courted and welcomed with smiles, a
new army of soldiers and heroes boldly enters,
and triumphs in the lists where the old pagan

world had sworn to conquer with fire and sword the new world, her rival, that confidently demands her place in the face of heaven, and aspires to nothing less than the inheritances of the ages. In this movement of transformation, chastity had also its appointed place. Though steeped in no blood, its palms will be not less glorious, its combats and triumphs, unseen by human eyes, shall only be the more brilliant in those of God. It, too, must have its heroes. Grasping the lily, symbol of soul purity, in order to make surer the road to heaven, they follow the way trod by the Queen of Virgins and the beloved disciple whose purity won for him the predilection of his Master.

Even as early as the time that St. Paul wrote his epistles to the Corinthians many Christians in every rank and station of life had made solemn vows to live in the state of virginity. These the apostle called the *betrothed* of the Divine Sponse; he applauded their choice; their hearts, he said, would not be divided in their affections; wholly occupied in pleasing God, they would escape the harassing cares and tribulations inseparable to married life. St. John, in his ecstatic visions, saw them in heaven following in the immediate train of the Spotless Lamb and heard them singing around the throne canticles of love unutterable to other lips.

At the date of our narrative the Church of Carthage was in a most flourishing condition,

and had long since blossomed and produced its
crown of holy virgins. Their modesty contrasted
singularly with the corruption introduced by paganism in that torrid climate, where bosoms are
as fervid as the air they breathe. As if to expiate
the abominations of the city, a number of young
maidens, bred under the refreshing shadow of the
cross, had embraced a life of perpetual chastity.
The bishop had solemnly consecrated them to
God. The gentle and pious Rufina, the orphan
from Gaul, was distinguished among them by
reason of her remarkable perfection and retirement of life. Another companion, a new sister,
was now about to join this choir of Christ's holy
spouses.

Her name was Angela; she belonged to a
wealthy family that had emigrated from Rome
and settled in Carthage for the better prosecution
of their commercial interests. Her parents were
Christians, and, being advanced in years, they
had retired from business some years previously,
in order to devote their whole lives to prayer and
good works. They gave freely in charity, but
they took especial care of the poor old people
whom the pagans remorselessly left to languish
in misery and neglect. Touched by such charity,
many of these unfortunates became Christians.

At an early age Angela gave evidence of a
natural tendency for piety and devotion. At the
time that ordinary children think only of play,
her greatest delight was to pray. During the

day she frequently retired to her room to kneel before the crucifix or a picture of Mary. With her little hands joined together or clasped on her breast, she used to pour out her soul before God. She was scarcely twelve years of age when her parents thus found her one day rapt in ecstasy. Her whole person shone dazzlingly bright, her countenance was aglow, and words of burning love fell from her lips. She seemed to be listening to and taking part in some mysterious conversation, to be gazing on her Beloved speaking to her. She pressed her hands on her heart as if to stay its flutterings, and to lose no word of what was being said to her.

There never was, perhaps, a more even or a milder temper than hers. On beholding her one felt irresistibly attracted to her. When in the company of her young companions she interested and held them captivated by the recital of some narrative borrowed from pious books or the Scriptures. In her company they forgot the amusements which they everywhere else sought with eagerness; the giddiness and petulancy so natural to their age gave way, for a time at least, to seriousness and attention. If asked the reason, they simply asked: "How could we help being good children with one who is goodness itself, and who has always so many interesting things to tell us?"

Angela had ever a horror for falsehood, and a lie never polluted her lips; when she was

only a child she used to make a candid avowal of
whatever she thought was a fault. She gave
ready and cheerful obedience not only to her parents but also to her teachers and governesses.
Later on in life she was heard to say that the first
time she read in the Gospel what was written of
the child Jesus, *he was subject to them*, the words
made such a deep impression on her that she had
resolved always to do the same, through love of
him, and so faithful was she to her promise that
one would have thought ever after that she had
no will of her own.

But what she was most remarkable for was her
extraordinary modesty and deep love of purity.
Even before she could have had any knowledge
of the nature of sin, she showed a wonderful delicacy on this subject, and must have been actuated by special and supernatural guidance. When
only five years of age she refused the assistance
of her maids and even of her mother when she
retired for the night or prepared to present herself in the morning. She used the bath only
when it was necessary or ordered by her parents,
and so sensitive was her modesty that she could
not brook the presence of even her own nurse.

At twelve she expressed her desire of consecrating her virginity to God. She spoke to the bishop and her parents with so much unction and
wisdom regarding her intention and the happiness of becoming a spouse of Christ, that they
melted into tears, for they felt that God spoke by

her lips and had visibly marked and singled her
out for that exalted honor. As a consequence,
the venerable pontiff had received her first vows
and had admitted her into the class of *postulants*,
according to the formulary then observed. Henceforth Angela lived in the most profound retirement, seldom appearing abroad except at the
celebration of the sacred mysteries. She spent
the greater part of the day in prayer, communing
with our Lord and seeming to see and hear him,
like the holy contemplative of Bethania. At
night she frequently arose to pray; often did
the light of day find her kneeling, her hands
raised towards the crucifix, her parted lips
wreathed into smiles through the happiness of
soul and the ecstatic raptures of her heart.

The days of her probation were past; Christ's
youthful spouse was now in her twenty-second
year; the dearest wishes of her heart were about
to be satisfied—she was called to consecrate and
give herself for ever to her *Beloved.* She was
standing in the presence of the bishop, surrounded by the virgin choir of Carthage, with the
saintly Rufina and a patrician lady named Marcella by her side. These stood nigher than the
rest, because they had been chosen to be her
sponsors. Although it was only just day, there
was quite a large gathering; every Christian
household in the city wished to do public honor
to the virtues and worth of the shrinking Angela. Hanno's noble lady and her daughter were

among the first to arrive ; in her quality of catechumen, Vivia had the right of remaining with
the congregation of the faithful up to the time
of the commencement of the oblation of the sacred mysteries.

The altar was arrayed in grand style as on the
highest festivals.   It was covered with a snow-
white cloth elaborately embroidered and fringed
with gold.   The most beautiful flowers of the
season were tastefully arranged in alabaster
vases and draped baskets, and filled the whole
edifice with fragrance and perfume. Gold and
silver lamps, the gifts of wealthy Carthaginian
Christians, hung at intervals and diffused a soft
and mellow light throughout the place. Not a
sound was to be heard ; the people held their
very breath, as if it were the dread moment
when, at the voice of the priest, God descends
among his children. Optatus had arisen with
the pastoral staff in his hand and the mitre on
his head.

In a few sentences he recapitulated all the
mysterious sublimity of virginity, which, "in a
body mortal and subjected to the humiliating law
of sin, raises man to the purity of the angel.
How beautiful and precious to the eyes of God is
that virtue which the immaculate Mary esteemed more than all the prerogatives of the divine maternity, which Christ glorified in his in-
carnation by suspending all the laws of nature
to be born of a virgin, and which he honored in

his beloved disciple—that virtue which gives even to the peasant's daughter the immortal king of Glory to be her Bridegroom and her Spouse! Henceforth she shall call him her *Beloved*, her *Only Love*. In return she shall be called by the sweet name of *sister*, *dove*, and *spouse*, holy and pleasing titles that will make her heart thrill with joy for all eternity, for then love will unite her more closely to her *Beloved* and she shall follow him inseparably and for ever in the train of her spotless companions in heaven.

"Such a vocation comes wholly from God's goodness, for he chooses whom he willeth; the creature has no right or title to selection. This is the highest vocation possible for woman, and hence it entails on her the gravest duties and the most exalted virtues. The Christian virgin must live by prayer, she must love retirement, she must fly from the world and its tumults, she must ever meditate on the law of God, watch over and guard her innocence, in order to keep herself *holy in mind and body*, and she must consecrate to Jesus Christ all the affections of her heart, because he is a jealous Spouse and will have no rival."

When the bishop had concluded his remarks, voices, melodious and sweet as those before God's throne in heaven, entoned a sacred hymn. "How beautiful and heavenly fair," sang they, "is the chaste Spouse of the virgin! How sweet is his countenance, how pleasing his voice! The heart throbs and beats for joy when it hears him say: *Arise, hasten, my love, my dove, come from Libanus,* and I will encircle thy brow with a precious crown, the symbol and pledge of our union. *O Beloved!* behold thy sister, thy spouse. She is like the flower refreshed by the dews of morning and tinted with the sun's rays, like the spotless lily growing in the silence and solitude of the hidden dell. Behold her who has sighed so long under *the shadow of him whom she desires,* seeking him so anxiously because *she languishes with love for him.* O Jesus, divine Son of Mary! O heavenly Spouse of virgins, to thee alone be honor, glory, and love for ever and ever!"

The choir of virgins ceased; Angela knelt before the altar; the bishop sat upon his throne.

"What do you ask, my child?" he said.

With downcast eyes and clasped hands she answered: "Father, if I be not too unworthy, I ask to receive the veil of consecration to Jesus Christ, the only object of my love in this world, and to be enrolled, to-day and for ever, among his holy spouses."

"Your piety is known to me, your virtues gladden the hearts of your parents, edify the Church of Carthage, and console its suffering and aged pastor; but, my child, the favor that you seek is very great, and, as I have said, the duties of a virgin are onerous. Have you seriously meditated on this before God?"

"Of what avail would be my thoughts, who am but a lowly maiden and the last of God's servants, did he not give light? Since I was twelve years old I have always sighed for the grace which I now implore from your consideration and kindness. I will never have any spouse other than my beloved Lord. He has wounded my heart with the darts of his sweet and chaste love."

"My child, the world presents only dangers and temptations. *The spirit is prompt but the flesh is weak*, are the words of Him to whom you desire to consecrate yourself. His nascent Church enjoys only a very uncertain peace, which at any moment may be disturbed by the storm. Do you feel yourself strong enough to be able to resist the world and yourself, to dye with your blood, if necessary, the veil which is about to be placed on your head, and to twine the palm of martyrdom with the lily of virginity?"

"Of myself, father, I am only misery and sin; but with the help of God's grace *I can do all things*. My Beloved has infused into my heart *a love strong as death*. I feel that the world and the flesh could not pluck it from my bosom. With that love what have I to fear? I could brave death and all its terrors. I should be only too happy, father, if, as you have just said, my Beloved should judge me worthy of reddening this holy veil with my blood, as the blessed Thecla did, and more recently the virgin Pota-

miena, almost whose martyrdom the holy Bishop
of Jerusalem has told us a few days ago."

These words produced a profound impression
on the entire congregation and lit up the face of
Angela with a heavenly radiance.

" Generous child," said the good Optatus, as
he brushed away a tear, " may your wish be accomplished. Christ receives you as his spouse, and
the church of Carthage admits you among the
number of her virgins."

The countenance of the youthful *bride* of
Christ regained its habitual calm. Her glance
seemed to settle again into that mysterious and
tender expression which it constantly wore during the hours of her ecstasies when she gazed on
her *Beloved.* Her parted and smiling lips lisped
words of gratitude and love which fell rather
on the heart than on the ear of the beholders.
She was noticed to press her hands nervously on
her heart as if apprehensive of being obliged to
succumb to the violence of her emotions and
heavenly raptures.

Then the bishop blessed the different portions
of the habit prepared for the young virgin, by
reciting over each the usual prayers already prescribed by the Church, and which are almost identical with those made use of to-day on similar
occasions. According as they were blessed,
Rufina and Marcella placed them upon the new
spouse of the Lamb. Angela was so rapt in
ecstasy that she neither moved nor seemed to

feel even the trembling hand of the bishop as he traced the sign of the cross on her forehead previous to placing thereon the veil, symbol of her solemn consecration.

Shortly after at a signal from her *sponsors*, she arose, ascended the steps, and laid her head on the altar to signify the oblation of herself to the Lord ; she then lifted up towards heaven the floral crown prepared for her by her companions as if to offer it to her *Beloved.* She returned, saluted the altar by a genuflection, and then proceeded to give the kiss of peace to her sister virgins ; meantime a hymn of thanksgiving was sung. . . . Soon after the Holy Sacrifice was begun.

When the deacon, in a loud voice, gave notice to the catechumens to retire, a young woman, weeping and holding her new-born infant in her arms, came and knelt before Angela to recommend herself to her prayers ; this was Vivia, who was touched to the depths of her soul upon seeing the young virgin consecrating herself for ever to the Lord. Angela knew and loved her ; she affectionately embraced the mother and the child. " Courage," said she in a low voice, " courage, Vivia, for you, too, will soon wear a glorious crown—more fortunate than myself, perhaps, for you will purchase it nobly at the price of your blood." Her prophecy was destined to be soon fulfilled.

CHAPTER XII.

THE REVOLT.

It was far in the night; the sky was overcast and the wind bore clouds of dust as it howled fitfully across the plain and echoed to the rumbling of distant thunder. The soldiers of Jarbas had been all day under arms by reason of a false alarm raised in the camp, and they now rested from their fatigues. No sound was to be heard except the monotonous step of the sentinels slowly pacing to and fro on their rounds.

An old man was walking rapidly up and down in a tent lighted by a flickering lamp. He had been watching and waiting so long that he had to replenish his little lamp. This man appeared to be restless and agitated; he glanced at the hour-glass often and impatiently, and listened at the tent door for the slightest noise.

"What can have happened to him," said he to himself. "Has he missed his way in the woods or in the sands of the desert? Could he have been murdered? Perhaps he has betrayed me? The wretch! he is ready to do anything for a little money."

Just then the movable curtain that covered the entrance to the tent was stealthily drawn aside, and Sylvanus—for it was he that we saw and heard in the tent—saw the black slave entering covered with sweat and dust.

" Why, Afer, what has happened to detain you so long ? I have been expecting you since yesterday. But, say, have you seen the chief of the Numidians ? How did he receive my message ?"

" Badly, very badly at first. I thought I had arranged matters so that there could be no difficultly ; but the bear ! just think, he coolly took me for a spy seeking to examine his troops and encampment. He would hardly listen to a single word from me ; he thrust me into irons, and put me to the torture in order to make me tell my business and my secrets. Luckily for me, I had nothing to conceal from him, else to escape such horrible torture I suppose I would have told everything. What a savage fellow is this leader of those savages ! I feel all my bones still aching and out of joint ; I suppose for the sake of this accursed business I shall not have the use of my legs for a long time to come !"

" How did you return to the camp, then ? You went on foot to avoid suspicion, you remember."

" By the chief's orders one of his horsemen took me up behind him and brought me to within a league of the camp. He would come no nigher, as it was already dark, and he was afraid of being surprised by some of the advanced pickets. Being thus left to shift for myself as best I could, I crawled along slowly and suffering torture at every step."

"Well, will he take advantage of the information that I sent him? Will he so arrange matters as to be here with his cavalry at the nick of time—that is to say, to-morrow, for then the revolt will be at its height? His co-operation, Afer, is indispensably necessary to us. I am well acquainted with the dispositions and feelings of our soldiers; at the first sign of a revolt many of them will side with Jarbas; unless the confusion which must necessarily arise from the sudden attack of the enemy's cavalry aid us, the success of the project will be next to impossible."

"When *the murderous fellow, that tiger with a human head,* saw that in spite of all his tortures I persisted unswervingly in my first declarations, he changed his tone and listened attentively to what I wanted to say. Then, after a moment's reflection, 'To-morrow,' he said, 'I will give you an answer.'"

"Well, what is it?"

"He will come with all his cavalry, and it is a strong force, as well as I could judge. At noon to-morrow he will assault the camp from the woods near by, and will fall upon our entrenchments like a thunderbolt. You know how Numidian horsemen can ride; their horses devour space without leaving a hoof-mark on the sand."

"Afer, the immortal gods are on our side, and

so to morrow my dagger will be steeped in the blood of the hated Vivia's husband! Go, take some rest; you need it sorely. Meanwhile, I will go to make final arrangements with some of the soldiers."

He left the tent after having cautioned his accomplice to preserve secrecy and silence. The black slave smiled at this advice; he knew full well that the least indiscretion would cost him his life.

After what we have just related, the reader will be at no loss to divine the object and nature of the mysterious interviews in which Sylvanus was occupied during the remainder of the night. We will pass them over, therefore, to come at once to the event whose issue was destined to result so fatally to the Church of Carthage, but especially to the Christian heroine whose glorious history we have undertaken to relate.

At about the third watch the storm came on with all that mad fury which belongs to hot climates. It soon passed away, however, so that at sunrise the clouds had rolled away and left the air refreshing and cool. The soldiers swarmed from their tents and formed themselves into groups to chat and while away the time. The false alarm of the previous day was the universal topic, and gave occasion to many jokes and much merriment. Soon, however, as if chance had so ordained it, there appeared to be an orator in every group; excitement, anger, and rage ran like wildfire among the troops, causing the wildest din and confusion.

"What sort of a life is this," cried some, "for brave men who are accustomed to fight and live like soldiers? We do nothing but yawn and lie in our tents, or, like blacksmiths, spend the day in furbishing our weapons for show and dress parade! Why do we never get a brush at the enemy?"

"Have we obeyed our country's call, left our wives and children," said others, "to leave our bones to bleach on the burning sands, where no one can live as soon as the hot weather sets in?"

"Our young general cares very little about the trouble and inconvenience of his soldiers. His own tent is proof against sun and rain; he has his own slaves to rig and trick it up for him. He can enjoy himself to his heart's content, for he can eat and drink and play as much as he pleases."

"This Jarbas is an effeminate young fellow, then? I never should have thought so."

"Would that were all! But he is a traitor. It seems he has been holding communications with the enemy. His messengers have been seen going stealthily to the Numidian camp. We are betrayed. The day has been appointed to deliver us over to the barbarians and to throw open to them the gates of Carthage."

"That is a lie! that is a calumny!" cried the soldiers who had not yet joined the revolt. 'Jarbas never was and never will be a traitor."

"The accursed Christians are the enemies of the gods and of the country, and are capable of any and everything. The man who betrays his religion may well betray his country also."

"Who dares to say that our general has gone over to the new religion?"

"Who is so simple and blind as to doubt it?"

"Were that so! . . . but no, that is one of the lies invented by his enemies. They are jealous of his fame, and cannot brook that one so young should have been selected by the senate to lead the expedition."

"Then, if he is not a Christian, why does he never show himself when the priests are offering sacrifice? Why has he selected his bodyguard from among those who are well known to belong to that abominable sect?"

The tumult became greater and louder among the troops. In their excitement a number of soldiers vowed and swore they would leave the camp. Just then appeared old Sylvanus, followed by priests clad in their robes of office.

Thereupon the ringleaders began to shout: "Here comes that good old man—that man loved by the gods, who came hither a few days ago like a messenger from heaven. Ask him and he will tell you what should be our opinion of Jarbas and what we ought to do."

"Brave soldiers," said the old mountain shepherd, affecting an air of inspiration, "the gods of Carthage are wroth. You seem as if you had abandoned their worship, for it is only rarely that their altars are now reddened with the blood of a few paltry and lean victims. A wicked and sacrilegious religion, of which they have a horror, threatens to dethrone them, and to convert to its own purposes the incense you formerly burned so lavishly in their honor. Their anger is ready to fall on you. They have called me from out of the desert to give you timely warning. They will give their protection to the Numidians, because these continue to worship them and to tolerate no traitor to the ancient faith. They will be their allies against you. Unless you hasten to propitiate Mars, the God of War, he will give them the victory, and the sands under your feet shall be your graves.

"Soldiers, follow me! I go to seek your leader, and to speak to him in the name of the immortal gods. He is said to be a Christian. The truth shall soon be known. He must declare, in the presence of the entire army, whether he has or has not embraced that abominable creed. Mars demands a solemn sacrifice; this is the only way to appease his anger; but he requires that the sacrifice be presided over by your general. If he refuses, then it will depend on yourselves whether you be crushed or not under the hoofs of the barbarians' horses."

As he ceased speaking a mighty shout arose that awoke all the echoes of the desert. The soldiers who had remained in their tents now rushed forth under the impression that the Numidians were upon them. In a moment the whole army was astir and saw how matters stood. Some captains vainly strove to quell the tumult; their powerless voices were drowned in the uproar. Confusion reigned everywhere; the sentinels abandoned their posts; it seemed as if the whole camp was suddenly seized with frenzy.

Jarbas was in his tent; but as some of his guards had apprised him of the attitude assumed by the troops, the shouts and cries of the revolters did not come upon him unawares. His great soul was not even disturbed. Without putting on his armor, or even his helmet, he strode to the door of his tent. Equally devoid of pride or dismay, he calmly viewed the surging crowd as they made the welkin ring with their seditious cries. When they came within speaking distance:

"Soldiers," said he, in ringing tones, "what would ye with your general?"

When lightning suddenly bursts forth and the sharp rattle of near thunder falls on the ear, the most animated discussions cease; the traveller pauses on his way in fear and awe. At the words, *Soldiers, what would ye with your general?* every sound was hushed; the heaving and swaying crowd appeared as if rooted to the ground; the rustling of the bird winging its flight overhead could have been heard. But the inexorable Sylvanus was there, and, lest a reaction should take place, cried out at once:

" General, the army is dissatisfied, and the immortal gods are angered."

" Who are you," replied Jarbas with dignity, "and who has authorized you to speak for the whole army ? Thank your white hairs, old man ; had I not been taught to respect that crown I should have you instantly arrested by my guards."

" My name ? it can matter little to you ; but in me you see a man inspired by the gods. They it was that sent me hither, and I stand here the interpreter of their sacred and dread will. Hearken to me therefore, O Jarbas ! and restrain your impatience. Already I have told you the army is dissatisfied ; it burns to meet the enemy, but instead of leading it against them you keep it here in disgraceful inactivity. It is even said that you are a traitor to your country, that you hold secret correspondence with the barbarians."

" Cease, old man ; Jarbas is above such slander, and can answer it only by contempt ! "

"Hurra ! well said !" shouted hundreds of voices everywhere through the crowd.

Sylvanus saw at once that he must shift his ground or his cause was lost.

"Such reports, of course, interest me but little," said he ; "it is for the soldiers to judge how much truth there may be in them. I have come to speak to you concerning the gods and their just displeasure ; they complain of having been abandoned for a new religion which finds but too much favor here. Mars, the terrible God of War, has sworn to fight in the ranks of the Numidians, to deluge the earth with our warriors' blood, unless solemn sacrifice be offered to him in the camp this very day."

"If there are cowards among my brave soldiers let them follow this man ; let them go and butcher a few harmless beasts and spill their impotent blood; I shall make no opposition. Go, poor old man, you have already said more than was necessary. . . "

"I would have you to understand that I bow to no power save that of the gods. I have not yet finished. You yourself, at the head of the army, must preside at this sacrifice ; such is the will of the invincible son of Jupiter. I await your answer."

"You will not have to wait very long. Jarbas is a soldier with an army at his back ; he is always ready to lead his brave legions to battle and to victory ; but he is no sacrificator, nor shall his sword be ever sullied by other blood than that of his country's enemies."

"Your words betray you, and I thank the gods for it. The report is therefore true ; proud Carthage, Juno's favored city, has, then, entrusted the honor of her flag to a youthful general, who secretly despises her gods and belongs to the accursed sect of the Christians ! "

"Obstinate old man, wisdom, I perceive, has fled from your bosom, for your lips traduce and malign innocent persons, who have done you no evil, who are just, law-abiding, and ask only to be allowed to follow in peace the dictates of their conscience."

" Do you acknowledge that you yourself are a Christian ?"

" Jarbas's lips have never been polluted by a falsehood. Yes, soldiers, the general whom you have seen fighting at your head, and who has some claim to glory, he whose ambition it is to lead you back in triumph to Carthage, after having achieved the overthrow of the Numidians— yes, Jarbas is a Christian; he is one because he had to acknowledge that the gods whom he formerly worshipped are no gods, and that the God of the Christians is the only true God."

There was so much dignity and conviction in these words, so much majesty in the speaker's attitude and looks, that the entire army seemed awed into silence and incapable of expressing its opinion and feelings. Sylvanus himself grew pale, and, forgetting the part he was playing, fumbled under his tunic for the poniard he had there concealed, when wild and discordant cries burst suddenly from all the ranks.

" Huzza! long live the general !" vociferated his faithful body-guard, who were all Christians.

" Down with Jarbas! down with the traitor! death to the despiser of the gods !" shouted the revolted pagans under the leadership of Sylvanus.

In vain did Jarbas calmly strive to quell the tumult, to drown the din of the storm. The thunders of the revolt made it impossible for his voice to be heard. *Down with Jarbas! down with the traitor! death to the despiser of the gods!* Swords began to leap from their scabbards and lances to be brandished; the more violent urged on the timid and those who still held back through respect for the authority of the general.

Just then the blade of a dagger gleamed like a flash of lightning. Urged on by the desire of revenge and burning for the glory of being first to strike Jarbas, Sylvanus rushed on him; but before the dagger could descend two guards had seized, disarmed, and carried, rather than dragged, the assassin to the general's tent, where they securely bound him.

With the exception of the soldiers of the bodyguard, who, like the general, stood facing the army, no one had observed Sylvanus's bloody deed. The others had merely noted the rush made by the guards and the hurried arrest of the prisoner, so that it appeared as if this had been done by the general's order. This idea fired the soldiers with the greatest fury and rage. "He has insulted and chained the messenger of the gods," cried they; "death to this wicked and sacrilegious man!" A thousand swords were raised to smite him.

But the faithful guards pressed around and

made him a rampart with their persons, determined to defend him against the furious soldiery.

As Christians they were meek and humble of heart, ready to die, to be slaughtered like lambs, for the faith; but they were fearless soldiers also, unwavering in discipline and obedience, and they now saw in their opponents only rioters and assassins, whose onslaught they were prepared to meet sword in hand.

A bloody, a fearful slaughter was imminent; on one side were numbers, rage, and blind fanaticism; on the other, courage, sense of duty, devotedness, and enthusiasm. Swords were being crossed, comrades, brothers in arms, were on the point of slaughtering each other, when suddenly the ground trembled and wild shouts rent the air; the Numidian cavalry were rushing like a whirlwind on the camp.

In presence of the enemy the soldier speedily forgets his bickerings and resentment; he only thinks of fighting bravely and winning the day. The revolted soldiers instinctively fell back and lowered their arms; the guards did the same. Profiting by this momentary lull, Jarbas cried out: "Soldiers, the barbarians are storming the camp; let us at them, and victory shall be ours." At these words the whole army faced about and rushed on the Numidians, who had already taken possession of the outer entrenchments.

The general, as we have previously stated, stood

unarmed at his tent door when Sylvanus first made his appearance. When the threatening soldiery surged towards him he had only time to seize his buckler and sword. Hastily demanding his helmet and breastplate, he marshalled his troops and placed himself at their head. They led out his war-horse, black as ebony, swift as the winds of the desert. The faithful steed came forth neighing, pawing the ground, and champing the bit; he had heard the sound of the clarion and the cry of battle. In another instant Jarbas would be at their head. His hand was on the flowing mane of his steed, when he was observed to stagger and grow pale; his hand dropped from the horse's mane, and he fell bathed in blood among his guards. They had scarcely noticed a diminutive, unknown negro, who had glided in like a snake and had rushed past the general. While he was being supported and led to his tent the black had disappeared.

CHAPTER XIII.

THE Numidians had profited by the information given them by Sylvanus. At the appointed hour the cavalry sallied suddenly from a neighboring thicket, flew across a short stretch of sandy plain, and found the camp unguarded. On that day the Carthagenian army had been undone had not the barbarians, in their love of booty, scattered themselves to pillage instead of making in a body for the tent of the general-in-chief. Jarbas's body-guard came up first and fell with such fury on the straggling bands that they had not time to rally; the legions lost but little time in forming their ranks and presenting a regular line of battle.

Meanwhile the youthful general lay weltering in blood on his cot. A skilful leech examined and prepared to bind the wounds. Guided by a steady and practised hand, the dagger had made a deep wound in Jarbas's side a little below the heart. The blade must have been thin and sharp, for the cut was narrow and the blood-flow small. Only three or four of the guard had remained away from the fight; their looks questioned the man of science and anxiously awaited the final decision he was about to pronounce.

In spite of the death-like pallor of his countenance, Jarbas had lost nothing of his unruffled calmness. His half-opened eyes seemed to follow his faithful servants and to strive to express his gratitude for their devotedness and grief. From time to time he pressed the hands of the aged physician as he bent over the bed, attentively watching the changes of the wounded general, while pretending to be occupied only in stanching with tepid water the blood that trickled from the wound.

Aruntius, so the leech was called, was not born at Carthage; he was a native of Lybia. After his first studies had been passed through at home, he visited Egypt, Greece, and Italy, gathering treasures of knowledge and laboring to perfect himself in his favorite art. After twenty years spent in travel, he returned to his native place to devote himself wholly to the noble profession for which he had so long and so laboriously prepared himself.

Being a man of profound research and loving the ways and manners of the olden times, he was superior to the prejudices that blind or rather tyrannize over the common herd of the narrow-minded multitude. The duties of his profession often brought him into contact with Christians. Their virtues had challenged his attention. He re-

solved to examine and study a religion that could
lift up the thoughts and aspirations of men beyond the powers of nature, and could, without
apparent effort, elevate their hearts and actions
to the noblest sentiments and most heroic sacrifices. As he sought the truth frankly and earnestly, grace perfected what study had commenced; accordingly he had received baptism
after the usual tests and conditions had been
complied with. Some years later his bishop had
judged him worthy of the priesthood, and had
imposed hands on him.

The Carthaginian army was preparing to march
against the Numidians when Aruntius came to
the city to consult with the metropolitan about
matters appertaining to the church to which he
was attached, and which had but recently lost its
first pastor. The holy prelate was persuaded that
he had discovered in him a man sent by Providence in the very nick of time. There was a con-
siderable number of Christians in the army, and
for these the presence of a priest would be a great
advantage and consolation. Vivia's husband had
been appointed to the command; he had decided
inclinations towards the new religion; the sweet
pleadings of his adored young wife and the important discussions had with the irresistible Tertullian had made a powerful impression on him.
The work must not be left half done, nor his
good dispositions be neglected. Hence the primate had proposed to Aruntius to accompany the

army, as he could pass for a physician; only the Christians and their commander would know that he was a priest. The self-sacrificing old man had readily accepted the offer, and so we now find him by the side of the illustrious victim anxiously striving to save his life.

Jarbas began to breathe more freely; his chest became lighter and found relief in the flow of blood, which Aruntius took good care not to arrest; but he grew sensibly weaker and his looks gradually assumed that languid appearance which indicates and measures, so to speak, the slow ebbing away of life. Jarbas himself was conscious of the approach of death; he understood it still more clearly under the mild workings of the grace that spoke louder than all in his heart.

"Father," said he in a weak voice to Aruntius, "what is your opinion of my wound? It is mortal, is it not?"

"God is all-powerful, my son! On the very threshold of death his breath can give new life when he will."

"Venerable Aruntius, fear not. Have I not faced death a hundred times on the battle-field! True, it is hard for a soldier to die by the hand of a base assassin! How much more preferable than this to have fallen gloriously by the steel of a brave enemy!"

"The glory of this world is naught, my son. God, who sees its emptiness, gives it not to those whom he wishes to crown with his own hand in heaven; adore, then, his blessed will; accept the sacrifice just as he requires it; his thoughts are wiser than ours."

"Father, forgive this suggestion of pride. I humble myself under the hand of God; but will you permit me to leave this world without having purified my soul by the sacred waters of Baptism?"

"The God whom you have so nobly confessed to-day in the presence of the whole army has already recognized and marked you for one of his. . . . Jarbas, do you believe in him? Do you acknowledge him to be the only true God?"

"I do, and I renounce with my whole heart all the false gods that I have worshipped in my blindness."

"Do you believe in Christ, his eternal Son, God and Lord like him, who for our sakes became man and died on the cross?"

"Yes, I believe in him; I adore, bless, and love this God of goodness who has suffered so much for me! His holy name fills my heart with confidence and joy. O sweet Jesus, Son of God, Son of the Virgin Mary, God of my beloved Vivia, thou art mine also!"

"Do you believe in the Holy Ghost, the Sanctifier, who spoke by the prophets, inspired the apostles and filled them with wisdom and strength?"

"Father, I believe all that you have taught me, as well as all the inscrutable mysteries of re-

ligion. Holy Church of Christ my Saviour, I
make profession of all thy faith, I receive every
article of thy wonderful and sublime creed."

Jarbas seemed to rally; his eyes became less
dim, his face less pale, his voice grew stronger
and firmer. To look at him then you would have
thought that he had simply swooned, and that his
life was in no danger. It was because there was
so much hope in his soul, and in his heart so much
love and happiness! The influence of grace had
momentarily overcome suffering and the sensible
action of the gradual sinking which was to end
so fatally. The venerable Arnntius was not deceived ; so he hastened for baptismal water, consecrated and kept ready for cases where baptism
was not given solemnly ; he poured it slowly on
the brow of the catechumen while pronouncing
the triple invocation prescribed by Jesus Christ
himself.

"Jarbas," said he, "heaven is now open to
you. If such be God's will, die in peace. Christ
awaits you and holds in his hands a crown infinitely more valuable than any that Carthage
could bestow upon you after your victories. All
your sins have been forgiven; imitate the mercy of
your Saviour—do you also pardon all your enemies, even the one who so basely murdered you.
Remember that your Lord on the cross asked forgiveness for his murderers."

"The grace of God has filled my soul, father,
and all hatred has died within me. Methinks I

can have done no evil to the man who lifted his dagger against me; I know him not. Let him be brought hither; I wish to say to him that I die pardoning him."

"He has fled, and is now in all probability far from the camp; but the old man who instigated the revolt and secretly fanned it for some days past has not succeeded in escaping, and awaits in chains the terrible sentence which the army will certainly pronounce upon him."

"Let him be brought; I shall be happy to set him at liberty. Perhaps some day he may remember that Christ's religion is one of charity and mercy, and may wish to embrace it."

The aged Sylvanus was brought in by the guards. The expression of his countenance was forbidding and savage. No tremor shook his frame as his cold glance surveyed the prostrate form of the general lying on his bloody couch.

"Friend," said Jarbas to him, "what have I done to you? why have you sought to take my life?"

"I had sworn to kill you. Afer was more fortunate than I, it appears."

"Who is Afer? You are, then, acquainted with the man who stabbed me?"

"I may have been wrong, perhaps, to have told you his name; it is enough for you to know that he has simply remedied my awkwardness, and that I took care to poison his dagger."

"Unfortunate old man, I pity you. But let me

ask once more what could have been the cause of your hatred to me, who never saw you before to-day ?"

"Are you not the husband of the base Vivia, of that accursed woman who robbed me of my child, sole object of my love—of that woman whom I hate with all the powers of my soul, and who, I hope, will soon go to meet you in the gloomy sojourn of the dead; for she, too, must die to sate my vengeance !"

The thought of Fatima now flashed on Jarbas's mind; he remembered all that he had heard regarding the implacable hatred of her father. Since his marriage he had often remarked the sweetness, modesty, and docility of that young slave, for whom, as we have already stated, Vivia entertained all the affection of a sister.

"Your daughter is an angel," said he to Sylvanus. "You cursed her, while she has never ceased to pray for you. She pardons you for the terrible injuries you have done her, for the bitter tears you have forced her to shed. May she never learn that her unhappy father has made her sweet mistress a widow ! Like her, I pardon you in the name and for the love of Christ, who pardoned me, and who, I hope, will pardon you also. Guards, respect the last will of your commander, and do you, venerable Aruntius, see that it be executed without delay ! Let this man be set free and let him depart from the camp this very hour."

He held out his hand to him, but the old man made no movement to seize it. His last glance at his generous liberator was one of hate. Jarbas raised his eyes to heaven, no doubt to pray for him. At that very moment, far from the tent where this scene occurred, in one of the wealthiest mansions of Carthage, a fervent prayer, accompanied by a flood of tears, went up to God's throne; a young slave was asking pardon for an obstinate sinner, whom she called by the sweet name of father, generously offering herself as a sacrifice for his conversion. God in his infinite mercy heard this two-fold prayer; the desire of martyrdom and of the gentle victim who immolated herself in spirit had found acceptance in his presence.

There had been too much agitation for the dying man. Moreover, the assassin's blade had been poisoned, as Sylvanus had declared with such savage exultation. The flow of blood began to cease in spite of Aruntius' efforts to make it continue, for he foresaw that otherwise the poison would act internally, and would speedily bring about the sad issue which from the beginning he saw was inevitable. He accordingly addressed himself to the duty of consoling and fortifying the last moments of the man to whom he had just now, by baptism, opened the way to heaven.

He drew from his bosom a small golden case divided into two compartments, which he habitu-

ally carried with him ever since he accompanied the army. "My child," said he to the dying officer, "I deem it necessary in your case to
forestall the time and end the prudent silence
wisely prescribed by the Church in the case of
catechumens. I have instructed you regarding
the marvellous and ineffable mystery which shall
proclaim to the end of time the charity of Christ.
On the eve of his death he took bread, blessed it,
and by his omnipotent power changed it into his
Body and Blood. He conferred upon his priests
for ever the power of working the same miracle
as often as they repeat at the altar the words pronounced by him at the Last Supper. Great is
your faith ; receive, therefore, the adorable Body
of your Saviour; may it be to you the pledge of
the glorious and eternal life that awaits you."

The dying man received the Sacred Host with
the most profound reverence and piety ; happiness and love beamed from and lit up his whole
countenance. Then, opening the second division
of his precious box he anointed him with holy
oil, repeating a prayer at each unction according
to the instructions given by St. James. "May
the peace of our Lord be with you," said he at
the conclusion of the holy ceremony, after which
he and the guards knelt in prayer at the foot of
the bed.

The pale, discolored lips of the Christian soldier continued to move in prayer, and fervently
kissed the crucifix as often as the priest presented

it. Summoning his strength : " My God," said he, in an almost inarticulate voice, " I return to thee; receive me into thy paternal bosom ; console my loved Vivia, protect my child, and have mercy on the man . . . "

His lips ceased to move.

" Heaven counts another soul saved," said the aged Aruntius, rising and tenderly closing the eyes of the youthful soldier who had just fallen asleep in the peace of the Lord and the glory of marytrdom.

Sylvanus was set at liberty beyond one of the entrances to the camp, with a warning not to return under penalty of forfeiting his head. Dark and silently he wended his way to his mountain home, revolving, as he plodded along, new schemes of vengeance.

His departure was not one minute too early, for the army was returning after a bloody victory over the Numidians, clamoring for possession of the old hypocrite who had induced them to revolt. They had learned the sad news of Jarbas's death, compassed by the dagger of a slave hired for that purpose by the impostor. Had he fallen into their hands he would not have had to wait for the slow process of a trial; his torn carcass would have been thrown outside the camp to feed the vultures of the desert.

We will not pause to describe the grief and lamentations of the army; the officers and the soldiers, even those who had been most violent during the outbreak, all mourned for him, and many, as they smote their breasts, acknowledged that they had been accessories to the crime to which he had fallen a victim. The tears shed by these iron-hearted warriors and these tardy regrets were doubtlessly a glorious tribute paid to the dead general; but he was insensible to the glory of a world whose nothingness he now fully understood. The Christian hero was now listening to the triumphal canticles of the angels and of his brethren the elect; with them he was celebrating the glory of God, the only Omnipotent, and, in the words of the priest Aruntius, Christ had placed on his brow a crown incomparably more precious than any that the gratitude of Carthage could award to him.

CHAPTER XIV.

PRESENTIMENTS. —

THERE has often been much discussion regarding the amount of credeuce to be given to *presentiments*, and by the term are implied certain strong, irresistible impressions which, without reflection or known cause, seize upon, hold, master the mind so that, do what it may, it cannot shake them off. As the etymology of the word implies, presentiments necessarily regard future events, or events which take place at a distance or under circumstances that preclude their knowledge.

Freethinkers, whose whole talent consists in scoffing at things that are and continue to exist without their avowal or consent, smile with pity at the word presentiment, especially if they see or suspect anything touching on the supernatural or divine. Presentiments, they will say in a magisterial and dogmatic tone, is only the result of imagination, enthusiasm, nervousness, or mental excitement. It is useless to enquire further of these extraordinary men, who pretend to know everything, and set themselves up for oracles among their benighted fellow-mortals.

It would be in vain to allege that learned, serious, well-balanced minds have not experienced these sudden, unaccountable impressions, and that they were incontrovertibly verified by the event —that a man young in years and of robust health has an irresistible foreboding of proximate death, another feels that some calamity is about to befall him. Well, these presentiments were felt, were repeatedly declared, and *were* true, for they were actually verified. But our self-appointed oracles will only answer by the same contemptuous smile, the same everlasting formula—*phantoms of the brain, dreams of an empty or excited imagination.*

Every man cannot be a freethinker at will; that requires so much knowledge and talent! We frankly confess that we are not one; that we belong to that unsophisticated class of people who candidly believe and admit *facts*, even though they may not be able to explain them by natural causes; so, even at the risk of being thought weak-minded and credulous, we will relate what happened at Carthage only a few hours after the general of its army died by the dagger of a hired assassin.

Two women, both of our acquaintance, are conversing together in a room. The one, in the humble garb befitting her servile condition, is seated and holds in her hands, in an absent and distracted way, a piece of embroidery just commenced; the other, by her bearing and attitude, seems to belong to a more exalted rank; she is standing, and holds in her arms an infant which she scarcely appears to notice, so deeply is she buried in melancholy reverie. Both women are pale, and their eyes bear the traces of recent tears. They are Vivia, the noble spouse of Jarbas, and Fatima, whom we shall in future call Felicitas, this being the name she received on the day she was received among the catechumens. These women had embraced each other, without, however, having exchanged the sweet words of affectionate salutation that usually passed between them.

Since her interview with the grave and austere Tertullian the young patrician lady has undergone a great change. She is more humble and subdued in air and manner; her garb is less stylish although still in keeping with her rank. She no longer wears those costly necklaces or golden, jewel-bedecked bracelets for which the Christian priest had so severely reprimanded her. Her long tresses, in which she formerly took so much pride, are arranged with less art and care. The rich and artistic furniture that we described on a former occasion has disappeared; her couch has been replaced by a plain, unornamented bed. The mother's heart still betrays itself, however, for the infant's cradle is still the same. Vivia had sold and given to the poor everything that was unsuited to the grave and severe tastes of a Christian, and was preparing herself by a more retired life, by prayer and good works, for the grace of baptism, which she was to receive at Easter-tide.

After a long pause she said to Felicitas:

"How late you have come this evening, and how long the time has seemed! Rufina, as you are aware, has gone into the country with my mother. I was all alone, and I never had greater need of a heart and a friend to share with me the strange uneasiness and anxiety that oppresses me!"

"What could one like me do for you, good lady? To serve you devotedly, to assist you in tending your child, to rock him to sleep in his cradle, to watch with you in his sickness, and to try and spare you a little fatigue, is all that a girl of my humble rank can do. Assuredly, it is not from one like me that you could expect any consolation in your sorrow."

"How quickly and often you forget the request so frequently made, and repeated only yesterday just before we separated? When I am alone with you I am not a mistress but a sister. Have we not a common Father in heaven? Do we not adore the same God? are we not preparing for the same baptism? Before long, shall we not be washed in the same waters, dear Felicitas? and shall we not enjoy together the happiness of sitting at the same table, at Christ's table, and partaking of that heavenly banquet about which we have been informed somewhat, but which I long to know more clearly and fully?"

" How sweet to my ear the name of sister—I, a poor orphan, who never knew my mother, and who for so many years have been begging of God to return to me the love and the heart of a father who abandoned me! Dearest sister, who can have annoyed you? why are you so sad and grieved?"

" Alas! do I myself know what is the matter and what is tugging at my heart-strings? What a crowd of frightful and sad pictures are passing through my mind! What mournful thoughts assail me! I have vainly striven to dispel these sad phantoms, but they follow me unceasingly. I have wept and prayed; but prayers and tears have failed to bring the relief they usually administer to the afflicted soul. O blessed, sweet Lord! if it should be so, if anything should have happened to my loved ones, to my dear, fond husband!"

" Why speak thus, Vivia? It is only a few days since you received direct intelligence from your noble husband, and were informed by him that the Numidians still remained hidden in their fastnesses; that they dared no longer to cope with our victorious troops; that he momentarily expected them to sue for peace, as they would be but only too glad to be able to retire with their shattered forces into their deserts and mountains."

" May God grant that my fears may prove to be groundless! But listen, dear sister, and judge for yourself. It was a short time after noon; my child slept quietly in his cradle, and I sat by his side. Suddenly I fell to trembling; I heard confused shouts and saw frenzied crowds of men rushing madly on. It seemed to me as if all this tumult was taking place in the camp and hard by my husband's tent. There were soldiers armed like ours, and sacrificators such as I remember to have seen in my childhood when my father occasionally took me to the pagan temple. They were led by an aged man of a dark and forbidding aspect, but whose appearance revived in me many early and half-forgotten memories. I vainly strove to turn away my eyes, but do what I would he was always before me. The sight of him made me shiver; it was useless to shut my eyes, to cover my face with my hands, for I could still see that horrid old man. My blood ran cold as ice and my limbs were bathed in perspiration."

" You must have fallen asleep, and some horrible dream—perhaps some reminiscence of the past . . ."

" No, no, Felicitas; I was as wide awake as I am at this moment. All that I tell you passed within myself, but appeared as real, and affected me as sensibly as if I saw it with my eyes and heard it with my ears. Oh! there can be but little doubt that God is preparing me for some imminent and terrible misfortune. I felt this so thoroughly that a cry burst from my soul as I called the name of Jarbas!

"Exhausted and beside myself, I fell on my

knees and threw myself prostrate in prayer.
When I arose I no longer heard the savage yells
nor the furious mob brandishing their swords
around my husband; the old man himself had
disappeared. A frightful spectacle presented
itself to the eyes of my soul. Pale and gasping
for breath, Jarbas lay stretched on a bed in his
tent. I saw blood, it was his; it flowed from a
wound in his heart. Another old man, a stranger to me, of a mild and venerable aspect, was
standing by his side. I saw him pour water on
Jarbas's head; he was doubtlessly a Christian
priest giving him baptism; I thought I even
heard the sacred words, Father, Son, and Holy
Ghost. I perceived also that he gave him something white to eat and then traced the sacred sign
of the cross on different parts of his body;
wherever these signs were made the flesh became
moist and shining. Will you believe it? I heard
Jarbas's voice most distinctly. With eyes lifted to
heaven he prayed, and in his prayer he mentioned
me and our darling infant! O Felicitas! my
noble husband is dead! In a few days his poor
remains will be brought back to Carthage."

"God is all goodness, put your trust in
him."

"He knows that in him alone I place all my
confidence."

"Your noble spouse will return to you well
and triumphant; heaven preserves him to your
affections, you and he will adore together for long

years to come the same God and the same Christ
his Son."

"Heaven does not give back its saints; it is I
who must go to Jarbas. May he not have long
to wait for me!"

"But these are nothing more than thoughts
which you yourself, perhaps, have conjured up in
your own mind by thinking of your husband and
his dangers. Must you for this abandon yourself
to grief and reject all hope?"

"Sister, these impressions come from God, I
verily believe. It was his hand that traced in my
soul those vivid pictures; they were so distinct
that even now I think I see them and Jarbas all
bloody on his bed, and can hear him pronouncing
my name and that of our child. No, I have no
longer a husband in this world! . . ."

She fell sobbing into the arms of Felicitas.

The two young women remained locked in
each other's embraces for a long time weeping
together. But after having vented their grief
they called to mind the great Consoler of the afflicted, and accordingly they knelt and prayed
fervently. Vivia's heart felt relieved from the
overwhelming load that weighed it to the earth;
prayer had brought to her soul the balm of resignation.

"Dear friend," she said, "our Heavenly Fa-
ther has had compassion on the *young widow!*
His tender pity has lifted up my downcast soul.
While we were praying I *saw* Jarbas in heaven,

smiling to me as the angels must smile on those
souls to which they desire to bring consolation.
May God give me the grace of being worthy of
my spouse, worthy of the eternal diadem which
he showed me.   But, beloved sister, you who are
always so calm and resigned, why did you look so
dazed and sad when you first came?   Occupied
with my own sorrows, I neglected to enquire the
the cause of your sadness.   Forgive my selfish-
ness!"

"As you are aware, my life is a sorrowful one;
I have long been accustomed to tears, and I do
little else than weep."

"But you are unusually sad to-day; you are
very pale, your eyes are red with tears, and you
tremble near me, who love you with all the affection of a sister; then that unusual delay in
coming, which I am at a loss to account for in you,
who are always so punctual and diligent.   Conceal
nothing from me, I beg and entreat!   Have you
heard any tidings?   Has anything befallen you?"

"What could I have heard?   I have lived quite
alone since Revocatus, the husband you gave me,
went to the camp with his master, and to-day I
have seen no one."

Felicitas appeared ill at ease; she turned aside
to hide the tears she could restrain no longer.

"What is the matter?" said Vivia, taking her
hands and drawing her to her bosom.   "If you
still love me, tell your sister what pains you so
deeply."

"How can I? how dare I? How can I tell to Jarbas's noble wife that the old man who seemed to appear to her, and whose scowling and forbidding look seemed to strike her with terror, and who perhaps—how can I tell her that he is the father of the poor unhappy slave whom your goodness has so highly favored, and whom you a moment ago called by the endearing name of sister? Have pity on him and on his unfortunate child!"

She fell on her knees and kissed Vivia's feet. The young patrician reeled as if thunderstricken; she buried her face in her hands; her heart beat as if it would burst, and to keep from falling she had to lean on the bed. As soon as she could collect her thoughts and strength she forced the young slave from her lowly position and said:

"What do you mean, Felicitas? Go on, I entreat you. Perhaps I have excited your imagination by my imprudent recital of what had alarmed me. Besides, did I not tell you that I did not recognize the old man, although it seemed to me that I had seen him before?"

"In the name of Jesus Christ, whom you have taught me to know and love, will you pardon *that man*, my unhappy father, for it is he?"

"Were he even the murderer of my beloved Jarbas I would forgive him, for Christ's sake and for the sake of obtaining mercy for myself."

She affectionately clasped the slave to her bosom.

"Blessings upon your head! may God bestow on you a hundredfold the generous pardon granted for his sake! I may now reveal to you the secret that I had determined to lock for ever in my bosom. Listen, then, in turn to what befell me. It was also shortly after noon; the most oppressive sadness came upon me suddenly and without apparent cause. My heart was steeped in an ocean of bitterness, tears streamed from my eyes; but, just as in your case, my tears brought no relief. My sadness was unlike anything ever experienced in all my sad life. I never before felt such anguish; I could scarcely breathe; I trembled for the life of my unborn child. In my terror and anguish I prayed to the Blessed Virgin, in the name of her beloved Son, to have pity on me. I lay motionless and prostrate on the ground. I know not how long I remained in this condition; can the man miraculously saved from the jaws of death tell how long his agony lasted? Mine was the agony of the heart.

"When I came to myself my sadness and tears were as great as ever, but I breathed with greater ease. I felt that my infant lived, and I fervently returned thanks to God. Every day I pray, as you are aware, for my unhappy father, that God in his infinite mercy would have compassion on him. I then heard an interior voice pronounce these words very distinctly: *Oh! pray for him; his last hour is come; he is falling into the hands of God's justice.* It seems to me as if these words are still re-echoing in thunder-tones in my heart.

"I know not who had spoken to me. Was it an angel from heaven come to warn me to avert by my prayers the anger of God about to fall on my guilty parent? or was it the Lord himself that paused in merciful pity before striking the blow? Who am I that God or his angel should come to me? All I can say is that the voice spoke as plainly as if I saw and heard the speaker with eye and ear.

"I drew forth and pressed to my trembling lips the cherished crucifix you gave me on the day of my reception among the catechumens, and which I always carry on my person. I bathed it with my tears, beseeching our merciful Lord to spare and pardon my father, as he on the cross pardoned the dying sinner at his side. I renewed the sacrifice of my life, so often offered before for the salvation of him who loved me so much and who has covered himself with guilt through excess of blind affection for me. '*Pray,*' repeated the voice, '*pray for him.*'

"Shortly after I lost consciousness, not suddenly, but as if I had swooned away; I know nothing about the ecstasies or raptures of which I heard you speak as being of such frequent occurrence with the saintly Angela ever since her childhood. Besides, God does not grant such privileges to a miserable sinner like me. These are doubtlessly reserved for pure, innocent souls,

for hearts burning with divine love. What I do
know is that the violence of my emotions and
agony exhausted all my strength so that I had
neither the will nor the power to move. At all
events, I saw my father as plainly as if he stood
within a few feet of me. His emaciated cheeks
were furrowed by deep wrinkles, his forehead
was bald, and a few thin, white locks fell straggling upon his bent shoulders. How very old
he had grown in a few years!

"His dark and forbidding countenance—just
the same as it was when he flung me from him
with an oath—breathed hatred and revenge. His
eyes, though riveted on some person whom I could
not see in the darkness, shot lightning glances
too terrible to be looked at. His hands and feet
were loaded with heavy chains; near him were
frightful instruments of torture and punishment.
The sight of them made my blood run cold, for I
felt they were brought for him. I thought, too,
that the ground was gradually opening under
him, revealing deep chasms, horrible to behold,
full of darkness and half lit up with lurid and
unnatural flames.

"In terror I shrieked: *Mercy, O my God!
for my unfortunate father*. Methought I then
heard a feeble voice, like that of a dying person,
gently utter the words, *Pardon him*. Suddenly
the scene changed; all the series of its horrible
pictures vanished; my father was alone, there
was sadness in his face, but there was also a cer-

tain calmness that lent to his appearance something of its former tranquillity. His eyes were
wet with tears, he was praying on his knees, as the
Christians do, before two plain tombs lit up by the
light of many lamps suspended from the vault.
When I recovered from my swoon and collected
my scattered senses I found myself quite exhausted and could scarcely drag myself hither to you.
But everything that I had seen in my strange
trance remained so stamped on my mind that I
still see them as plainly as I did then. What
can all this mean? what are those two tombs at
which my father prayed and wept? I am perfectly bewildered. Does our Lord condescend to
warn and prepare us for the accomplishment of
his designs? Can it be possible that your noble
husband has been assassinated? And if so, was
he regenerated by the saving waters of Baptism?
Is he now in glory as he appeared to us both?
Has my father spilt blood in his hatred of our
holy religion? Or rather, has not the spirit of
illusion and fear come to disturb the peace of our
souls and to shroud in grief the pure joys we feel
in the Lord since we were informed that we
should be admitted to the holy mysteries next
Easter? We shall soon know. God will have
pity on us; let us hope in him and commit ourselves to his paternal providence. But, oh! do
you not abandon the poor orphan; give me your
affection, you shall ever have my gratitude and
devotedness; may God ever guard you, who have

been so kind to me; may he soon þring you back your fond husband, and may his angels watch around the cradle of your infant! If God requires a victim, behold I am ready; I would gladly lay down my life for you, sister dear, since you will that I call you so, and for my poor father, that he may one day find mercy. . . ."

After having joined in prayer, they bade each other "good-night" and both retired to rest.

CHAPTER XV.

NEWS of the death of the gallant young soldier Jarlas speedily reached Carthage. A faithful and trusty messenger, in the person of the slave, Revocatus, was despatched from the camp by Aruntius to bear the tidings to Vivia. After official notification, the senate, even before appointing a successor to take command of the army, had solemnly decreed the honors of a triumph to the youthful hero so prematurely stricken down by death. By virtue of this decree his remains were to receive the same ovation and honors that would have been given to himself were he living, and a laurel crown was to be placed on his tomb as a mark of the country's gratitude. The legislature of Carthage, while it honored in this manner the memory of Jarbas, was as yet ignorant of the fact that he had died a Christian and a martyr to the faith.

Although the presentiments of which we have spoken in the preceding chapter had partially prepared Vivia, still the news of her husband's tragic end was a terrible blow. She shut herself up in her apartments with her mother, the pious

Ruffina, and Felicitas, and found consolation only in prayer and in the tender and kind words of the saintly Julia. Bishop Optatus and Tertullian came to visit her. The powerful exhortations of these men of God animated her faith and gave strength to her wounded heart. She wept, but who could blame the tears of a young woman so soon a bereaved widow? but her grief was devoid of violence, murmuring, or impatience. She had every reason to believe that Jarbas had gone to heaven, where she hoped to be able to meet him speedily; this confidence not only lessened the bitterness of her tears but filled her soul with that pure and heavenly peace which is known only to those who have the hopes of eternity.

After having stabbed Jarbas, Afer, taking advantage of the confusion and excitement, slunk unnoticed from the camp. Although still suffering from the effects of the torture, he travelled solitary by-ways until night fell. He then rested a little. Being a child of the desert, the course of the sun and the movement of the stars were unfailing guides to his feet. He had a double advantage in travelling in this manner: he ran less risk of being overtaken by the soldiers in case they should be on his track, and by following a straight line he would reach the city more speedily; he was so impatient to clutch the double reward he so well deserved, plenty of gold and freedom! On the fifth day he descried the

domes of the city, but out of precaution he kept
aloof until the streets were deserted and the
houses closed ; thanks to the darkness, he reached Jubal's house unperceived.

Old Sylvanus, however, had not been quite as
careful or swift as the black slave.   As Jarbas,
before expiring, had ordered his release, he knew
that nobody would molest him on his journey.
So he trudged along leisurely, found Fatuma
very much alarmed on account of his prolonged
absence, because he had not acquainted her with
his visit to the camp, and, having quieted her
fears, sought a few hours' rest in his tent.   He
then repaired to Carthage, where he was known
to none except his old comrades.   His first step
was to present himself at the house of Afer's master, under pretext of informing him of what had
taken place, in case his accomplice had not been
able or had not dared to inform him about the
result of his mission, but in reality to carry out
his oath of revenge on Vivia herself, after having first stabbed her through the object of her
tenderest affections.   The deadly hatred he entertained for her could be sated only by her blood.
Jubal had liberally rewarded the fidelity of his
slave by bestowing on him more money than he
had promised ; but, reflecting that he might still
need his services, he always deferred his liberation from slavery.   In vain did Afer remind him
of his bargain ; in vain did he urge that Carthage
was no longer a safe place for him ; that he might

be questioned at any moment about his long absence from the city ; that, in fine, he was of no
further use since those Numidian rascals had
maimed him with their accursed tortures.   The
choleric young man flew into a rage and made
answer that he had power of life and death over
his slave so long as he had not signed the instrument of his manumission.   Afer knew his
master's temper too well, so he had to resign himself to await patiently better dispositions and
more favorable opportunities.

The high-priest, continually occupied in nursing schemes of vengeance against Tertullian, was
speedily informed by old Sylvanus of the occurrences that had taken place in the camp the day
of Jarbas's assassination by the negro slave.

Felicitas' father narrated to him the history of
his wrongs, the reason of his sworn hatred to
Vivia and the detested Christians.   The vindictive
priest lauded him exceedingly, commended his
zeal for the sacred cause of the gods, and took
especial pains to portray to him the abominable
practices of the Christians, in which, of course,
his unhappy daughter participated.   The old
hypocrite had too much interest in arousing the
fanaticism and fanning into flame the mad passions of the mountain shepherd.   He saw in him
a tool very useful in the scheme he was now
planning.   His greatest hope, however, was in
Jubal's mad recklessness with regard to Vivia ;
so he sought him secretly one evening.

"The holy work has been happily commenced, it seems," began he at once; "two men under your roof-tree deserve well of the gods and the country. Vivia's husband, as you are probably aware, had betrayed his religion, and this explains his secret interviews with Tertullian, that detestable priest who, were he let alone, would end by sweeping the people from our temples and the sacrifices from our altars. But now that we can prove, and that the whole city will soon know, that Jarbas was a Christian, that the revolt in which he perished was caused by his attachment to that accursed sect, the opportunity must be seized to stir up the people and to force the governor and the senate to proscribe, once for all, this new religion, as the edicts of our pious emperors direct and command."

"Jubal is not accustomed to bother himself with religion," answered the hot-headed youth. "If your Jupiter is a god, let him take vengeance on his rival, the Christ of the Christians; that is his business, not mine. The arrogant Vivia has insulted me; you told me, if you remember, to take revenge on the man whom she had the assurance to prefer to me. I committed my cause to the tried fidelity of Afer; his dagger gave me the satisfaction I wanted. But as for *her*, my vengeance must reach her too; she must be mine, were it only for one instant. Her pride I will pull down, I care not how, or I shall go to the shades with the husband for whom she

mourns. Then put aside, I beg you, the ridiculous subject of religion and worship. Upon this
condition I am prepared to listen to your advice,
although it has been my invariable custom to
follow only my own."

"When years shall have made you wise, perhaps you will not think as you do at present.
But if you take no interest in the struggle in
which the future of our ancient religion is in-
volved, at least pay attention to what interests
you personally. The haughty Vivia, whom I de-
test as much as you do, has insulted you ; she rejected your name and hand, while I have heard
more than one patrician lady say that the woman
of your choice might well be envied by the
highest and best in the land ! But are you aware
of the real reason of her disdainful contempt for
you ? "

" Her heart, I believe, had been already given
to another ; she loved, and perhaps her love was
returned ; for, mind you, I am no fool to give
credence to nursery tales of virtue, nor have I
ever believed one word about her hypocritical
chastity. Virtue ! where is it ? It is a high-
sounding, pretentious word, behind which proud
people strive to screen their weaknesses."

" Jubal, you may be right in not believing in
virtue, especially when it shrouds itself in such
external asceticism. Our gods are not so severe
and savage, and I confess I can hardly bring myself to believe that the heart of a girl can be

stronger and do more than they. You deceive yourself when you attribute Vivia's conduct towards you to the fact of her having loved some one else and her love having been reciprocated. I can tell you she had entirely different reason, and I have it on the very best authority."

"In humbling and rejecting me, could Vivia have possibly any other motive? Please explain yourself, I do not like hints and half-way revelations."

"Nor will I hide anything from you. Know then, Jubal—and she herself has boasted of it— she ignominiously refused you only because you were not a Christian."

"That is not so; at the time she was not a Christian herself."

"That was dissimulation on her part, for she had long before secretly embraced the new religion. Are you not aware that her mother has been a Christian these many years?"

"At any rate, Jarbas was no more a Christian than I when she accepted and married him."

"True; but she had stipulated the conditions; being smitten with love, he swore he would become initiated. Remember the story of the old camel-driver; his account of the death-scene leaves no room for doubt."

"Well, what do I care if, to please his new wife, Jarbas, with or without sincerity, changed his religion? Who says that Vivia rejected me because I was not a Christian?"

"I, or rather she herself. I remember the exact words as they were at the time repeated to me. 'Jubal,' she said, 'is a noble youth, well educated, of good disposition, wealthy, and of illustrious lineage; but a man of his disposition and habits cannot be expected to become a convert to our religion; it would necessarily appear too austere for him. I shall never, however, marry any man except a Christian or one who will promise me to become a Christian.' Is not that plain enough to remove all doubt?"

This was a deliberate falsehood, of course, but the pagan priest when he invented and put these words in Vivia's mouth imagined that the choleric Jubal would fly into a rage and would swear an implacable hatred to the whole sect of Christians. To his surprise, however, the young man did not yield to one of his usual fits of passion, but fell into silence and seemed to be occupied with his own musings and thoughts.

"Jubal," said he in a slightly mortified tone, "do you think I am simple enough to listen to idle hearsays like a child, or so mean as to betray by a falsehood the respect I owe to my office and to my hoary head?"

"I have no motive to suspect your seriousness or sincerity; hence I do believe your words. What a wonderful change they have suddenly produced in my mind! So, then, Vivia did not despise me! If, on a certain occasion, she wounded my pride by a stinging rebuke that may scarcely be forgotten, the reason was because I made a mistake and thought she was like all the young women with whom I was acquainted in society. I wounded her delicacy by a thought-less and imprudent sally; this was the construction she put on it herself when she afterwards refused my hand. So, then, her only objection to me was on the score of religion! Am I justi-fied in imputing that to her as a crime? O Vivia! why did I not understand you better then? I would not have hated you; perhaps we would have been united by sweet and holy bonds. By your side would I certainly have found the hap-piness which I seek in vain in the thousand fleet-ing attachments in which my poor heart has grown weary and exhausted ever since my boy-hood."

"What do you mean, Jubal? To please Vivia would you have embraced the abominable religion of the Christians, at the risk of making yourself a by-word and a laughing-stock to all your boon companions throughout the entire city? Or rather, would you have essayed the task of un-deceiving and bringing her back to the worship of the gods of her childhood?"

"I have told you a hundred times that I do not believe in your gods. I know too much about them, you see; they are no better than myself, and you may rest assured I have no ambition to be worshipped on an altar or to have incense burned in my honor."

"Still, there is no middle course; either you must believe in our immortal gods with all the wise men of every age, or in the man named Christ, that miserable Jew, who was crucified for his crimes, and whose impious doctrines have hitherto succeeded in seducing only a handful of poor slaves and a few women from the common herd of the people."

"Vivia is neither a poor slave nor a woman of the lower ranks; she is a patrician lady, and it is conceded on all hands that she is distinguished by education and character as well as by birth and position."

"She is young and inexperienced; it was no difficult matter to dupe a woman like her. How could she resist the attacks of that fanatic, Tertullian ?"

"If Tertullian is a fanatic I am not aware of it. What I do know is that Carthage may well be proud of being able to reckon him among her sons. I have heard him plead in cases of the utmost importance; his remarkable eloquence swept everything irresistibly before it. I assisted at his lectures when he was professor of rhetoric. I remember how we admired his great talent, his wonderful genius. The day that witnessed his conversion gave the new religion its most noble and glorious conquest."

"You have certainly lost your senses, Jubal ; you are no longer yourself. I make no doubt you will soon forsake your pleasant ways ; you will bid adieu to your gay comrades, and will affect a melancholy and austere sort of life, just as all these Christian hypocrites do."

" Just now, at all events, I am not in the humor of doing anything of the sort. But even if I were, where would be the great harm ! Olympius, put a stop to these base recriminations of men who are not here to defend themselves. After all, they are as free as you or I."

"They must have gained you over somewhat, to make you side with them so earnestly. Oh ! indeed, what astonishing news for the whole city to learn some fine day that the gay Jubal, the leader of all fun, the hero of all the routs and revels of the town, has suddenly turned Christian ! "

"I have said, and I repeat, I have not yet gone quite so far ; but Vivia is a Christian, you must remember."

" She is your enemy."

" She may have been ; she is so no longer."

" What ! only a moment ago you swore a mortal hatred to her ! You sought her dishonor and blood ! "

" My hatred has vanished. The honorable assurances given by you a little while ago have produced a revolution in my feelings. Now I feel I love her with a love worthy of her."

"Gods ! can it be possible you could love the woman that insulted you so grievously ! How long is it since the *loathed hawk* has become so enamored of *the gentle dove ?* "

This reminder, so maliciously evoked by the pagan priest, made Jubal turn pale with anger ; his breast heaved, his heart seemed ready to burst, as it did when the haughty patrician first spoke those stinging words. His lips quivered and gave forth hoarse, inarticulate sounds, and his eyes shot fire like those of a wounded tiger. The old man gazed on him with diabolical satisfaction ; he had evidently touched the right chord, and had lit up all the fires of hatred in that heart, that had begun to open itself to better impulses. In his frenzied rage Jubal's first thought was to rush out and say to his slave : " Afer, seize your poniard once more. I must have the haughty Vivia's blood ! " He paused, however, on his way to the door, and, bridling his rage by an effort that surprised even himself, he approached the high-priest, and, looking in his face, cried :

" Olympius, beware of ever uttering one word of what you have just now said to me ; you may not do it with impunity ! "

The words were accompanied by a threatening gesture which made the hoary old coward tremble.

" Why fly into such a passion ? " he asked. " I protest I had no intention of offending you. Learn to know me better ; I am always anxious to aid you by advice and place at your service the weight of my influence and office."

" I tell you plainly I look upon your advice as very questionable. As for your influence, I can well afford to do without it. Do not imagine you can inveigle me into the perpetration of a new crime, for you shall not. I begin to see your aim. You hate the Christians; you hate Tertullian. Every word you utter clearly proves that your object is only to instigate a bloody persecution against those who refuse to adore your gods in order to ensure the destruction of the man you hate. The fate of the Christians concerns me but very little; I shall not accuse nor defend them. But if Vivia's head is endangered beware, for I shall hold yours responsible. You know me; Jubal does not say things twice!"

The pagan priest saw the futility of further dissimulation, since Jubal had read him so thoroughly. Having, however, shrewdly calculated all the possible difficulties of the case, he came to the conclusion that the moment had arrived to try his last resort—intimidation. He was confident this new plan of attack would ensure success.

"Yes," cried he vehemently; "yes, this accursed sect must perish; this detested priest must atone for the insult done me, for I also have been outraged. But as you refuse to aid my plans, know that you shall not save *your Vivia.* I swear to you by the immortal gods that I myself will demand her blood."

" False and cruel man ! had I my dagger about me that would be your last speech. But Vivia

shall not perish; I will protect her, and woe to
the wretch who would dare to touch a hair of her
head!"

"Rash youth, how could you help her? Would
she herself condescend to accept your impotent
protection? She despised and rejected you; now
she abominates you with all the powers of her
soul."

"Vivia is too good, her heart too noble, to
hate; when she will see that my love for her is
as pure as it is sincere she will not reject it."

"Do not deceive yourself, Jubal; betwixt you
and her there is an impassable gulf; there is
blood! Do you imagine she does not know that
her husband has fallen by the dagger of your
slave? Everybody believes and says it. It is
reported that his sudden flight did not prevent
some of the guards from recognizing him.
Listen to me, Jubal," continued he in a more in-
sinuating and milder tone, "in spite of what has
passed between us, I still desire to serve you.
Even in the supposition that these reports result
in nothing, that Sylvanus and Afer remain silent,
I am in possession of your secret; what guaran-
tee have you that I may not betray it? There
will be no difficulty in obtaining the avowal of
your *bravo*, as he is called. A slave, especially
one of his stamp, is not going to die on the rack
rather than betray his master. But you will
enter a protest. Of what avail will that be? Is
it not known that Afer is only a pliant tool in

your hands—that it was he who struck the blow, but that it was you who designated the victim? Your name, your influence, your father's reputation have hitherto been able to restrain the stern severity of the law. A few insignificant slaves and obscure women, by falling victims to Afer's dagger, could not, of course, have appeared of much importance in the eyes of the magistrates. But in the present case it is a question of a young nobleman, of the general of the army! His family has power, his wife has influence. Carthage feels for her misfortune. Let me say but one word and Jarbas shall be avenged. You must, therefore, see very plainly that my silence has the right of exacting the observance of certain conditions."

The man who is clean of heart, whose conscience has nothing to fear from human justice, can afford to be resolute and independent. But he who has perpetrated a grievous crime and has incurred the high penalty of the law, belongs no longer to himself; he is at the mercy of his accomplice, or of any one who may inform against him. In spite of his repugnance, a word or beck is capable of compelling him to perpetrate new crimes, and to descend even to the lowest depths of infamy. Jubal found himself in this predicament; he understood his position perfectly.

"At least," said he timidly, "let Lady Vivia incur no danger. Promise me this, I beseech you!"

"Then you love this woman very much ? "

"More than everything else in the world. Oh ! do not thwart my affection ; my heart feels as if rejuvenated ; she fills it to the brim ever since you taught me to know her better. A moment ago it would have been a satisfaction to see her dying at my feet, and now I tremble at the bare thought of any danger befalling her."

"Jubal, her fate depends on yourself."

"I thank you for the assurance ; you can now speak, I shall comply with all your demands."

The young man was at his mercy, and the hoary old hypocrite had succeeded beyond all his hopes. He hated Vivia from the simple fact of her being a Christian, and he confidently hoped to involve her in the common ruin as soon as he should have no further need of Jubal's assistance. Had the latter been able to note the wicked smile that contracted Olympius' lips as he gave the assurance of Vivia's safety he might have plucked up some courage and spirit ; but he was too busy with his hopes to see anything.

"Jubal," continued the pagan priest, "my conditions are very simple and easy, if you give proof of cordial co-operation. You can dispose of your black slave as you please ; he has compromised himself too much, so I leave him to you. But you have received and now shelter under your roof a man who may be very useful to me—I mean old Sylvanus ; I wish to have him near me ; besides, it is his own desire."

"He is yours from this moment; you are aware, however, that I have no claim to him. He is my guest, not my slave."

"Your friends are many and influential; your rank opens to you all the doors of the aristocracy of the city. Use them and your best efforts to bring odium on the Christians; do all in your power to stir up the people against them. Pay particular attention to the fanatic Tertullian; hold him up as the mainstay of the sect and the most ardent propagandist of the new doctrines. Speak boldly against the apathy of the senate, the indifference shown by the magistrates and governors in spite of the severe laws enacted by our august emperors."

"Although the part you assign me is not suited to my tastes nor habits, still I will do as you command."

"This is not all—nay, what I have still to say is perhaps the most important. Jarbas's remains are daily expected. Preparations have been made to receive them with grand public demonstrations; it is of vital importance that no such honors should be paid to the corpse of a vile Christian. Cost what it may, either the blind decree of the senate must be revoked, or the people, in their sovereign capacity, must take the matter into their own hands and do the needful. Be up and doing, therefore, Jubal, lose not a moment, and remember that to ensure success all means are legitimate."

"To insult the remains of Jarbas were to affront Vivia herself. I have already informed you that I love her, that the happiness of my life depends on her. Moreover, what is the use of such savage vengeance on a dead body?"

"How badly you understand your own interests, Jubal, by yielding thus to such mistaken delicacy and puerile sensitiveness! Can you not understand that Vivia's pride must be humbled, that she must begin to fear for herself, which she never will so long as she continues to imagine herself protected by her husband's name? But the moment she begins to feel her weakness and isolation, rest assured, she will become more tractable and mild. The ivy thrives and grows only so long as it is supported by the trunk to which it clings; let the tree fall, with it the ivy falls to the ground and is trampled under foot. So, too, if you love Vivia, if you judge her worthy of bearing your name, you must first humble that pride of which she has no small share; she must feel how isolated, abandoned, and unsupported she is in her widow's weeds; you will then tender her your protection, and, you can rest assured, she will be but too glad to receive it. You see I have not only kept my word, but I also prepare the way for you to arrive at the heart of the woman whom you love."

It was thus the cunning old man flattered the young patrician's passion the better to enlist him in the furtherance of his schemes. Jubal allowed himself to become the dupe of these wily promises and pledged himself to follow all the instructions of Olympius. That very day he sent Sylvanus to the priest and manumitted Afer. The negro quitted Carthage without delay, for he felt he was not safe within its walls. Olympius did not meet with the like success with the governor of the province, whom he had gone to see in hot haste. In spite of all his endeavors, he had not succeeded in inducing him to take measures against the Christians. As we shall see further on, he found less resistance on the part of another magistrate.

CHAPTER XVI.

THE CHRISTIANS TO THE LIONS.

So long as the Emperor Severus had had competitors for the crown, he permitted the Christians to practise their religion unmolested. He was perfectly aware of their fidelity; he knew he had nothing to fear from them; moreover, his army had no better or braver soldiers. But as soon as the death of Niger and Albinus had left him undisputed possession of the empire, and the revolted provinces had been brought to subjection by his victorious legions, his previous policy was cast aside. Had he come to the conclusion that the atrocious calumnies laid to the charge of the Christians with redoubled malignity were true? In blind attachment to the worship of idols, had he grown afraid of the daily progress made by the Gospel? or did he, through pride, seek to add new glory to his name by overthrowing a religion that had withstood all the power of mighty Rome, and all the efforts of four great persecutions? On this point history is silent. Be this as it may, in the tenth year of his reign he published the most severe edicts against

the Christians ; this was a signal for a fifth persecution, and, although the blood of martyrdom
was not shed in some provinces, it raged with
such fury that people began to think the time of
Antichrist had come.

Egypt, the home of every sort of superstition,
had received and rigorously enforced the imperial
edict. The celebrated Christian schools of Alexandria had become widely known and had drawn
scholars and students from every land to that
city. A great number of martyrs here suffered
for the faith. The illustrious Clement, to avoid
death, fled to Cappadocia, where he governed a
church whose bishop was languishing in prison. Origen's father was among the confessors
who gave their blood for the name of Christ.
We have already related the glorious end of the
virgin Potamiena, the sister by adoption of the
noble Julia.

At Carthage, where the interests of commerce
and the frequent inroads of the savage tribes of
the desert principally occupied the popular mind,
there was less prejudice and less hatred of the
Christians. It was a common saying, however, that they had infallible *charms* to win
over those whom they desired to attach to their
religion ; they attributed the many conversions,
which they could not otherwise explain, to the
power of magic. This was the popular opinion,
and it satisfied the masses. Upright and reflecting persons, however, did not allow themselves

to be deceived by such idle and frivolous reports. When they examined and became more intimate with the Christians, they could not help admiring and protecting them when necessary. The edict for the persecution might accordingly have lain, like its predecessors, in the archives of the state, had not the pagan priest's pride been wounded. On what do not the most important events often depend ?

The day after his interview with Olympius, Jubal, in the hope of obtaining the hand of Vivia, set to work with a zeal worthy of a better cause. At table, at play, in his evening or rather nightly revels, he never ceased to attack and inveigh against the Christians. Being naturally clever, and commanding a wonderful flow of language, he constantly turned into ridicule their morals, manners, and customs. To the depraved society which he frequented he depicted the followers of Christ in the most odious colors; he represented them as so many execrable monsters whose accursed race should be destroyed without delay and without mercy.

"Look at these hypocrites," used he to say; "to give themselves the semblance of virtue they keep aloof from all social gatherings; you never find them at the theatre, the games, or the public baths. They shut themselves up in their homes like bears in their dens; when necessity happens to drive them forth you would know one of them among a thousand by their plainness of attire, the

affected modesty of their looks, and their studied
soberness of gait. They despise us for knowing
how to enjoy life without bothering ourselves
about that mysterious and unknown future that
never troubles people of good sense. In reality,
they are no better than ourselves; they have all
our vices minus our frankness; they shroud
themselves in mysteries and secrets, and they do
well, for they ought to hide such a mass of tur-
pitude and infamy!

" Those men of so much external austerity and
mortification are well known. In private among
themselves they unblushingly give full scope to
abominations that would horrify even us, although we do not pretend to be models of
virtue. They affect to be very humane, to have a
horror of blood, while in their nocturnal conven-
ticles, when gorged with wine and meat, they
slay a child and drink its blood.* In fact, the
lions and tigers of our mountains are less cruel,
and I do not see why we wage a war of ex-
termination on those animals, who are ferocious
only by instinct, while we tolerate men incomparably more savage.

" My friends, we have hitherto had pity for
this impious sect, and saw it grow without alarming ourselves; now, however, it threatens our

* This was one of the calumnies forged from the doctrine
of the Real Presence by the ignorance or malice of the ancient
and pagan enemies of the Church. What a state of society
does not this reveal! What must have been the position of
the Christians! *Ex pede Herculem.*

ease and our future. We shall soon be obliged
to square our pleasures and pastimes according
to their notions of public propriety. The women,
who love laughter and pleasure as well as we,
leave us one by one, attracted no doubt by the
novelty of the thing, and they take with them
their fairest slaves. Let the contagion go on
spreading a little while longer, and we shall be
driven perforce to politics and philosophy, and
must resign ourselves to spend our days in dis-
mal celibacy; indeed, all our patrician ladies vie
with one another in embracing the new religion,
so that they now make it a point of honor to wed
none but Christian husbands. After a while, if
we wish to marry, we shall be obliged either to
cringe and beg to be received into that hypocritical sect, or to bestow our name on some plebeian
or poor slave. What do you think of this? what
would our ancestors say were they to wake from
the slumbers of the tomb?

"In my opinion," he added, "it is high time
to put an end to this growing evil.

"You all know me. I do not care for the
gods any more than ye do, but we must not permit ourselves to be robbed of what constitutes
our happiness. Let us boldly stand up for our
pleasant enjoyments; they are about to be
wrested from us. We are all in the full vigor of
youth; we have power, gold, and slaves, and let
us make the best use of them. Let us attack
this new religion, then, by every means in our

power; let us assail its superstitions, and the impieties, the disorders, and the crimes that it teaches and practises. In the name of our only god, Pleasure, let us dethrone the false God called Christ. The undertaking is worthy of us.

" The opportunity is most favorable ; fortune evidently favors us. In a few days, as you are aware, Jarbas's remains will arrive in Carthage, where they are making every preparation to receive them with the utmost pomp and display. But there is something which perhaps you did not know: it is that Jarbas was secretly a Christian. It was in hatred of that detested name that the army revolted and he was stabbed. Let us all make joint protest against the decree of the senate ; let us boldly brand it as a disgraceful and infamous act. We can produce a perfect panic in the city. The Christians will soon crawl back to the obscurity whence we allowed them to emerge. Their wives and daughters, to-day so proud and haughty, will return to throw themselves into our arms. . . . War, then, to Christ! Glory and victory to sweet Pleasure! "

Aided by lust and wine, Jubal's words electrified the heads and hearts of the young men over whom he always had such influence. Goblet in hand, they swore hatred to Christ ; even some, more impulsive or more heated by wine, shouted the savage cry to which the Roman amphitheatres so often re-echoed: " The Christians to the lions! "

On his side the old shepherd of the mountains was not idle. In his implacable hatred he had gone on blindly obeying the pagan high-priest. One thought occupied him day and night—to glut his vengeance, to shed the blood of the detested woman who had robbed him of his treasure, of his beloved Fatima. He used to go occasionally into the fields to visit the slaves at their toil. He pretended to pity them in order to gain their confidence, and when he thought them willing to listen, "Poor fellows!" used he to say, "you toil for masters who have nothing but severity for you, while it only depends on yourselves to throw off their heavy yoke. Your proud oppressors are Christians either overtly or secretly; in any case they are outlaws, and can have no rights over you. Denounce them to the magistrates, demand that they be punished according to the wise edicts of the emperors, that they be exiled or condemned to death. Freedom for yourselves, your wives, and children, together with a portion of the fertile lands you cultivate with your sweat, will be the reward of your courage. But let there be no delay, for your cruel masters know their danger and might provide against it. You are well aware from experience that they have but little scruple to make a *vile slave* die under the bloody whip and thong."

At other times he crawled slowly towards Vivia's residence or seated himself on the public way. His emaciated limbs made him look like a skeleton, his frowsy beard and hair, his livid and careworn countenance were calculated to produce the impression that he was one of those unfortunates whom the pagans imagined were pursued by the fates. When accosted or offered shelter he invariably refused assistance with the dolorous exclamation: "Interrupt not my grief; what can any one do for a wretch condemned to suffer without consolation or hope?" And then the crowd was entertained by a repetition of the history of his grievances and woes. They never failed to win him sympathy, and the eyes of many a listening mother were moistened with tears for the loved and lost daughter of the sorrowing old man. But when his hatred found vent in curses and imprecations on the Christians, and especially on Vivia, his impassioned cries for vengeance never failed to lash the crowd into fury and to draw forth a wild, unanimous shout of: "Death to the Christians! Death to Vivia!"

The pagan priest kept himself fully informed regarding the state of affairs throughout the city. He wrote Jubal the most flattering letters to encourage him in the prosecution of the work he was so ably conducting. He was not equally well satisfied, however, with the proconsul. Firmilianus, the governor of the province of Carthage for a number of years, had never had any reason to find fault with the Christians. He was on intimate, nay, friendly terms with

many of them. Being naturally of a mild disposition and, on principle, indifferent to matters
pertaining to religion, he could not understand
why people should be molested or persecuted simply because they believe this or that doctrine.
In common with the other governors, he had, received the late imperial edict; but, despite the
murmurs of some pagan zealots, he was in no
hurry to publish it.

Had Firmilianus been a younger man, ambitious, the desire of pleasing Cæsar, or the fear of
losing his place might have induced him to act
in contravention to his own inclinations and
wishes; but he was now advanced in years and
tired of the honors that began to weigh upon
him. His failing health was beginning to cry
rather for retirement and rest from office. He
had always led a quiet life and he wished to end
it in peace.

In vain did the malignant old priest urge him
on; nothing was gained by pleading the constantly
increasing exasperation of the people, the evil consequences to the city of a popular outbreak, the
intention entertained by a number of the senators
of denouncing him to the emperor in case of a
longer postponement of the publication and enforcement of the edict against the Christians. The
old man's invariable answer was: "The emperor
is mistaken; the Christians are neither wicked nor
dangerous." Or again: "At my age a man
needs rest; wait awhile. I am old and infirm;

when I am gone they may do as they like." But *to wait* was precisely what Olympius did not wish to do, hence he resolved to make the people speak, confident that their mighty and terrible voice could not be ignored or resisted.

In the principal square of Carthage, situated at a short distance above the harbor, lying at her feet, there stood a white marble statue of Juno, the Queen of the Gods, and chief protectress of the city; a costly diadem of precious stones was placed on her head, and sparkled with dazzling brilliancy in the sun's rays. In her right hand she held a golden sceptre, as a symbol of her power; in her left the model of a ship bearing the proud inscription, *Carthage, Queen of the Sea.* This statue had stood in its present position for centuries; the Romans had respected it through fear, no doubt, of incurring the anger of the haughty and implacable goddess. The entire population held it in the greatest reverence. Previous to their departure for a campaign the soldiers were drawn up in line of battle, and in its presence the senate officially delivered the insignia of command and the standard of the city to the general, charging him to return it unsullied and victorious. It was customary also to place there votive offerings, crowns, necklaces, bracelets, etc.; a bronze railing protected them from the rapacity of marauders and thieves. There was not a single pagan family in easy circumstances who did not consider it a duty to

make some offering. At night an armed watchman guarded the sacred monument.

Now it happened that one morning, at break
of day, the watchman was found dead in a pool
of blood; he had been stabbed to the heart, and
had fallen near the railing. All the votive offerings had been carried away, and the statue itself
was terribly mutilated; its uncrowned head and
right hand lay on the ground; the golden sceptre
was broken; its scattered and battered fragments
proved that the perpetrators of the deed were
animated by a spirit of hatred and contempt. In
a moment the great square was crowded by hor-
rified spectators; some raised their hands and
eyes to heaven supplicating the Queen of the Gods
not to be enraged against the city which she had
always protected; others fell prostrate on the
ground to testify their abhorrence of the terrible
and sacrilegious deed. Before long, however, it
began to be circulated among the crowd, no one
knew by whom, that " *it was the Christians
that had been guilty of the sacrilege of breaking
Juno's statue !*" Indescribable rage took the place
of consternation and terror; an ominous and wild .
cry burst from every lip: " *Down with the Chris-*
tians! the Christians to the lions ! " For more
than an hour all the echoes reverberated to that
terrible shout; in the privacy of his distant home
Tertullian's enemy heard it, and his heart bound-
ed with fiendish satisfaction.

All day long the city remained a prey to agitation; the streets, the squares, and the quays were filled with excited crowds. The great crime of the past night was the universal topic, and, as it was universally taken for granted that the Christians were the criminals, the question was where would their rashness stop if not checked by swift and condign punishment. The more moderate, or, rather, to speak with more exactness, the less rabid, demanded that the guilty be arrested without delay and put to death. With a little diligence they could be easily discovered. Rumor unanimously singled out the names of some. Tertullian and Vivia had too many implacable enemies not to be at the head of the list; hence it was currently reported that the one had advised and that the other, wholly led by his influence, had carried out his instructions. It was reported, furthermore, that the slave Revocatus had been seen during the night skulking on the way leading to the great square. There could be no question but he was the instrument employed by the patrician lady.

The Christians could have no difficulty in understanding the significance of this popular movement; the shouts and cries for their death fell constantly on their ears. They retired to their houses to pray and to prepare themselves to give testimony for the faith of Jesus Christ, for they had no doubt that they were on the point of being dragged before the tribunal. Kneeling before the altar and surrounded by some of his priests, Optatus offered himself as a victim for his beloved flock, and besought God that his life might be taken for all. Clad in deep mourning and sorrow, yet calm in her grief, Vivia busied herself with her mother, Rufina, and Felicitas in making preparations for the funeral of her noble husband. In the silence of his humble abode, and heedless of what was passing abroad, Tertullian, with a genius knowing no repose and a soul above fear, was working at his celebrated treatise, "Against the Gentiles," and collecting the irresistible thunders destined to give the death-blow to idolatry.

Night at last put a truce to the agitations of the day; the crowds gradually dispersed, and people began to think of preparing for rest. The Christians began to hope; even the good bishop returned home under the impression that his flock was no longer in danger. In a little while the whole city was hushed. It was like a sea after a storm, when the winds cease and the waves fall, and calm settles on the bosom of the deep.

Suddenly an ominous reddish glow, accompanied by murky volumes of smoke, appears. The fearful glare spreads clearer, broader, and higher; it lights up the heavens and the harbor, and is reflected even by the distant waves of the sea. The temple is on fire; its lofty porticos, marvels of art, its stately marble pillars, splinter, totter, and fall one by one in thundering ruin to the ground. The greedy flames envelop the whole building from the foundations to the dome, and could be seen for miles at sea. Soon the entire structure is but a shapeless mass of fire. Its destruction was as speedy as if it had been surrounded by pitch, sulphur, and the most inflammable materials. In the short space of a few hours there remained nothing of this costly and beautiful temple save a heap of black and half-calcined stones.

The burning of this building having followed so closely on the *sacrilegious* mutilation of Juno's statue, it became evident to the minds of all that there existed a plot and a set plan ; such coincidences do not spring from accident nor does it co-ordain facts in this manner. But who could have framed this plot and carried it out so skilfully 1 In the popular mind there was not even the shadow of a doubt—only the Christians would have been guilty of such a crime. Emboldened by the impunity so long accorded to them, seeing their ranks increasing from day to day, and their numbers swelled by the most influential citizens, they doubtlessly imagined they were now strong enough to be able to brave the terrors of the law and give full scope to their hatred of the old religion and of all that it held most holy and sacred. Hence the people rushed to the fire with increased rage and bitterness, and as the crowd grew so did the shouts: *Down with the Christians! the Christians to the lions!* and every time a fragment of the temple fell in the progress of the conflagration their savage yells grew louder and louder. The slaves and the rabble were particularly fierce; they were on the point of attacking the houses of the Christians when the lieutenant-governor, or procurator of the province, appeared on the scene. His presence checked the movement, though not the shouting, nor could the mob be induced to disperse until they had been assured that severe and speedy punishment would be inflicted on the godless Christians.

CHAPTER XVII.

For a long time the attention of the emperor had been frequently called to the fact that Firmilianus, governor of the Carthagenian province, was too old and feeble to be the representative of mighty Rome in the metropolis of Africa, hence Severus, while leaving him the title which he possessed at the time of his own advent to the throne, had associated with him a young procurator, a man firm, but ambitious, ready to do, or rather to stoop to anything for the sake of ambition. To those masters of the world who bought the venal crown of the Cæsars at the price of gold, treason, or murder, it was of prime necessity to surround themselves with unprincipled, cringing men, who would be swayed by ambition or avarice to support every whim of the prince on whom depended their future and advancement.

The name of the above-mentioned procurator was Hilarian. Having been bred in the camp, he had all the roughness and all the vices of the soldier of that time. As he was avaricious and

a libertine, gold and pleasure were to be had no
matter at what price.   To satisfy his passions he
shrunk from nothing, no matter however base or
tyrannical it might be.   He knew that Rome had
lost the right of questioning the uprightness of
those whom she appointed to the government of
her provinces, and also that she winked at their
most crying exactions providing there were no
rebellions, and that the usual tribute to the mother country was duly paid.   Woe to the wealthy
who had occasion to bring a cause to his tribunal !
They had to pay dearly for the justice required
at his hands !

Chance, if, indeed, it has anything to do with
the affairs of men, so had it that, a few days previous to the events just narrated, Hilarian met
Angela with her parents, on her way to a meeting of the Christians.   Struck by her modest air
and beauty, he enquired who she was, what her
condition, whether free or bond ; for the plainness
and sober color of her attire did not permit him
to imagine for a moment that she could belong
to one of the wealthiest families in Carthage.
Great, consequently, was his surprise when he
learned that her parents had amassed a conside-
rable fortune in trade, and that for many years
their merchantmen were well known to every
port on the shores of Greece, Italy, and Gaul.
From the indagations made by one of his confi-
dants, he found out that Angela, as well as her
parents, were Christians, and that it was doubt-

less for this reason she wore no rich or brilliant
stuffs like other young ladies of her rank.

So long as he had served in the Prætori·n
Guards, Hilarian shared in the popular prejudice
regarding the Christians, considering them to be
simply fanatics or hypocrites who, under the semblance of a mortified life, concealed the deepest
corruption. But since he had been installed as
colleague in the government of the province he
had learned to know them better; he had discovered that their virtues were many and real
and their morals irreproachable. He was aware,
therefore, that he should meet invincible resistance on the part of the young Christian if he
resorted to the vulgar means of seduction; but
as in his bosom avarice vied with lust, after a
little hesitancy he decided to ask for her hand;
he would thus become possessor of her immense
fortune. But Angela was a Christian, and he
who even now aimed at becoming the successor of
the old and decrepit Firmilianus could not marry
a woman belonging to a religion proscribed by the
laws of the empire. To attempt to persuade the
young heiress to renounce Christ was, on the
other hand, equally dangerous and futile. He
had power, and he flattered himself he should
succeed by means of intimidation and threats.
It is evident he did not know the Christians very
thoroughly as yet.

Accordingly, on the day of the mutilation of
Juno's statue some soldiers repaired at noon to

the house of Angela's father. Hilarian, thinking
that this afforded him an excellent opportunity
to further his plans, had commanded them to bring
her quietly to his tribunal. The young virgin
was at prayer, or rather in sweet ecstasy with
her Beloved. She had been informed of the events
of the past night, the clamors of the savage mob
for the slaughter of the Christians, and, in the
persuasion that this was the signal for a bloody
persecution, she had lovingly offered herself to
Jesus Christ. She longed so ardently for martyrdom that, yielding to her pious transports,
she speedily fell into one of her usual ecstasies.
Being recalled to consciousness by her mother's
voice, she no sooner heard that the procurator
of the province summoned her to his tribunal
than she exclaimed joyfully: "The day so ardently longed for has come at last; I am going
to heaven to meet my Beloved and to love him
for eternity." After having sought the con-
gratulations of her mother on her good fortune
and happiness, she placed herself at the discretion of the soldiers, who had begun to grow impatient at delay and to fear that she might have
escaped by some secret passage. In spite of all
her efforts to the contrary, her father could not
be induced to let her go alone.

Upon her arrival Hilarian was found seated on
his tribunal, clad in the insignia of his office and
surrounded by soldiers and lictors. He arose and
said in his most winning tones:

"Angela, be not afraid, and look upon me rather as an indulgent friend than a severe judge."

"I fear nothing, my lord," said the young virgin. "*He* who is with me is all-powerful; I know He will not forsake me."

"Of whom do you speak? I cannot certainly suppose that it is of this old man, who, I presume, is your father. Who, then, can this all-powerful protector be?"

"You know him not, but I know him. I see him; *He* is here by my side; *He* smiles on me in love; *He* bids me take courage."

The young Christian's face shone with supernatural radiance, and her lips lisped loving and tender words, unintelligible to the procurator.

"Angela," continued Hilarian, "let us not lose time in useless words. Strive rather to prove yourself worthy of the interest inspired in me by your youth, and frankly answer my questions. Are the reports that have reached me true? Can it be possible you are a Christian?"

"You have not been misinformed. Yes, I serve Christ, and I will serve him to my latest breath."

"How could you have allowed yourself to be duped by this newfangled doctrine? What motive can there be for abandoning the ancient creed of your fathers?"

"Our religion is not new; it remounts through the prophets and patriarchs to the crea-

tion of the world. It was God himself that
founded it. As for your religion, or rather your
wicked system, it is the work of demons, and
your gods are no gods."

"But the Christ whom you adore was condemned to the shameful death of the cross on account of his impostures and crimes! This you
are aware of; how, then, can you hold ·him for
your God?"

"I know that Christ, the eternal Son of God,
died on a cross for my sake; but he was holy
and innocent. They who condemned him were
blind and wicked. Oh! had they but known
the God of all goodness and love, they would
not have crucified my *Beloved ;* they would have
loved him as I love him."

"It is you, Angela, who are blind. You are
wealthy, and richly endowed with all the gifts of
nature, and you join a religion that proscribes all
pleasure and enjoyment. You hold yourself
aloof from the world, where you may find all
the amusements suitable to your age and the
homage due to your birth and beauty."

"We have pleasures purer than yours, enjoyment infinitely greater than any you can boast
of; but they must be tasted to be appreciated.
In my retirement I am not solitary, as you imagine. There is *One* with me that holds the place
of all. He is my happiness and my life ; *he* fills
my whole heart. I feel that *he* is all mine and I
am all *his.*"

" I cannot understand your strange language. Our emperors have proscribed your religion, as you are aware; their will is that our gods be reverenced and honored throughout the whole empire."

" I am Christ's hand-maid; I will never adore your gods."

" Angela, I have compassion for you on account of your youth; I am resolved to show mercy to you in spite of yourself. Be saved by me, and renounce all those miserable superstitions; cast off those lugubrious garments, so unbecoming to one of your rank and fortune. The entire city will honor you as you deserve, and a befitting marriage will soon be the reward of your wisdom."

" These garments I prize because I received them from *Him ;* I would not exchange them for the costliest silks and purple. Why speak to me of honors ? All my glory consists in despising them. As for your vaunted espousals, what are they in comparison to those to which my heart has ever aspired ! "

Hilarian felt himself worsted by the young Christian; her mild and modest answers attested her calmness and firmness alike; but as she seemed not to have understood the sufficiently clear allusion made by him to his own wishes, on the score of a befitting marriage as the reward of her abjuration, he judged it necessary to come to the point openly and plainly.

"Angela," said he, "listen attentively to what I going to say; the law empowers me to treat you with severity. The occurrences of the past night can be laid to the charge of the ungodly members of your sect alone, and they make it incumbent on me to have recourse to stringent measures. I had resolved and I still am determined to save you. It depends on yourself to profit by my clemency; I stipulate one condition, however. The very first time I saw you I felt irresistibly drawn toward you. I vowed to exalt you to my own height and to bestow my name on you; but it is necessary that the wife of the procurator Hilarian be of the same religion as himself. This is the price of your safety."

The young virgin cast her eyes on the ground; a holy modesty suffused her face with deep blushes, but she uttered not a word.

"It is well," exclaimed Hilarian, interpreting her virgin blushes and modest silence as a tacit sign of consent; "I am delighted to find you so reasonable."

Descending from the tribunal, he attempted to kiss her hand, but before his lips could touch it she recoiled and said with calmness and dignity:

"My lord, if the laws make it your duty to condemn me as a Christian, although I have done no evil, behold I am ready; my every aspiration is to suffer and die for *Him* who has suffered and died for me. I beg, however, that you will do me the favor of not even requiring an answer to the extraordinary proposition just made."

"Then you despise me, Angela! Whence, let me ask, so much haughtiness and pride?"

"I despise no one; you are come too late; another has forestalled you, and I have given him my heart."

"Ah! here is a true specimen of Christian hypocrisy! So, Angela, under the semblance of straitlaced modesty, you, too, hide an intrigue. Then you are in love?"

"Yes, I have long loved *my dear Betrothed.*"

"No matter what be his name, were he the most influential man in Carthage, I swear to you he shall never have you."

"*My Beloved* is beyond your power; your rage can never reach him. To him have I given my troth and all the love of my heart; to him shall I ever remain faithful."

"Now you add insult to contempt; this is more than enough! I ask now, and for the last time, will you consent to become the wife of Hilarian?"

"I neither will nor can; ask me no more questions."

"Angela, you wish to deceive, to impose upon me; you are still free."

"I am not, you may rest assured."

"Since when? No one ever heard of your having been betrothed or married."

"Only a few days ago *He* whom I have loved since I was a child has solemnly taken me for his spouse. It was of him I spoke when I told you that all your power and anger could not reach him."

"Angela, either you are mocking me to your grief, or else you are laboring under some hallucination."

"Were you a Christian you could understand, perhaps. But why so many questions? I repeat, I am a Christian, and I will never have any spouse other than *Him* to whom I have plighted my troth and my love."

Under the belief that her firmness came principally from her father's presence, Hilarian commanded him to be led from the court. Angela, however, gave no sign of alarm or perturbation.

"Fear not," said she to the old man; "*He* who is with me will sustain me to the end."

"We shall see that," cried Hilarian in a menacing and angry tone. "Demented woman, do not persist in your folly; renounce your impious creed, consent to become my wife, or I shall confiscate to the public treasury" (he dared not say to his own) "all the wealth of your family, so that you and yours shall be reduced to beggary."

"It is written: *Blessed are the poor, for theirs is the kingdom of heaven.* *He* whom I adore, *he* whom I love, lived in poverty, having not even where to lay his wearied head. You may deprive us of the goods which we value not, and which we must leave sooner or later. We have treasures a thousandfold more valuable, but these you cannot take away."

At the word *treasures* the passion of avarice awoke in the procurator's heart, and his eyes lit up with the fire of covetousness.

" Where do you keep these stores of wealth ? " cried he.

" In heaven ! it is there we daily lay them up."

" If you fear not poverty, at least fear exile, or a still worse fate. I can make you a slave, Angela, and you had better reflect upon this seriously."

" The whole world is the Christian's fatherland ; he is free even in chains."

" The haughty tone you now assume may belie itself when tested by the horrors and loneliness of a dungeon. You will there regret the pleasing companionship of your friends and the light of yon fair sun."

" You are mistaken, for even in your dungeons I shall not be alone. *He* will come down and will remain with me. His sweet words will flood my soul with joy, his light will dissipate the darksomeness of my prison."

Galled as well as humiliated, Hilarian ordered the instruments of torture to be brought forth in the hope of intimidating the young virgin. His intention, however, was not to torture her, but to see what effect the sight of them would produce upon her. Angela looked at them fearlessly for an instant and then raised her eyes to heaven, as if to say: "Be thou blessed, O Beloved of my heart! it has been given to me at last to have some part in thy sufferings, after having so long sighed for this happiness!"

"You see these terrible instruments," said the procurator; "they wring groans and cries of pain from the stoutest. Do not wait to have your limbs torn and to see your delicate body bleeding from every pore; obey."

"*He* who is with me will enable me to suffer courageously for his sake."

The torturers advanced to seize and lay her on the rack. Accustomed as they were to such harrowing scenes, they could not help a feeling of involuntary pity. An imperious gesture from Hilarian made them pause, and, turning towards Angela, who was calmly praying to God:

"Your insolence and obstinacy," said he, "deserve the severest punishment. Nevertheless, I still entertain a hope that you will have pity on yourself and on your aged parents. Plunge them not into inconsolable sorrow, and ruin not yourself. Angela, I give you until to-morrow to make up your mind. Think of yourself and of all that you hold dear; remember the happy and honorable life that lies before you if you hearken to the voice of reason. If, however, at this hour to-morrow, you will not sacrifice to the gods and become my wife, I swear by our divine emperor that I will cast you to the wild beasts in the amphitheatre, after having first caused you to be dishonored. We shall then see if your Christ, or this mysterious protector that you have so often cast in my teeth, shall be able to save your body from dishonor and the bloody fangs of the lions."

A ray of heavenly joy beamed in the eyes of the young Christian when Hilarian spoke of exposing her to the wild beasts, but at the mention of the other threat the chaste virgin grew suddenly pale; her limbs trembled and tears gushed from eyes half closed by an instinctive movement of shame. Her modesty became so alarmed, she felt such a fearful revulsion of feeling, that she had to lean on the back of a seat to keep from falling. The procurator felt overjoyed; he congratulated himself at having struck on, or rather at having borrowed, such a happy idea from the olden persecutors of the Christians; he was satisfied he had triumphed over all her reluctance and opposition. But his joy was short-lived; the youthful virgin had seen and heard *her Beloved*. Her countenance became once more smiling and radiant.

"Until to-morrow, then," said she. "*He* who is with me will be able to protect me. Oh! the fair, the glad day when I shall go to him to begin my eternal espousals!"

Accompanied by her father, who had awaited her at the door of the protorium, she sped home to allay the fears of her anxious and weeping mother. After having affectionately embraced her, she related all that had passed between Hilarian and herself, as well as the threats made by him in his private interview. When she mentioned the menace of dishonor previous to being exposed to the wild beasts, she shook and trembled from head to foot, even though she assured her parents that her Divine Spouse would save her from that shame and indignity. "He promised it to me," she said, "and I believe in his promise; my heart's only *Beloved* knows I fear not torture and death, and that I have long and ardently desired to suffer and die for *him*. But he will never permit his spouse to suffer such a disgrace; I am confident he will not; I know not how he will save me from it, nor have I asked him. He has informed me that I shall reach his foot-stool to-morrow white as the lily of the valley, pure and spotless as the sainted Potamiena, whose virginity he preserved and protected."

In those times of living faith fathers and mothers were not driven to despair when God demanded a martyr out of the family; they accompanied him to the tribunal, and exhorted him to confess boldly the name of Jesus Christ; in prison they visited him and respectfully kissed his chains and wounds. On the way to the place of execution they walked by his side, recommended themselves to his prayers, and pointed to that heaven whether he was going to be crowned by

God's own hand. The father, suppressing his
sighs, smiled on his son, and, if he complained,
it was only because he was not allowed to share
in his child's glory and happiness. Triumphing
over the human heart, even the mother restrained her tears. Happy and proud of the
glorious confession of her daughter, she sought
to assist at her final combat, or rather at her final
triumph. When death had done its work on the
body of the youthful martyr, she descended into
the arena, and on her knees collected his blood
with a sponge or veil ; with her own hands she
bore the sacred remains to the family tomb,
whenever the executioners did not deprive her
of them by casting them into the fire or scatter-
ing the ashes to the winds.

Moreover, Angela's parents, being encouraged
by the holy exhortations of their daughter, thought
of nothing but of offering to the Lord his own
chosen victim. They never dreamed of saving her
by flight from Hilarian's sentence; and had the
thought presented itself they would have rejected it through fear of causing a general persecution of the Carthagenian Christians, or of
seeming to refuse to Almighty God a victim so
pure, a virgin so undefiled, a spouse so tender and
loving, and who had but one aspiration—to unite
herself to her Beloved inseparably and for ever.
Towards evening they sent a secret message to
inform the bishop of what was taking place.
The saintly prelate hastened to visit the young

Christian, to fortify her for the combat. Having provided himself with the holy mysteries, Angela obtained his blessing and the sweet consolation of receiving for the last time *Him* who constituted all her happiness, her only Love, and whom on the morrow she was destined to contemplate face to face in heaven.

CHAPTER XVIII.

HATE had but too well inspired the soul of the pagan high-priest. While Jubal, the blind instrument of his will from the time of his having conceived a passion for Vivia, kept the people excited by fiery harangues against the Christians, the old mountain shepherd, Sylvanus, following the instructions of the haughty and vindictive pontiff, had broken the statue and fired the temple of Juno. Slaves hired for the purpose had aided him in the accomplishment of the hellish deed. We have already seen the effect produced on the masses by this double *sacrilege*.

Even the senate became excited and its deliberations stormy. The very leniency shown to the Christians in the past now became a reason why they should be summarily and severely dealt with. The majesty of the gods had been publicly outraged; such a crime demanded solemn reparation; the profanation should be expiated by the blood of the guilty in order to appease the just anger of the goddess. Even the venera-

ble members of the senate trembled in their curule
chairs; the whole city looked as if a hostile army
was at the gates ready to slaughter all the inhabitants unless every man rushed to arms to repel
the assault.

The senate had been in session two hours.
Hitherto the rostrum had been accustomed to
calm debate, and, even when earnest and impassioned language had been used, due regard to
decorum and dignity had always been observed;
now, however, it thundered with mad invectives
and atrocious calumnies against the Christians.
According to some fanatical young declaimers,
the followers of the new religion, ungratefully
abusing the liberty accorded to them, plotted
against the state in the very face of day. Being
the enemies of the gods and the emperors, they
aimed at nothing less than the overthrow of the
government, the destruction of the senate, the
corruption of the army, the exile of the wealthy,
and the blockading of the city to foreign commerce. It was high time, therefore, to thwart
their nefarious plans. Besides, had not the gods
spoken by the voice of the people? *Death to the
Christians! the Christians to the lions!*

"The Christians to the lions! What is their
crime?"

The words rang out in tones deep and loud as
thunder. The audience trembled as if the ancient vault had been suddenly rent and was about
to fall crashing upon their heads. The speakers

in the rostrum were struck dumb, and for an instant the senators gazed at one another with evident signs of terror ; they had not yet realized the man who had thus suddenly interrupted their deliberations.

Without giving them time to recover from their astonishment, Tertullian—for it was he—flinging back his cloak and casting on the assembly that peculiar glance of his, so expressive of lofty genius, had ascended the steps of the hemicycle with flashing eye, raised head, and heaving breast. To those who knew him it was evident that a very flood of ideas filled his bosom ; that an irresistible storm of eloquent vehemence was about to burst forth.*

"*The Christians to the lions!*" began he. "Upon hearing this savage cry as I entered this assembly, I might well imagine I was in a Roman amphitheatre, in the midst of a mob drunk with fury, thirsting for blood, and impatiently waiting for the wild beasts to tear in pieces a few old men or young women for adoring Christ, the only true and living God! And it is in a senate-chamber where I see congregated noble and wise patricians, the glory and light of this city, that these savage shouts are heard! What, then, has become of that honor and justice on which you so prided yourselves until now ?

"*The Christians to the lions!* Of what so great

---

* In this and the following chapter we do little else than give a synopsis of Tertullian's celebrated *Apologeticus.*

and so odious a crime can they have become guilty
to be thus summarily condemned to a punishment
from which ordinary humanity spares the vilest
slave ? Is it the name alone you persecute with
such unflinching rigor ? But why should a name
in itself so harmless, and which simply implies that
those who bear it are the disciples of Christ, excite more odium than that of Platonist or Pitha-
gorean, which no one has ever dreamed of calling
a crime in the case of the disciples of Plato or
Pythagoras ? Here is a man who is confessedly
a good husband, an upright, law-abiding citizen,
honest, peaceable, and charitable to all ; simply because he calls himself a Christian, does the very
name, forsooth, render him unworthy to live ?
A modest, mild, chaste woman, the honor
and the model of her sex, is a Christian, and for
this is she deserving of death ? What is there so
evilly ominous and criminal in the name of Christian that it must needs be proscribed and wiped
out with torrents of blood ? When and where
has a name ever before provoked such deadly opposition ? Is not this the height of injustice and
madness ?

"*The Christians to the lions !* Their name
comes from Christ, whose stupendous sanctity
even Tiberius so far recognized as to wish to
dedicate altars to him, forbidding under the
severest penalties the molestation of his disciples ;
these lived in harmony and peace under the protection of the laws of the empire. The first to

draw the sword against us was Nero, the enemy
of every thing great, noble, and pure. But the
condemnation of such a man, or rather of such a
monster, is our justification, his hatred is our
glory, and the best proof of our innocence in the
eyes of the whole world. Of all the wise and
good princes who sat on the throne of the Cæsars,
not one sided with our enemies against us. Mar-
cus Aurelius publicly returned thanks to the
Christians for having, by their prayers, saved the
Roman army from the Quades and Marcomans in
Germany ; he did more—he made it a capital
crime for any man to prosecute them on the sole
score of religion.

"*The Christians to the lions !* But before
making them the food of the wild beasts kept in
your amphitheatres, have you given them a hearing ? Have you examined them juridically ?
Have you, as justice demands, afforded them the
power and the means of defending themselves ?
If a person be accused of murder, arson, or parri-
cide, does your lictor's axe smite him before he is
examined and tried ? Before you condemn the
blackest villain, you demand the proofs of his
crime, you admit the testimony of witnesses, you
allow the accused to say openly whatever he may
deem useful to his cause ; he can summon to his
aid the assistance even of learning and oratory.
Nor is this considered a favor ; it is only justice ;
meantime the barbarous laws that you invoke
against us deprive us of all that is granted to or-

dinary criminals.   Because we are Christians all
legal procedure is set aside in our case ; we are
neither citizens nor men, and hence other penalties, other executioners, are here necessary, and
so our case is referred to lions and tigers, the
worthy enforcers of such justice !   This is a
novel sort of legislation that you now wish
to introduce against us, and how subversive
of all received rules of procedure !   Let the accused deny the crime laid to his charge, let him
protest before the judge that he is not a thief or
a murderer, he is not discharged on the simple
plea of his not pleading guilty, but, after having
exhausted all the ordinary means of conviction, if
all doubt be not removed from your minds, you
order him to be put to the torture, to wring from
his lips the avowal which was held back through
shame or the fear of death.   In our case it is
just the reverse ; if I am summoned to one of
your tribunals for being a Christian, I need only
say that I am not one and I am discharged ;
the law requires nothing more of me, and in
case I am so disposed, I can drop manacles to
don honors.   On the contrary, if I refuse to
dishoner myself by a lie, and I persist in declaring myself to be a Christian, I am subjected to tortures the most barbarous and un-
heard-of to compel me to say I am not what
I really am.   But if my being a Christian
makes me deserving of death, why should I be
discharged on the strength of a simple denial

that would be futile in any other suit ? or why
employ such violence to compel me to say I am
not guilty of what you deem so heinous a crime ?
It is plain, therefore, that such a method of procedure is palpably absurd. Why do you not
adopt what would be a better plan, and write as
a heading over your new laws : ' It is forbidden,
under penalty of death, not to be, but to style
and declare one's self, a Christian ? ' You would
at least have the merit of frankness.

" *The Christians to the lions !* But why do
they deserve to be so hated, so abominated ? We
live among you ; our houses are as open as yours,
you may enter them at any hour of the day, for,
having nothing to hide, we fear not the most inquisitive eyes. Our homes, as you are well
aware, never re-echo to effeminate or voluptuous
strains ; there silence is broken only by prayer
and hymns to the God who created the universe.
We abominate all debaucheries, all that may flatter and foment the passions. We interdict all
banqueting and feasting, where pride and sensuality so often and so gayly squander the patrimony
of the needy and the orphan. Our meals are
frugal ; the beggar or the stranger never solicits
in vain his share of the homely fare that satisfies
our appetites and wants. Honorable magistrates,
consult your archives, send or go yourselves to
the grim prisons where lie in chains those who
dared to insult the majesty of the law, who steeped their hands in blood, who brought disgrace

and dishonor on their families, the parricides who clutched through crime at their paternal inheritance, the unnatural mothers who murdered their sin-begotten offspring, the turbulent or thieving slaves—among all these off-scourings of society you will not find a single Christian; ours keep themselves free from all crimes.

"Do we not live in submission to the laws? Is it among us that the spirit of revolt revolves sanguinary projects, thus paving the way for the dismemberment and ruin of the empire? We pay punctually and without complaining our share of the public taxes. Being lovers of peace, which we consider a precious boon from God, we nevertheless do not refuse to bear arms whenever our country calls us to her defence; our soldiers fight by the side of yours, and the enemy finds them no less brave or intrepid. The country has no better citizens nor the Cæsars more faithful and reliable subjects; you are well aware that it is not the Christian soldiers who dethrone and murder those whom they previously helped to nominate for the crown, nor are they of those who sell to the highest bidder the dishonored diadem of our emperors.

"As for our morals, they are pure and irreproachable; we abhor the very semblance of vice, and everything that trenches on immorality is banished from among us; chastity is the governing principle of our matrimonial alliances and guards them against other affections. Our young

men are conspicuous for uprightness of character; from infancy they are trained in the
school of virtue. Our daughters are modest and
reserved; they retain unsullied the candor of
childhood under the ever vigilant eye and shield-
ing hand of their chaste mothers. In order to
find time for prayer and contemplation many of
us lead a life of perfect continence; death may
find them old in years but children in innocence.
We prize purity so much and honor it so far that
we halt not even at the limits laid down by duty
and precept.

"Ignoring your gods as we do, it follows as a
consequence that we keep aloof from your temples. We have a horror of the abominations
committed in them under the cloak of religion;
these abominations are such that my tongue refuses to name them, and their very thought
makes me blush for shame. Neither do we take
part in your games, because, in the majority of
cases, to do so would entail the loss of modesty
and virtue. We shun your theatres, because they
are the public school of every vice and obscenity.
While you, victims of a shameful and insatiable
passion, go thither and sacrifice the honor of your
wives and daughters, we shut ourselves up in the
privacy of our homes to pray or to read *the law
pure and undefiled* of our God, in order to render
ourselves still more holy and pure.

"Magistrates, I appeal to yourselves; will
you refuse to accept your own testimony? 'Be-

hold,' say you every day, ' here is a man whose
excesses were known to the entire city ! Since
he became a Christian his life has been regular,
his habits exemplary.' ' This youth, heretofore
the leading spirit in every licentious gathering,
the first in every mad frolic and debauchery, by
becoming a Christian he has become another
man ; his deportment, his conversation, his whole
life has become redolent of modesty and decency.' ' This woman, who had been so reckless of her reputation as a wife, of her duties as
a mother, from the moment she embraced the
new religion she has led a life of strict seclusion ;
the world now seeks for her in vain at its festivities ; she eschews all its pleasures in willing punishment for incense and enjoyments so sought
after in the past.' It is thus that truth forces
even yourselves to proclaim the purity and holiness of our morals.

"I am aware that blind hatred lays to our
charge the most awful crimes. This is done in
Rome and it is done in Carthage ; these reports
have been spread to the ends of the world, and,
as usual, the calumny goes on increasing from
day to day. It is said that in our assemblies we
deliberately butcher an infant torn from its mother's bosom ; that we greedily devour its flesh
and steep our lips in its still warm blood; that
after this horrible feast is over dogs trained for
the purpose upset the lights, and that, under
this opportune darkness, we indulge in the most

diabolical and unnatural deeds. Through a sense of shame and respect for you I would fain pass over this imputation in silence, but the demands of our cause compel me to ventilate it.

" That we have our meetings I do not deny, nor that we strictly refuse access to the profane —by this we designate those who belong not to us—they alone can be present who have been initiated after long and severe tests. How, then, and through whom can you be informed of what takes place in them ? Let me ask has any one here witnessed it ? If so let him arise, let him speak and say what his privileged eye saw and ear heard on a subject about which the public speaks with so much assurance. At least let the deserter be named who could and did divulge those secrets of blood and infamy upon his own personal knowledge and experience ! Why skulk in the dark ? Such a man would be a benefactor to heaven and earth if he could convict us, and put an end, by clear and public proof, to crimes which must interest, because they disgrace, our human nature.

" The youngest infant must utter cries upon being put to death in such a barbarous manner ; these cries ought to be heard outside, and should find an echo in the breast of every mother. What woman can say she has trembled at such heart-rending cries ? Death invariably leaves some remnants of its victims ; blood leaves some accusing marks ! But who has ever seen any ?

Who has ever gathered and preserved them for a
proof of the crime? A child cannot disappear
without the family noticing the loss of one of its
members. Where are the mourners for a child
taken by its mother in the evening to one of our
assemblies and never again brought back to the
paternal roof? But to drink and relish the blood
of these tender and innocent little ones! You
cannot be aware of the fact that we are forbidden by our law to eat the blood of animals or the
flesh of anything strangled? Noble senators, the
wives and daughters of many of you are Christians and are instructed in our mysteries. Arise
and say whether, upon their return from our assemblies, you have detected the odor of this pal-
pitating flesh, or found traces of this foaming
blood upon their lips! Tell us if you have even
seen anything in them to cause you to suspect
aught of all these horrible excesses which are so
calumniously laid to our charge!

"You have a soul and a heart! Well, then,
permit me to invite you to bury your knife in the
breast of this infant, who is incapable of even
producing hatred in your bosom; tear it in pieces
with your hands in order to partake of it; carefully collect every drop of its blood; dip your
bread into and eat it; but as you eat note well
where your mother or sister is seated! Senators, you shudder with horror at the bare thought.
I flatter myself I know why; it is because you
are men! But we are men as well; our nature

is not different from yours! How, then, could we do what you would be incapable of doing even if you had the will?

"Spurn, then, for ever this calumny, out of which hate makes capital with such incredible persistency in order to draw upon us the fury of the mob. Let us be informed once for all what is our crime, why those cries for our blood which so plainly harbinger the deadly scenes that are about to disgrace your city? As for us, we live at peace with *those outside* as well as with our brethren. We do evil to none; if we are insulted we remain silent; if we are plundered, we complain not; we make no applications to your tribunals for redress nor for the restoration of what has been unjustly wrested from us. If we are hated, if we are reviled, we cordially pardon and repay good for the evil received. We have enemies because people persist in being so, while we give offense to none; meantime we pray for them and cease not to love them. This is the Christians' revenge. Display and luxury being interdicted to us, our wants are few, and hence we give the superfluous to the poor, to whom it rightfully belongs. With our gold we purchase liberty for the captive and the slave and a home for the wanderer and the houseless; we bestow especial care on the aged, the orphans, and the sick; we refuse not food and raiment to those whom you so heartlessly abandon to misery and want. Indeed, our charity is so well known to you that you yourselves say commouly : *See the Christians how they love one another; their own poor are not enough for them; to our shame, they support ours also.*

"In order to compass our destruction it would seem as if every means were good, and even lying against us were praiseworthy. Because our religion forbids us to sacrifice to the emperors, who are only mortals like ourselves, and although, by reason of the power given them by God, we regard them *as secondary majesties*, we are branded as their enemies. Although it is a notorious fact that we never enter into conspiracies or revolts, no matter, a pretext must be trumped up to deprive us of the protection of the laws; it has been found, and people cling to it persistently. I shall not repeat what I have said regarding our loyalty to the emperors. Our instructors in the faith have taught us to pray daily for them. While, through flattery or fear, you coldly offer vows to your deaf and powerless gods, or deluge your temples with the unavailing blood of oxen and sheep, we, with eyes raised to heaven, with hands uplifted, because pure, with bared heads, because we have nothing to be ashamed of, we supplicate the only true and omnipotent God to grant the Cæsars a long life, a peaceful reign, security in their palaces, courage for their legions, wisdom and justice for the senate, virtue for the people, and peace for the whole empire. We alone can obtain from him all these favors, because we alone

adore him, because we are ready to lay down our
lives for his law, because we offer him the most
pleasing of all sacrifices—prayers emanating from
a chaste body, a spotless soul, and a pure heart
animated by the Holy Ghost. We enemies of
the emperors! Ah! may they never have any
other! The sceptre shall never more tremble in
their hands, nor the crown on their heads; they
shall no longer have to fear the secret plots nor
sanguinary revolts that daily threaten their lives.

"It is asserted that our religion is new. Yes,
in Rome and in Carthage I grant. But in Asia,
the cradle of the human race, it remounts to the
remotest antiquity; it reckons more than fifty
centuries, and its birth is coeval with that of the
world. The religion that, in your opinion, has
but just been established was taught by God to
the first man. Christ, from whom it derives its
present name, only confirmed, consecrated, and
raised it to its full perfection. But even were
it a new religion, would that be a sufficient reason
to proscribe it without examination? Has not
everything in this world had its beginning—laws,
institutions, empires, and kingdoms? Is your
own religion eternal? do we not know the very
day when lies began to contend for the mastery
against the eternal truth held by us?

"Before condemning us, justice would demand
that you know us thoroughly; it is absolutely
unjust to hate what you do not know, as well as
to blaspheme what you do not understand. Then

what do you when you curse and clamor for our death for the reason that we are Christians? Through blind hatred and groundless prejudice, you assail people whom you cannot call guilty, from the fact that you do not know them. But take heed, this ignorance will bear witness, and plead against you; it will convict you before the tribunal of reason and conscience, and, from age to age, will tell to unborn generations that the senate of the second greatest city in the world proscribed thousands of men, women, and children, that it did this *through prejudice*, and for the sole reason that they went by a name the meaning of which that senate did not understand. Noble magistrates, before you stigmatize and fulminate that name by your contempt and might, learn its import as I have done. Think not that I ask any favors for that religion; no, persecution can neither dismay nor terrify it; it knows that it is destined to find enemies in the world; being the offspring of heaven, its hope, glory, rest, and throne are in heaven. The least you can do is to examine it; it fears not the light; being confident of victory, it simply demands that it be not judged and condemned without a hearing. The justice denied by an infuriated mob you will not refuse; here, and in your presence at least, I am persuaded its voice shall not be drowned by the mad cries that only a few moments ago I had the mortification of hearing.

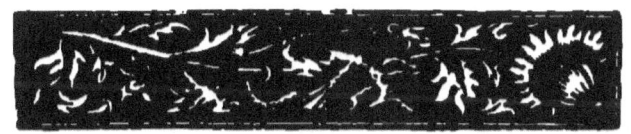

CHAPTER XIX.

THE TWO RELIGIONS.

" You deplore the fact that the number of the Christians is constantly increasing; the city, say you, is becoming filled with them; they are everywhere—in the rural districts, in the fortified places, in the island as on the mainland; and you say the truth. Men and women, the young and the old, the great, the rich, the poor, and the needy alike are leaving you in crowds and openly coming over to us. *We are but of yesterday,* and yet we fill every place—cities, castles, towns, councils, camps, tribes, companies, armies, the palace, the senate, and the forum. Your temples alone have escaped this invasion; they are the only places we leave you, and you are at no loss to ascertain the reason. At Rome and in the provinces, where persecution has been essayed, the sword, the axe, fire, water, the cross, the mines, everything has been put into requisition; thousands have been slaughtered; the innocence of childhood, the helplessness of womanhood, the hoary and venerable circlet on the brows of the aged—nothing was respected, nothing spared.

They wished to drown in blood *the accursed Christian race.* But God in his omnipotence turned that blood into a germ and a seed so fruitful that it gave to the Church thousands of new children. You are as .well aware of this marvellous and astounding fact as I am; if it does not make you reflect, I pity you.

"Noble senators, your so-called religion is pleasant and accommodating; it puts no restraint on the inner man nor on the desires of his heart. Pride, pleasure, intemperance, and all the passions are allowed full scope; every man is at liberty to give free rein to all his thoughts and desires; your religion knows no barrier save the impossibility of further enjoyment. To it belong enjoyment, pleasure, festivities, public games, theatricals, luxury, display, and banqueting; to it belong, too, the peace of the nation, the protection given by the laws, position and honor in society—everything, even the crown of the Cæsars. Our religion is the reverse of all this. Her creed requires the silent submission of the understanding, her precepts the obedience of the heart and of the will. To embrace it we must renounce every inordinate desire and devote ourselves to a life of retirement, prayer, and abnegation. Ours are contempt and revilings, and the future has in store for us only exile, prison, tortures, and death. According to all the laws of nature and all the aspirations of the human heart, we should increase your ranks,

we should demand of your religion what is denied
to us by our own, we should seek in your company all those enjoyments that embellish life and
from which we have voluntarily estranged ourselves ; and it is you who take refuge in our
camp and come to be enrolled under the humble
and blood-stained standard of the cross ! There
must be a reason for this. We are of your own
stock and nature. We were made, not born,
Christians. We have lived among you and have
taken part in your rites and sacrifices. But we
separated from you because the light has shone
in our souls. We have been convinced that the
gods whom we formerly worshipped with you
are not gods ; that what we hold and practised
as a religion in the past is unworthy of any upright and enlightened mind, and more unworthy
still of every honest and pure heart. It would
be cowardice and a crime to resist our convictions. With erect heads and hearts we have
ranged ourselves on the side of truth and have
pledged to her cause our honor, our liberty, and
our very lives.

"Noble magistrates, hear me without prejudice,
as men of your wisdom and exalted position
should. We are told to sacrifice to the gods and
to acknowledge them as such. I appeal to your
consciences ; let us be judged, let us be condemned by them, as we should certainly deserve to be,
provided you can deny that all those whom you
style your gods were men like you and me. If

you admit it, we are acquitted, and you shall have
no alternative but to imitate our example. If,
despite the testimony of your conscience, you
question this fact, take heed, for all the monuments of the past rise up against you as so many
incontestable witnesses; they will give you the
names of the cities where those men were born,
the countries where they lived, the places where
they died and where the graves may still be
found that cover their ashes. I shall not weary
you with the ridiculous history of each of those
gods; it would be interminable, for there are gods
old and new, barbarian, Grecian, Roman, Carthagenian, private, public, urban, rural, naval, and
military. I shall reduce the question to a single
point, which you would fain forget because it over-
whelms you.

" You avow, and it is universally admitted, that
Saturn is the oldest and the first of all your gods.
He heads the catalogue, and accordingly it is from
him you derive all the leading and most honored
gods of your interminable calendar. But what is
true of the first or father of your gods is equally
so of all his descendants. Question, therefore,
your most ancient historians, examine the monuments of antiquity—they are impartial and irre-
fragable witnesses of the facts. Saturn was born
and lived in Greece, whence he came into Italy
at the time of King Janus. He gave laws to
that country, then in a state of barbarism. Like
all men born of woman, he grew old and died

there. Fable loves a wide range and deals in fancies, not facts, and thus it made Saturn the son of heaven and earth, as if they had blended and brought forth an offspring. In common with us, you have classed this absurdity as belonging to the domain of poetry, and you know full well that it arose from the fact that Saturn was a stranger from a distant country and of unknown parentage. Even to-day we say of a person who comes suddenly and unseen that he *has fallen from the sky or clouds.* And so it was with Saturn.

"But if Saturn was only a man, a fact that no one can seriously doubt, those born of him, your Jupiter and the rest, were men like their father, or else the ridiculous absurdity must be admitted that the immortal gods owe both existence and godship to miserable mortals. Besides, you yourselves recount their birth; you tell what woman or what goat suckled them; you find diversion in narrating their exploits and adventures. I am aware that, to avoid the crushing arguments derived from the more than humble part played by them, you assert that *godship was communicated to them after death.* You admit, therefore, in spite of yourselves, a supreme, absolute, self-existing God from the fact that, as you say, he can communicate divinity to those who previously had it not. By what name, then, will you call this omnipotent, self-existing, eternal Being? How do you worship him? What sacrifices do you offer to him ? Is he in Carthage, as at Athens, *the unknown God*—the God without a name ? What a shame for those who call themselves wise men !

"The divine nature is *incommunicable;* it is essentially eternal, *one*, infinite, and indivisible; but were it otherwise, and could it be supposed, by an impossible hypothesis, that men could be made gods, although the eternal God needs no one, much less the dead, to assist him in the government of a world which he created and which existed long before your Saturn and your Jupiter, assuredly it would not be those whom you senselessly adore that he would have chosen to raise to such a dignity. We know all about those so-called gods; we have read your theologians and poets, and we blush even now at the thought that we were once capable of burning a single grain of incense on their altars!

"Is it necessary to remind you of what your priests still repeat every day to you in your temples ? The gods are unparalleled for cruelty, avarice, knavery, hatred, bickering, adultery, and incest. This one eats his children lest they should verify the prediction that they would one day take up arms against and dethrone him ; that one defiles his own sister's bed, and lends himself to every degradation and meanness to satisfy his brutal passions and lusts so infamous that they would disgrace the most degraded debauchee among men ; one is treacherous and a thief; another delights only in murder, riots, and blood. Sarentina has altars erected to her, although she outstripped a *Lais* or a *Phyrne* as a prostitute. Some of your gods are always drunk and reeling with wine, like those besotted, degraded beings whom your children mock and bespatter with mud in our streets. It must needs be acknowledged then that God, who is infinite, and from whom, too, the future cannot be hidden, was sadly mistaken in making such a hasty selection and that he closed heaven to men infinitely preferable and more meritorious.

"Strange inconsistency! you say there is a *Tartarus*, a prison or place of punishment for the wicked, to which you consign unnatural children, adultcresses, persons guilty of incest, rape, or cruelty, thieves, murderers, corrupters of children, cheats, perjurers—in fact, all those who most closely resemble some one or other of your gods. Ah! hearken to me and rid your heaven of this infamous rabble, consign them to hell, their proper place; it is far more just to bring back from Tartarus and enthrone in heaven all those men so unreasonably condemned to suffering, since their crimes are incomparably less heinous than those of your so-called gods. Blasphemy! sacrilege! you will perhaps exclaim. You may rage and fume as you will; you know in your hearts that we say but the truth and that shame alone restrains us from enumerating many and far worse crimes.

"To these powerless, godless divinities you have been able to attribute only contemptible parts. One of your oldest and most esteemed poets, whose verses grace all your festivities, has immortalized their imperfections and absurdities. In one instance your gods, having sided with the Trojans or the Greeks, fight each other like so many gladiators; in another a goddess, with *a name synonymous with lust* would pollute our lips, complains and weeps like a child at seeing herself bleeding from a wound made by a soldier's arrow. Mars, your invincible Mars, allows himself to be detected and bound hand and foot by a lame blacksmith; for three months does he pine in bonds and in the fear of death. The all-powerful Jove barely escapes the conspiracy formed by the gods against him and his despotic tyranny; like a drivelling old man, he can only bestow tears on his son, Sarpedon, when he could not save his life. Apollo tends the flocks of King Admetus; Neptune hires him as he would a mason to build the walls of Troy; his grandfather strikes Esculapius with lightning for the venality and avarice with which he practised his art; a contest for the palm of beauty takes place between some of the goddesses, precisely as might have been the case among so many vain courtesans, and they leave the decision to the judgment of an effeminate stripling; even the grave Cybele languishingly sighs for a scornful swain. Such are the sort of gods for whom you claim our re-

verence; your very comedians turn them into
ridicule on the stage, and by so doing give proof
of having better sense than you can lay claim to.

"Would that they were only criminal and ridiculous! But they are also your teachers; in
their school what can you learn except crime, and
how can you honor them worthily unless by imi-
tating their excesses and debaucheries? Do you
believe we know nothing about your disgraceful
mysteries? We are perfectly aware that it is in
your temples, at the feet of your altars, in the
name of your gods, and to please them, that
shrinking modesty is basely immolated; it is with
brows bound with sacred fillets that your wives
and daughters prostitute themselves *in the name
of religion.* Your rites and ceremonies demand
and consecrate the most frightful abominations;
your gods invite you to commit them; they
smile on your crimes; their festivals, to be pro-
perly celebrated, must become wild orgies, mad
revels, where all decency is publicly outraged.
But I will pursue no further a subject so disgust-
ing and vast. . . . One day when wisdom shall
have enlightened the nations, when that light
from above that even now shines for us shall
have dissipated the filthy darkness that still
shrouds the human race, posterity will ask with
surprise and awe how could it have been possible
that men could have accepted and adored such
gods, and, in the face of day, could have offered
them a sacrifice immeasurably more awful than

human blood—the sacrifice of modesty and chastity.

"We spurn and abhor those gods of human invention and make with whom you have peopled your Olympus. Our God (and may he soon become yours!) had no beginning; his age is eternity. Infinite in his perfections, essentially holy, or rather holiness itself, it was he who, by his word, wisdom, and omnipotence, created the world and all its array of elements, bodies, and spirits, in order to show forth his power and glory. He is invisible, although he appears constantly in the marvels of creation; impalpable even while stamping in us his image; incomprehensible to our weakness, even though human reason may arrive at the knowledge of him; perfectly known only to himself, since he alone is infinite and illimitable. Nothing conveys a more magnificent conception of him than the very impossibility of that conception, his infinite perfections and transcendent greatness revealing and at the same time hiding him from the minds of men, and thus rendering him both known and unknown to human ken.

"If the heavens, the earth, the ocean, the day, the night speak eloquently of him and repeat his glory to every attentive mind, the soul, despite the prison of the body and the tyranny of the passions, when it awakes as if to sudden consciousness, pays homage to his name and proclaims faith in him: *Great God! Good God!*

As God wills! God wills! Oh! testimony of the soul naturally Christian. His name frequently starts unbidden and unthinkingly to your lips, and when this happens is it not a fact that you then turn your eyes, not towards one of your temples, but towards heaven! The reason is because the soul knows that it is in heaven that God, that he who alone merits this name, has his dwelling-place and his throne; that it is from heaven it derived its origin, since it derived it from God.

"Besides the Scriptures, whose simple and yet sublime pages were inspired by him, from the beginning and through every age God delegated certain men who, by their virtues and merits, were made worthy of knowing him and of making him known to others; these he enlightened by his Spirit to proclaim to the world that there is but one God who created all things, and moulded man from the dust of the earth, who governs the seasons, whose ministers and avengers are the elements, who has given precepts and laws, the violation of which shall entail eternal punishment, and their observance everlasting reward, when, at the end of time, he will summon the dead to his tribunal. The men who received this divine mission we call *seers*, because the secrets of the future were unveiled to them. Their prophecies and the miracles wrought by them in proof of their mission are narrated in our sacred books, which antedate by many centuries your

most ancient records, your gods, your oracles, and
your sacrifices; one of them named Moses pre-
ceded your Homer by more than five hundred
years, and yet there were many prophets previous
to his day.   They all foretold the establishment,
progress, trials, combats, and triumphs of Christ's
religion.   Seeing what comes to pass in our own
day, we call to mind the fact that they had been
foretold, and our faith only grows stronger.   I am
not surprised that you scoff at these things; I
myself did so formerly, but then I was blind like
yourselves.

"Long beforehand our prophets had foretold
that, in punishment for their pride and infidelity,
the Jowish people, banished from their country,
dispersed, wandering, without a God, king, or
altar, would show to every nation on the globe
the awful malediction that pursued them; you can
verify the truth of this prophecy for yourselves.
But it was foretold that God would then choose
to himself more faithful followers from the East
and West, that the new Lawgiver who was to come
to enlighten, reform, and save the nations would
be God's own Son, not a son that would have to
blush for the wickedness of his father, who
should owe his existence to the incest of a sister,
to the weakness of a seduced girl, to the infidelity of another man's wife, but a Son eternally
begotten of his Father, and in the plenitude of
time born of the purest of virgins without man
having had any part in this marvellous conception.

" For five thousand years heaven announced
Emmanuel, the Man-God, to the world; the
world awaited his coming with trembling anxiety ;
the time and the place of his birth were known ;
at the specified moment *the Desired of the nations*
appeared. To accommodate himself to our weakness and wants he clothed himself with our human nature; but under its lowly garb his divinity remained not entirely hidden. Under the
carping scrutiny of a prejudiced people he gave
repeated proofs of his divine origin. By the
same word that created the world and shall one
day renew it, he put demons to flight, gave sight
to the blind, cured the leper and the sick, made
the paralytic walk, commanded the elements and
the storm, and called the dead from their graves.
He foretold the manner of his death, and when
the hour was come he voluntarily delivered himself up to his enemies, and died on the cross—on
the cross the object of your derision, because
you know not its glory or power. His death
was accompanied by miracles that demonstrated
his divinity; he gave up the ghost at his own free
will and with his own word, thus anticipating
and rendering unnecessary the usual office of the
executioner; the sun veiled himself in his meri-
dian splendor and grew dark ; the heavens were
draped in murky clouds, the hills shook, the
rocks were rent, the veil of the temple was torn,
the dead arose and appeared to many. Christ
lived like a God and he died like a God. A cen-

turion and some Roman soldiers were the first conquest of the *Crucified* One.

"He had said, '*I lay down my life;* on the third day I will rise again.' Accordingly, at the dawn of that day, and notwithstanding the precautions taken by the Jews and the guard watching the sepulchre, the stone rolled away from it, to the terror and dismay of the soldiers; in the empty tomb there was found only a winding-sheet; Christ, death's conqueror, had arisen. Forty days after he ascended gloriously to heaven in the presence of his apostles. Pilate, a Christian by instinct, but by policy the murderer of the Just One, transmitted to the emperor Tiberius an exact account of all this. This document is still preserved in the archives at Rome and is widely known. The Cæsars would have become Christians long ago had they not been necessary for the world, and still more necessary for the designs of God upon his nascent Church.

"The men chosen by Christ to preach his doctrine were but humble fishermen. They had neither the learning of philosophers nor the eloquence of orators; nevertheless, aided by strength from on high, they confidently divided the whole world for their future spiritual conquest. All the nations have heard their voice; the islands and the continents have witnessed their miracles and marvellous progress. Even Athens and Rome have paid homage to their irresistible words. When death put an end to their glorious career other apostles moulded by them continued the work of regeneration and salvation, and you know what rapid strides it has made. The worm-eaten throne of your gods is crumbling everywhere; the demons who have caused themselves to be worshipped under the name of those would-be gods acknowledge their discomfiture. If you desire to persecute us you must lose no time, for in a few years the whole world will be Christian. Take our blood if you will, that will only hasten the day of victory.

"Believe and say what you will, Christ is the true God. Despite all human opposition, his pacific reign shall embrace the East and the West, and no power can wrest from him the sceptre of the world. From the moment of his death on the cross the movement began, and all the nations, drawn by an irresistible power, shall come in turn to fall at his feet, until he will descend upon the ruins of the universe to crown those who shall have believed in and served him in faith and purity of heart. Noble magistrates, if you believe not my words, believe at least those whom you revere as your gods; you cannot question their testimony. In the name of Christ, we compel them to acknowledge that they are nothing more than unclean demons. In the name of Christ, their conqueror and maker, we · oblige them to come forth trembling from the bodies of the possessed; by the omnipotence of that sacred name we compel their oracles to become mute.

Test it, the experiment may be easily made. Even I, the last and least among Christians, am ready to stake my head that I shall exhort that avowal in your presence from any of your number who, by inhaling fumes at the altar, shall show the usual signs of being, as you say, *under the influence and inspiration of the god.* There can be no danger that your gods will lie to their own detriment and confusion.

"Such, then, is our faith. We believe in one God, eternal Creator and Sovereign Lord of the universe. We believe in Christ, his only Son, his word, his wisdom. Consequently we are forbidden to acknowlege or honor the gods that you have made. And if you should like to know something regarding what you so unjustly style *the Christian faction*, I will here briefly state what we are and what we do; this will show you even yet more plainly that to persecute us is tantamount to the perpetration of one of the most awful crimes—namely, that of persecuting innocence itself.

"We keep aloof from all intrigues; we never mix in politics; our aims, like our hopes, are on a higher plane than this world. We shun your public games; they are born of superstition and beget corruption and deceit. We take no part in the excesses and follies of the circus, in the obscenities of the theatre, the cruelties of the arena, nor in the improprieties of the gymnasium; we cheerfully leave all your pleasures to yourselves; ours are quieter and purer, and suit us better. Besides, if it is our pleasure to shun all amusement, what harm is this to others? And if it were a privation, the loss and the regrets should affect only ourselves.

"Having but the self-same faith and hope, we form but one family, or rather body. We meet on certain days to worship God; we pray for the emperors at our meetings, although we are accused of being their enemies; we do the same for all those in office, for peace, for our friends, and even for all who hate us without cause. We read our Sacred Scriptures with due respect, and draw from them the light and instruction required by our wants and circumstances. The holy Word strengthens our faith, animates our hopes, nerves our courage, and fortifies us in the performance of our duties. Aged men preside over these assemblies; having undergone a long probation, they are appointed to that honor as a reward and a public recognition of merit; for with us the priesthood is not a prize to be won by intrigue and bribery.

"Nevertheless, we have a sort of treasury; we have no cause to blush, however, on this score, for we have made no traffic of religion in order to form it. Each of us, according to his means and will, makes a small monthly contribution. This is a pious fund that runs no risk of being squandered in feasting and banqueting; it is used for the maintenance and support of the needy, pen-

niless orphans, decrepid and abandoned slaves,
and those who have lost their all by shipwreck.
When one of our brethren is condemned to the
hard toil of the mines, chained in the dungeon,
or transported to some island on account of his
faith, the religion to which he has generously
borne testimony follows him and provides for his
wants.

"We live in the greatest harmony and union,
and like brothers we share the goods which
among you cause so much domestic contention
and strife. Having but one heart, everything is
in common between us—everything except our
children and wives. We are divided only on the
sole point that unites all other men. Marriage is
sacred and has inviolable rights among us. With
you it is different. You do not blush to treat
your wives as Socrates and Cato did theirs; the
children of your wives may well not be yours
when the wisest of your philosophers and the
shrewdest of your censors have set the example
of rendering paternity doubtful.

"Among us chastity is required of all; God
himself taught it to us; we practise it faithfully
because such is the command of a Judge who
cannot deceive and who inflicts eternal punishment on crime. How could it be possible for us
to shed our brothers' blood when we are forbidden to harbor even anger? How could we defile
ourselves with adultery when our law condemns
lustful thoughts and even looks. So far are we

from injuring any that we are forbidden to resent even injury itself.

" We are accused of being useless members in society; nevertheless, we do not live in the woods like the Brahmins of India; we live among you, travel with you, we bear arms, we till the soil, we trade, we ply the same trades and professions; we purchase in your warcrooms the flour we eat and the stuffs we wear; we reject none of the things made by God for man's use; we simply avoid excess and abuse. As to the feasts that we are accused of celebrating, their very name indicates their object; we call them *agapæ*, or love-feasts, for charity is their end and aim. They do not cost enormous sums of money as yours do; our table is served with becoming frugality, and the poor man sits at it by the side of the rich, for with us the poor are the friends of God and our most pleasing care.

"Senators of Carthage, pay attention to my concluding words. A brave soldier, while he does not fear danger, does not seek it; when it comes he does not flinch. We do not invite persecution, but if it does come we will face it boldly; it is our glory. We do not rush into the jaws of death like madmen; if it comes we receive it cordially and gladly; for us death is a triumph, the entering into the possession of that life eternal for which we constantly sigh, so that by depriving us of the little place that each of us holds in this world we receive in exchange

a throne in heaven.   Do you thirst for our blood?
Take it ; but at the same time learn to know who
are those innocent and unoffending men that are
so relentlessly persecuted !   Were they so disposed, a single night and a few torches would be
enough to make Carthage a heap of ashes ! Were
it our rule to do evil for evil, we would have no
occasion to retaliate in the dark ; we could act
overtly, and to-morrow—nay, this very day we
might marshal an army so great, brave, and devoted that your thinned legions would find it no
easy task to cope with it ; fortunately, however,
it is one of our principles that it is better to be
slain than to slay.   Instead of rushing to arms,
all we need do would be to leave you and seek
some other country ; you would then stand amazed at the solitude and desolation to which your
paralyzed city would be reduced.   I have made
known to you the God whom we adore, and who
is your God, no matter whether you will or not.
I have defended our religion against prejudice,
ignorance, calumny, and hatred.   Judge now
whether *the Christians deserve death !* "

And Tertullian slowly withdrew, leaving the
assembly spellbound by his arguments and eloquence.

CHAPTER XX.

AT his departure from the senate Tertullian plainly saw that the crowds around the doors were greatly excited. Although he readily surmised the cause, still he calmly made his way through the press and bent his steps homeward ; it was about the ninth hour of the day. The pagan priest was coming from the opposite direction, and as he recognized Tertullian's retreating form all the hate of his envenomed soul broke loose. He strove to harangue the mob in order to set them on the hated victim whom he had sworn to ruin ; but the words died on his parched and quivering lips, anger so choked his utterance as to render him incapable of speech. The mob laughed at his vain efforts and the contortions of his red and bloated countenance ; some even hissed him. When the opportunity presented itself, the pagans freely bestowed their contempt and sarcasm on the venerable representatives of their immortal gods.

Meantime the senate resumed its deliberations but with its wonted calmness and dignity. Ter-

tullian's eloquent harangue still rang in their
ears ; they seemed to hear the echo of the triumphant proofs of the innocence of the Christians, of the blind, fanatical injustice and hatred
shown them on all sides. On the other hand,
they still seemed to gaze on the beauteous and
heavenly form of that religion which, in God's
name and by his commission, revealed to the
world doctrines so simple and sublime, and a code
of morals that could have been framed only in
heaven. The ominous terms *proscription* and
death were mentioned no more. To conciliate
the mob, however, the more timid advised the
arrest of some of the more zealous and leading
Christians, but the majority opposed the measure
as being the outcome of timidity and fear. " If
the Christians are guilty, said these, let them be
condemned without discrimination and in accordance with the imperial edicts. But if no
crime can be proved against them, justice and its
own honor makes it incumbent on the senate to
protect them boldly against their enemies ! " At
Rome, as it is well known, the senate did not act
in this way; it basely bowed to the will and caprice of its *master.*

Instigated by the violent harangues of the implacable Sylvanus and some slaves who were
simple enough to credit his fair promises, the
mob sent message after message to the senate to
inform them that the people would brook delay
no longer, and had determined to take the law

into their own hands if the laws were not immediately and sternly enforced against the Christians. It was urged that no time was to be lost, as the day was already far advanced, and vengeance should not be delayed until the morrow. But it was in vain, the senate remained firm, and made answer that in justice to itself it could not yield to threats and language that breathed rebellion and insolence. The senate would have had to pay dearly for their courage and firmness had not Hilarian opportunely made his appearance on the scene. It was to his interest to postpone matters to the next day; he hoped to succeed with Angela. Upon repetition of the assurance that he would do full justice to all their reasonable demands, the mob agreed to disperse. The old mountain shepherd was furious; headed by a band of the more turbulent, he rushed to the gate through which the remains of the hapless Jarbas had just been brought into the city under the escort of a detachment of troops and a guard of honor.

A most wicked and barbarous deed was there perpetrated; at the sight of the urn containing the ashes of the late commander all Sylvanus's old hatred of Vivia waxed stronger than ever. " Vengeance ! " screamed he ; " vengeance, O my friends ! Will you allow more honors to be paid to the accursed remains of the villain that betrayed his country and religion for the sake of a base woman ? " So saying he rushed like a madman through the guards, snatched up the urn, shivered it into atoms, and flung the ashes to the winds. The applause and yells of his companions made the scene the very picture of a pandemonium. The news of this barbarous deed soon reached the ears of the unhappy Vivia; of the man she had so deeply loved she had now nothing to weep over save his sad memory!

Still the generous neophyte murmured not. Her faith and courage came to her aid, and soon dried her tears. What cared she more what happened in this world? All her thoughts and aspirations were now fixed in heaven, where she would soon meet her beloved husband. The presentiment that her end was nigh grew stronger than ever; she felt that her sole duty now was to make ready for the *glorious testimony* which she was called upon to give to Jesus Christ.

But what had become of Angela, the pure, tender virgin, whose honor and life were equally in jeopardy? Let us turn from the howling mob, thirsting for blood and desecrating the ashes of a brave soldier who died asking pardon for his murderer; let us return to the Christian maiden condemned to dishonor and death by Hilarian, in case she will not renounce Jesus Christ as her God and Spouse.

It was late at night when Vivia heard what had happened to Angela. Since her final conversion the patrician lady had conceived a most tender affection for the young virgin. She took pleasure in visiting and conversing with her on spiritual subjects, but especially on the happiness of loving God.   Many long hours were spent in these sweet communings, but they seemed short, they were so pleasant and so full of consolation. Angela, too, seeing how worthy and generous was that soul, now that it had emancipated itself from the vain things of earth, often denied herself by leaving the retirement in which she loved to dwell to seek the society of her young friend. Vivia appreciated this mark of friendship all the more from the fact that she was fully aware that this was an exceptional favor in her behalf.   Full of anxiety, therefore, on account of the dangers that threatened Angela, she could not think of retiring to rest.   Before dawn, therefore, she set out, under the escort of Revocatus and Felicitas, to seek her friend.   Having arrived at the door, she dismissed her attendants with a message for her mother and Rufina, lest they might be alarmed at her absence.

After having received the Holy Mysteries at the hands of the venerable Optatus, Angela prepared to spend her last night in prayer.   On her knees, rapt in ecstasy, with her hands crossed on her bosom, she seemed to hold sweet converse with some being invisible to other eyes, yet plainly visible and present to hers.   A heavenly smile played upon her lips, and by an occasional movement seemed to be addressing the mysterious object of her affections.   As a preparation for the immediate celebration of her eternal espousals with the Spotless Lamb, for the signing with her blood of the eternal contract of love, she had bedecked herself in the white robes of a *bride*; she had placed on her head the white veil received at the time of her consecration, together with a crown of roses and lilies. In the mellow light of the lamp that fell upon her she seemed like an angel gazing with rapture and love on the very face of God.

For a moment Vivia stood spellbound at the sight. She was loath to interrupt the deep meditation and recollection of her friend, but remembering that she had come to listen and speak to the generous maiden for the last time, and to gather strength for her own confession of the faith, she drew nigh, and, calling her by name, fell weeping into her arms.

"Why, Vivia, is this you?" said the young virgin, as she aroused herself from her ecstasy. "Of course you have come to congratulate me on my good-fortune. Oh! how happy am I to die for *my Beloved.* A few hours more and I shall go to him; I shall see him; I shall gaze face to face upon his adorable countenance and shall be received into his loving arms!"

"Angela, why are you so anxious to leave us all, to depart from a world that you edify by your good example and many virtues?"

"It is *His* will; *he* has heard the plaintive cooing of the dove; *he* stretches out his hand to

restore her to the ark where he dwells, to the
mystic cell where he reposes. My captive, exiled
soul yearns for *him*, to fly to *him*. If you but
knew *my Beloved* as I know *him!* I saw him
only for a little while, alas! How indescribably
beautiful *he* is! What sweetness in his looks!
How ravishing his smile! how tender and loving
his accents! In him everything is incomparable,
everything is pleasing, everything is ravishing,
everything floods the heart with happiness and
love!"

"But can you not live and love as you have
always done in the past?"

"Vivia, for the ten years that have elapsed
since He *wounded my heart* I have been languishing, not living. And you, who are so kind,
would you desire to drop gall into my cup of
happiness? But hark! *He* is speaking. *He* calls.
He bids me hasten."

The young virgin suddenly assumed the attitude of one listening to a voice speaking to
her. With feelings of awe, Vivia broke not the
solemn silence. Though she heard no sound, the
atmosphere seemed to be gently moved and laden
with unearthly fragrance. A brilliant glory en-
circled Angela's head; her face became radiant
with indescribable beauty; the blush of the rose
and the whiteness of the lily were there blended
in marvellous perfection.

"Did you hear Him, Vivia?" said she after a
short pause. "Did you see *my Beloved?* Never

was his voice sweeter; never did he seem to me more fair and lovely. His hand touched mine, and I felt as if he placed a ring upon my finger; his lips were pressed to my brow. How can I explain the heavenly raptures that deluged my soul? I thought I should have died of happiness and love; what, then, shall it be in heaven, when I shall contemplate him in the fulness of his beauty, when I shall possess him with all the strength of my affection and love?"

" Beloved Angela, do not take umbrage at the words of a poor neophyte. I understand the earnestness of your desire ; death will bestow upon you the *heavenly Spouse* whom you so ardently love. But who will console your parents for the loss of their idolized child?"

" He who never forsakes his own, who turns to joy every anguish that is offered to him with humility and resignation. My parents! Ah! you know how I love them. For a little while my heart was tortured at the thought of being separated from them. But my *Beloved* is still more dear to me ; *I am his ; he* calls me ; besides, *he* has informed me that I shall precede them only by a few short days."

" Great is your faith ; still greater is your love, Angela. Why am I not like you? But as you are determined to give your life for the faith of Jesus Christ, I only ask you to defer your happiness for a short time. You have heard of the events that have caused so much excitement among the people. The mob is everywhere clamoring for our death; a persecution is inevitable, and many of our brethren will be called on to lay down their lives for the faith. As, through hatred of our holy religion, Jarbas was assassinated, persecuted, and insulted even after death, it is but natural that his widow should be singled out by the fury of our enemies. For the sake of our brethren and my sake consent to live a little while longer. You will encourage us by your example, you will console us in prison, and, by leading us on the day of trial, you will preserve us from yielding to cowardice or weakness. In the name of Christ, your Spouse, I conjure you not to forsake us, more especially myself, who am but a weak catechumen and a too fond mother. What would become of me without you?"

"What God shall will, and as it may be pleasing to his providence. By his grace I shall lead the way. He has been pleased to choose me for the first offering of the Carthagenian Church; seek not to deprive me of this privilege. This very day, Vivia, I am destined to be truly espoused to the *Beloved* of my heart. The altar is ready, the Spouse awaits me; in a few moments Hilarian's guards shall be here to lead me to his tribunal."

"It is not yet day. Come home with me, Angela; the privacy of my house will save you from molestation. Together we can there pray and wait for the time marked by Almighty God; we

will die together, for I also am to give my life for
the cause of Christ. My husband is awaiting me
in heaven; he appeared to me and offered me a
crown similar to his own."

"Blessed be God! What greater fortune or
happiness than to die for Him who died for us?
Prepare yourself, Vivia, for that glad hour. I shall
intercede with my *Beloved* that he render you,
worthy of the glory prepared for you. I may not
await you; behold, I am clad in my bridal robes,
and have my nuptial crown on my head! What
would the *Bridegroom* say were I to delay even
for one moment that eternal union so yearned for
by my heart? I am called by *him* to the altar.
Oh! may the messengers sent to take me thither
come speedily. I see him; *he* beckons to me,
and his melting voice whispers in my ear: *Come,
my sister; arise, hasten, my beloved; come and
receive thy bridal crown.*"

"But have you forgotten that before you shall
be cast to the wild beasts you are to be exposed
in a place of infamy? Angela, how can your
pure soul contemplate the possibility of what is
a thousand times worse than any death? Oh!
save, save yourself from such a horrible fate.
The wretches seek to rob you of purity, your
greatest treasure!"

"Vivia, remember the virgin Potamiena, your
pious mother's companion and friend! *He* will
be with me, as he was with her. He can change
the place of infamy into an impenetrable sanc-

tuary. Has *he* not thousands of angels to protect me under their wings? When the judge
condemned me yesterday to undergo that sentence, I confess I trembled and wept; but *my
Beloved* told me not to fear, that he himself would
take care of my honor and purity, and that I
should come to him without blemish or defile-
ment. I have confidence in his promise. No,
dear Vivia, he will not permit me to be put to
shame. . . . But hist! I hear the footsteps of
those sent to seek me. Farewell, and pray for
me."

Vivia, hearing no noise, imagined that this was
a mistake. Besides, it was scarcely daybreak,
and it was not likely, as she thought, that the
officers of the law should come at so untimely an
hour. But upon opening the window she descried in the distance a band of armed men hurry-
ing silently along the street. There was no room
for doubt; she was at a loss to account for her
friend's knowledge of their approach, for it hardly occurred to her that some *invisible monitor*
had secretly warned the young martyr of the approach of the soldiers. Overwhelmed with grief
at the thought of their separation, she fell weeping upon Angela's neck, entreating her to fly
while there was yet time.

"Dear Vivia," answered the youthful virgin,
with a winning smile, "your affection for me
makes you forget yourself. Fly! fly from *my
Beloved* when the moment so long wished for is

come to be united to him for eternity! Why
should I do him such a wrong! Pray, Vivia, we
shall soon meet near him in heaven."

Quietly disengaging herself from Vivia's arms,
she fell once more upon her knees. The patrician lady made no further efforts, but contented
herself with gazing on her and silently joining
with her in prayer.

Meanwhile the guards had surrounded the
door. Pudens, their officer, bade the slave who
had come to know who had knocked to deliver to
him a young Christian named Angela, whom he
had orders to bring to Hilarian's tribunal. The
terrified slave ran trembling to his master; the
latter immediately presented himself to the centurion.

Pudens was a brave soldier; although he was
but the son of a freedman, his gallantry soon
distinguished him among his companions in arms,
and had won for him the rank of officer in the
Roman legions. But years of hard service and
many wounds had rendered him unfit for further
duty in the field, and so he had been assigned to
the command of the prison guards. Being penniless and without means of support, necessity
obliged him to accept the position, no matter
however unwilling he might have been. He was
of a very gentle disposition, full of kindness, humanity, and tenderness; he was stern only in
battle. As may be easily imagined, he had great
compassion for the hardships and privations of

the prisoners, and was often seen mingling his tears with theirs. It was only with reluctance that such a man could have undertaken the painful task in which we now find him engaged.

Upon seeing the sad and pale face of Angela's father he hastily brushed away a tear with the back of his hand, saluted him courteously, and, with a voice that betrayed the agitation of his bosom, said :

"Venerable sir, pardon me for being a messenger of woe to your house. Being a soldier, I must obey my officers, and, no matter how regretfully, I am obliged to execute my orders. The lieutenant-governor, Hilarian, has charged me to conduct forthwith to his pretorium the maiden who made her appearance there yesterday."

"Kind sir," answered Angela's father, "I sincerely compassionate you. It is indeed a painful duty to be obliged to tear from the arms of a father and mother an innocent child in order to lead her to death. But my religion forbids me to bear you any ill will ; you are at liberty to carry out your orders. I have but one request to make : put no chains on my beloved child. She will follow you unresistingly. I conjure you, in the name of your own mother, in the name of your sisters, if you ever had any, respect, and make your soldiers respect, her modesty. Oh ! our Angela is so timid and pure."

" Have no fears for the honor of your daughter ; she shall be under my protection until I deliver her to the lieutenant-governor, and woe to the man who would dare to insult her delicacy even by a word ! It would cost him dearly, for I am a soldier. My orders were to put manacles on her, but as this would pain you, and is, as you say, unnecessary, she shall walk untrammelled by my side. Hilarian may say what he pleases about it ; I am used to being twitted on the score of my excessive soft-heartedness."

" May God reward you for your humanity and respect for modesty ! May his grace bring the light into your soul ! Worthy centurion, you deserve to know him ! "

" I am no believer in your God, but, as he has done me no evil, I do not join the crowd in insulting him. It is said that those who worship him are upright and charitable ; so far I shall always respect them, even though I believe them to be mistaken. But, by your leave, I may tarry no longer in idle speech ; time presses and Hilarian does not like to be kept waiting. Where is your daughter ? I have confidence in your word and shall remain here with my soldiers. Go, then, I pray you, and bring her forth without delay."

" Spare, oh ! spare me the anguish of announcing to my child that the moment of separation has come. Do you accompany me, and upon seeing you she will understand the motive of your coming, and will follow you."

So they went up together to Angela's chamber.
The young virgin was still on her knees, seemingly rapt in deepest meditation. As usual, her
hands were crossed on her bosom; her eyes were
raised towards a picture of Christ, her heavenly
Bridegroom. There they remained, motionless
and rayless, wholly devoid of that living sheen
that habitually revealed all the burning emotions
of her heart. Her lips were still; the smile that
had parted them seemed to have frozen on them as
if on the lips of a statue. She neither moved nor
stirred. Her brow had the whiteness of the lily;
her face was pale, but it wore that calm, subdued
pallor that belongs to sleeping innocence, calm
repose, and angelic dreams. A heavenly beauty
sat upon her brow similar to that which God will
stamp on the persons of the elect on the morning
of the resurrection. Hard by her mother and
Vivia knelt and wept awaiting the fatal moment.

At the sight of Angela the centurion Pudens
stood still through amazement and awe; he
dared not so much as even to enter the chamber.
Never before had he seen anything similar to
this. That indescribable beauty; that air of candor, innocence, and calm repose; that preternatural reflection of a joy and happiness which sensual paganism could not conceive and had never
been capable of bestowing on its goddesses; the
snow-white dress that, with equal grace and modesty, enshrouded the entire person of the youthful virgin; and that attitude of deep recollection,

made such a picture and produced such a deep impression on him that he was struck dumb with astonishment. After some moments of silent contemplation, and remembering the orders he came to execute, he motioned to the father to announce to Angela that it was necessary she should now follow him to the lieutenant-governor's tribunal.

"My child," said the unhappy parent, "arise and say good-by to your mother. I shall accompany you as far as I shall be permitted to go. I trust God will give me the necessary strength. I shall be as near as possible to you during your final combat, and shall lovingly gather up the torn fragments of the meal left by the hungry lions of the Amphitheatre."

Angela seemed not to hear him, although she usually awoke from ecstasy and returned to consciousness whenever any one addressed her. Twice did her father call her by name, but she stirred not; he took her hand to lift her up, but her hands remained rigid and immovable on her bosom. "Angela!" repeated he in a louder tone, "arise; the Lord calls you."

"Angela has gone to heaven," exclaimed Vivia, as she fell upon her knees; "her fair, pure soul has taken its flight to Christ, her Spouse. He has saved her from shame and dishonor and has kept his promise to her."

She was not mistaken; the young virgin was indeed dead! She had just breathed her last, or rather had calmly fallen asleep in the Lord. Ardent longing and fervent love had consumed the shackles that bound her soul; or rather, as Vivia had just said, the divine Spouse, jealous of her virginal purity, had taken her to himself, had received her into his bosom. Heaven alone holds the secret of her death, and it is not given to us to peer into its mysteries. One thing we do know and firmly believe—that God can, and sometimes does, derogate from the laws of nature in favor of those whom he loves.

Angela's parents blessed God as they wept over their beloved child. Vivia became animated by a still greater desire of laying down her life for the faith of Jesus Christ. Amazed at what he had witnessed, and glad to escape from so painful a task, the centurion affectionately pressed the old man's hand and said: " I would willingly give twenty years of my life to be the father of such a daughter. I do not know what to think; such things never happen among us, and I am tempted to believe that, after all, your God may be the true God."

That night, by torch-light, the young virgin's body, clad in white, with its crown of roses and lilies, its crossed hands, and half parted lips still wreathed with the angelic smile they were at the moment of death, was laid in the family vault. The venerable Optatus was pleased to preside in person at the funeral service. The Christians who had been able to be present knelt and prayed with the parents around the lowly grave. That consolation was not granted, however, to Vivia; for her the hour had come to give her *glorious testimony* to Christ.

CHAPTER XXI.

WHEN the centurion Pudens had narrated to
Hilarian the strange scene he had witnessed the
lieutenant-governor's first impulse was to dis-
credit the whole affair; his mind was filled with
a thousand conflicting thoughts. Had the officer
lacked nerve to carry out his instructions? Had
he not yielded to the tears and entreaties of a distressed family? Might he not have been bribed
by valuable presents, and thus have connived at
the escape of the Christian maiden? Might it
not be possible that, at the instigation of her parents, the girl had feigned to have swooned away
or to be dead? What proof was there that the
extraordinary state in which the officer stated he
had found her, and what, in his simplicity, he
imagined to be death, was not the result of magic,
in which it was *well known* the Christians were
such practical adepts? He resolved to test the
truth by personal examination, and arrived at
Angela's late home just as Vivia and her favorite
slave, who had returned to rejoin her, were
issuing from it.

The dead body was lying on a bed. Its appearance was so unchanged that Hilarian thought for a moment he had found Angela in a tranquil slumber ; but the hands and brow were cold, respiration had ceased, the heart was still, although the limbs were as pliant as if she were yet alive. Hilarian made a long and careful examination, and, seeing there was no room for doubt, he departed without uttering a single word. His hatred and anger against the Christians became greater and more envenomed than ever, as if they had been instrumental in his discomfiture and had thwarted his designs ; but as Vivia and Felicitas had crossed his path they must be the first and chief victims of his resentment. As they had met him, there could be no doubt that they had recognized him, and would laugh at his discomfiture and report it throughout the entire city.

At his return home he found the pagan priest, Olympius, waiting for an interview. He took very good care not to inform him of what had occurred ; he could not hide his bad humor, however, and accordingly launched forth in invectives against the accursed Christians, who continued to be protected by the senate in spite of the outspoken sentiments of the people, and whom the governor of Carthage was afraid to punish notwithstanding the positive commands contained in the imperial edicts. Nothing could have been more palatable to the rancorous heart of his visitor.

"Why, then," said Olympius, "do you annoy yourself so much about what the senate thinks? Do we not all know what it is? It is composed of a few nobles crazy on the score of lineage, mad in the pursuit of pleasure or wealth, and absolutely indifferent to the interests of the city and province. A few decrepit drivellers, whose whole ambition is to die in peace, and who tremble like children at the bare thought of seeing a single drop of blood shed in Carthage. What matters to them the cause of the gods and the stability of our religion, provided they be allowed to arrive peaceably at the goal of their mortal career? As for Firmilian, *who is governor only in name*, his days are drawing to a close. A short time ago another and a more severe crisis has set, and I have hurried hither to bring you the *good news*. You are thus at liberty to act with as much impunity as if he were actually dead. By using his name and seal you can placard the edict of persecution on the senate doors and throughout the entire city. The people are anxiously expecting it, and will hail it with universal satisfaction and rejoicing."

"You can rest assured," answered Hilarian, "that it is not through fear of the governor's authority that I am held in check; in a few hours, or, at latest, to-morrow, he will be no more. But you must remember we live at a great distance from Rome; who knows but the emperor's disposition toward the Christians may

be changed ? He favored them for a long time;
he may have acted in a sudden ebullition of passion, or to gain the good will of persons whom it
was his interest to conciliate ; and who can tell
but that he has already returned to his former
and more lenient policy ? You know nothing
about princes ; they are swayed only by egotism ;
they give it a more specious name, but in the
end it is invariably self-interest.   Their only aim
is to secure to themselves the possession of a
throne obtained by intrigue.   The interests of
religion and the good of the state—forsooth !
These are but empty, high-sounding words that
dupe the common herd, but mean quite another
thing in the bellowing mouths that constantly repeat them ! "

"For all that, it is no less a fact that our
august emperor has spoken those words; you
hold in your hands an unrevoked edict of recent
date.   What can you have to fear if you publish
and enforce it ? On the contrary, you will have a
stronger claim on the emperor's favor, and, mark
me well, you cannot fail to become successor to
old Firmilian."

"I lay no claim to hypocritical disinterested-
ness; since my arrival at this post I have been
expecting promotion and have claims to the gov-
ernorship of the province.   The position is an
honorable one ; your city ranks next to Rome in
importance ; it is also lucrative, and that is a very
important consideration and an excellent reason

why I should not like to make a mistake. If I treat the Christians with severity there can be no doubt, after the events of yesterday, that the senate will oppose me. It may bring an action against me at Rome as an enemy to the public peace, nay, even as an enemy to the emperor, for bringing his name and government into disfavor by my harshness and cruelty; and who knows but my head should be the forfeit I should have to pay for my officiousness, in case it should be adroitly forged into a crime? When princes demand blood they must not be obeyed too readily, unless people want to become the victims of their inconstancy or remorse. Were he Nero I should not hesitate an instant; before this I would have had all the Christians of Carthage in prison. But you can rest assured that, with a man like Severus, too great haste is very dangerous."

"And still, in other provinces there was none of this hesitancy, yet, so far as I am aware, not a single governor has been reprimanded."

"That may happen later; besides, elsewhere the governor's authority is not counterbalanced by the arrogant pretensions of an all-powerful senate, backed by a large and faithful army."

"I see how the matter stands, Hilarian: you are afraid of compromising yourself. It appears to me, however, that there is a very simple way of shirking all responsibility, even in the very improbable supposition that the emperor should happen to change his mind or his policy."

" And what may that be, may I ask ?"

" Firmilian is still alive. In his name and
under his seal issue orders at once for the arrest
of a certain number of the most influential members of this abominable sect. In case of demur or
protest from the senate you can say it is only a
precautionary measure imperatively demanded by
the present state of things and the agitation produced by recent events in the city. The initia-
tive having been taken, things will take their
natural course, and you can wait and bide the
issue."

As it will be observed, the artful old man never
lost sight for a moment of the object he had in
view ; he wanted the blood of the priest who had
wounded his pride, and he essayed the same hypocritical part with the lieutenant-governor that
had served him so effectually in the case of young
Jubal. Hilarian fell the more readily into the
snare from the fact that he yearned to be revenged and sought to strike terror into the Christians, so that they should have neither time nor
opportunity to turn him into ridicule.

" Well, you may be right," said he to Olympius ; " let us try it. You know the Christians
of Carthage better than I do ; give me the names
of some of them, of those whom you judge to be
the most dangerous on the score of influence
with the sect or zeal for the spread of the new
doctrines. Would it not be best to begin by the
one they call bishop ? "

"Optatus is so old that he is almost harmless. Notwithstanding his title and office he has very little influence. In his case we need be in no hurry. Optatus is thrown into insignificance by the towering genius and restless activity of one of his followers. This man is looked upon as an oracle by the Christians; he is the greatest champion of their cause and the most redoubtable enemy the gods ever won from them by the new sect. Since his desertion from among us this man, in his implacable hatred, has never ceased to use all his eloquence and efforts in the cause of error. He leads astray entire families by his keen and powerful arguments; in his pride he has vowed to pull down and destroy every one of our altars in Carthage. This is the fanatic that caused the mutilation of Juno's statue, and made her temple to-day a heap of smouldering ruins. It was his violent harangue that intimidated the senate yesterday and brought about such a change that it would seem almost the work of magic. You will cover yourself with glory, Hilarian, if you rid religion and the empire of this hated monster; you will become the benefactor of the gods and of the Cæsars. Only smite his head, and the blow shall fall on and be felt by the entire body. You know the man; his name is Tertullian."

"I pledge myself, then, that before the day dies Tertullian shall be in chains. But we must find him companions; a single victim would not

be in keeping with the *tardy seal* of our dying
governor. You must not forget that it is in his
name I act, and it is necessary that he now make
ample amends for years of connivance and inactivity."

"I fully agree with you, and, as you are so
kind as to consult me, I would call your attention
to a certain Saturninus, a great propagandist of the
new tenets among slaves and the masses, emulat-
ing, no doubt, among this class Tertullian's efforts among the aristocracy and men of letters.
Only a short time ago, by dint of promises and
cunning, he succeeded in gaining over to his sect
a number of mechanics employed on the docks.
These tradesmen, joined in a secret and thorough-
ly-organized alliance with a numerous band of
slaves, must necessarily be a source of alarm and
danger. At any day or moment they might, at
the beck of their leader, fall upon us like wild
beasts. This organization should be broken up
before it is too late."

"This is the first mention I have heard made
of this Saturninus. But no matter; he shall go
to prison with Tertullian."

"Secundulus is the friend and fellow-laborer
of Saturninus; ought he not share in the reward
as he has shared in the labor?"

"It is nothing more than right that he should.
But this makes only three, and that is altogether
too few."

"Not so fast; there is a woman in Carthage

who is almost as haughty as Tertullian himself.
Still young and very wealthy, she plumes herself
on being able to despise the gods and turn them
into ridicule.   Being allied to all the patrician
families infected by the poison of error, she has
obtained such influence over all their female
members that, by her advice, all the marriage-
able ones have sworn to wed none but Christians.
This, as you see, is a new plan to draw over the
élite of our young men.   As she is an enthusiastic admirer of Tertullian, she looks upon his will
as the exponent of Heaven's command; hence
it is the firm conviction of everybody that both
recent profanations were the work of this woman,
and that she acted in obedience to the commands
of her unscrupulous adviser.   Both sacrileges were
perpetrated, at her instigation, by one of her
slaves named Revocatus ; the crime is deplored
by the entire city and will inevitably draw down
upon us the anger of the gods unless the guilty
be severely and swiftly punished.   This haughty, impious, and sacrilegious woman would richly deserve a thousand deaths, were they possible."

"What is her name?" asked Hilarian, concealing his satisfaction.   "From what I have
heard among the people I have but little doubt
that you mean Vivia, Jarbas's young relict."

" Yes, your surmise is correct.   And what is
more, let me further inform you that this woman, in spite of the tears and entreaties of a

father, by dint of cajolery and bribes, influenced one of her young slaves—a child almost—to embrace the Christian religion, and then gave the poor girl in marriage to this very Revocatus, the blind executor of all her caprices and commands. This unfortunate female slave is the daughter of old Sylvanus, of whom you have often heard me speak, no doubt, for his hard lot is known and pitied throughout the entire city. Let not the haughty Vivia with her two devoted slaves be divided from her dear master and guide ; let her follow him to prison and to death also !"

·"But," rejoined the lieutenant-governor, assuming an air of hesitation and reluctance, " Vivia is the daughter of a senator."

"It is well that the senate be taught to fear ; it will only be the more pliable and tractable."

"Hanno might enlist in his cause the sympathy of his peers, and in this case may there not be danger that the legislature might have recourse to extreme measures and use force to deprive us of our prisoners ? "

"I know Hanno. Upon learning the news of his daughter's arrest he will fume and talk for a while ; that will be the end of it. Besides, I know for certain that he felt pained at Vivia's change of religion, and frequently threatened her with his direct resentment if she would not retract. There is therefore nothing to be feared from him."

" To speak candidly, I should not be sorry to humble that woman's pride. I know not why I feel such a deep dislike to her, and, as you assure me that I can do so without risk, I shall give immediate orders for her arrest and of the others whom you have named. I shall try them tomorrow, and then we shall see if they will all be as obstinate as that zany Angela, who had the mad folly to attempt to browbeat and resist me openly. I may add, however, that it is now commonly believed that the attempt resulted in her eventually dying of fright."

Hilarian turned aside to hide his blushes, and even the old hypocrite himself could not wholly repress a smile of derision. Hereupon they both separated; the lieutenant-governor betook himself to prosecute his designs in the name and under the seal of his superior officer, while the pagan priest hurried to bear the good and welcomed tidings to the old mountain camel-driver, as well as to gloat over the sweet prospect of soon enjoying a revenge so long and persistently sought after. " The time is come at long last," said he to himself; " we shall now see if his haughty mien will not quail before the judge and the executioners. Oh! how happy I shall be at the sight of his blood and severed head. Tertullian! Tertullian! you shall find out before long that the High-priest of Carthage may not be bearded with impunity!"

At about the same hour an old and a young

man some seventeen or eighteen years of age
were leisurely sauntering together in a beautiful
villa on the sea-shore. It was only a short time
after sunrise ; the cloudless firmament gave promise of a fine day ; the air was fragrant with the
sweet breath of morning ; the birds, shaking the
last dewdrops from their wings, seemed to be on
the point of finishing their usual matin service to
the God that gave them life and food. The man
whom we see drinking in all the fragrance and
sunshine of the early morning is the fortunate
owner of this magnificent villa. Being a senator,
rich in lands and slaves, caring little for politics,
tired of the routs and pleasures of city life, he
gave his whole attention to the care and embel-
lishment of his favorite seat. His ambition was
to die one day quietly and slip from the world's
stage without leaving a single trace behind. The
youth who walks with him and seizes his arm
from time to time, as if to ensure more marked
attention, is called to occupy a more prominent
part in the world. His name shall be great one
day among men and shall be pronounced with
respect and admiration from age to age.

The wealthy senator is named Thascius Cypri-
anus, and his young companion is called after
him.

"Father," impetuously cried the youth,
"what think you of the debate that we heard
yesterday in the senate !   What is your opinion
of the man who for a whole hour held the entire

assembly so breathlessly spell-bound? For my
part I can think of nothing else ; all night I was
not able to close my eyes, my mind was so full
of him and his arguments."

" For a long time past, my son, Tertullian has
given evidence of extraordinary ability. When
he taught rhetoric, students flocked to hear him
from every side, and as a forensic orator he had
no equal. Since he embraced the new religion·
he is said to have written marvellous pages in its
defence ; at Carthage, and even on the other side
of the Mediterranean, he is looked upon as the
oracle of his party."

" Father, your praises are too tame; that man
is the glory of mankind. What sublimity of
genius ! What nobility and grandeur of character !
What irresistible eloquence ! What loftiness of
thought ! To my mind the so-vaunted Demos-
thenes and Cicero dwindle into insignificance
when compared to him ; even the sublime, the
divine Homer pales before him ! "

" Perhaps you exaggerate, my son. Admiration is near akin to enthusiasm, and enthusiasm
magnifies everything."

" I know it ; and that is why I am so mis-
trustful of myself and so afraid of being carried
away by my imagination ; besides, my sympathies
are not on the side of the cause that he advo-
cated. Nevertheless, his eloquence gradually
mastered and swept me on in spite of myself.
I felt as if I could willingly fall at the feet of

that man and beg him to teach me to speak as he spoke—if, indeed, eloquence may be taught and acquired by study."

"At any rate you have made a fair start, Cyprian; although you are as yet only a stripling, you are spoken of in Carthage as a very clever student; only continue as you have already done and you will one day become as great an orator as Tertullian."

"Would that you were a true prophet! But alas! that can never be; the gods have not given me such talent, although I would willingly give the brightest years of my life in exchange for it. Oh! for one single day like yesterday for Tertullian. My happiness would be complete! At the close of one such day I would willingly die, for I would be certain to live for ever in the memory of all future generations."

"Well, enough on this subject, Cyprian. I presume your sole object in seeking this interview was not to extol the unquestionable genius of Tertullian. You have something else to say to me. Be not afraid; you know your father. Speak frankly."

"You are right, father. Well, I wish to save Tertullian. I know that his life is in danger. Yesterday, as I was passing through the square around the senate, I heard the mob crying out against him and clamoring for his blood. There is a report that the Christians are about to be persecuted on the strength of an imperial edict. If such a thing should happen Tertullian would inevitably be one of the first victims. And, oh! what a disgrace that would be to Carthage, what an irreparable loss to the whole world! It would be like blotting out one of its brightest stars from the firmament."

"But, Cyprian, how could you save his life if, notwithstanding the veto of the senate, the imperial edict be enforced? Up to this we have done all in our power to protect the Christians, because, if the truth must be told, they are the most submissive and law-abiding citizens in the empire. The only objection that ever was or can be made against them is on the score of religion, and that is not our business, but theirs. It may be that we have endangered our lives by refusing yesterday to yield to the demands of the people. What more could we have done?"

"I only ask you, father, to let me carry out my own plans in this matter. I am confident of success. Our old female slave, Jucunda, has been a Christian for a long time, as I recently found out from one of her companions. Just now Jucunda is laid up with a severe fit of sickness. I am told that it is usual among the Christians to visit each other in such cases, and that they invariably desire to see one of their priests whenever they are in danger of death. If you will permit me I will call on Tertullian, and will request him, on the part of poor Jucunda, to come hither immediately. You and I are the only persons in the villa that know him. He could easily remain here with us until the persecution shall have blown over. I confess I would be very glad to avail myself of such an excellent opportunity of informing myself regarding the doctrines of this new religion."

"Why, Cyprian, what do I hear? That you desire to save the life of a man whom you admire and believe to be guiltless I can well understand and fully approve, but to wish to examine a religion that is said to be so full of mysteries is, in my opinion, entirely out of the question for a youth of your age."

"Truth belongs to every age, and I desire to know the truth."

"That the Christian religion may have many excellent points I do not pretend to deny; but why should you begin to doubt about that in which you were bred, and which was the religion of your ancestors and is still that of your country ?"

"Hitherto, I confess, it had never entered into my mind to examine if the gods we worship were really and truly gods. Since I heard Tertullian, however, that doubt has arisen, and I must needs satisfy it."

"My child, do not trouble yourself with such a bootless study. After all, is not our great Jove just as good as he whom they call Christ ?"

"If Tertullian is right, Jupiter is not worth one grain of the incense that is burned on his altars, and it would be a positive disgrace to worship him. But, on the other hand, what a grand, noble, and perfect figure does not Christ present as he was represented to us yesterday! What innocence and holiness of life! What sweetness and mildness in his speech! What omnipotence in his works! What charity and love in his sacrifice! Oh! if ever the Deity did descend from his throne, if he ever did put on human flesh, it was thus, truly thus, that he must have appeared among men!"

"See, Cyprian, how your imagination is again running away with you! Will you never correct yourself?"

"Imagination! the word is easily said. But Tertullian adduced incontrovertible facts—facts universally admitted by all our poets and historians; can they be denied? Are we not obliged to admit, father, that every assertion made by him regarding the gods was strictly true?"

"The main facts were, although he may have exaggerated somewhat; poetry, as you are aware, does not lay claim to scrupulous precision, its object being less to instruct than to please."

"Let us prescind, if you will, from the inventions of poetry and fable; they certainly are not very creditable to our gods; but if Jupiter and the rest of them were born, lived, and died as common mortals did, was not Tertullian right in asserting that they were not gods, since eternity is a necessary attribute of the godhead?"

"I freely confess I never carried my examination or thoughts so far; my invariable maxim was ever and always: Be good and honest; that is enough."

"No, not for me at least; I feel something in my soul that revolts at the thought of giving my homage and adoration to beings that have no right to them. My soul requires such a God as the Omnipotent Being so well described by Tertullian—a God self-existing before time or creation began; absolute creator of the myriad things and worlds of which we see but a fraction; supreme lord and master over all his creatures, and from his lofty throne moderating and guiding the whole with paternal love and care."

"Are you, too, thinking of joining the new faith? Could you give me such pain?"

"I do not say that I will become a Christian; nevertheless, it must be acknowledged that it forms a code of belief and morality that has no equal, and that its votaries are virtuous and charitable. Were you not as much surprised as I was at the wonderful picture presented to our minds by Tertullian yesterday? What extraordinary men must those be who know no distinction of nation or caste, and whose love embraces the whole world! But by what process can a person be born again so as to lead a new life and become quite another man even while preserving the same body? How break through old and cherished habits in a day, turn from luxury to abstemiousness, cast aside gold and purple to wear coarse and humble garments? Oh! why was I not born a Christian? Perchance I exaggerate the difficulty of the change. Tertullian will instruct me; for I am resolved to question and confer with him. But above and below all I will save this great man; to-morrow it may be too late, and if any mishap should befall him I would never forgive myself."

. "You are no longer a child, Cyprian, do as you please; but I am very much afraid you will one day rue this hasty zeal."

" O dear father! thanks, thanks."

The young man embraced him with transports of joy and gratitude. In a short time he was hastening to Carthage in his splendid chariot. Having arrived at Tertullian's humble abode, he made known the object of his visit. The priest made no delay; a poor dying slave had a sacred right to his ministry; moreover, the young man's frankness and avowed desire for religious instruction had at once produced a very favorable impression on Tertullian. He accompanied Cyprian therefore without loss of time.

It is much to be regretted that among the numerous writings that have come down to us from the pens of both, no mention is made of what passed between them during the prolonged stay of Tertullian at the villa. It is highly probable, nevertheless, that even then Cyprian became fully convinced of the truth of the Christian religion, even though he had not sufficient courage to embrace it; the fiery passions of youth had already tainted his heart, and so influenced him that, like the youth in the Gospel, he could not summon resolution enough to make the sacrifice. But the good seed had fallen on his soul and would not fail to fructify. The day shall come when the young patrician will generously resolve to break the shameful bonds that bind him, and to be free from their thraldom; Carthage will call him her greatest and most illustrious bishop; the Church will honor him as one of her noblest martyrs and will enroll him in the exalted ranks of those whom she styles her doctors and fathers.

CHAPTER XXII.

A FEW hours after Tertullian's departure for Cyprian's villa the great city of Carthage was thrown into the most violent commotion. The edict of persecution had been formally published and proclaimed. The implacable hatred of old Sylvanus gave him a certain right to be one of the heralds of the bloody tidings. He had the satisfaction of being appointed to placard the decree on the doors of the senate. It was hailed with wild shouts of joy from the crowd of slaves that blindly followed him in all his movements. A large body of troops were detailed to scour the city; these burst into the houses of the Christians, and dragged away in chains all those whose names were inscribed on a list that bore the official stamp of the governor. It is hardly necessary to state that the tender-hearted Pudens had not been appointed to the command this time; care had been taken to select a tribune of remarkable *sternness* of character, and one who had made himself conspicuous for his detestation of the Christians.

By one of those sudden changes that so frequently come over men who are actuated by impulse and passion, Hilarian determined to strike a blow that would effectually intimidate the senate, and would make it appear as if he set at naught their opposition to the adoption of violent measures. Accordingly, in addition to the names supplied by the high-priest, he ordered the arrest of a great number of persons without distinction of rank or sex. Their names are written in their blood in the Book of Life, but are lost to us, with the exception of those of Jucundus, Artaxis, and Quintus, mentioned by Saturus in his account of a vision seen by him a short time previous to his martyrdom. Had it not been for the authentic Acts, which happily are still extant, and which describe the bloody tragedy that then took place, we should never have known that, during the few days which elapsed between the publication of the edict and the death of Vivia, a whole host of martyrs had gloriously died for the faith in Carthage.

It was a harrowing sight to see the unhappy Christians dragged in chains through the streets and squares of the city, buffeted by the rude soldiery, maltreated by a frenzied mob that cursed and jeered and cast mud upon them. Bound hand in hand, the noble Vivia and Felicitas were as badly treated as the rest; regardless of their youth and of the helpless state of Felicitas, who was about to become a mother, their veils were torn away and they were hurried forward with blows and kicks, so that they were dragged rather than led along the streets.

The martyrs—for such they may now be called—appeared not to heed their barbarous treatment. Serenity and joy beamed on their countenances; they opened not their mouths, save to thank God for having made them worthy to suffer for his name, or to encourage each other to give steadfast testimony to him before men. Both women felt a momentary confusion at being thus rudely exposed to the insolent gaze of the soldiery; but they speedily recovered self-possession, and, with downcast eyes, continued to pray with as much recollection and fervor as if they were hidden in the retirement of their oratory. By a last remnant of shame Olympus kept aloof from the crowd; but he watched anxiously from a hiding-place on the roof of his house for the approach of the confessors. He gloated over the thought that he should soon see the object of his sworn hatred manacled, trembling with fear, and pale with terror. The instant he saw the crowd coming his eyes sought at once for the tall form of Tertullian; but oh! the cruel disappointment! Tertullian was not among the prisoners, and then came the bitter news that he had left the city in the company of an unknown young man, and had gone with him nobody knew whither. This came upon the unhappy old man like a thunder-clap, and almost deprived him of life.

The city prison was filled with malefactors of every grade—fugitive slaves, thieves, and murderers—condemned to the mines, and now awaiting the execution of their sentence. From this circumstance the Christians had to be confined in a separate building, where they had the twofold advantage of enjoying plenty of air and light. The priest Saturus lost no time in visiting the prisoners. His first act was to embrace his brother Saturninus and bind the wounds and bruises received by the latter on his way to the prison.

Saturus's name had not been put on the list, either because he had been overlooked or had been reserved for a future occasion. This zealous priest had spent twenty years of his life in converting pagans and instructing the catechumens. No sooner had he been apprised of the fact that some of those whom he had been preparing for baptism had been arrested for the faith than he hastened to bear them company in prison, the better to prepare them for the approaching conflict.

Saturus was greatly loved and esteemed in the Carthaginian church. His piety, amiability, gentleness, and kindly disposition made him an universal favorite with all, and hence his appearance among the prisoners was the signal for much congratulation and rejoicing. They all pressed around him to enquire how it had come to pass that he was not brought with them to prison. "I was not worthy of that honor," was the an-

swer of the humble priest, who feared the very
shadow of vainglory, and who envied the martyrs what they had already had to suffer for the
name of Christ. It was only afterwards they
discovered that he had voluntarily surrendered
himself to the tribune in charge of the prisoners.

From the beautiful histories called the " Acts
of the Martyrs," which used to be read publicly
in the olden Church, we learn that, when in
prison, the confessors of the faith used to make
the dungeon vocal with the accents of prayer and
psalmody; these strains not only pleased God
and his angels in heaven, but filled men with such
amazement and admiration that not unfrequently
the very jailers became converts. Our glorious
confessors did not fail in the observance of this
sacred custom of the ancient martyrs; having
given each other the kiss of peace, they all fell on
their knees and joined in prayer with the priest
Saturus.

Their devotions were interrupted by half-
smothered moans; Secundulus, with his eyes fixed
on heaven, lay motionless and dead. Being of a
weak and delicate constitution, he had succumb-
ed under the cruel treatment received on his way
to prison. Upon opening his tunic it was found
that he had been mortally wounded; his breast
was all bruised and bleeding from the blow of a
heavy stone flung by some vigorous hand.

The martyrs wished to honor and give decent
burial to the body in the garden that surrounded

their temporary prison. The savage tribune in charge sternly refused them this consolation. In vain did Vivia proffer him a well-filled purse that she happened to have on her person at the time of her arrest. Her offer was rudely rejected; the dead body was hurried away with orders to have it cast into the sea. Soon after the confessors were led to the tribunal of the lieutenant-governor; the mob, more violent than ever, followed after with renewed savageness and violence.

The examination opened with Saturninus. With head all bruised and covered with blood, he made answer that he was a Christian and was ready to suffer and die sooner than sacrifice to gods that were nothing but foul demons. All the rest made the same declaration. Saturus, although his name was not on the list of the accused, now came forward, and, raising his voice, exclaimed: "I also am a Christian and will not sacrifice to your so-called gods." Hilarian was dumfounded; he could not understand how a man could voluntarily surrender himself and be willing to suffer the most cruel tortures and even death. Vivia was reserved for the last, less on account of her distinguished rank than for the purpose of intimidating and humbling her by a protracted and public trial.

"Well, and what may your name be?"

"You know my name," answered the noble patrician, "and consequently the question is useless. I shall answer the question, however, not to glorify myself, but that all who are present may know who I am. My name is Vivia Perpetua; I am the daughter of Senator Hanno, and, since a few days past, the widow of the brave Jarbas who died a martyr for his and my faith."

"You acknowledge, consequently, that you are a Christian?"

"I am a Christian, and, by God's grace, I will remain one as long as I live."

"But are you not aware that our august emperors have, by solemn edicts, proscribed that wicked superstition, and have commanded uniformity of worship throughout the whole empire? Their will and the laws require that you adore the gods."

"There is but one only God, who made heaven and earth and all things therein, and one Christ, his only Son, into whose kingdom I most ardently desire to enter. Speak not of your gods to me; I blush at the thought of having ever worshipped them."

"Our gods are great and immortal, while the Christ you insanely follow was only a contemptible impostor, who was deservedly condemned to die the death of a slave."

"Blaspheme not what you do not understand. Christ was condemned by wicked men who knew him not. He, who by a single word opened the tomb and brought the dead to life, could have come down unscathed from the cross and covered his enemies with confusion; but, in his charity, he was pleased to lay down his life for our salvation. He it is whom I adore, as I have already told you, and I will adore no other."

"Vivia, you, like the rest of your sect, have permitted yourself to be led astray by false teaching."

"God is truth. He deceives not the innocent and confiding soul that sincerely seeks him."

"In good sooth, if you were to be believed, it would seem as if you heard a voice from heaven; I recognize in this the usual fanaticism and folly of all your co-religionists."

"I look upon myself as unworthy of being addressed by the Lord my God, for I am one of the last of his servants, one who has only to-day begun to be really and truly a disciple of Jesus Christ. But I know that God has spoken by his prophets, and, in these latter days, by his only beloved Son himself; on his word my faith is founded."

"Say rather that you have blindly given ear to the teaching of a certain Tertullian, whom you look upon as the oracle of your sect."

"Before I knew or heard him I was a Christian. He simply comfirmed me in my belief."

"He would have done far better had he undeceived you; but he basely plunged you into deeper error, and now, like the coward that he is, he abandons you in the hour of danger; he should have been here had he not run to hide himself where he cannot be found the very moment he received intelligence of the stringent measures about to be enforced against his dupes and godless companions."

"Tertullian is no coward; it is very evident you do not know him. He fears neither chains nor tortures. True, I know not what has become of him, but I do know and assert that he is incapable of harboring the base sentiments attributed to him by you."

"Let us say no more about this man; he cannot escape me very long, at any rate. Do you persist in declaring yourself a Christian?"

"I have been taught not to tell a lie, even to save my life; yes, I am a Christian, and now more than ever I bless the God of goodness and charity for having called me to the inestimable light of his Gospel."

"You are a lady of high birth and refined education, Vivia, and you should reflect that this religion has hitherto won over only slaves and vulgar persons. Your family is one of the first in this city. Can you have the lamentable hardihood to disgrace your name and your own father?"

"Slaves and the poor should be the first in the Church of Jesus Christ; of this our apostles have informed us, in order that the world should see clearly that it is the work of God's power. The wise and the powerful ones of the earth will come also in their turn, but that shall come to pass only when it shall have been made manifest that the Church had succeeded without them. Nevertheless, you must know that, in Carthage as everywhere else, the cross has obtained a footing among the most distinguished and noblest families. You remind me of my birth and my father; you say I dishonor my name, while I hold that I add to it more lustre than it ever received from all the noble deeds of my ancestors. To know the true God, and, if needs be, to die for him, is the climax of all glory and my sole ambition."

"Vivia, I see I have not been misinformed; you are eaten up with pride, and to such a degree does it go that, even in chains, you affect an air of haughtiness and bravado."

"Before I knew the degradations and humiliations to which Christ subjected himself for love of me I was the willing dupe of vanity and pride; now I glory only in the Lord my God, and hence it is that I prize these chains more than jewels and gold."

"A truce to all this folly; you have youth, education, rank, and wealth, and you may live happy and respected in the world. Your husband's death has made you free once more; who can hinder you from wedding as you please among the most eligible of the nobility?"

"The goods and honors of this world have no longer any value for me, and my affections shall never again be given to any creature. But what boots all these questions? I am a Christian, and nothing can induce me to renounce my faith."

"That remains to be proved; in the agony of torture and in the presence of grim death you will speak very differently and will cry to me for mercy; but it will then be too late."

"You know not God's power and how he can give strength and courage to the hearts of his servants. Put me to the torture, if you will; condemn me to the most painful death. I am ready. My last word shall be but a repetition of what I have hitherto so often declared: *I am a Christian!*"

The lieutenant-governor was pale with anger; for the second time did he find himself overcome by a woman. As he was about to give the signal to bring forward the instruments of torture, an old man was seen making his way through the spectators; his hoary locks fell dishevelled upon his shoulders, his eyes were haggard, and his whole countenance stamped with grief; he held an infant in his arms.

"Vivia," cried he, as he fell sobbing on his knees, "O my darling Vivia! in the name of your own child, have pity on your unhappy father. If I have always been to you a loving father and doated on you as the most idolized of all the family, spare, oh! spare me this disgrace. Forget not those who call you by the sweet name of sister. Remember the mother whom your death will leave without proper consolation. Behold

your own infant! He stretches out his little arms
to you for mercy and life—for without you he
cannot live. Forget, I conjure you, this horrible
pride that would fain undo us all; such a death
as this would inevitably brand us with disgrace,
so that we could never more show ourselves in
public."

The guards, and even the very executioners,
were moved to compassion. As Vivia wiped
away her tears and convulsively clasped her infant to her bosom, Hilarian and his satellites
were so fully convinced that she would yield that
they began to prepare the incense which she was
to burn in proof of her having renounced Christ;
but strength from on high sustained the noble
martyr. As a daughter and as a mother her
heart was moved to its depths, and who would
dare to impute this to her as a crime or to
accuse her of weakness? As a Christian, however, her great faith wavered not for an instant.

"Father," answered she, "the Lord is my witness that I love you tenderly; nor do I forget
how you watched over me always and singled
me out as the object of your predilection. My
mother and my little brothers know how deeply
I love them. Need I say how I yearn for, and
how my heart-strings cling to, this helpless babe
that to-morrow shall have no longer a mother?
But my religion commands me to put God before
all that I cherish here below, and I shall never
betray my faith. He for whom I suffer will take

care of you; he will console my mother and my brothers. In his hands I place the child that he gave me; he will be his protector and father."

"'O Vivia! let me entreat you not to forget what you owe to yourself and to your family. What matters it of what faith you be. It is all the same, provided you be good and virtuous. In our religion, in the religion of your youth, are there not many women and matrons both chaste and deservedly honored? For pity's sake! I do but say that you are not a Christian—you are required to do nothing more."

"Say, father, can that precious vase before you, brought hither, I presume, to make me an idolater, change its name?" *

"Assuredly it cannot."

"Neither can I style myself other than what I am—namely, a Christian. Far from being ashamed of the name, I glory in it."

"Cruel daughter, heartless mother, die, then, if you will! But I here renounce and give you a father's curse."

In his rage and blind fury the old man rushed upon Vivia, as if to tear her in pieces. Rage gave way to shame; bursting into tears, he again flung himself on his knees before her as he cried:

"Vivia, pardon an unhappy father who can no longer call you by the name of child! Excess of grief made me forget myself."

He wildly kissed the hands stretched out to raise him.

"Vivia," exclaimed Hilarian, "can you resist the entreaties and tears of your venerable and honored father, the pleading helplessness of this child whom your obstinacy will deprive of its mother? Sacrifice to the gods and for the prosperity of our emperors."

"I am a Christian; I will not sacrifice!"

"Death to the wicked Vivia!" cried a spectator, the savage, implacable Sylvanus.

"The Christians to the lions!" shouted the mob.

"Blessed be God and his only Son, Christ Jesus!" answered the brave martyrs.

Meantime Hanno continued his entreaties, hoping his daughter would yield through compassion for his grief and pity for her infant. Hilarian began to lose patience and made a sign to an usher to take him away. As usual, the officer proceeded to obey by striking Hanno with his rod. Vivia noted the act and trembled from head to foot at the insult done to her aged father. Tears started to her eyes. She was ready to fall on his neck when Hilarian cried out:

"Guards, take back the accused to prison and let them be treated as state criminals!"

The confessors withdrew with joy on their countenances and acts of thanksgiving on their lips. They had given public testimony to God and to his Christ.

CHAPTER XXIII.

THE BAPTISM.

THE aged Firmilian breathed his last the night after sentence was passed on the confessors, and Hilarian became governor of the province without more ado, as the emperor had promised him the position previous to his departure for Africa. This gave the new governor full power and confidence; but as he mistrusted the senate, he immediately despatched a message to Rome to inform Severus of what had taken place. As it may be easily imagined, he took good care to put forward his zeal for religion and the empire, his solicitude and determination in enforcing the edicts, despite the opposition of the very men who should have been the first to aid him in his efforts. But what he emphasized most was the danger that would arise if the Christians should be allowed to go on unchecked in committing overt acts of treason. The sacrilegious mutilation of Juno's statue and the burning of her temple, of which he openly accused them, were facts which showed how bold they were becoming and how necessary it was to lose no time in putting them down.

In the belief that Tertullian had escaped to some far-distant country, Olympius's disappointment and vexation permitted him to think of nothing but the detested object of his undying hatred. Buried in the seclusion of his house, and refusing to see even his most intimate friends, he accused the gods of apathy to their own interests or incompetency to defend them.

Upon learning that the Lady Vivia had been cast into chains, insulted by the rabble, and dragged before Hilarian's tribunal, Jubal flew into one of his usual fits of passion and rage. Equally incensed against the high-priest who had so basely deceived him as ashamed of the ridiculous part he was made to play, he withdrew to a friend's house in the country.

The old herdsman, Sylvanus, brooded alone with glad anticipation over his near prospects of revenge. He looked calmly on the daughter he had once so loved, as she walked, chained to the woman he hated, to receive her death-sentence at the tribunal of the governor. She was a Christian, *and was, therefore, his child no longer;* besides, she was the favorite of that Vivia for whose blood he thirsted. That ulcerated heart had room for nothing save fanaticism and hate; all the kindly feelings of nature had died there long ago.

Our brave confessors still remained in the abode to which they had been consigned until they could be received into the public prison.

Heedless of their cruel treatment and the brutality of their pagan and not unfrequently drunken
guards, they spent all their time in prayer and in
preparation for the glorious death that awaited
them. Their meals were taken in common ; and
whenever they were permitted to walk in the
gardens around their prison-house, they either
conversed about heaven and heavenly things, or
read the " Acts of the Martyrs," brought thither
by the priest Saturus. As for Vívia, she usually
remained in-doors with Felicitas, for the delicate
state of the latter kept her confined to the retirement of the prison. The two mutually encouraged each other to remain steadfast in the
faith ; yet this did not save the slave-girl from
betraying occasional fits of despondency and
weeping.

"Why are you so sad, and why do you weep ?"
said Vivia to her one day. "Is your father the
cause of your distress and tears ?"

"Of course, dear sister, I can never forget my
poor unhappy father. The thought breaks my
very heart. But God knows that I have borne
my sorrow with resignation, especially since he
gave me the sweet assurance that he will one day
have mercy on him."

"Then why this great sadness ? You certainly cannot regret that you embraced our holy religion."

"May God preserve me from such a wicked
thought ! I daily return thanks to him for hav-

ing called me, and I bless your name, since it was
through you that I have the happiness of knowing him."

"We are all so happy, and our hearts leap for
joy at the thought that we are so soon to suffer
for the love of Christ! You alone sigh and
weep!"

"And that is precisely the thought that wrings
tears from my eyes!"

"What do you mean? I do not understand
you."

"That I shall not have the happiness of suffering and dying with you; and at the thought of
this separation I cannot help feeling an overwhelming sense of sadness."

"But why should we be separated? You need
fear no weakness on my part, dear sister. I feel
that God has given me strength to suffer and die
for him. He will give a like courage to you also.
Have you not invariably told me to put my trust
in him?"

"I know that God is good. But I shall not die
with or near you. At my last hour my eyes shall
seek yours in vain; the noble and pious Vivia
shall have gone to heaven ere then, and her hapless slave shall be left behind to weep and moan
in solitude and abandonment."

"What can put such thoughts into your mind?
Have you not, like all of us, borne testimony to
the faith? Has not the sweet promise of martyrdom been given to you as well as to us?"

" Yes ; but are you not aware that the law does not allow a pregnant woman to be put to death until after her delivery ? Before that time shall have come for me you will be a conqueror, crowned in heaven."

" Wholly wrapped up in my own happiness, I never gave that a thought; and, dear Felicitas, you never brought it to my mind."

" I was afraid to sadden you by making you think of your own absent babe."

" God gave me the consolation of seeing and embracing him two days ago, as you know. My mother received permission to visit me, and took that opportunity to bring him to me. You need have no fear of reminding me of my darling boy. I hope he will be restored to me before long ; nevertheless, if God requires that I make him the sacrifice of my child, may his holy will be done ! "

" I admire your courage, and I feel brave when I am near you. But when I shall be alone, who will sustain me ? "

" God will ; so keep up your courage. Besides, unless I have been misinformed, our execution, or rather our triumph, is to be delayed until the celebration of the games ordered by the emperor in honor of his son's elevation to the throne ; your delivery may happen previous to that time."

" The celebration you speak of is to take place in a few days, while my delivery will not at least for another month."

" The Lord is all-powerful ; we will pray to

him, Felicitas, and I feel confident he will hear
us. No, no, dear sister, we shall not be separated. The same day will witness our regeneration
by baptism, and the same day shall also date our
entrance into heaven."

"It is God himself that puts these sweet assurances on your lips. O Vivia! how your words
give me courage."

And the two women knelt and prayed long
and fervently together.

The captain of the guards was, it will be remembered, impervious to every feeling of kindness and compassion. For the first few days,
therefore, he did more than carry out the orders
of the governor: he treated the martyrs with excessive cruelty. But the invariable mildness and
patience with which his savage treatment was always met resulted in producing a marked change
in his bearing and manner. He saw so much
harmony among them, such decorum in conduct
and speech, such calmness, or rather such cheerfulness, in the very presence of the most frightful
torments and death. All their words and actions
bore the impress of such deep earnestness and sincerity. His old prejudices began to be shaken,
his hatred to grow less, and his severity to relax;
still, he dared not protect them openly from the
brutality of the soldiers.

The priest Saturus took advantage of these
happy dispositions. Two deacons had succeeded
in gaining admission to the prison; they brought

from the bishop chrism for the baptism of the
catechumens, together with a chalice and an altar-
stone for the celebration of the Sacred Mysteries.
As Vivia and Felicitas ardently desired to be
baptized previous to their second appearance before the governor's tribunal, they had been privately prepared for the grace of the sacrament.
They were also to receive the Body and Blood of
the Christ whom they had so generously confessed.

In the dead of night, when the guards were
asleep and everything quiet, the confessors noise-
lessly crept to a room where Saturus was awaiting
them. An altar had been prepared; it was as
poor and as rough as the crib that received the
Infant Saviour. It was simply a plank raised on
four piles of stones by way of props, with Vivia's and Felicitas's veils for altar-cloths. The
two dingy bronze lamps that lit the prison now
served to light up the altar. The two catechumens
knelt at the door and prayed fervently.

In the first centuries the Church wisely required a long and severe probation previous to baptism. This was because at that time the name
of Christian was synonymous with proscription
and death; it was necessary, therefore, to test the
faith and courage of the candidates, and to guard
against the admission of persons who might demand baptism under evanescent and momentary
impulses and might fall away from the faith in
the hour of trial. Where some of the members
of a family were Christian and had given proof

óf fidelity to the faith, as well as in the case of
infants, these precautions were deemed unnecessary; but otherwise, whenever a pagan candidate
presented himself for baptism, the bishop put him
on trial for a longer or shorter period, according
to circumstances. In the first place, he had to be
instructed, and, as a rule, this had to be done privately; then came the far more tedious task of
disabusing him of all the vain superstitions in
which he had been brought up, of uprooting all
the habits of self-indulgence and pleasure that
formed the staple of pagan life; after that he had
to be taught to cultivate a taste for the pure, the
noble, the spiritual, and the supernatural—things
altogether at variance with his former tastes and
habits, and equally distasteful to his pride and
passions, which had hitherto known neither dic-
tation nor restraint. It was requisite also that
the candidate should give proof that he could and
would brave the resentment and opposition of
his family, that he would be ready to make the
sacrifice of all his worldly goods, to become an
exile from home and country, to be buried alive
in the mines, to bear the rack, the dungeon, and
death—the usual termination of the Christian's
career in those times of bloody persecution. If
the Church, always guided by the Spirit of God,
had not followed this rule of prudent deliberation
and delay, every day of her life would have been
saddened by numberless apostasies from her fold
and the faith.

This disciplinary conrse had been observed in
the case of Vivia and Felicitas. They, too, had
to prepare themselves for baptism by prayer, rig-
orous fasts, and the constant practice of all the
Christian virtnes. The bishop had appointed the
approaching Easter for their reception into the
Church, for at that time baptism was solemnly
administered only on that day and the Feast of
Pentecost. Bnt, as they might be condemned
and put to death at any moment, the bishop had
anthorized Saturus to shorten their probation and
baptize them in prison.

Onr readers are aware that, in those times,
the ordinary method observed in the administration of baptism was immersion, thrice repeated
in honor of the Blessed Trinity. The deacons
then pnt a white garment on the newly-baptized
person, and this dress was to be worn for the
next eight days. This custom is still observed in
some churches of the East, notwithstanding the
fact that they have been separated by heresy or
schism from the Roman Catholic Church for
more than twelve centuries. In some ancient
churches in the West are still to be seen stone
steps leading to cisterns or wells; these were the
baptisteries of former times. But in cases of
sickness, imprisonment, or when the churches
were closed in times of persecution, baptism was
administered by *infusion*, with the exorcisms
and prayers still in nse in our own day.

Previous to commencing the Holy Mysteries

Saturus approached the catechumens and asked them what they sought.

"We desire," they answered, "to be received by baptism into the communion of Christ's servants."

"You believe in him ; you have given public testimony to the faith. You have courageously braved insults and injuries, and in a few days you will be summoned to seal with your blood the testimony you have already given. By what deeds and practices have you endeavored to prepare yourselves for the due reception of the grace you demand ?"

"Good father," immediately answered Vivia, "and you all who have long edified the Church of Carthage by your exemplary lives, bear with me in your charity. The prayers and self-sacrifices of one of my mother's pious slaves have brought me to the knowledge of the true God. But, alas ! even while I made profession of him and his law, I long refused to give him my heart. I was proud, haughty, and a slave to vanity and my own ease ; my whole life was a ceaseless round of pleasure and vain display that was a scandal to others and a mockery of the example and poverty of Jesus Christ, my Saviour. I denied myself no indulgence or gratification, blindly alleging in defence or extenuation of my conduct that I acted only in accordance with the requirements of my rank and position. I was the cause of much annoyance to the fatherly heart of our zealous bishop; I was a scandal to

the Church of Carthage, and cost my mother
many bitter tears. The priest Tertullian was the
instrument employed by Almighty God to deliver me from my deplorable delusion and apathy.
I sincerely deplore my past folly and crimes. I
have long and secretly prayed God to forgive
me, and I again implore his pardon in your
presence ; I ask yours also, holy confessors ;
take pity on a poor sinner ; do not cast her off
on account of her sins ; imitate the goodness of
that God who, in his mercy, has been pleased to
associate me with you in your sufferings and
chains. This I beg of you in the name of Christ,
who died for the salvation of sinners.

" Unlike me, this young woman has no painful
declarations to make or pardon to ask of your
charity. She was always mild, humble, and irreproachable ; ever since she became a Christian
I have seen nothing in her but eminent piety
and marvellous perfection. Like all the saints,
God has purified her by making her pass through
the crucible of great suffering. For over seven
years she has borne a long martyrdom from the
anger and malediction of a father whom she loves,
but who has renounced and hates her because she
became a Christian. For seven long years she
has borne her sad lot without a murmur, and has
constantly prayed and wept and offered herself
as a sacrifice for her hard-hearted and cruel parent. Felicitas is indeed a saint !"

" Vivia's great charity and affection for me has

made her blind to my faults," said the slave. "Alas! she is sadly mistaken. Until I was fifteen years of age I adored vain idols, I ignored and blasphemed the true God. Up to the present I have done nothing that could redound to his honor or glory. Still, his mercy is infinite, since he has deigned to invite me to suffer for his name. Oh! how good is God to have thus condescended to bestow a glance of his merciful eye on the most abject of all his creatures."

So saying she buried her face in the dust. Humility has a modesty and a noble sort of confusion all its own.

"Arise, daughter," said the priest. "Return thanks to God, the fountain of all virtue as well as of all light, and to his Son Jesus, *the author and finisher of our faith.* Blessed are you because you have believed, but more blessed still because you have rendered your life conformable to your belief; to God alone be all the glory! As for you, Vivia, the humble avowal made by you in the presence of your brethren has found acceptance in the sight of the Lord. Be of good cheer; the Christ in whom you believe and whom you have confessed before men pardons you all your sins; the Church forgets and forgives you whatever sorrow you may have momentarily caused her; and your pious mother, consoled by your generous sacrifice, has only one wish—to see you persevere to the end."

"May the God of all goodness be praised and

blessed!" exclaimed Vivia, as she raised her streaming eyes to heaven.

The priest now proceeded to repeat the prayers prescribed by the Church and to sign the catechumens with the hallowed sign of the cross. In the name of the three Persons of the Blessed Trinity he commanded *the spirits of darkness* to depart for ever from those who were now marked with the sign of salvation and become the heritage of Jesus Christ. Then, upon a signal made by Saturus, both the young women advanced and knelt near the altar.

"Let us lose not a moment," said the priest; "the hour for the holy sacrifice is at hand. Vivia and Felicitas, in the presence of God and his angels, who will record your promises in heaven, and in the presence of your brethren here present in chains for Jesus Christ, do you solemnly pledge yourselves to adore Him alone, and to renounce for ever all worship and veneration of idols?"

"We promise to do so," said they; "and with God's help we will faithfully keep our promise."

"The struggle has already begun; the Lord has hitherto given you strength to resist courageously. But do you feel that you will be willing and able to confess your faith in spite of suffering torture and death?"

"We love God with our whole hearts; we are ready to suffer and die for him."

"Brethren, what think you?" said Saturus,

turning to the confessors. "Do you judge them worthy of the grace of baptism?"

"The Lord himself has spoken. We judge them to be worthy."

The sacred waters of baptism fell upon the heads of the two catechumens amid the fervent prayers of the assembly.

Immediately after Saturus began the Sacred Mysteries and the Omnipotent from his exalted throne in heaven descended upon that humble wooden altar. After having given the kiss of peace to one another, as was then the custom, all the confessors received the Body and Blood of Jesus Christ from the hands of the celebrant. Trembling with joy and love, the two neophytes approached the Eucharistic banquet in their turn. Vivia was so overwhelmed with happiness that she could not contain herself for joy; while the rest were occupied in the recitation of the thanksgiving hymn she fell weeping into the arms of Felicitas. "O beloved sister!" she cried, "how I long to see face to face in heaven the God who has so generously given himself to us. What a happiness to contemplate and love him with one's whole heart and soul! To be united to him I would willingly die a thousand deaths, were it possible."

As the dawn was approaching, the objects that served for the altar were restored to their places, and the confessors separated to take a little rest. Vivia and Felicitas were too happy to think of sleep. They lay down together on a mat to hold sweet converse on the graces received and the thoughts that filled their glad hearts during that memorable night.

CHAPTER XXIV.

FROM the moment he quailed under the withering glance of Tertullian, Olympius had lived only for revenge. Having failed to induce the old governor to issue a decree for the persecution of the Christians, he addressed himself to the base task of arousing all the bad passions of Jubal, and of urging him to the commission of the most cowardly of all crimes—assassination. He had made a confidant of the old mountain herdsman, because he found him to be as good a hater as himself. He used Sylvanus to stir up a sedition among the slaves, and to hound on the populace against the Christians; the savage shouts of the rabble filled his soul with joy; but when he was about to touch the goal of all his happiness and ambition, to hold his *enemy* in his power, Tertullian had evaded his grasp. All his hopes were, consequently, dashed to the ground.

If he even but knew where Tertullian was concealed! For he never doubted for a moment that fear was the cause of his flight. But he could find no clue to his hiding-place, and all his efforts in that direction had proved abortive. In his vexation he refused to take food. When night came he flung himself on his couch and vainly tried to sleep; instead of sleep the ever-present figure of the *detested priest* came to his eyes and made him fill the whole house with his howlings and curses. Besides, he was terrified at the thought of Jubal's resentment upon finding that he had been made a dupe and a tool; he knew but too well how that youth usually treated those who had incurred his displeasure, and he constantly imagined he felt the cold blade of the dagger piercing his heart. The old man could bear it no longer, so he had recourse to poison to end his life.

In the meantime the confessors had been transferred to the city prison and were placed in a horrible dungeon that had to depend on one narrow opening for light and air. The dampness of this place, together with the foulness of the atmosphere, rendered the darkness still more horrible. Narrow cells honeycombed the walls of this dark prison, and into them the Christians were thrust with nothing save the bare floor to sit or rest upon. They were seldom allowed to leave their cells except at meal-times, when they were marshalled in a long gallery, half-lit by two dingy lamps, whose feeble gleams revealed only squalor and mouldy walls that never saw the sunlight. They had no fire to warm their benumbed limbs, and all human wants were turned into suffering in that pagan prison. Such privations were especially irksome to a person of Vivia's habits and antecedents; it required all the power of faith to enable her to bear them unrepiningly. Her greatest trial was separation from her child, and she confessed that *this had caused her hours of bitter suffering.* But God took pity on her anguish. Her mother's purse found means to have the child restored to her. "*From that moment,*" said she, "*I became quite contented, and my prison so pleasant an abode that I preferred it to any other.*" Such a candid and child-like declaration fully revealed all the heart of a mother.

Hilarian, having learned that the tribune treated his prisoners in a more humane manner, threatened to deprive him of his office unless he obeyed his orders more carefully. Taking advantage of this, the soldiers maltreated them more than ever; and as they did so in the presence of the officer, it was natural to infer that they were only carrying out his wishes. Fired with indignation at such treatment, Vivia boldly remonstrated with him one day by asking: *How dare you treat so harshly prisoners who belong to Cæsar, and are reserved to grace the arena on the day of his coronation? Why do you refuse to allow them to enjoy in peace their short reprieve? Will it not be to your credit if we are found in good condition when we shall be exposed in the circus?*

With meal-time, however, recurred the most painful ordeal of the whole day; even in their cells they could pray at least. At night their cloaks partially protected them from the cold and damp, and they slept calmly under the watching eye of God. But whenever they went to the gallery to their meals they invariably found a crowd at the door waiting to enter and surround the table; some were drawn by curiosity, but the majority came to enjoy the pleasure of mocking and insulting them. Drunken slaves, young libertines, and abandoned women jeered and howled the most obscene songs; for, of course, only the lowest dregs of the populace came daily to enjoy and amuse themselves with such a spectacle. The confessors hung their heads in silent shame, or occasionally raised their eyes imploringly to heaven ; these ribald songs were more painful than all their other sufferings. They were torture unutterable to the chaste ears of Vivia and Felicitas, that had never before been polluted by such sounds. They hid their burning faces in their hands, while their tears not unfrequently moistened the hard crust given them for food.

On one occasion, however, the martyrs' supper was spared the usual scenes of ribaldry and insult that we have vainly endeavored to describe. Along with the crowd there came into the gallery a man who, as soon as he entered, fell on his knees at the prisoners' feet, and cried:

"Glory to you whom the Lord has made worthy of suffering for his holy name! Woe to me, a miserable sinner, to whom he has denied that glory and the eternal honor of sharing your chains!"

This man was Tertullian. As usual, that trumpet-toned voice, the eagle-glance and lofty bearing, inseparable to him, awed into respect and silence even that vicious rabble of depraved men and women. But how came he thus suddenly into the prison?

On the day after, the occurrences that had taken place in Carthage became known at Thascius's villa. The young Cyprian requested that the news should be carefully kept from Tertullian, lest he might, as he certainly would, have insisted on hastening to the assistance of his brethren. His suspicions were aroused by some hints dropped by a freedman whose occupation was to do errands between the villa and the city. The priest took him aside and demanded to be informed of the exact state of affairs—to know the whole truth. The freedman tremblingly blurted out the entire secret.

At the recital of the indignities and insults heaped upon the Christians Tertullian's noble soul was filled with anguish at the thought of having lost his opportunity of sharing the sufferings of the persecuted Christians. All his thoughts aimed at the topmost pinnacle of human effort and superhuman virtue; he panted for the

contest, for dangers that would afford full scope
to his courage and indomitable energy, and for
victories laboriously achieved. He longed to
come to a death-grapple with paganism; his
dream of happiness was to be able on some grand
public occasion to brand the vile system with infamy, sarcasm, and contempt, and then to die
with the sacred name of Christ, his God, upon
his lips. Accordingly, without waiting even to
take leave of his hosts, he returned to the city
and went straight to the prison.

All the martyrs were overjoyed at the presence
of Tertullian, and ran to give him the kiss of
peace; Vivia and Felicitas humbly prostrated
themselves to receive his blessing. As his eye
fell on the plain mourning dress of the noble
lady whom he had once so severely reprimanded
for her vanity and display, it lit up with joy; for,
in spite of his severity, he had a kind heart, and
his first impulses were always the outcome of a
naturally sympathetic and generous nature. As
his gaze rested upon her for a moment, he seemed
like an overjoyed father finding a beloved and
long-lost child. But, as if afraid of betraying
his feelings, he took her infant into his arms,
blessed him, and kissed him on the forehead.
For the first time it was remarked that a tear
glistened in Tertullian's eyes; that precious tear
seemed to Vivia to fall upon her heart like dew from
heaven. Never had she felt so proud and happy
in being a mother as she did at that moment.

She was on the point of giving utterance to her feelings when the priest checked her by a forbidding gesture, and with his usual air of severity thus addressed them *:

"Blessed martyrs, you are on the eve of coronation by the hand of Almighty God himself, and hence it would be but presumption in me to claim any right to exhort you. I am emboldened, however, by the reflection that not only the trainers and overseers of the circus, but even the unskilled—nay, all who choose—are wont to shout and encourage by their cries the most accomplished gladiators, and that from even the onlookers useful suggestions have not unfrequently come. First then, O blessed! grieve not the Holy Spirit who has entered the prison with you; for if he had not come with you you had not been here to-day. And do you give all endeavor, therefore, to retain him, and thus to let him lead you hence to your Lord. The prison, indeed, is the devil's house as well, wherein he keeps his family. But you have come within its walls for the very purpose of trampling the wicked one under foot in his chosen abode, as you had already in pitched battle outside utterly overcome him and his human agents.

"I have full confidence in your courage; it has been tried, and was not found wanting; nevertheless imprisonment, especially if it be

* We do little more than give a synopsis of Tertullian's "Exhortation to the Martyrs."

protracted, is necessarily so irksome and full of
trials that even the stoutest may succumb. Constant suffering, separation from home and kin-
dred, being shut out from God's sun and air, the
entreaties and tears of friends and family who
know not the glorious inheritance of Christ, the
insults of the mob blindly mocking the chains
that they should kiss with reverence had they
not been carried away by prejudice and hatred,
the brutality and maltreatment which you daily
suffer at the hands of the military guards, and
which would not be practised or permitted even
against prisoners of war, make up a dread catalogue of suffering, and fills the enemy of your
souls with joy and hope. Blessed martyrs, put
him to confusion by your unflinching patience;
let him quake and tremble before you, let him
fly as the serpent does from the snake-charmer or
the fire, and so thwart him that he shall plunge
into the lowest depths of the pit to hide his
shame, discomfiture, and rage.

"Everything that could be an obstacle to your
soul's interests and detachment from earthly
things should have been left at the prison gates.
There and thenceforth you were severed from
the world and all its affairs. Nor let this separation from the world alarm you. For if we
reflect that the world is more really the prison,
we shall see that you have gone out of a prison
rather than into one. The world has the greater
darkness, blinding men's hearts; the world im-

poses the more grievous fetters, binding men's very souls. Your prison is full of foul odors, but they cannot be compared to the fetid exhalations of the world's lusts and vices. The world, too, has worse and greater darkness than any prison, and the host of its sin-bound prisoners is incomparably more numerous.

"The pro-consul who summoned you to his tribunal is as much a mortal as the lowliest slave; in a day or two death will breathe upon him and he shall fall into his own littleness and the oblivion of eternity. The day will come when the haughty and powerful Hilarian shall stand trembling like a child before you. The judge of the world is our Omnipotent God, is Christ the conqueror of the world; he is the just, all-powerful Judge, whose wrath and vengeance are eternal; he alone is to be feared. Wherefore, O blessed! call not this place a prison, but rather a holy refuge whither God has brought you for a little while, and of which he is the guardian. It is full of darkness, but ye yourselves are a bright light; my eyes see bonds and chains, indeed, but my soul sees the blessed liberty of the children of God. Unpleasant exhalations are here, but ye are an odor of sweetness. The judge is daily looked for, but ye shall judge the judges themselves. Sadness may be here for him who sighs for the world's enjoyments. The Christian outside the prison has renounced the world, but in the prison he has renounced even the prison also.

It is of little consequence where you are in the
world—you are not of it. And if you have lost
some of life's sweets you but imitate the thrifty
merchant who is willing to suffer present loss that
after gains may be the larger.

"Thus far I say nothing of the rewards to
which God invites the martyrs. Meanwhile, let
us compare the life of the world and of the prison, and see if the spirit does not gain more even
here than the flesh loses. Your eyes are not
pained by the sight of idols, nor do they obtrude
on your daily walks; you have no part in heath-
en holidays, for you can neither see nor hear their
mad orgies and celebrations; you are not annoyed by the foul fumes of their idolatrous sacrifices; you are not pained by the noise of public
shows, nor by the frenzy or immodesty of their
celebrants; your eyes do not fall on the filthy
stews of obscenity and vice; you are free from
the occasions of sin, from temptations, from un-
holy reminiscences. The prison does the same
service for you which the desert did for the prophets. Our Lord himself spent much of his time
in seclusion, that he might have greater liberty
to pray, that he might be quit of the world. It
was in a mountain solitude that he showed his
glory to the disciples. Let us drop the name of
prison; let us call it a place of refuge. Though
the body is cooped up and the flesh confined, all
things are open to the spirit. In spirit, then,
roam abroad and wander in imagination, not

along shady paths or colonnades, but on the way
that leads to God.   You will be in no bouds as
often as you walk on that path in spirit.   The
foot feels not the gyve when the mind is in heaven.   The mind encompasses the whole person,
and whither it wills it carries him.   But *where
thy heart shall be, there, too, shall be thy treasure.*   Then let our hearts be placed where we
would have our treasure.

"For argument's sake, blessed confessors, let us
grant that even to Christians the prison is irksome and unpleasant.   But we were called to the
warfare of the living God when we pledged our
baptismal vows.   Well, no soldier goes to a campaign laden with luxuries, nor rushes to action
from a comfortable chamber, but from a rude
and narrow tent where he has had to bear all
manner of privations and hardship.   Even in
peace soldiers must inure themselves to war by
toil and fatigue—marching, running, drilling,
digging trenches, regardless of heat and cold and
fatigue.   All this is borne without a murmur for
the sake of glory and fatherland.   Blessed martyrs, will you be less generous than they ?   You
are preparing for a noble struggle, where the living God will be your captain, the Holy Ghost
your trainer, whose prize is an eternal crown, co-
citizenship with the angels in heaven, and glory
everlasting.   The Lord invites you to, and now
prepares you for, the conflict.   He strengthens
you by the ordeal of previous suffering and pri-

vation, that, when the hour of battle comes, you may be ready and able to meet it. See how the athletes are prepared to fight and wrestle in the circus; no luxuries or ease or delicate food for them! They must fast and exercise and toil incessantly; the harder their labors the stronger their hopes of victory. 'And they,' says the apostle, 'that they may obtain a corruptible crown.' We, with the eternal crown before us, regard the prison as our training-ground, that the hour of trial may find us prepared; for virtue is acquired by patience and endeavor, and is lost by effeminacy and indulgence. .

"We have God's testimony that the flesh is weak; it has its terrors as well as its weaknesses. It may quake and tremble for a moment when it sees the drawn sword or hears the hoarse roaring of the lion. But God assures us also that 'the spirit is willing.' Invoke its assistance to bear up against the weakness of the flesh. See how for a little glory and notoriety many worldlings have borne torments and death! And this not only in the case of men, but of women too; and I make the remark, Vivia and you other holy women, in order that you may pluck up courage and be worthy of your sex. The world has its heroines as well as its heroes: Lucretia, in the presence of her kinsfolk and neighbors, plunged the knife into her body to win renown when chastity had been lost; Dido despised the flames, lest she should be compelled to marry again and forget her love for her dear husband ; and so did the wife of our own Hasdrubal, who, when this city was burning, leaped with her children into the conflagration and perished with it, preferring death to the degradation and shame of seeing her husband a suppliant at the feet of the proud conqueror Scipio.   Cleopatra, too, wooed the rage of the deadly asp sooner than fall into the hands of her enemy.   But you may allege that death is less terrible than the fear of torture. Did the Athenian courtesan flinch under torture and betray the secrets of the conspiracy and the names of her confederates ?   Even a woman of such a character not only triumphed over pain, but ended by biting off her tongue and spitting it in the tyrant's face to show her determination and the futility of his torments.   Who has not heard of the religious ordeal to which the Spartans submit their children ?   These are beaten with rods before the altar, and bear stripes without a groan amid the applause and exhortations of their parents and relatives.   There can be no doubt that it shall ever be counted more honorable and glorious to suffer mental than corporal stripes.   But if so high a value is put on earthly glory that men should seek it at any cost and despise the sword, the fire, the cross, and the wild beast for its sake, assuredly these sufferings are but trifling where it is question of gaining a divine reward and a heavenly kingdom.   If the bit of glass be so precious, what must be the

value of the real pearl?   And is it too much to
ask us to give as cheerfully and as much for this
as others do for the imitation?

"But let us put aside all these human con-
siderations and incentives to glory; they belong
to a world to which we have bidden adieu and in
which we have no interest.   We also have our
own history, and it reckons its heroes by thousands.   From the hour that Christ, the King of
Martyrs, consecrated suffering and death for us,
who are fed by his teaching and fortified by his
example, pain and death have no terrors; they
find us ever smiling and always ready.   The
apostles, our teachers and fathers, rejoiced in
their bonds; rapt in prayer, filled with joy, and
gazing upon heaven opened, Stephen scarcely
feels the shower of stones that crushed him;
Andrew gladly hails the cross so long and so
ardently coveted.   At Rome, Peter and Paul
triumph over Nero's cruelty, and gladly lay down
their lives for Christ.   Ignatius of Antioch so
longs for martyrdom that he determines to pro-
voke the fury of the wild beasts in case they refuse *to grind him like wheat;* the aged Polycarp
thanks God in gratitude for being brought to the
stake, and is so overjoyed at his lot that his request not to be tied to it is granted; the virgin
Thecla rejoices to die for her Heavenly Spouse,
and Sabina willingly sheds her blood for the
faith; two mothers (one of them a slave and
your namesake) calmly witness the death of their

seven sons, and exhort them to constancy, thus suffering a sevenfold martyrdom, like the mother of the Maccabees, before they received the glad signal for their own deliverance.   What shall I say of the thousands who, for two hundred years, bore testimony to Christ and received the triumphal palm from his hands?   Recall their memories, beloved brethren ; they have marked out the path for you ; they have taught you how a Christian should answer before the judge and the tribunal, and how he should look upon their racks and their tortures.   Like them fight the good fight ; like them resolve to suffer and to die for God and his holy cause.

"Far be it from me to tell you that blood enough has been shed for Christ ; that our enemies have drunk thereof to satiety ; that you have room to hope for your lives, if not from their clemency, at least from the weariness of slaughter.   No, they still thirst for blood ; he who was a *homicide* from the beginning will never cry, *Enough !*   They have sworn to destroy the Church ; they will smite as long and wherever they find a forehead marked with the sign of the cross.   Poor fanatics ! they cannot see that man's efforts can never prevail against God's will and work, and that by pulling down the stones they only enlarge, strengthen, and embellish the edifice reared by his hands.   No, your judges will have no mercy ; they are now maddening with hunger and exciting the rage of their lions and tigers, and you are destined to follow in the footsteps and share the fate of an Ignatius. Martyrs of Jesus, rejoice! prepare yourselves by prayer for the hour of combat! God will be with you and will strengthen you in your trial. We, your less-favored brethren, will be there to witness and to celebrate your triumph. I, too, will be there, and will repeat the words with which I saluted you when I entered: '*Glory to you, blessed martyrs, whom the Lord has made worthy of suffering and dying for his holy name. Woe to me, a poor sinner, whom God in his justice has rejected from the lists!*'" Having prostrated himself anew at the feet of the martyrs, Tertullian arose and departed through the crowd, that fell back to make way for him. Such was the effect produced by the man and his words that profound silence fell on the guards as well as on the bystanders. The martyrs felt wonderfully consoled, and returned thanks to God as if he had sent an angel to visit them in their prison. Vivia's courage increased so wonderfully that she burned for martyrdom, exclaiming: "May the hour for the final combat come soon! Would that we were to be sent to the amphitheatre this very day!"

CHAPTER XXV.

FROM the very beginning God revealed himself to man. In the Garden of Eden he made known to him his glorious destiny and laid his command upon him. Adam was so accustomed to hear God's voice that he knew it, and so, after his fall, recognized it as it came to him in the thicket, whither he had flown to hide his shame and nakedness. We read in the Scriptures that God spoke to Cain to upbraid him for his crime and to intimate to him his terrible chastisement; also that he revealed his future designs on the world to Noah. The patriarchs, too, were honored by sundry messages from Heaven. Jacob beheld two mysterious visions. All the prophets have declared that: *The word of the Lord came to me; The vision of Isaias, the son of Amos.* Such are the prefatory words of the seer of the royal race of Israel as he prepares to announce the important events of the future. The chaste spouse of the Blessed Virgin heard in sleep the heavenly messenger directing what should be his future course and conduct.

Who does not know the marvellous visions of
the Apostle St. John in the solitudes of Patmos ? The combats and sufferings of the Church,
her joys and sorrows, her struggles and triumphs,
her career through the ages, the apostasy of the
nations, the conversion of the deicide people, the
tyrannical, wicked, and bloody reign of the blasphemous monster, Antichrist, are all present to
that eye whose light is from above. The Lord
makes him mount up *in spirit* even to the foot-
stool of his throne; the heavenly Jerusalem
opens to him her twelve gates and shows him all
her marvellous splendors; he contemplates in his
glory the Incarnate Word, whose eternal genera-
tion he unfolds; he hears the choirs of heaven
repeating their glad songs of thanksgiving, praise,
and love.

In every age God's friends have been favored
by such-like communications or visions, as may be
seen by the uninterrupted testimony of Church
history. The grovelling and materialistic spirit
of the world cannot conceive such things, and
consequently sneers at them. It can tolerate
nothing that trenches on the *supernatural*. But,
we are writing for Christian readers; to them we
will relate what is narrated in the "Acts of the
Martyrs," as they have been preserved and handed down to us from ancient times. They are
among the most precious monuments of the ages
of faith and heroism, of the times when God
multiplied prodigies, as well for the consolation

of his people as for the conversion of unbelievers.

Our readers are aware that Vivia had two brothers, both catechumens, and both preparing themselves secretly, under the guidance of their pious mother, for the grace of baptism. Still they continued to attend the public schools of Carthage—such was their father's wish—but they avoided all intimacy with their pagan schoolmates and kept aloof from their games and amusements. They listened attentively to the instructions given by their professors, took practical lessons and exercises in what was then the chief study—namely, rhetoric—and then hastened home, where they were sure to find plenty of innocent recreation and amusement, thanks to the solicitude and care of the gentle and pious Julia.

The brothers found no difficulty in obtaining permission to visit their sister in prison. Far from exciting fear, it was thought that their motive could only be to shake her faith, for her tender attachment to them was well known, while they were believed to be zealous partisans of the ancient worship. Meantime both youths profited by their access to prison to encourage Vivia and to receive edification from her.

On one occasion, when the elder brother had come alone to visit his sister, he said to her: "Sister, a very strange report has been circulated to-day in the city ; it is said that the emperor has suddenly changed his plans and has issued orders for the stay of the persecution, and that those who, by virtue of the first edict, had been already cast into prison should be merely sent into exile. Father has heard this news with great joy; for, in case it should prove to be true, he hopes to obtain your liberation from the governor, in consideration of your birth and youth."

"God's holy will be done!" answered Vivia; "my dearest wish is to die for his holy name, and I rejoice as the hour approaches when I shall be permitted to give him this last proof of my love. Still, if it be his will that I should live for the consolation of my mother and the Christian education of the child that he has given me, I am ready to obey. *Whether we live or whether we die, we are always his.* But what can have given rise to this strange and unexpected report?"

"I cannot tell; all I know is that it is all the news throughout the city. Some are glad of it; for even among the pagans there are persons who are not devoid of feeling and have no desire to see blood spilt; others—and they are the majority—find fault and speak their minds openly; it would even seem as if they intended to petition against the emperor's clemency, as nothing less than *cowardice* and *treason*. From violent and wicked men of this stamp, who are nearly all from among the rabble, only the very worst may be expected."

"Well, brother, it matters but little how men

may fume and rage ; God's omnipotent hand
holds them, and they may not overstep the limit
that he has been pleased to prescribe for them.
As for myself, at the very first sound of the storm
I have had the most intimate conviction that it
had been given to the powers of hell to assail us.
Until God's angel shall be sent to drive them into
the bottomless pit, the evil spirits will continue
their work of hate and revenge against Christ,
their eternal enemy.   For reasons which they
cannot understand, and which will inevitably redound to their discomfiture and confusion, God
has been pleased to permit them to shed our
blood, and they will do it."

While uttering these words Vivia seemed like
one inspired.

" Can it be, dear sister," rejoined the youth,
" that God's angel has visited you as he did Peter
in his prison ?   Has he revealed all that you have
just now said with such positiveness ? "

" You know your sister ; does she deserve that
the blessed spirits should leave God's throne to
come down to her ? "

" Nevertheless, you believe you will lay down
your life for Christ ? "

" I do ; I have that sweet, nay, firm conviction.   God has chosen me to be the first out of
our family, and I bless him for it with my whole
heart."

" Who has told you so, then, since you avow
that it was not an angel ? "

"They who told me are in heaven ; it was my dear husband, Jarbas, and Angela, Christ's holy virgin. Before she fell asleep in the Lord she assured me that before long I should shed my blood for the faith. Perhaps I may have said already more than enough; let us not dispel our father's hope. As for my mother, I am confident she would gladly give her first-born to God."

"I shall do as you please ; but then you must promise me what I am going to ask. I know you are in God's favor ; beg of him, therefore, to make known to you by some vision if you are to suffer martyrdom, and let me know the result."

"I am the last of God's handmaids; but, in spite of my unworthiness, he gives me many proofs of his infinite goodness. I will do what you require of me. Return to-morrow and I will inform you of the result."

The night being now far advanced, one of the guards came and curtly told the young man to depart, and to take heed in future not to remain so late, unless he should have the curiosity to spend the night in prison.

But what were those especial proofs of love and kindness that God was pleased to give Vivia, and which inspired her with such unshaken confidence ? The acts of her martyrdom are silent on the subject, and hence we are fain to respect a secret established by her own reticence and hu-

mility. It is only through obedience that the
saints divulge the extraordinary favors conferred
on them; their invariable wish is *to hide the
secrets of the king,* to bury with themselves those
secret confidences of God that belong rather to
the next than to this world.

Sufficient to say that Vivia, upon regaining
her cell, prayed long and fervently as usual, and
then fell into profound slumber. Hard by the
pious Felicitas, ever tormented with anxiety for
her unhappy father, unavailingly wooed rest and
sleep. Suddenly a soft light shone in the cell,
and she heard, as it were, the slight rustling of
wings. The light centred full on the head of the
unconscious Vivia; but her face was aglow with
gladness and joy. All amazed as she was, the
slave concluded at once that the Lord had sent a
messenger to her sleeping mistress. Hence she
bent forward, and with bated breath listened to
see if she could catch the sound of any voice; but
she heard nothing, and, after a few moments, the
light disappeared. Vivia continued to sleep
tranquilly.

When she awoke it was broad day, and Felicitas had gone down to prepare her mistress's
morning meal; for, in spite of Vivia's remon-
strances, she persisted in waiting on her mistress
as if she were in her own opulent home, and on
this particular day she had a little feast for
Vivia. The tender-hearted Pudens, observing the
delicate condition of Felicitas, had made her a

present of some cake, dried fruit, and a little wine. Just as she was on the point of returning to Vivia's cell somebody called her by name.

" Where is my sister?" asked a well-known voice.

" She has not come down yet, but she will be here in a moment; I am just going to her."

After a short delay Vivia and Felicitas came down together.

" Dear brother," said she, " to satisfy you I have prayed to God according to promise, and here is the vision I have had : While I was asleep our cell appeared to me to be suddenly flooded with a bright light, and a voice as sweet as an infant's called me by name and said: ' *Vivia, behold !* ' And I looked and saw a golden ladder of prodigious height; its feet rested on the earth while its top reached heaven, but it was so narrow that only one person at a time could find room on it. Its sides were bristling with naked swords, sharp lances, knives, and hooks, so that no one could possibly go up any distance unless he used the utmost circumspection and kept looking up constantly. A horrible dragon was coiled at the bottom of the ladder. This frightful monster belched forth torrents of lurid flame from his gaping jaws, and threatened destruction to any one that would dare to approach.

" The priest Saturus, who was not arrested with us, but who had the courage to surrender himself voluntarily to the persecutors, came for-

ward, fortified himself with the sign of the cross,
and was the first to go up the rounds of the ladder. I saw him climb up cautiously, yet fearlessly, until he reached the top, when he turned
towards me with a smiling countenance and outstretched hands, and cried out : ' Vivia Perpetua,
I await you! Fear not; you have only to beware lest the dragon bite you.' ' In the name
and by the almighty power of Christ, our Lord,'
I made answer, ' the beast shall not hurt me.'
As if afraid of me, the monster immediately
lowered his head as I prepared to mount, and it
thus served me for a first step. Filled with holy
confidence, I pressed on without faltering. When
I gained the top of the ladder I beheld a spacious garden teeming with fragrance and flowers.
A majestic old man with snow-white locks appeared in the centre. He was of lofty stature
and wore the dress of a shepherd. Round about
him I descried a countless multitude, all clad in
spotless garments. This venerable old man
called me by name and said to me : ' My daughter, you are welcome.' He then put into my
mouth a small piece of curd, which I received
with clasped hands and swallowed. All the bystanders answered, 'Amen.' Thereupon I awoke
and found my mouth full of something far sweeter than the purest honeycomb. The vision had
disappeared, and I immediately relapsed into
slumber."

"Are you certain that you did awake at all ?"

interposed Felicitas; "I was watching you very attentively, and it seemed to me that you neither awoke nor stirred even."

"Then tell me, dear friend, did you hear or see aught of that beautiful vision?"

"I heard no voice, but I saw the light that appeared to you; it fell on your head as if it were a sunbeam coming through the vault of the cell."

"Did the Lord reveal anything to you, also, dear friend?"

"I am unworthy of such a favor. God's angels do not speak to so undeserving a creature."

"Console yourself, Felicitas; this vision is for us both. I have already told you, and I am firmly convinced, that we shall die together and shall go to heaven together."

The patrician youth had hitherto uttered no word, but sat listening in profound silence; he now exclaimed: "Dear sister, I now know and see that our name and family is to receive a new and an imperishable glory that will eclipse all the fame acquired in the past by civil and military honors; I hail our heavenly nobility in you, glorious and happy martyr of Christ!"

Flinging himself on his knees, he reverently kissed his sister's hand and departed to convey to his mother the knowledge of the glad tidings he had just received.

On the same day the confessors were again brought to the tribunal of the new governor, where they were subjected to a second examination. Hilarian made use of promises and threats in the hope of shaking their faith. He reminded them that they had been condemned to be exposed to the wild beasts in the amphitheatre, and that the execution of the sentence had been deferred only to make the games decreed by the emperor more attractive and interesting. The unanimous answer made was that they were Christians ; that they would never sacrifice to the gods nor to the emperors ; and that they were ready and willing to die. Furious with rage, the governor ordered the prisoners to be immediately scourged. Vivia and Felicitas were so cruelly beaten that their faces were torn and covered with wounds and blood. The holy martyrs never ceased to confess and thank Jesus Christ. On their return to the prison they fell prostrate in prayer.

During the following night the angel of the Lord again visited Vivia in sleep ; let us listen to her as she narrates this second vision to her mother:

"Yesterday while we were all praying it so happened that I unconsciously mentioned Dinocrates's name. I was surprised at myself for having done so, because I had never once thought of him since my imprisonment. Tears came to my eyes at the thought of him and his sufferings, and I felt urged by some strange impulse to pray for him. I did so with the greatest fervor. The thought of Dinocrates haunted me during the whole day, and I repeatedly and earnestly recommended him to the mercy of our Heavenly Father.

"The instant I fell asleep, in the evening, I thought I saw him coming out of a dark place in which there were many other persons. He was tormented by a burning thirst; his face was pale and disfigured. The hideous cancer that had tortured and killed him was still there. I would have spoken to him and gone to his assistance were it not that he was too far off and I could not approach him. Hard by him there was a basin full of clear and cool water, but its banks were so steep that a child could not reach it to quench his thirst. I felt the deepest compassion for him. Thereupon I awoke, bathed in tears, yet not without a hope that I might be able to alleviate his sufferings. Accordingly I besought the Lord to grant that favor, and I continued to pray until the night was far advanced and sleep once more fell upon me.

"God had pity on my tears; the vision reappeared, but a great change had taken place. The scene was still the same as before, but the darkness had disappeared and was replaced by a soft and pleasant light. Dinocrates appeared washed, smiling, and elegantly clad. There was still, however, a slight scar where the hideous cancer used to be. The banks around the basin had become so low that the child could easily reach the water. I also noticed on the brink a little vial from which he drank, and when he had slaked his thirst he ran to play with some other children. I then awoke, and, in my confidence that his sufferings were now over, I knelt on my bed and gave thanks to God.[*]

"O dear Vivia!" cried the weeping mother, "after God, how much gratitude do we owe to the pious Rufina. It was she who baptized our little Dinocrates a few days before he died. But why was it that the dear child came to be detained in that abode of darkness and suffering? What faults could he have possibly committed?"

"One must be so spotless to enter heaven! You yourself have often told me, mother, of the searching ordeal and purifications required by God's justice of the souls that depart out of this world. Perhaps Dinocrates was guilty of some slight fault after his baptism, and God . . ."

"Enough, Vivia, enough! I only consulted the bias of a mother's heart. I have offended God by seeking to fathom the mysteries of his justice. May he pardon me for my lack of faith! Thanks to your prayers, my poor darling is now happy with the angels in heaven. God of goodness and mercy, can I ever thank and bless thee sufficiently? And you, dear Vivia, who are destined to enjoy his presence before me, do not for-

---

[*] This is taken from the Acts of St. Perpetua's Martyrdom, and clearly shows the antiquity of the belief in Purgatory.

get your poor mother at his holy footstool. May I soon be united to you both in heaven! But may God's will be done. Farewell, Vivia, farewell, beloved daughter. The day of your happiness is nigh; I shall not return to disturb your retirement or to interrupt your prayers. At your entrance into the amphitheatre, where the crown I envy you awaits you, I shall meet you to bless and embrace you, and also to place in your hands the blessed and blood-stained veil of the virgin Potamiena. After it shall have been dyed a second time in the blood of martyrdom I shall place it in my bosom in memory of all that I loved most in the world."

Julia and her daughter remained long locked in each other's arms and shed many tears. Such tears are not displeasing to God; is it not he who puts into the heart that tender and strong love that binds together the mother and the child?

CHAPTER XXVI.

OF all those who had been arrested on the same day for the faith there remained but Saturus, Saturninus, Revocatus, Vivia, and Felicitas. Two —Secundulus and Quintus—had died in prison; the others, to satisfy the mob, had been burned alive. The eve of the day had now come when the few remaining members of that glorious band of Christian heroes were about to win the immortal crown, the dearest object of their souls' ambition. The pious slave alone was inconsolable; in spite of Vivia's kind words and assurances she feared she would be denied the glorious privilege of sharing in the next day's combat. The governor had apprised her that she should be delivered before she would be put to death. He even thought of having her separated from her companions and putting her in a place by herself.

During the previous night Vivia had another vision, which she related in these terms:

" It seemed to me that the Deacon Pomponius

had come and had knocked loudly at the prison
door and that I had run to open it. He wore a
white dress ornamented with a countless number
of gold beads. He immediately took me by the
hand and led me along a narrow and rugged
pathway. Breathless and exhausted, we at last
arrived at the amphitheatre. Pausing in the centre, he said to me: 'Be not afraid; I shall be
with you in a little while and will share with
you the combat.' He then left me there standing
all alone. Knowing that I was to be exposed to
the wild beasts, I could not understand why they
delayed to set them upon me. Then there appeared a hideously ugly Egyptian, who came to
fight me, accompanied by some other persons
equally deformed. At the same moment I saw a
band of young men coming to my assistance. They
rubbed me with oil, and I found myself changed
into a strong and stalwart gladiator. Just then
there appeared a remarkably tall personage, clad
in a flowing robe, down the front of which there
hung two purple bands. He held a wand like
that borne by the master of the games, and a
green branch from which hung clusters of golden
fruit. In a loud voice he commanded silence,
and I heard him say : 'If the Egyptian gain the
victory over this woman he shall slay her with
the sword. If the woman be victorious over the
Egyptian I shall give her the green branch.'
Then the Egyptian and I drew nigh to each
other and the combat began. I flung him flat on

his face and put my foot on his head. The spectators began to applaud and my abettors raised the pæan of victory. But I went up to the master of the games, who had smilingly watched my struggles and victory. He kissed my brow, bestowed on me the green branch, and said : *' Peace be with you, my daughter !'* I then awoke with the conviction that I was destined to contend, not with wild beasts, but with Satan."

This as well as the preceding visions were written *in extenso* by Vivia herself ; at a later period they were published in the Acts of her martyrdom, and for many years continued to be read publicly in the churches.

From the moment of her imprisonment the soul of this great lady burned with the desire of martyrdom ; this was her only thought, her sole desire, the subject of all her conversation, the grace petitioned for in all her prayers ; she never ceased to return thanks to God for having permitted her to suffer for him. She never lost courage for a single moment, and nothing had been able to ruffle the peace and happiness that filled her soul. And yet she must have suffered more than the other confessors ; she had exchanged an opulent home for a dark and loathsome prison ; a life of ease and enjoyment, with troops of slaves to wait upon her, for a life full of privations, and rendered more irksome still by the insolence and brutality of her jailers. But faith and charity made her strong—nay, made her glory in her chains and rejoice in privations, poverty, insults, and tortures. On the eve of her death she seemed scarcely able to control the tide of happiness that filled her soul and would fain communicate itself, out of its very abundance, into the listening ear of her beloved slave, when her father suddenly appeared before her.

"Vivia," cried he, as he cast himself on his knees and tore his white locks, "are you aware that to-morrow is the day appointed for the games?"

"I am, father, and that is what fills my heart with holy joy. Yea, to-morrow your daughter shall be crowned by God's own hand. Arise; a father should not kneel at the feet of his own child."

"Are you still my child? Am I still your father? Unfortunate man that I am! For the past month I have been begging you with prayers and tears to consent to live with me, for the sake of your mother and for the sake of your child. But you have despised all my entreaties and tears, although you were well aware that you were breaking the heart of an old man who loved you so much."

"I know your affection, I pity your grief, and I love you with all the tenderness that a child can have for a father. But I am a Christian and cannot betray my faith."

"Alas! always the self-same obstinacy and blindness."

"Always the self-same fidelity and wisdom, and I owe both to the wonderful mercy of God."

"But you, Vivia, whom I have always known to be so proud of your birth and rank, how will you be able to stand the insolent gaze, insults, and jeers of the vile mob?"

"Just as I have done already; for I have learned that true nobility consists in being derided and mocked for Christ's name and sake."

"Well, but when you shall hear the lions roar and shall see them rushing into the arena, what will become of all this mock courage? Then you will tremble and grow pale with terror, I am sure; you would gladly cry for mercy, but you shall not be able, for your tongue will be palsied by fear. Do you not remember how you used to tremble like a child whenever you heard, no matter how far off, the howling of the wild beasts in the amphitheatre?"

"God had not then prepared me for the glory of martyrdom. But now that he has given me his grace I can hear without fear the roaring of the lions, and I would gladly give them my body to be torn for his sake. You know not what invincible courage Christ infuses into his martyrs."

"O Vivia, dear Vivia! there is yet time. Bring not shame and sorrow on the last days of your unfortunate father. Have pity on *us* at least; can your God be displeased with you for this? You need but pretend to offer sacrifice in obedience to the orders of the emperor."

"As the daughter of Hanno I will never purchase my life by a dastardly deed or action ; as a Christian I will never practise dissimulation regarding my faith."

"If you will only allow me I will call on the governor and say that you ask for a short delay, for a reprieve of a few days. I will offer him money, every obolus in my possession ; nay, if necessary, I will kneel and kiss his very feet."

"You shall do none of these things, for even if you did I would publicly declare my refusal to offer sacrifice and my desire to be exposed in the amphitheatre. Farewell, dear father, and may God give you the grace to see the truth ! "

"Your God is cruel and pitiless ; and I swear he shall never be the God of Hanno ! "

And the old man departed without casting a look upon his daughter.

It was only by dint of doing violence to herself that Vivia succeeded in checking her feelings. But the moment she found herself alone with Felicitas she gave free scope to the tears she had restrained in her father's presence, and which had started to her eyes especially at his parting words. After a little while she repaired to seek the priest Saturns, telling her companion that she would not be long absent and to wait for her in her cell.

"Father," said she to the priest, "I come to request that you call Saturninus and Revocatus, in order that we join in praying to God to hasten the delivery of our sister Felicitas. She has shared our chains and sufferings; it is just that she share on to-morrow our triumph and happiness. I have the fond conviction that God will have pity on her sorrow and will hear our prayer."

Accordingly the four martyrs knelt together in prayer. Scarcely had they begun when Vivia heard a subdued cry of pain.

"The Lord has heard us," exclaimed she; "return him thanks; I must hasten to our sister."

It was indeed true: the pains of travail had seized Felicitas a full month before her time, so that when the patrician lady returned to the cell she found her moaning on her pallet.

" Oh ! how good God is," exclaimed Felicitas, as she saw her mistress. " So I shall be able to die with you to-morrow. As your prayer for my speedy delivery has been granted, pray also that I may have strength enough to be able to go to the amphitheatre."

" The Lord will perfect the work he has begun. Have courage ; I shall be strong enough to support you in case you require assistance."

"I know how good and kind you are. . . . But in case the governor should decide to postpone the day of my execution ! If, in consideration of my paleness and weakness, the crowd should demand that I be removed from the arena ! "

"Hilarian is not so compassionate, and the crowd that will come to enjoy the spectacle of our death-throes will have for us nothing but insults and cries for our blood."

"Then I have nothing to do but to give thanks to God. On my way to martyrdom I shall carry no anxiety for the fate of my infant; your pious mother will take charge of it, as she has already promised me, and my little one will grow up near yours. Together they will learn to know and love our holy religion. . . . But, sweet Lord, how much it costs to become a mother!"

A violent pang here surprised her into a scream of pain that was heard even by the guard at the door.

A soldier drew nigh, and, peering into the cell, cried: "What! you weep and lament like a child. What will you do when you shall find yourself before the wild beasts in the amphitheatre?"

"It is I who suffer these pains now," mildly answered the slave. "God's justice requires that I, in common with all mothers, should bring forth in pain and travail. But in the amphitheatre *Another*, whom you know not, will suffer for me, because I shall suffer for Him. Only a few days ago I was cruelly scourged until I was covered with wounds and blood—it may have been your hand that did it—and did you hear me complain?"

The abashed soldier retired in silent confusion.

A short time after Felicitas was happily delivered. Vivia remained by her all day. Towards nightfall the good slave, feeling much better, expressed a desire to rejoin the other martyrs.

For some time past the rabble that had been admitted to the prison while the confessors were taking their meals had been refused admittance. Hilarian had been obliged to yield to the earnest protestations of some senators who considered it a disgrace to the city and the empire that such wretches should be allowed to come constantly and insult persons who, though they might be criminals, still had a right to the protection of the laws against the hatred and blind passions of the rabble. The prisoners gave thanks to God for this, for among all their sufferings the greatest was to be thus paraded for the amusement of an abandoned, vulgar mob that annoyed them by their blasphemies and scurrilous songs.

At this time it was customary, at least in Africa, to give what was called *the free supper* to criminals on the eve of execution. This, like many other usages belonging to the period, was a barbarous custom which would fain force the wretch to pretend to smile and enjoy good cheer as he stood trembling on the brink of a future without hope and of a death full of torture and agony. Hilarian gave orders for the observance of this custom in the present instance, and signified his intention of assisting at this last meal of our martyrs. The people came in such numbers to take a good view of those condemned to the wild beasts that the guards had great difficulty in restraining them.

The banquet was sumptuously served, and the table was laden with a profusion of the choicest and most exquisite meats. Massive cups of embossed silver shone between crystal flagons full of the rarest wines. Magnificent candelabra and bronze lamps shed a flood of light on all sides. It looked like a feast got up for the celebration of some great family rejoicing, or a grand banquet such as the rich prepare when they desire to satisfy their pride even more than their sensuality But the grave and recollected appearance of the guests contrasted singularly with all this pompous display.

"God be thanked!" said Suturus, as he signed himself with the sign of the cross. "*Amen*," answered the martyrs. In imitation of the example set by the priest, each one took only a little bread and some dried fruit. None partook of the proffered wine. Even Felicitas, although weak on account of her recent delivery, limited herself to a little water. The crowd looked on in amazement at such incomprehensible abstemiousness, and the still more incomprehensible composure manifested by the women. The governor, who had confidently expected a scene, became visibly embarrassed and began to regret having come, when a sepulchral voice at the lower end of the hall exclaimed:

"The cowards! fear has deprived them of their appetite. What a fine spectacle they will present to-morrow in the amphitheatre, pale, trembling, and half-dead with terror even before the beasts will be let loose!"

Felicitas shuddered and closed her eyes.

"Who calls us cowards?" said the priest Saturus. "True, we refuse to partake of dainty meats and generous wines; we need them not, like criminals who seek to stupefy themselves by gluttony. We can look death in the face; instead of being an object of dread it is our dearest wish and hope. Let the man who accuses us of fear come to-morrow, and he shall see if we will quail before the lions and tigers!"

The manly tone in which these words were pronounced made a deep impression on the crowd. Pity smote the hearts of some, while even those who had come to insult and mock the martyrs felt restrained by a feeling of awe and respect. All were hushed into silence and contented themselves by gazing in silent wonder at the strange beings who were going to die and still could be so calm and self-controlled.

"Note us well," resumed Saturus, "so that you may recognize us on that awful day when Christ, our God, shall judge all men. To-day you blaspheme his name, because you know him not; you have clamored for our lives because we refuse to adore your false and foul gods, and give all our homage to the true and only God

who reigns in heaven ; but, on the last day, you
shall tremble before the angry face of that great
Judge ; then he shall have only words of malediction and wrath for you, and his omnipotent
justice will hurl you into that bottomless pit
where it has already bound the demons, your
masters ; note us well, then, I say, for you shall see
us crowned with glory and inundated with joy
and happiness ; then God shall have avenged his
servants and martyrs.

" There are some of you who now seem to be
moved to compassion, but who to-morrow will inevitably applaud our persecutors and gloat over
our sufferings. It would be far better for them
to reserve such momentary compassion for themselves. As for us, we need not your pity. From
the day we enrolled ourselves under Christ's
standard we made him the sacrifice of our lives,
and have ever since looked upon ourselves as victims doomed to death. As you well know, we
might have remained free by uttering one word ;
nay, nothing has been left undone to wring that
word from us in order to shield us from your so-
called justice ; and we have not consented to
speak that word. We have been loaded with
chains, beaten and tortured in every possible
manner. Have you heard our lips utter a single
complaint ? We were happy and glad to suffer
for Jesus Christ. For a whole month past we
have longed impatiently for the day—the greatest of our lives—when we shall be permitted to

consummate our glorious combat. Come, then, to-morrow, and you shall behold us marching to death as to a banquet or a long-wished-for festival."

"Yes, until to-morrow!" screamed the same voice that had previously spoken from the crowd; "to-morrow, at the amphitheatre, to enjoy the sport! At last, Vivia, I shall behold your blood flowing and your bones ground to dust!"

Felicitas fell fainting on the bosom of her noble mistress; she recognized and knew that that was her father's voice. The crowd dispersed without a word, while the guards, at a signal from the governor, led the martyrs into the interior of the prison.

CHAPTER XXVII.

FOR many a day the great and busy city of Carthage had not presented such an animated scene of excitement and bustle. From all the country and towns round about the people flocked in to see the games, so that the vast amphitheatre, where the martyrs were to be exposed to the wild beasts, was at a very early hour filled to overflowing. All work was suspended; the wharves were abandoned and silent; so that, save in the neighborhood of the circus, the city looked like one abandoned by its inhabitants at the approach of an enemy or through fear of an earthquake.

The sun rose bright and fair; it was the time appointed for the departure of the confessors from the prison under a strong escort. They had arisen a short time before cock-crow, and, when the altar that we had seen once before had been prepared, the priest Saturus had celebrated the Holy Sacrifice. Saturninus, Revocatus, Vivia, and Felicitas had received the Bread of

the Strong as a preparation for their last journey. Before setting out they knelt to receive
the priest's blessing, after which, as was then
customary, they gave each other the kiss of
peace.

Saturns walked first. His beautiful and sweet
countenance seemed to wear a fairer and nobler
stamp than ever; his eyes were often raised to
heaven and beamed with a wonderful expression
of happiness and joy. Saturninus and Revocatus
followed next; from the movement of their lips
it was evident that they were praying. Felicitas
was so full of gratitude for her speedy delivery
that she could not restrain herself, but burst out
into acts of thanksgiving to God. By her side,
with tranquil mien and firm foot, like one confident of God's protection and love, walked Hanno's noble daughter, Vivia Perpetua. Her eyes
were slightly bent towards the ground, not so
much through a motive of shrinking modesty as
from a desire of hiding from the spectators the
holy emotions that agitated her soul and filled it
with heavenly rapture. As the martyrs entered
the arena she suddenly fell on her knees, saying :

"Mother, bless your child for the last time
and rejoice with her."

A woman, still young, and evidently a lady,
bent over and embraced her, saying :

"Yes, Vivia, your mother blesses you with all
her heart. Courage, darling of my soul; prove

yourself worthy to the last of Christ our God. I shall pray for you during the combat."

So saying, she conveyed to her the veil stained with Potamiena's blood. Vivia kissed it reverently and put it on her head. Just then she recognized by her mother's side the holy Rufina.

" Farewell," cried she to her, " my darling sister! I am going to give *my glorious testimony* to Christ."

She embraced her tenderly.

The spectators began to lose patience.

" The Christians to the wild beasts!" shouted a thousand voices.

"Glory and benediction to the holy martyrs!"

The utterer of this courageous exclamation arose to address the multitude, but a venerable old man made him a sign to sit down again. This was the impetuous and ever-ardent Tertullian; the imprudent ardor of his zeal would have cost him his life had not the attention of the spectators been absorbed in watching the scene taking place at the entrance to the amphitheatre.

An effort was made to compel the martyrs to don the costume usually worn by those who fought at the public games. For men this consisted of a scarlet cloak, and was the garment peculiar to the priests of Saturn; for women it was a band around the forehead, and was the distinctive badge of the priestesses of Ceres.

The martyrs, however, positively refused to comply with this idolatrous ceremony: " We are here," said they, "simply to maintain our liberty untrammelled; we are Christians, we have acknowledged it, and it was on that indictment that we have been condemned. We cheerfully make the sacrifice of our lives, but we have, as you must admit, the incontestable right of refusing to do whatever is forbidden by our holy religion. We will never consent to wear the badges of your false gods, whom we abhor and abominate. Let us be put into the arena just as we were when we left the prison; we are ready to die, but not to dishonor our faith."

The governor was afraid to use coercion, so they passed boldly through the gate of the amphitheatre.

"All my confidence reposes in God, and what can the power of men avail against me? In their presence I have not been ashamed of Christ, my Saviour; him do I glorify by my testimony. For his love do I enter the lists; he has promised and will reward my *agony* with a crown. Oh! how sweet to die for him who has died for me. *I see the heavens opened;* Christ Jesus is gazing on me and encourages me with his glance; my heart and my flesh are filled with gladness because the hour so long and ardently desired has come to sacrifice my life to him whom I love."

So chanted in her sweetest tones Vivia Perpetua, as she advanced into the arena. The humble Felicitas, whom she led by the hand with all the affection of a sister, joined in this canticle of

love. The amazed spectators looked on in silence
at the marvellous spectacle of two young women
rejoicing on their way to meet a frightful death.

"He for whom we suffer is alone great, is alone
powerful. The blood of his martyrs cry to him as
in the beginning did the blood of the innocent
Abel. Though you revel to-day in our sufferings,
you shall be made to tremble before the justice of
the Omnipotent. We know that death shall usher
us into an eternal life of bliss and place us
on glorious thrones to reign with him for ever.
As for you, he will soon demand of you a rigor-
ous account of your cruel and unhallowed deeds;
for his vengeance is terrible against those who
blaspheme him and persecute his servants and
friends in this life. And you, Hilarian, who, by
an abuse of power of whose origin even you are
ignorant, have judged and condemned us, our
omnipotent God shall judge and condemn you in
turn."

So spoke Saturus, Saturninus, and Revocatus
as they passed before the elaborately-bedecked
balcony where the governor sat in state. Hilarian grew pale with rage; the people were filled
with indignation.

"Ply the whip on the insolent fellows," cried
a thousand voices. "Let the *venatores* * give
them their deserts!"

---

* The *venatores* were men armed with whips who took
charge of the *bestiarii* — the combatants with the wild
beasts — and spurred them on or punished them, according to
circumstances.

"May Christ, who was scourged for our sake, be blessed!" calmly replied the martyrs.

Full of joy at being treated like their Master, they cheerfully bore the blows upon their naked limbs until they were covered with blood.

"Let loose the wild beasts," now roared the mob, frenzied by the sight of human blood,

"Loose them all upon me," cried Saturninus.

This he said in accordance with a desire expressed by him in prison one day when the conversation fell on the different sorts of torments inflicted on the Christians; on that occasion the good old man said he would prefer to be exposed to all the beasts in order that the number of his combats would be reckoned by the number of the wild beasts. Revocatus agreed with Saturninus, but Saturus said, with a smile, that had he the option, he would *object* to the bear—for whom he had a cordial dislike—but would be far more partial to a lion, tiger, or leopard. God heard and remembered their wishes on the day of combat.

"Saturus's choice is mine too," cried the undaunted Revocatus; "I hope they will set all the beasts in the amphitheatre on me."

The tigers and leopards, with glaring eyes and opened jaws, seemed anxious to jump upon their prey. Goaded on by hunger and the lances of their keepers, they sprang up with a savage growl and put forward their bristling claws.

Saturninus and Revocatus drew closer to the

cages of the wild beasts, and the signal was given.

A leopard and a bear rushed upon them and sent them rolling in the sand. Their limbs were bruised and torn, and the blood burst forth on all sides. Every time they arose, a new spring and new gashes hurled them to the blood-stained ground.

"It is high time to pay attention to Saturus," yelled the spectators, "those fellows must have had enough."

As if to give variety to the spectacle, they set a wild boar upon him; but the animal savagely turned upon his keeper and tore him open with his tusks; he then flung Saturus on the ground but did not wound him. The boar then returned to his den, where he obstinately remained squatted and could not be forced to leave it again.

"A bear will do the business better," yelled the crowd; "bring out the bear!"

Saturus shuddered and had to summon all his faith to his assistance so as not to betray any signs of fear. But the bear that had rushed with so much fury on Saturninus and Revocatus now refused to stir, and remained in his den as if held back by some invisible power.

"I thank thee, O my God, for having had compassion on the weakness of thy servant." This prayer of the martyr was heard only by Pudens, who then happened to be very close to him. This veteran tribune of the imperial army,

whom we saw brushing away a tear at the home
of Angela, and who since then had changed the
position of captain of the prison guards for the
more humble one of jailer, had been much impressed by the confessor's great virtues. His upright, frank mind naturally received the truth the
moment it appeared, and, consequently, only a
few days before the martyrs were exposed in the
amphitheatre, he had put his name on the list of
the catechumens.

Seeing that the bear persisted in remaining
obstinately sluggish, he began to entertain the
hope that the rest of the animals would also refuse to molest the man whom he looked upon as
a father.

"God," whispered he to him, "does not want
you to die yet."

"You are mistaken, friend," smilingly answered Saturns. "Remember what I told you in
prison; the first time the beasts will not touch
me, but I am to undergo another ordeal, and
then you will see how quickly I shall be torn by
the fangs of a leopard. But as for you, remain
steadfast in the faith, and let not the fear of men
ever induce you to betray it!"

"Put Saturus to another trial," said the governor; "bring forth a leopard this time!"

In an instant the martyr was rolling on the
arena; at one snap the animal had made such a
deep wound that Saturns's body was immediately
covered with blood.

"He is well *washed* at all events," yelled the spectators, clapping their hands.

"Pudens," said Saturus faintly, "give me the ring on your finger."

Having dipped it in his blood, he returned it to him.

"Keep this always as a pledge that will ever animate you in the faith. Farewell, my friend; may my sufferings, instead of intimidating, strengthen you. Remember our conversations; you now see the verification of all that I have foretold you. Be strong, therefore, in the faith; you will also one day give your life for Christ."

So saying he expired in the catechumen's arms. Thus it came to pass that the priest Saturus was crowned first, in accordance with what the Lord had revealed to Vivia in her vision.

"Let the women now come forward," said the governor.

The two martyrs advanced and embraced each other.

Paganism, as is well known, found delight in insulting modesty; hence it very seldom happened that female martyrs had not been made to suffer on that score. The Christians' predilection for that virtue was no secret, and, therefore, to bodily suffering was almost invariably added some outrage to their chastity. It could not be expected in a case like the present that our martyrs would be permitted to escape a confusion and shame incomparably greater than death; accordingly at a preconcerted signal from Hilarian Vivia and Felicitas were stripped naked and enclosed in nets to be tossed and gored by a wild cow. God, however, espoused the cause of his chaste servants; they were so filled with the unction of his fortifying grace and presence that they took no note of what was taking place; nay, he so disposed the minds of the spectators when they perceived the weakly condition of our two heroines that they cried out against this treatment and declared they would withdraw from the amphitheatre in case of refusal. The governor dared not persist, so a loose and flowing garment was put on each of them. The instant the cow was let loose she sprang upon Vivia, lifted her into the air, shook her for a moment with her horns, and then flung her prone upon the ground. The youthful martyr, seeing that her robe was torn, modestly drew together the edges of the rent; she then gathered up her hair, which had fallen loose by the violence of the shock, so as not to appear to imitate women in distress, who usually wore their hair dishevelled in sign of mourning; finally she adjusted on her head the veil given her by her mother at the entrance to the amphitheatre. From her calm and smiling appearance she looked like a modest maiden attiring herself in the privacy of her closet previous to making her appearance in the family circle.

Suddenly her eyes turned to look for Felicitas.
She descried her lying motionless and horribly
mangled by the horns of the infuriated beast.
Vivia hastened to her with outstretched arms,
crying :

" O sister ! how came you to fall in this manner ? The combat has not yet begun, and you
are all bloody ! " Then in a louder tone :

" Why do you delay to let loose the wild
beasts ? Why do you not carry out the sentence
pronounced upon us ? "

" No, no ! " cried the mob, " that will do ; " let
the sword do the rest."

The popular will was all-powerful in the
amphitheatre.

Accordingly, Vivia and Felicitas, together
with Saturninus and Revocatus, were carried to
one of the *vomitoria*, or gates facing the public
square. The priest Saturus having been pronounced dead, officially, Pudens obtained permission to take away the body.

" May the peace of the Lord be with you, sister," said a man close to the gate as Vivia came
up.

But she paused not.

" What ! do you not know Rusticus, the friend
of your mother and of the holy Rufina ? "

" Say, when shall we be exposed to the beasts ?
What is the cause of the delay ? "

" But, Vivia, you have been exposed already ;
I saw how the wild cow tossed you into the air

and flung you on the ground. Do you not see
on your garment the glorious marks of the ordeal ? ”

The brave woman awoke to consciousness as
from a dream and saw upon her person and
dress the marks of a conflict endured so unconsciously that she remembered absolutely nothing
about it.

“ Where, then, was she ?” asks St. Augustine,
in a panegyric, still extant, on the martyrs of Carthage. “ Where was Vivia when she was attacked
and mangled by an infuriated animal, being so
unconscious of the assault as to enquire, when it
was ended, when it would begin ? What saw
she that she perceived not what a whole multitude saw ? What felt she not to have felt such
violent pangs ? By what movement of love, by
what ecstasy, by what mysterious draught was she
transported, ravished, and inebriated by Heaven
to make her seem impassible in a mortal and so
delicate a body ? ”

Faith alone can answer the question ; human
wisdom can give it no solution. The perfect and
ardent love of God and his omnipotent power can
raise man above and beyond himself and make
him insensible to all that may pass around and
even within his own body. The history of the
saints and martyrs furnishes us with many and
striking instances of this.

Meantime, one of Vivia’s brothers had succeeded in making his way to her to bid her a

last farewell. Consulting only his affection for
his sister and his zeal for the faith, he strove to
fly to her arms, to declare himself a Christian and
to die with her; the guards frustrated his inten-
tions, however, by hemming in the martyrs from
the crowd preparatory to leading them away.
Saluting her brother and Rusticus with a sweet
smile, Vivia had only time to say: "Be steadfast in the faith of Christ, the only true God.
Obey his precept of loving one another; be not
grieved at our sufferings. The Church of him
who died for its establishment needs to be
watered with blood before it can arrive at full
maturity and fruitfulness. Blessed are they
who cast into its bosom the precious seed that
multiplies children unto her!"

The guards paid no attention to these words;
they were too anxious to get through with their
work.

At the farthest end of the amphitheatre stood
the *spoliarium*, where the *confectors* despatched
those whom the wild beasts had not entirely deprived of life. There, too, our martyrs would
have finished their sacrifice had not the mob vo-
ciferously demanded that their execution should
take place in the amphitheatre. Saturninus,
Revocatus, Felicitas, and Vivia had, therefore, to
retrace their steps to satisfy the blood-thirstiness
and caprice of the mob.

The sword did its work well and speedily in
the case of all except Vivia; she had fallen into

the hands of an inexperienced *confector* who was
a novice in such bloody work. Trembling and
beside himself, he was scarcely able to hold his
sword or find the spot where to strike. Seeing
him fumbling with the edge of his sword she
said in her sweetest accents:

"Friend, you seem to be very inexperienced
at your trade ; do you not see that your companions have already performed their task ? Pluck
up courage, then ; you need be no more afraid
than I am."

"Hurry up!" yelled the mob; "do you want
to keep us here until night ?"

The sword cut through the flesh and soon en-
countered the bones. Vivia uttered a cry of pain
and tottered, but immediately recovering herself
and regaining her presence of mind, she guided
to her throat the trembling hand of the bungling
gladiator.

"That is the place to strike," she said to him ;
then in a louder tone: "Sweet Jesus, what a
happiness to die for thee !"

The sword severed the entire neck—the body
sank slowly to the earth, while the soul, borne on
angels' wings, ascended to heaven.

"Glory to our gods! Glory to Cæsar !" rang
out from the multitude. "Glory to Christ!
Glory to his martyrs!" cried Tertullian as he
slowly retired from the amphitheatre.

"I am avenged at last ; I have looked upon her
blood !" yelled the fierce Sylvanus.

"Noble and chaste Vivia," murmured Jubal, "forgive me."

He drew nigh and looked silently on the dead body, while Julia placed in her bosom the veil steeped in the blood of her beloved daughter.

A few moments' later the amphitheatre became silent and deserted. The populace went to spend the rest of the day in dissipation and amusement, without bestowing a thought on the sad drama and scenes witnessed in the morning.

CHAPTER XXVIII.

EXACTLY two years after the events just related Julia was conversing with the holy Rufina regarding the heroic and happy death of her beloved child. With pious enthusiasm she declared she would gladly go to meet her in heaven, even though she had to follow in her footsteps and win the crown at the same price in the amphitheatre. The humble freedwoman had but that one aspiration and desire in her whole soul; she yearned to be united to her Divine Spouse, the sole object of all her thoughts and affections. Vivia was no longer there to require her advice and assistance; Revocatus, her brother, the friend of her childhood, the sharer of her sorrows, was no more. One sole tie bound her to life—attachment to the noble mistress who loved and treated her like a sister.

A little slave-girl, almost a child, timidly drew aside the *velum*, or curtain, that served for a door, came across the room on tiptoe to the noblewoman, and said:

"Kind mistress, a poor old man, who looks

very tired and unhappy, asks to see you. I
know that this day brings sad memories with it;
the noble Vivia was so very good; I shall never
forget all she has done for me, a poor little waif.
I thought that maybe you would prefer to be left
alone with Rufina, and then, again, I thought
that, as you are so kind and condescending to
those in affliction, I ought not to take it upon
myself to send away this stranger without letting
you know. I noticed that he trembled all over and
big tears fell from his eyes. I felt pity for him,
so I told him to wait a little while, that I might
be able to come and ask you what I ought to do."

This slave was a Christian whom Julia had
taken into her service shortly after Vivia's martyrdom; she had an excellent disposition, with a
slight tendency, however, to be over-talkative;
but that might be, and was, easily pardoned in
one so young and so full of life.

"It would have been wrong, Thesba," said the
noble matron, "to turn away such a poor old
man; you say he is in want and in tears—these
are two sacred claims to our consideration. Always remember, my child, the lessons and example of your sainted mistress; you loved her, I
know. Be always kind, Thesba, and always
good to the poor and the afflicted. So you may go
and bring hither this stranger."

"That is just what I told Jucunda; if our
mistress should ever find out that the door of
her house remained shut to a poor person

through our fault, she is so anxious to help the needy and the suffering that I am sure she would scold us roundly; so I came right away, without waiting to hear all the rest of what she wanted to say to me. You say I did right; I am delighted to hear it, for my happiness is to please you; I am glad, too, for the old man's sake, for I am sure that after having seen you he will be less unhappy."

So saying, she bent down to kiss her mistress's hand.

"That will do now, Thesba; do not keep that poor stranger waiting in this way. You are a good girl, and I am glad to be able to say so; but you do not know how to moderate your tongue sufficiently."

Thesba pouted a little, as if to say: "*After all, I am no chatterbox. . . .*"

A moment later the old man entered and the door-curtain fell behind him.

"Pity," cried he, falling on his knees and bending his face to the floor—"pity a poor, miserable man."

"Good and venerable old man, I entreat you to arise and say what is your trouble."

"In the name of Him who pardoned his murderers with his latest breath, and of her who died a martyr and now prays for us in heaven, pardon me!"

"Whoever you be, and if you have injured me in any way, I freely forgive you for Christ's sake."

So saying she held out her hand to him.

"Generous lady, I perceive very plainly you know not the guilty man at your feet. Oh! no, my hand shall never touch the hand of Vivia's holy mother."

He sobbed aloud and violently smote his breast. Seeing such deep grief, even Julia herself could not restrain her tears.

"Brother," said she gently, "for your words make it evident that you are a Christian, I repeat that, if you imagine you need my forgiveness, it is yours even were you the slayer of my own beloved child."

"He who shed the noble Vivia's blood in the amphitheatre is less guilty than I, and even his presence ought to cause you less loathing and horror. You see before you the hard-hearted and unnatural father who cursed his daughter for being a Christian, the wretch who implacably hated and persecuted her whom you loved so well!"

The old man's brow again smote the floor as he repeated in sobbing accents: "Pardon, pardon and mercy!"

Julia and Rufina could not help experiencing an involuntary feeling of pain as they recognized the hoary herdsman of the mountains, but it soon yielded to a deep feeling of compassion and pity.

"God be praised!" exclaimed the pious lady. "He has had mercy on you, brother, and his grace has finally touched your heart also. Both martyrs have prayed for you.   Let us forget everything, then, except gratitude to Almighty God.   Henceforth, good Sylvanus, let Vivia's mother be regarded by you as a sister."

The old man looked up with eyes full of tears and gratitude.

"Noble and holy woman," cried he as he clasped his hands, "my sole motive for leaving my lonely mountain-hut was to ask your forgiveness and to make ready to die in peace. But what bond can there ever exist between the pious Julia and her daughter's life-long enemy?"

"The same faith, brother, the participation of the same sacraments, and the hope of the same heaven.   But be pleased to satisfy my curiosity on one point: how came you to become one of us?"

"I can refuse nothing to the woman who so generously granted me her forgiveness. I witnessed the shedding of Vivia's blood with savage joy and satisfaction, and—shall I say it?—I looked calmly and with dry eyes upon that of my own child, whom I then hated as intensely as I once loved her. My vengeance was satisfied; I was, or at least I thought I was, happy ; it seemed to me as if my heart had been eased of the terrible load that weighed upon it for so many years, and that I should now begin to enjoy peace and contentment in my desert home and among my camels—all the gifts of your generosity and bounty.

" I turned my steps, therefore, to the mountains
I had left to execute my schemes of bloody vengeance. Old Fatuma, who had been in the
greatest anxiety on account of my protracted and
unaccountable absence, received me with transports of joy. I hardly deigned to notice her protestations of affectionate welcome, and, without
even enquiring about the condition of things at
home, I pleaded fatigue and want of rest although
it was still early in the day. I longed for solitude; I felt restless and agitated; I began to look
upon myself with shame, and terror, and loathing.
The two nights that had elapsed while I was on
my way home had been passed in the most horrible dreams. I heard unearthly sounds, the mad
cries of frenzied multitudes, the hollow roaring of
wild beasts, like that which the lion utters at
night in the desert. I saw them by hundreds
rushing open-mouthed on their prey; naked
swords flashed, and blood smoked and ran in
streams on the ground. Even when I awoke I
could not dispel the horrible picture; nay, it arose
before me always, and, if possible, more vividly;
I quaked in every limb and a cold prespiration
oozed from every pore. I called upon the gods
and reminded them that it was for their sake I
had sacrificed my own child. Vain words, that
were not only not heard by those to whom they
were addressed, but which ascended, like so many
blasphemies, to the throne of that Eternal Justice
that I still so recklessly defied !

" In the day-time I used to wander, like a madman, on the mountains, recklessly leaving my
camels to stray where they would. My sole aim
was to divert my thoughts from the horrid chan-
nel in which they eternally ran; but at every
step I used tò halt, terror-stricken. In the quivering leaf, in the sound of the mountain torrent,
in the very echo of my own sighs, I thought
I heard an angry voice crying out in thunder tones: *Wretch! what have you done
with your child?* In the evening I used to return home worn out with exhaustion and suffering. I had warned Fatuma not to ask me any
questions; but as I often found her weeping, I
began to suspect that she had been informed by
some stranger of what had taken place at the
Carthaginian camp; more than once was I
tempted by this surmise to plunge my dagger
into her bosom ; her presence was hateful to me,
and her sorrow a constant reproach.

" For seven long years I had borne the consuming rage of the most intense hate ; I believed
that the human breast could bear no greater tor-
ment and agony than I did. I had gloated over
the blood—all the blood I had thirsted for. And
yet I became a thousandfold more miserable. At
last I discovered what remorse was. It clung to
me like the talons of a vulture to its quarry.
Remorse !—the invisible witness that day and
night accompanies the guilty, no matter how
speedily he fly, that seats itself at his board to

make little the crust he would strive to swallow
as he trembles, that bends over his bed to fill his
slumbers with the terrible representations of his
crime. Remorse!—the implacable and ever-ac-
cusing judge that thunder-strikes with eye and
voice, the hard-hearted executioner that mocks at
sighs and tears, that smites and torments with
savage glee and riots in the throes and mortal
agony of his helpless victim. Remorse! I found
out what it was at last; I carried it with me like
a barbed arrow rankling in my heart's core. My
eyes saw blood everywhere, while my ears rang
eternally with savage yells and threatening voices.
God was punishing me for the innocent blood
that had been spilt, while I, instead of humbling
myself under his hand, obstinately persisted in
hating and blaspheming him. Pardon me, good
and gentle lady, if I shock your faith and alarm
your piety; but I feel obliged to make known all
the depths of my wickedness. The more did I
feel tortured by remorse, by so much the more
did my heart overflow with hatred and vent itself
in blasphemous imprecations against Christ and
his followers. I could have found joy in the total destruction of all the Christians in the world;
I envied the happiness of the executioner appointed to put them to death. How often, in my
frenzy and blasphemous rage, have I looked up
to Heaven and shouted: O crucified One! strike
me dead if thou be God. If, as thou boasteth,
thou hast the power, if thou wieldest the thunder,

and death obeys thy vengeances, why delay
the punishment of a tottering old man that defies
thy wrath?   Poor blind maniac that I was!
Christ heard my blasphemies and mad defiances,
and still the thunderbolt rested quietly in his
hands.   Blessed martyrs! you were then kneeling
before his throne and praying for pardon for your
persecutor and murderer.

"One evening, during a fearful storm and while
the mountains shook and re-echoed to the thunder, as I was plodding my way homeward I descried an old man stretched on the ground at the
foot of a tree.   Having approached, I saw that
his hands were crossed on his breast and that he
stirred not, so I came at once to the conclusion
that he was dead.   I strove to lift him up; he
opened his eyes for a moment, his lips moved as
if trying to speak, but he again fell back unconscious on the earth.   That morning Fatuma
had fortunately given me some dates and a flask
of excellent wine.   A few drops of this administered to the old man caused him to revive gradually.   After having partaken of the fruit, he
rallied sufficiently to be able to walk with my
assistance, and in this manner succeeded in coming home with me.   Fatuma made a blazing fire,
and its genial warmth not only dried his dripping
garments but infused life into his benumbed
limbs; in due time he recovered completely.
Until then I had paid no attention to the stranger's appearance; I had looked upon him simply

as some belated traveller who had been overtaken
by the storm in the mountains and had succumb-
ed to exhaustion and fatigue. But now in the
firelight his appearance struck me. I had certainly seen this man before, but where or when I
could not tell. I ransacked my memory in vain
and could evoke only vague and confused sur-
mises. At last I adopted the expedient of enquiring how he came to venture all alone among
those desert mountains; this I did in the hope
that I might be able to recognize him by his
voice.

" ' There are,' answered he, with a pleasant
smile, ' many things in life so imperatively forced
upon us that we have no control over them, and
so must take them as best we may. In such
cases the old and the young alike must quit the
roof that shelters them. And so was it that I
had to wend my way to these mountains in the
hope that I might meet some hospitable family
that would take pity on me and give me a place
at their hearth. My strength failed me, and for
two days I wandered about aimlessly until Heaven
sent you to my assistance; a few hours later you
would have found only the corpse of an unknown
stranger who had died of exhaustion and hunger.'

" That voice I had certainly never before heard,
and still as I listened it touched my very heart to
its depths.

" ' Poor man !' I answered, ' I suppose the gods

have deprived you of your children, else, no
doubt, they would have come to your assistance
and given you a home.'

" 'Many of them are, indeed, dead,' rejoined
he, 'and the survivors are no better provided for
than myself.   They are in chains, or, like me,
are obliged to conceal themselves in the hope of
seeing better days.   May the Lord take compassion on them !'

" Evidently this man was a Christian; there
could be no doubt of it, and I myself had
brought him to my tent and had made him my
guest !   In an instant my trembling hand clutched my dagger hilt, my eye scanned the way to
his heart.   I was going to strike when the old
man, baring his breast and casting himself upon
his knees, said calmly : ' There are no soldiers
here to wrench the dagger from your hand.
Strike, strike Sylvanus ; the noble Jarbas pardoned you, the priest who taught him to have
mercy pardons you as well.'

" The dagger dropped from my hand.   I
thought I heard a double cry in my heart :
Mercy for my father ! mercy for this man !   I
was conquered ; I fell at the feet of the venerable
Aruntius and besought him to pray to his God
for me.

" ' She who was your daughter here below,' said
he, ' and who now beholds the Lord face to face
in heaven, has prayed for you ; she has lifted up
the all-powerful voice of her blood ; nay, more, in

the arms of Christ she has prayed that the father she never ceased to love should be restored to her.'

"I spent the greater part of the night on my knees at the old man's side. His grave yet mild words not only poured light into my soul but infused new thoughts and feelings into my bosom, and with them a peace such as I had never known before. The more he spoke the more lively grew my sorrow and confidence, and a longing to hear and learn more about the God that I had so long blasphemed. But when he came to speak of Christ's wonderful life, his meekness, his tender charity, his marvellous mercy for sinners, his sublime sacrifices for a world that scornfully rejected him; when I heard the history of his long and mysterious sufferings, and then that cry of love and pardon for his enemies that burst from his lips, I could restrain myself no longer and I cried out in my grief: 'Wretch that I am! I also hated him, and in my blind hatred clamored for innocent blood. O noble Vivia, and you, sweet child, whose name I dare not pronounce, pardon me, and your God shall be my God!'

" Aruntius instructed me as he would a child in the doctrines of that wonderful and sublime religion which cannot be known without being loved. The aged Fatuma came and listened as often as her occupations would permit. Her unprejudiced soul opened itself unresistingly to the new doctrine, and we began to prepare ourselves by prayer and penitential exercises for the grace of baptism. The old man was anxious to rejoin his children; he had learned that the persecution was ceasing and that he might again resume his place among his flock. In vain did I conjure him with tears to tarry yet awhile in our mountains, to strengthen us still more in the faith.

"'A bishop,' replied he — for such was his dignity—'a bishop belongs to his church.' Three days ago he gave us his parting blessing; he had administered to us the sacrament of regeneration.

"God, I hope, has pardoned a poor sinner; from his exalted throne he has seen my repentance and tears. And even you, kind and pious servant of the Lord—you have not spurned the implacable hater of your own daughter; you have received and called me by the sweet name of brother, and forgiveness was in your heart even before I came to implore it of your generous compassion. In the name of Jesus Christ, grant me a further favor—to bathe with my tears the hallowed resting-places prepared for their precious remains by your hands."

So saying, the old man knelt and lifted his imploring eyes to Julia.

A few moments found him prostrate on the sepulchral slab of the saints' tomb. Deep was the old man's grief; his frame quivered with emotion, and with broken accents he called on the names of Vivia and Felicitas:

. "Pardon! pardon!" sobbed he, while tears streamed from his eyes. He continued thus prostrate at the tomb for a long time. Julia and Rufina dared not interrupt such deep and overwhelming grief.

When he finally arose to depart he had recovered something of his usual composure, and thus addressed the patrician lady:

"Blessings upon you, kind lady, and may God reward you for all your goodness to me, the least and last of his servants! I can now die in peace: I have been forgiven in heaven and on earth. No doubt I have not many days to live; I shall devote them to prayer and penance. I shall now retrace my steps to my mountain home, never more to leave it except to visit from time to time the venerable Aruntius, and to strengthen myself in the faith and in my reliance on God's mercy."

Although pressed to rest for a day or two by Julia, the old man departed. Nor was he mistaken regarding the nearness of death. A few months after, exhausted by mortification and compunction, he died in the arms of the pious prelate who taught him to know and love the merciful and consoling religion of Jesus Christ.

There remain but a few words to be said regarding the other personages that have occasionally appeared on the scene of which we have been writing the history.

Pudens did not long escape being pointed out

to the governor as a partisan of the new sect; having been questioned regarding his faith, he boldly avowed himself a Christian, and gladly heard the sentence that condemned him to perish by the sword. In prison he found awaiting him Angela's parents, both bound in chains for the same glorious cause. The same day also witnessed the shedding of their blood. This was but a few weeks after the triumphant martyrdom of Vivia and Felicitas.

Unable any longer to live in Carthage and look upon what would constantly bring to his mind so many harrowing recollections, Jubal continued to live in the country. Reflection even more than years gradually tempered the fiery impetuosity of his character. Ever full of the thought of Vivia and of admiration for her virtues and heroism, he conceived a desire to study the tenets of a religion that had raised her so much and so far above the weakness of her sex; retirement had prepared him to be able to appreciate it, and so this votary of pleasure and debauchery, this cold contemner of every belief, became a model for his Christian brethren by his purity and holiness of life. Nothing was ever after heard of his former slave; Afer died in the desert, and in all probability died as he had lived—without remorse for, or a thought of, all the blood he had spilled.

God accorded a long life to Julia. She was denied the consolation of seeing her husband open his eyes to the light, and this was for her a lifelong sorrow; still, her declining years were gladdened by the pious lives and filial devotedness of her two sons. They and the sainted Rufina stood by her death-bed, and buried her remains in the same tomb with Vivia. The poor orphan from Gaul survived her only a short time. As to Verecunda and Thesba, who only flitted for a moment before us, they never forgot the lessons and example of their holy mistress; the first was judged worthy of receiving the virgin's veil at the hands of the bishop; the other married a freedman and became the mother of a large and pious Christian family.

Tertullian, after having attained the greatest prominence and fame, relaxed nothing of his zeal and herculean combats. The ancient fabric of idolatry crumbled stone after stone under his unremitting assaults. Heresy, too, slunk away and hid itself from the thunders of his voice and pen; the world stood amazed at his learning and genius, and the Church hailed him as her most intrepid defender. But human genius, no matter how great it may be, is never safe from a fall; while human knowledge, even though it approximate to that of God himself, may end in confusion. *One day the powers of the heavens shall be moved and the sun shall be hid in darkness.* Tertullian allowed himself to be led away by the illusions of pride; he lost that faith on whose wings he had soared so high. This great man, whose fall causes us a pang of sorrow even after the lapse of so many centuries, not only fell into error, but he attacked the Church that he had so often and so successfully defended, and thus became the champion of the most deplorable and absurd ideas. God, who permitted him to fall because of his pride—did he lift him once more into the light? The answer is still hidden among the many secrets of heaven.

Cyprian never forgot the important lessons received in the villa of his father, Thrascius. Although a Christian in conviction and conscience, he gave ear to the seductions of youth, and for years continued to lead the life of a pagan ; but at last the divine seed broke through the clod that smothered it, and burst into flower and fruit; from the moment of his conversion he made a vow of continency, sold his vast possessions, and distributed all his wealth among the poor. When a priest, and subsequently the Bishop of Carthage, he undertook and achieved for the Church labors that would seem beyond the power of any man to accomplish. The sanguinary persecution set on foot by the Emperor Decius, to which he was destined finally to fall a victim, brought into bold relief all his apostolic firmness and character ; from his retreat in exile he ceased not to watch over his flock, and by his exhortations to infuse strength and courage into those who suffered for the faith. His youthful imagination wove golden dreams of torensic glory ; nor was he disappointed. From the moment that he sought, in the study of the Sacred Scriptures, the secret of the *true sublime*, he became master of an eloquence that was manly, natural, and persuasive; it was a torrent that swept all before it. There was, indeed, something of the African style about him, of the harshness and ruggedness of Tertullian, whom he always called his *master*, and whose writings he constantly studied, even while at his meals; but apart from these faults peculiar to his age and nationality, he is looked upon as the leader and prince of Christian writers; more fortunate than Tertullian, he remained unswervingly attached to the unity of the Catholic Church. If, in his differences with Pope St. Stephen, he was sometimes wanting in moderation and docility, the ardor of his zeal, the energy of his convictions, the fire of his character must militate as an excuse; at all events, his glorious martyrdom has wiped out all his short-comings. Accordingly, for sixteen centuries the Christian world, oblivious of Cyprian's aberrations in youth and of whatever mistakes he may have unwittingly made in the heat of controversy in after-years, has placed upon his brow the twofold crown of learning and virtue. God bestowed on him that of martyrdom.

St. Cyprian was beheaded in the year of our Lord 258, fifty-four years after Vivia Perpetua's glorious martyrdom, of which event, consequently, it is possible that he may have been an eye-witness in his youth.

APPENDIX

BY THE TRANSLATOR.

The readers of the foregoing pages will be pleased, no doubt, to read the lessons of the Office for the festival of SS. Perpetua and Felicitas, the more so as they contain a long extract from the written account left us by the pen of our glorious heroine herself. The simple words and unvarnished tale cannot but prove most acceptable to those who lovingly linger over the last pages of this book and the hallowed memory of its heroine.

"Under the Emperor Severus there were seized in Africa a number of young catechumens. Among these were Revocatus and his fellow-slave Felicitas, Saturninus, and Secundulus; also Vivia Perpetua, a lady illustrious by birth, education, and marriage, who had a suckling infant. She was about twenty-two years of age. She has left an account of her martyrdom, written by her own hand. "While we were in the hands of our persecutors," she says, "impelled by his affection for me, my father constantly endeavored to persuade me to change my resolution. 'Father,' I answered, 'I can say nothing else than that I am a Christian.' Enraged at this declaration, my father thereupon rushed at me to pluck out my eyes. He contented himself with abusing me, and went away foiled in his efforts and in the artifices of Satan. A few days after we were baptized; during my baptism the Holy Ghost gave me to understand that I should now look for nothing but bodily suffering. A few days later we were thrust into prison; I was greatly frightened, because I had never before experienced such darkness. Shortly after this the report was spread that our trial was going to take place. Haggard with grief, my father came from the city to see me and to shake my resolution. He said: 'Have pity, O my daughter! on my white locks! Have pity on your father, if I am worthy to be called father by you. Think of your brothers! think of your mother! think of your child, who cannot survive your death! A truce to this foolish obstinacy, or you will kill us all.' My father said these things out of love for me; falling at my feet and bathed in tears, he addressed me, not as 'his daughter,' but as 'his lady.' I mourned over the white locks of my aged father, at the thought that of all my kin he would be the only one who would not rejoice at my martyrdom. To console him I said: 'Nothing shall happen except what God may ordain; you must reflect that we belong not to ourselves but to him.' He retired full of sorrow.

"One day, as we were taking our repast, we were suddenly hurried to be tried. We came to the court and were placed in the dock. The others were questioned and made their declaration. Then my turn came. All of a sudden my father rushed in with my child; he drew me aside and entreated me, saying: 'Have pity on your infant.' Hilarian, the procurator, added: 'Spare your father's white locks; spare your tender child; offer sacrifice for the welfare of the emperors.' I made answer: 'I will not; I am a Christian.' Then the judge pronounced sentence and condemned us all to the wild beasts, and we went down to the prison rejoicing. As I had been in the habit of suckling my infant, and had had him always with me in the prison, I immediately sent to demand him of my father. But my father refused to give him to me; God, however, so ordained it that the child did not require to be suckled, nor did my breasts pain me."

"In this way did the blessed Perpetua continue the narrative of her sufferings up to the eve of her martyrdom. As to Felicitas, being eight months gone in her pregnancy at the time of her arrest, she was greatly alarmed as the day appointed for the games drew nigh, through fear that her martyrdom might be postponed until she should be delivered. All her fellow-martyrs felt great sorrow, fearing that they would be obliged to leave on the way to a common hope so good a companion. On the third day previous to the celebration of the games they joined together in offering their tears and supplications to the Lord. No sooner was their prayer ended than she began to be in labor. Hearing her moaning with the pain, one of the turnkeys said to her: "If you complain now, what will you do when you will be exposed to the wild beasts that you pretended to despise when you refused to offer sacrifice?" She answered: "At present it is I who suffer; but then there will be Another with me who will suffer for me, because I shall be suffering for Him." She gave birth to a girl, who straightway was adopted by one of our sisters in the faith.

"The day of their victory had dawned; the martyrs left their prison for the amphitheatre as if for heaven—full of joy, radiant with happiness; and if they trembled it was from gladness, not fear. Perpetua came last; the serenity of her countenance and the majesty of her carriage betrayed the noble matron and the noble Christian. While on her way she kept her eyes bent to the ground to hide their brilliancy from the spectators. By her side walked Felicitas, full of joy at having been delivered in time to be able to encounter the wild beasts. The devil had prepared for them a most infuriated wild cow. When they had been enveloped in nets they were brought forth. Perpetua was put into the arena first. She was tossed into the air and fell prone on her back. When she came to herself and perceived that her dress was rent down the side, she drew it together, heeding rather modesty than pain. Having recovered from the fall, she bound up her dishevelled hair, for it would be unbecoming in a martyr to suffer in that plight, lest she might seem to be in mourning in the hour of her triumph. Having regained her feet, and perceiving Felicitas lying bruised on the ground, she approached, gave her her hand, and lifted her up. They remained standing side by side awaiting another attack; but the stern spectators were moved to pity, and both the martyrs were led away toward the Sanavivarian gate. So profoundly rapt in spirit and ecstasy had Perpetua been that when she arrived at that place she began to look around her as though awaking from sleep. To the amazement of everybody she said: "I should like to know when we are to be exposed to that wild cow?" When she was informed of what had taken place she could not credit it until she perceived on her person and dress the marks of the ordeal through which she had passed. Then having summoned her brother and a catechuman named Rusticus, she addressed them saying: "Be firm in the faith, let there be mutual love among you all; and be not scandalized at our sufferings."

"God had spared Secundulus the ordeal of the amphitheatre by taking him out of this world when he was still confined in prison. Saturninus and Revocatus were exposed to a leopard, and ended by being mangled by a bear. A wild boar was set upon Saturus; then he was cast to a bear, but the bear refused to leave his den; having thus passed unscathed through two ordeals, he was withdrawn. Toward the close of the games he was exposed to a leopard, and at a single snap was all covered with blood. Seeing him in this condition, the people, in allusion to this second baptism, shouted: "Saved, washed! saved, washed!" The dead martyr was then thrown among the rest at the usual place where persons were despatched by the sword. But as the peo ple demanded that the martyrs should be brought back to the centre of the arena, that their eyes might be feasted with the sight of their murder and watch the sword as it pierced them, the martyrs of their own accord arose and went to the place where the spectators would have them go. Before doing this, however, they embraced one another, so as to seal their martyrdom with the holy kiss of peace. Motionless and in silence they all received the death-blow; as for Saturus, he was already dead. That she might have the merit of suffering some pain at her martyrdom, Perpetua uttered a cry as her ribs arrested the point of the executioner's sword. She herself guided to her throat the bungling hand of this novice in the gladiatorial trade. Perhaps it was that such a woman could not be otherwise slain than by her own consent, for the unclean spirit feared her."

CONCLUSION.